THE HEART OF THE CENTURY

The Heart of the Century

A novel

by

EUGENE CHRISTY

Adelaide Books
New York / Lisbon
2020

THE HEART OF THE CENTURY
A novel
By Eugene Christy

Published by Adelaide Books, New York / Lisbon
adelaidebooks.org

Editor-in-Chief
Stevan V. Nikolic

For any information, please address Adelaide Books
at info@adelaidebooks.org

or write to:

Adelaide Books
244 Fifth Ave. Suite D27
New York, NY, 10001

ISBN: 978-1-954351-09-7

Printed in the United States of America

For Rodney MacDow

Contents

VOLUME III

OF THE TWENTIETH CENTURY QUINTET

Who is it that can tell me who I am?

– William Shakespeare
King Lear

Pa's Story

1952 Revere, Massachusetts

All I ever wanted to do was try and make an honest living.

Like a stray cloud's shadow crossing a meadow, this thought floated into his mind unbidden, as Tony LaStoria, trying to keep his head from swooning, sat up, slowly, carefully, painfully, on the edge of his bed, one day in 1952.

Merely to rise in the morning seemed a struggle these days. He was far removed from the reckless 10-year-old runaway who started down the mountain, on foot and alone, from the village of Alta Villa, in the province of Campania, in the year 1899. His beloved wife Gigi had been dead for a year. *How could a year have gone by already?* Now he was afraid. Now he had to endure another day waking alone in their bedroom, in the house on Payson Street in Revere, the very room where she lay dying for so long while their daughter Gerry tried to administer comfort measures, and he stood helplessly by. Now he knew he was no longer the man he used to be.

Tony LaStoria had not felt so angry and guilty, so desolate, since the last time Gigi gave birth, when Anna was born, their seventh child, in 1927. With Gigi's death, he knew that he had killed her. In his mind, it was a fact. Which hit him with full force, in the face. He had killed her beginning in 1927, with that final pregnancy. *That's how long it took her to die.* A canyon opened up in their bed and he fell into a deep pit in the ground. But into that void swept the spirits of all those he had ever loved. Alongside those he had stopped loving. And one that he hated. And one that he longed for.

He dragged himself into the kitchen. He sat down as if the effort was overwhelming. Gerry, the daughter who had never left home, the dutiful one, was there, waiting on him, as always, with his grandson, little Nicky, now five years old, obliviously playing, under the clawfoot kitchen table.

"Pa, have your coffee. What can I get you?"

Little Nicky Big-Ears, who heard more that they thought he did, wondered again, out loud, muttering to himself, as he played toy trucks beneath the table, why he wasn't allowed to call him "Pa," since everybody else did, Daddy, Ma, his Uncle Augie, *but no, I have to call him "Papanonni," or else be scolded again for asking so many questions all the time.*

Pa said, "A little bread, a little oil."

"Same thing every day. Let me make you an egg at least."

"Why should I eat an egg? If I'm lucky, I'll die today."

"Pa!—don't say such things. Right in front of Big Ears!"

"Why not? It's the truth. Ah! I'm too mean to die. I'm just hanging on to torment everyone. Just ask your sister Peggy."

"Pa. Come on."

"I hope you locked the doors. I don't know how many times I told you, I don't want her in my house. But no—you gotta let her in."

"Pa, what can I do? I feel sorry for Henry and Ronnie. Where are they gonna go when they're not at their father's?"

"You don't see how she's taking advantage of you?—your own sister. She parks those kids on you while she goes off gallivanting."

Gerry was wiping the table yet again. She placed the sliced Italian bread and miniature bowl of olive oil before her father, but he didn't seem interested. "What are you gonna do today, Pa?"

"It's Saturday, no? Don't I always do the shopping in town on Saturday? And then I'm going to the track."

"Pa! You know what Doctor Graham said! No excitement!"

"No excitement. No excitement. That's what life comes down to. You can't die peacefully in case you'd get excited. I'm not supposed to smoke, I can't eat provolone and genoa in a spuckie anymore! Maybe I'll get lucky and take another heart attack!"

Yet, when he went outside, onto the back porch, he stepped into a world of such surpassing strangeness, that he knew he did not want to die. Not today. The world was so beautiful, how could one leave it? He knew every grass-blade in this, his own backyard, with the familiarity of one who spent hours in the dirt, lovingly tending plants and animals. Yet, though it was a warm July morning, still it seemed as if he had stepped into an unexpected snowfall. A screen, slanting regiments of flakes, blinded his eyes with a drifting veil. Through that mist, he saw everything in a blizzard whiteness. But it was the sun, the humid July sun, and he shielded his brow with one hand.

Yes, there was the garage, domicile of the lumbering beast, his big black '47 Buick sedan. The garage doors were properly closed, as they should be. The beast was locked away, with the long-handled spade and the other garden implements. With that spade you could dig potatoes or dig your own grave.

Behind the garage, he knew, he would find his dogs in their kennel. From the back steps, when he glanced to his right, there was Gigi's flower garden, running the length of the house, kissing up against the chain-link fence.

This was his domain, the world he had made.

Though Gigi's gardenias and sunflowers and tulips bloomed brightly, she herself was under the ground, miles away, in the Holy Cross Cemetery, in Malden, waiting for him. His car, too, waited for him. *Hmm. All your life you been driving a black car. You own a hearse. The car and the ground are waiting for me. All I lack is the coffin, and a dead body to place in it.*

Tony LaStoria called back over his shoulder for his grandson.

Little Nicky came running and slipped his hand into the old man's hand, where his fingers felt they belonged, where they fit, comfortable, warm and cared-for.

Tony looked down and smiled for the first time that day. "Let's go see Daisy," said the old man.

She was just one of a dozen dogs, retrievers and pointers, hunting birds which Tony used to work in the Lynn marshes, but when he had said to young Nicky, 'She's yours,' the boy's eyes got big and brown. After that, they were inseparable, boy and dog.

But his dogs were of little use to Tony now. He had never believed in pet animals. Only women kept canaries and cats. His dogs were not allowed in the house. His dogs had to work for their keep. And yet they were more faithful and trusting and grateful than many a human relation. He would carry a bowl of scraps or bones out to them in their kennel himself.

What was he to do with them now? The neighbors had been complaining for years. His bird-gun lay leaning idle in his bedroom closet. He had no heart for hunting anymore.

He wandered with Nicky into the garden, seeking shade. It was going to be a hot one. He climbed the single wooden step up into the grape arbor, which he had built with his own two hands, behind the garage, along the chain-link fence, an oblong built-up box with sodded earth and long green grass, green as emerald, in the blooming shade of trellised grape vines overhead. In better days. During the war.

Awful to think of how, in some ways, the war was the best time of their lives.

The war and its four gallons per week brought him back to the city, and gave him this house, close enough to the trolley lines to commute by streetcar and subway every day to the shop in Boston where he managed the floor, the stitchers, the cutter and the pressers, making overcoats for the Russian army, and Eisenhower jackets for the Americans, on government contracts in Harry Spritzka's sweatshop.

Now Tony LaStoria knew that if he had to build that grape arbor all over again today, he had not the energy, nor the will, not any longer.

And yet the war had brought anguish to poor Gigi, who had three sons overseas, three boys of her own bosom, in daily danger, in mortal straits, which she could never for a second let slip from her mind, and her daughters, the only true sisters she had ever had, had grown up to be strangers in her own house, and the war, the war, the war, weighed down on all of them like those bundles on the backs of refugees you saw in news photos in the papers, those images which turned your mind into a bulletin board of misery.

Always, such thoughts came to Tony, these days, in this, his sanctuary, the grape arbor, a vale of peace hidden away from the street and passing cars. Here the quiet was deep and cool and profound, shutting off the world. Once or twice a week, every week, on creaking wagon wheels, the ragman still came passing down Payson Street, his horse, with lowered head, pulling; the ragman was a relic now, passing down Payson Street between rows of cars parked on both sides, a curio–"Rags! Good money for your rags!"

The old world was passing. Nowadays nearly nothing was left of the life he had grown up in. With it had gone his youth and his struggles. And where would he find peace, if not in the grape arbor? Perhaps in the ground, at last. If there was in the end, any peace.

Feeling guilty, he knew not what for, it occurred to him that he ought to be weeding the garden. But more and more it was difficult to get up off of one knee. Just the other day, he had almost dragged down a tomato pole trying to haul himself up. Now Tony thought of his nakedness. He had come outside in a pair of dress-pants wearing an undershirt with no sleeves. What was he thinking? He ought to go back in and put on his white shirt. *Madone.* What to do with the day? He didn't feel like going to the track. Not really. He didn't feel like anything.

But he loathed with every muscle the vacuum of indecision. He would do what he always did with his Saturday. "Come on, Nicky. We drive into town and do the shopping."

"Can I say good-bye to Daisy, Papanonni?"

Nicky's mother was watching from the kitchen window. Her father, and her son, were standing in the driveway. For one blinding moment, Gerry was overwhelmed with sadness. She was expecting, and soon little Nicky would have to share his life, and share his grandfather, with a little sister or brother, and this tableau she was observing now from her window, this tender closeness between grandfather and grandson, she knew, was destined not to last. She thought of her poor mother, and believed her father missed her mother, terribly. The old man had reached out to her son for a lifeline, a reason to go on. When she thought of how those two, her mother and father, had loved one another, day after day, she wanted to cry. She felt it in her bones with all her might.

Little Nicky clung to his grandfather. Still, before they could leave in the big black Buick, the boy would have to have a romp with his very own golden retriever, and squeeze Daisy's tail and hug and kiss her and get his face licked.

While the dog-show was on, Tony went back inside to put on his clean white shirt and fasten a different pair of clean pants on, and buckle his belt, and adjust his suspenders. He thought he was alone in his bedroom till he felt Gerry was standing in the door behind him, with her arms folded.

"A little privacy?" he complained, turning to face her.

"Pa."

"What? What now?"

"I wish you wouldn't go to the track today."

"I wish you would stop making such a fuss all the time. I'm not an infant."

As he stepped through her, past her, in the doorway, he said, "I know what I'm doing."

Now as the big black Buick reversed down the driveway, Gerry was watching. She did not know how to drive. Her father had always said to her, "Anywhere you need to go, I'll take you." She always marveled at how smoothly he backed up the big black Buick, and, spinning the steering wheel, angled it gracefully into the street between rows of parked cars. As it pulled away in the street, taking her son and her father, she ran out to the front hall to call her brother.

"Patsy, can you get outta work this afta? You know, for the daily double? Pa's goin' to the track. He won't listen to me."

As Gerry replaced the receiver on the hook, she felt tears come welling up in her eyes, and she was dismayed because she could not understand why or where that came from or what it might mean, except that it worried her, and she went back out to the kitchen to sit down with a cup of coffee and get ahold of herself.

On the highway there were signs. While the boy Nicky practiced deciphering route numbers and place names, the man Tony read meaning into roadside vegetable stands: Adamo's tomatoes were blood-red today, in boxes, in rows, plump and juicy, bright in the hot sun, heart-shaped valentines propped in rows in a display case of cards. As they passed along C-1 past Orient Heights and Beachmont and approached the side-road leading to the gates of Suffolk Downs, Nicky was leaning his chin on the dash of the Buick, excitedly getting dizzy.

Suddenly, the horses pounding in the dirt, straining for the finish line, the thoroughbreds racing across the newsreel screen of Tony's windshield, vanished, erased by the still stone of two stationary statues, St Peter and St Paul, on pedestals high on the wall above a confessional.

It was an image of St Anthony's of Padua, his parish church in Revere.

Seized with a piercing apprehension, Tony pictured Father Spinelli, the pastor. He heard the hollow stone echo of words rebounding: *forgive me, Father!*

It was Saturday. He must go to confession today: it was Saturday. He could do anything he wanted, as long as he did that. It was Saturday.

Five-year-old Nicky was sighing with ecstasy as they dove into the sudden dark pit, down, down, down, spiraling under the harbor in the tube of the Sumner Tunnel. Soon, the boy's favorite part of the trip would arrive, and he was filled with anticipation as they burst from the dark shadows upward suddenly into the dazzling day and congregated buildings of Boston.

Around them the North End closed like a vise. Tony piloted the big black Buick with one finger barely pressing the pearl-white steering wheel. Cruising these narrow, crooked streets chocked with jaywalking shoppers, he could see the outside world through glass; he was floating in a transparent ocean.

This was the intimately familiar neighborhood where Gigi had lived, on Prince Street, when they were young, and there, on the corner of Hanover Street, St Leonard's, where they had been married, long, long ago, *before so much, before so much.*

There, behind them, the stalls and step-down fish-and-meat-and-cheese shops of the Haymarket, which you could smell, even several streets away, mingled with sea-breezes from the harbor, so close by; the markets, which you could feel, behind you, alluring, inviting, promising delights, tempting your senses; there, his formidable father-in-law, the butcher, Fabrizio, long dead now, had once held sway, a Haymarket merchant. With all his heart Tony felt the happy nostalgia of those distant days flood his eyes.

They parked on Prince Street, quite a ways down, and made their way hand in hand, the old man and the boy, through the quiet, shadowed street, past the Brinks warehouse, of recent infamy, to rejoin the Saturday crowds drifting into the funnel of Hanover Street.

This weekly expedition was something they both looked forward to. At 62 years of age, Tony now filled out his measure of waistline with an air of prosperity. He still had his mane of silky hair, still with the part down the middle, as had been the style of four decades in the past, but now no longer black and gleaming, now snow-white and pillowy. The shopping trip, to Tony, was mandatory: only he could search out and select the meats, vegetables, fish and oil for the week. It was his self-appointed role in the family. He was the head, he was the provider. No one else was allowed. Still, he thought with considerable satisfaction, no one ever complained. Well—*that was not allowed either, to tell the truth.*

At five, little Nicky was the adored scion of a ship captain, a Columbus of the parkways, his grandfather, who once a week, on a Saturday, brought him along on a voyage of exploration, where he would get a treat, at some port along the way, but also lessons in geography, in family affairs, in worldliness, in the craft of haggling, in the art of seamanship, in the captain's duties of the wheelhouse, in history, politics, and, of course, horse racing.

"Come on, Nicky. Would you like a little dish of spumoni?"

As they sat sharing a small circular table in the sidewalk café of DiLeo's on Hanover Street, Tony found himself wandering in thought across a meadow, following a lamb, who stepped from tuft to tuft, diffidently: the she-lamb unlocked the garden door, and, appalled, found it over-run, the earth un-tilled, gaunt vines forsaken. Tony called his three sons, and immediately they fulfilled his wish, digging with all their might. He called four sisters, and each one was his daughter, and they were rocking, back and forth, on the piazza, in rocking-chairs, beside a small, circular end-table *with a pack of cards.*

"Papanonni, I'm done."

Little Nicky had looked up to discover a faraway look in his grandfather's gleaming eyes, so he called to him, by the affectionate name of *Papanonni.*

But the old man did not answer immediately. He had not yet returned from where he had been. A garden where a woman came, who sensed his adoration: and immediately, the garden filled with flowers. *Laura.*

"Fra poco," Tony whispered.

"What?" said Nicky.

His grandfather looked at him. "Oh—nothing."

He was back. Tony said to his grandson, "Okay, *andiamo,* there's lots to do, before we can go home."

Nicky placed his spoon down and looked longingly at the empty dish, which he wanted to lick with his tongue, but did not dare.

His grandfather led him by the hand while he performed his quiet miracles, with a look, a word, a gesture. The old man picked apples and oranges, he selected peaches and pears, mushrooms, pork and chicken, lamb and pastries, a bottle of zinfandel, a bottle of muscatel, as he explained, "These two we mix, Nicky, half and half." Oregano, fresh, garlic in bunches, handsome cheeses and black-eyed olives, enough to last the week, wandering, tasting, touching, pinching, squeezing, testing, appraising with his practiced eye, pricing with a touch of peasant canniness, which came from God knows where; enough to feed an army, more than enough, more than they would ever need or want, always more, *my eyes are bigger than my stomach,* but, *it's only money, you can't eat copper coins, only close the eyes of the dead, basta!* . . . a slight rain drizzling on the tin eaves of the corrugated marketplace, like the *sprezzatura* of a mandolin. *Food enough to last the week, or a month, or anybody's lifetime. But what if we run out of time, money, time* . . . ah, there, under a black umbrella, drifting by in the sweet rain of the bakery door opening, a beautiful woman, *ah, divine lady, my angel* . . .

Long ago, his first love, Laura Antonelli, had died. Long ago, in 1911, she had passed through the flames of hell, was purified in the purgatory of a wedding night, and then passed beyond the blue empyrean, into a heaven where she waited, until such a time as the time when Tony could rejoin her, beyond his corporeal body, in the pure love of paradise.

Food for the living, flowers for the dead.

This was the belief that Tony LaStoria fell into, to fill the emptiness left by the death of his wife, Gigi, a year before: when Gigi died, then Tony no longer had to hide his own thoughts from himself, for fear that Gigi, with her powers, reading his mind, would overhear him.

When man and boy returned to the house on Payson Street in Revere, that Saturday in 1952, Tony rested, swinging the door of the Buick wide open, to get some air, and swing his legs out. It was the heat. He pulled out his white handkerchief from his back pocket, on the right, to wipe his brow. On the left was his wallet. Everything was in order. *Let's sit for just a moment.* On the highway there was a breeze, but now they were standing still in the driveway, and the sun was baking the interior of the big black Buick, despite the solid black sun-visor, trimmed in chrome, over the windshield. He called to Gerry to take in the groceries from the trunk.

She did, but she was alarmed to see him sitting there, defeated in the driver's seat.

Her father was ruminating, as he often did. The questions of right and wrong in this life. Certain powerful personal superstitions ruled his thinking. *You did not touch your money with your right hand.* Whosoever did so grasped his money with greed. *Money was a thing of the left hand.*

Gerry didn't want to say anything to him, stationary in the heat, on the edge of the car-seat, obviously lost in thought. She was afraid to upset him. These days the littlest thing could set him off. His heart condition made her stop and think better of making a federal issue of the race track with him. He would get angry, lose his temper with her. That she could not risk. Instead, inside, she dumped the bundles on the kitchen table, and ran to the front hall again.

On the phone she told her brother Patsy she thought he should be there by post time for the first race, to keep an eye out on the old man.

As she put the receiver back on the hook, she felt the shadow of a black umbrella pass over her.

But Tony did not go to the track. Not now.

He ushered little Nicky out of the car with a word. When he had caught his breath, he pulled his legs in, started it up again, and threw the hydramatic into reverse.

The boy looked after the old man. "Papanonni! Can I come?"

"Not this time, Nicky."

He backed down the driveway, headed down Payson Street, and turned left onto Beach Street, the way you would take to go to the track, but when he reached Bell Circle, instead of turning right for Suffolk Downs, he looped around the rotary and went the other way. He might have been driving aimlessly, because he was not conscious, not aware of driving, of the corner he had just turned, or the traffic lights up ahead.

Instead, he was sitting on a train traversing the coastline of Connecticut, during the war, returning home from New York, with his head against the rattling train-window, tired unto death, helpless to hope for a word of news from any of his three sons. To know they were all right was all he wanted. Without that word he was sunk in worry. As far as he had known, from their letters, Augie was somewhere in England, Patsy somewhere he could not disclose, and Gene—Gene hadn't written. For months. For quite some time. Forever. Was he dead? Alive? Broken in pieces somewhere beyond the reach of help? The last he had heard the boy had written from a hospital in North Africa somewhere, maybe Algiers, maybe not, complaining of the embarrassment and repulsiveness of dysentery. But he had been alive. Why could Tony now, sitting on this train, not see his face, not hear his voice, not receive some word, any word?

It was then that Tony had bargained with God.

If you save my three sons, if you let me see them again, if you bring them home to me, I will repay you.

At that time, he had not known how. But a response to his vow was received.

It came from a previously unknown source in his life, the new pastor of St Anthony's in Revere, Father Vito Spinelli, who had been sent by the Vatican in Rome, in the middle of the war, to Cardinal O'Connell, to serve in the ranks of the Archdiocese of Boston. Father Spinelli, as an Italian refugee, was assigned by Cardinal O'Connell to an Italian parish, rendering the refugee from the Vatican out of sight and out of mind. After conversing with the Cardinal, in English, Father Spinelli decided that the war made for strange bedfellows. But the Cardinal turned out the wiser on one count: of all the Italian parishes in his jurisdiction, St Anthony's in Revere needed this new Italian-born pastor the most.

The parish in Revere had begun construction on an ambitious edifice, overly ostentatious, thought O'Connell, as was typical of their kind. It was planned to be an exact replica of a Renaissance church in Siena, in the north of Italy, to be built by immigrant Italian stonemasons, imported at great expense from the quarries of Barre, Vermont, where they had been re-settled for a generation. Construction of the church, begun in 1924, was still only approaching completion in 1943. Over the decades, and during the Depression, hundreds of Revere families, working-class Italians, immigrants and their sons and daughters and grandchildren, had pinched and filched from their weekly grocery bills to pledge pennies for the construction of a church they could not afford.

The Cardinal wanted a strong administrator, and fund-raiser, to get the job done.

When Father Spinelli first stood in the wide windswept plaza before the tall oak doors of the church, he found himself faced with a most curious conundrum. He was flanked by a brace of sentinels, two statues standing on pedestals at the corners of the broad flat expanse of the main approach: St Anthony cradling the Christ-child, portrayed in stone, on the one hand, and Christopher Columbus, holding in his hands a cracked globe of weather-greened bronze, on the other. Above the main doors, above the Roman arch, a circle, intersected with stone piers framing stained glass, formed the enormous rose-window which dominated the façade of the building.

On a day of perfect blue sky puffed with white clouds, you could stand in this place gazing upward at the tall campanile in the rear looking over the shoulder of the red tile roofline and become transported into the past of a glorious Renaissance, translated into the rocky language, the rusty orange and glinting mica, of New England granite.

Inside, the pillars of sunlight slanting down from the rose-window, the cold marble of the holy water bowls, the smell of the oak-wood pews, brought the new pastor home, home to his new abode on earth.

Indeed, the rectory, his domicile-to-be, was attached to the side of this magnificent edifice, precisely in accord with the architect's plans borrowed from Siena, an exact copy down to the last detail, and to pass from the church's vestibule to your office, bedrooms, kitchen, you need only pass through a Gothic arch.

In the aftermath of his promise to pay back God, when Tony La Storia knocked on the front door of this rectory, he was ushered into the presence of the new pastor, Father Spinelli. It was the first time they had met. The war was all round them. The war was raging all around the globe which lay in the hands of the bronzed-green Columbus outside. The discoverer of America stood on his pedestal on the left as you went up the gently terraced steps to the tall oaken doors of this Renaissance relic of a church. On the right was the old world, the saint himself quietly cradling the Christ child in his arms, looking down at him with a mystic beatitude. The war was inscribed on the bronze globe of Columbus, where weathering had seamed it with a jagged crack; and the war was also imprinted on the minds and hearts of two men, two strangers, meeting one another for the first time.

Tony had his own special connection to this church because it was called St Anthony's of Padua, the same name, the very same, as the parish church of his long-ago childhood in Little Italy, in New York. Ever since Tony had acquired the house on Payson Street and relocated the family patriarch's domicile to Revere, he had become quite intimately involved with, and comfortably at-home-with, this new parish.

So much of the war, his round-the-clock, three-shifts-a-day war work, his sons in the Army, the decline of Gigi's health, her increasing decline, was burdensome to Tony; and he was not accustomed to petitioning God, quarrelling with Him, or even speaking to Him, in prayer or in revolt, and therefore, only the church, with its rhythms, its rituals, its ceremony, it's Sunday Mass, gave him comfort, or escape.

Only within the walls of St Anthony's of Padua could he feel something that was transcendent because it was eternal. A life on the battlefield of this war could be snuffed out as easily as one of the red or gold candles at the altar rail of this *chiesa sacrata. And it could be the life of your son.*

Meeting this way, for the first time, Tony was surprised to find the English of the new native-Italian pastor to be quite polished, equivalent, almost, one had to say, to Tony's own. And also, the priest's story intrigued Tony.

Spinelli came from a small town near Rome called Montefiascone. He was the youngest of four brothers in a family of ten and he had left behind six sisters and his mother. His three older brothers were all killed in the war, serving in the Italian Army, two of them on the Russian front, one at El Alamein. He was his mother's only surviving son, her salvation, the priest she had given birth to. His mother petitioned the Vatican to have him expatriated, to preserve the life of her only remaining son from any possible harm as long as the war went on. Thus Father Spinelli was reassigned to oversee the completion of an Italian church in America.

"It's very strange," said Tony.

He was sitting with the priest in his tiny reception room, sipping an anisette poured by Spinelli himself.

Tony was marveling over his first impression of the man. This person could have been his younger brother. Except for a more receding hairline, and with the addition of the wire-rimmed glasses, which Tony himself also had lately begun to wear, which Father Spinelli had worn since childhood, each of them was looking at himself in the mirror.

"It's strange," Tony continued. "You have lost three brothers, and I have three sons in the war."

"May God preserve them."

"I can tell from your face, right now, exactly how I would feel if anything happened to my boys."

The priest had that kind of openness about him, about his features, his direct, fresh gaze, that communicated kindness, without words, a benevolence towards his fellow humans which came natural to the boy and the man, and which was the thing which had caused his mother to love him so deeply and want to save him.

That was not the kind of love from a mother that Tony had ever known.

But why did he accuse his mother of this—this lack of loving-kindness?

Tony said, "Father Spinelli, what can I do to help? I want to do something."

"My friend, there is something you can do. We have one pedestal left, above the confessional on the left, where we had hoped to put statues of St Peter and St Paul, flanking the booth. Would you like to be the one to sponsor them?" And so, with this pledge of money for the statues of St Peter and St Paul, Tony LaStoria placed his faith in God's ticket-window at the big racetrack in the sky. And, of course, in his first available private moment, he informed the Deity, solemnly, "Now I'm taking a gamble here. I'm trusting you. You gotta come through for me."

Two dollars on the Daily Double, betting that Patsy, Gene and Augie would cross the finish line and come in winner, place and show.

Now, eight years later, on this hot July day in 1952, when Tony veered left at Bell Circle, he was again going to an appointment with Father Spinelli. But the priest did not know that it was an appointment in search of absolution on the part of the man who had long since become not another parishioner, but his friend, his confidant, in the New World. This time, when they were sitting together, almost knee to knee, in Spinelli's tiny reception room, Tony did not know where to begin.

"Father, forgive me!" he blurted out.

"Why, Tony? What's wrong?"

"Can you give me absolution, now, please! I'm asking you."

"Tony, why this fever? You are a good man. What's come over you?"

"I can't wait for confessions at three o'clock. That's why I came to see you now."

Tony was thinking, with horror, that all his life he had defied both God and man. But he had escaped his punishment for so long. Until the life of his sons were put in danger—by him. He who could not save his own sons from the perils of bullets and bombs. He who could not save his own wife from the compulsions of his carnal desires. Only then had he returned to the confessional, to the communion rail, after a lifetime of lapses. And what had he confessed? That he disobeyed his parents? The same trivial, venial sins he had been accustomed to accuse himself of as a child going to his first catechism classes, only to be told to recite his Act of Contrition and three Hail Marys, while he hid from the world the hatred in his black heart, and the forbidden love he harbored in the same black heart. Of those sins he could not accuse himself.

He who could not save his own wife, his own sons, his own beloved Laura on that distant day when she dove to her death in flames, could not now on a hot July day in 1952 speak his soul to save himself. He could neither tell the priest how he had hated his own father, nor how he had turned his back on his own mother, nor how he had loved a woman not his wife.

These were his sins.

Of these things, he had spoken to no one—not even to Gigi, who had loved him.

Gigi had loved him, and made a home for him, and gave him sons, and daughters, here on earth, and so she did not deserve to know that there was another, one he could never forget, before her, one he had loved and would never stop loving, who had gone to heaven, when she died in a fire in New York, in 1911—before Boston—before Gigi—before everything—*before the world was born.*

And so Tony LaStoria had spent his life torn apart by loving one woman present and one woman absent, one woman on earth, and one woman who would never again be looking into his eyes.

Now he reached out blindly, wildly, to the native natural uninhibited kindness of the priest, who could not help himself. And he received his absolution. Even though it was not yet three o'clock on a Saturday.

Then Tony LaStoria fled from the rectory of St Anthony of Padua and drove, speeding, from stoplight to stoplight, to Suffolk Downs, in mortal terror that he might miss the seventh race. But he was much too early. He had missed the Daily Double but it was still only the third race. He wandered from the grandstand to the paddock in his customary white shirt, which felt tight on him in the hot July sun. This immaculate-colored shirt he wore today with an open collar and short sleeves. He had a closet full of them, to ensure that each and every day he had a clean white shirt to wear. Ever since his childhood ended he had done this. As a tailor by profession, as the son of a tailor, as a middle manager who had made his living and raised his family in the garment industry, it was his uniform, his badge. To look in the mirror he would not know himself without this trademark.

But today, in this heat, under this sun, morbid thoughts strayed into his mind as he wandered the paddock, as if the shadows of clouds were deepening on the meadow under the horses' hooves, though there were no clouds this day, though the sky was a penetrating clear cloudless blue as sharp as the edge of a knife. Did he wear his white shirt to hide a black heart? Did he veil from the suspicious distrustful eyes of the world a secret soul?

Who could save him now? Who could save him from himself? He needed a cigarette, badly, and he was out. He withdrew the crumpled pack of Chesterfields with its cellophane wrapping from the breast pocket over his heart. He knew he shouldn't smoke, but—how could he have used up the last one, and not–? Another stupidity, another mistake with which to chastise himself, another failure. He remembered that they had installed a couple of those new-fangled cigarette machines at the track. He deposited his quarter and struggled with the mechanical slot-handles, rocking the machine until finally a pack of Chesterfields fell into the dispenser-tray.

He went back to the Buick out in the lot to find the matchbook he had hidden from his daughter Gerry for just such a case as this. Back inside, he found his fingers too nervous to fumble open the pack. He bought a race program and the first thing he did with that was to roll it up so that, when the race went off, he could beat the palm of one hand with the rolled-up program in the other. Then he began to smoke. He found a seat. In the grandstand. He looked around to make sure no one he knew could find him. He could not now speak to anyone. If they saw him, he would run the other way. He lit one cigarette and then another. He needed to win today. He needed to bring home a winner to the family. He needed a victory to validate himself. He needed to know that he was good and honest and true and right. *He needed a sign that he was forgiven.*

Finally it was post-time for the seventh race.

At the last second, he went to the two-dollar window and put his money on *Shadowbrook* to win, place and show. It was long past three o'clock when Tony LaStoria went down to the rail at the finish line with the rolled-up program in his fist. He had 12-1 odds. If the horse came in, he had put enough down to win groceries for a week. He wished he had bet the house on it. He felt sure he was going to win. He knew it. Couldn't lose. It was a longshot, but he liked a longshot. Why bet unless you stood to win a bundle? If he lost, he would do what he always did, work harder the next week and make up for it. The family never went wanting for anything because of his gambling, he had always made sure of that. And when he walked in the back door with a new raincoat for his daughter Gerry and toys for little Nicky and all little Nicky's cousins to boot and a big smile on his face, it was worth it, to hear himself say, "Well, I felt lucky, you know, and I bet the longshot, and wouldn't you know—the horse came in!"

So with the rolled-up program in his hand, there at the crowded finish rail, Tony LaStoria watched impatiently, craning his neck, to see if he could catch the exact split-second when the gates clanged open and they were off, but he blinked, and missed it. A bad omen. *Nevermind. We're gonna do it.*

The seventh race was the featured race of the day and there was a field of nine going a mile and a quarter. Tony narrowed his eyes to squint through his specs and try to identify his horse all the way across the oval as they crept across his field of vision, approaching the eighth pole in a cloud of dust like a silent movie in slow motion. They were too far away to make a sound. A voice behind his ear in the jam at the rail said, "Who ya got?"

"Number eight."

"Good luck."

"Ah, whadda you know?"

"He ran fourth his last three starts at Aqueduct. He's a wagon-horse. Why do you think he's 12-1?"

Now Tony was angry. They were coming up on the quarter pole and he still had not picked out Shadowbrook. This bastard in his ear, this good-for-nothin' know-it-all, had to get his needle in. We'll show him! Under his breath, he let loose the first, urgent "Come on, Shadowbrook!"

And the program rolled up in his right hand tapped the palm of his left.

And he ripped the lit cigarette from the corner of his mouth and threw it down and tried to step on it, he was so angry, but in the jostling ranks at the rail, he couldn't be sure, so he let it go, because now the race was coming on and he could feel the excitement surge through the crowd with a bolt and enter his body like electricity.

They were coming around the far curve and they were lifting their knees and dropping them down with a thump and a clump of spitting muddy dirt on the sprinkled dry track and there was Shadowbrook on the outside with Tony DeSpirito on board, coming on, coming on.

Tony had the whip hand out. He was a good jock. Good Italian kid. *Whadda's the guy know from nothin', it's not the nag, it's the jock I'm bettin'!*

"Come on, Shadowbrook!" Tony roared, and the voice leapt out of his lungs with a hoarse cry, a flag waved red.

And Shadowbrook came on, on he came on, and his knees were pumping on the forelegs and his hindlegs were up under his belly on the gallop and he was coming on and DeSpirito's right arm was hinged at the elbow and he was shaking the reins in his left fist and his right arm up and down and up and down was pumping and he was beating his horse with the whip and Shadowbrook's neck was plunging as he lunged after every step to pull it out and Tony LaStoria's right hand was pumping as he beat his left palm with the rolled-up program and the tears were coming in his eyes as he smelled the clumps of earth while the horses pounded in the dirt right in front of him a thunderous climax at the finish line and it was Shadowbrook by a nose and Tony LaStoria shot his right arm up in the air with the rolled-up program a baton of triumph and he went to cry out his victory but the voice caught in his throat and he could not breathe.

Slowly, Tony sank down to his knees.

He grasped for the rail to pull himself up but his armpit stabbed with pain and his chest felt like someone was tightening metal barrel staves across it with a vise-like force tighter and tighter and he looked up at the sky and the twist of his neck flipped him onto his back on the ground but he still could not get a breath and he realized what was happening and he dropped the program from his hand and reached out with ferocious futility and caught only someone's pants-cuff in his loosening fingers but he had not strength to grasp it and the weight on his chest was like a thoroughbred standing on him with all four hooves and snorting hot breath in his face to force him to breathe but he could not take it in he could not get his lungs to expand and he felt his back settle into the ground beneath him and his legs go slack as spaghetti and as he looked at the sky it seemed to be melting from a clear hard brilliant hyacinthine blue into a widening diaphanous white as if the sun were expanding blossoming and spreading open with an inner intensity a pulsating heartbeat the thrumming heat that should have been inside his chest behind his clean white shirt but which now hovered high in the air above the agonizing crowd where he could look down on them from above and see himself stretched out, twitching.

But when he raised his eyes from this strange distance, from this place apart, where he was prone in the crowd, buried in the tangle of arms and limbs, eyes and silently moving lips, he was then conscious of a form emerging like a shape from the womb of the white glow in the sky, a form assuming a shroud-like outline that was not a garment of death but a mantle of light, vibrating, and it seemed to Tony LaStoria that in the midst of struggling to breathe he was floating upwards towards this apparition.

Then, suddenly, he saw a woman standing in a doorway dressed in gypsy rags with the paints of a harlot coloring her cheeks as she crooked her finger and whispered, come and have a drink, and he wanted to smear her kiss from his lips with the back of his hand and when he did it was not rouge but blood that came away on his flesh, and a canyon opened up and he fell back into a deep pit in the ground.

It was the second time that day he had felt he was dying. No. Not the second, the third. The second time was when he had tried to sit in the chair in the kitchen. So. This was the third time. *And he knew what that meant.*

Yet he did not wish to die. Not now. Not now when he was holding tight to the winning ticket in his hand. When he was clutching it into his fist as surely and tightly as once long ago he had tied his mother's poor few coins to his palm with a knotted white handkerchief. *Was there no one who could save him?*

From the sky the radiant lady in the diaphanous white mantle bent her knee and reached out her hand toward him asking him with this gesture to rise but he could not and she then reached out both arms towards his supine body and he felt his body go slack as his essence was drawn from his chest like a thread, a slender thread into which his entire soul poured, from the remote shoulders to the calloused knees, drawn upwards towards the light and he was mounting higher and higher on this winding staircase, this spooling thread, into the sky on the strength of rails no more solid than a cloud, on a ladder of vapor, as the woman in the white mantle smiled down on him with utter pity and heartbreaking love and, and, and a sadness in her eyes, a century of sorrow, a thousand rains of regret, and as he felt her tears wet his cheeks, almost without his knowing, he realized whose eyes those were, whose eyes were weeping, and beyond his volition, it seemed, her name escaped his parched lips. *"Laura!"*

At half past noon-time that hot July day Patsy LaStoria brought down the cover of the steaming press on the leg of a trouser miles away in Spritzka's sweatshop in Gloucester. He wanted to get out of there. It was Saturday. His sister Gerry had called twice that morning, from his father's house in Revere, anxious about Pa. But Patsy needed this job. How much longer it would be there for him he did not know. Spritzka was a pal of his Pa's, from the old days in New York, but from everything Patsy had ever heard, the guy had more money than King

Midas, but he had closed up every shop and storefront he had in Massachusetts, for a long time now, except for this one.

Patsy owed his job to Pa's connections with Spritzka, but the rich industrialist, or stockbroker, or banker, or whatever he was, had gotten tired of playing with his old toys and wanted some new ones, so he had sold off, a dump of his properties, a corporate divestment.

Pa had gone to work for Paparelli's, managing the floor for them in their sweatshop in the Everett Mills, up in Milltown, up on the New Hampshire line, a thirty-mile commute, one way, every day, from Revere.

It was killing Pa.

The way Patsy figured it, Pa had given his life making money for that lousy Jew from New York, and now he was thrown aside, like an old oil-rag.

A year ago, their mother, Gigi, had passed away, and these days, Gerry, his sister, was a bundle of nerves, figuring the old man was not long for this world after that.

And besides, she was pregnant. With a five-year-old already. And the only money of her own coming in these days was the little her husband could make in Page's woodworking shop on Broadway in Revere.

You didn't have to tell Patsy. He lived in Revere, too. Halfway up that awful steep hill on Reservoir Ave. He had two of his own at home. He knew how hard it was to make ends meet these days. What with inflation and a war going on Korea. *They called it a police action, but*—Sgt. Patsy LaStoria, MP, late of General Patton's Third Army in Germany, knew better.

Which brought us to this Saturday and Gerry's nervous-Nellie phone-calling, which took him off the floor and out to the dock where the payphone was—*a regular pain in the ass.* But there was nothing for it. Patsy wiped his brow with his sweat-soaked hankie, lit another cigarette, and worked for another half-hour. Then he called it quits. *That's all the blood, sweat and tears they're getting outta me on this Saturday. Time and a half, they call it. Time to go!*

He started up the jalopy in the parking lot. He was driving one of the repair jobs this week off the lot at Leo's Garage in Saugus, where he worked his second job, evenings. *Gotta take care of little Anthony and Linda at home. Can't let my Mary down. Don't even get to see them no more. Now I gotta spend time on my free Saturday afternoon on Pa, all because of Gerry.*

Well, whaddya gonna do? She's your sistah. You know how the girls are—weepy, all the time weepy. That's why we love 'em, cause they're soft, and this life is hard.

He pulled out into traffic on 128, the new road they were building, forever, it seemed, in a ring around Boston. You could drive till you got to Rte 1 South, and then as far as Saugus, and then, it was a Saturday afternoon parking-lot. After the war they developed this stretch of Rte 1 like crazy, both sides, up and back, and on a Saturday shopping day, you couldn't move. Stop and go, stop and go, in the hot July sun, with all the windows rolled down, and the jalopy's skin burning up too hot to touch. *Can't even hang your arm out the door and try and get a wind. Jesus.*

When you got to Revere, it was that much worse.

On C-1, at every goddam stoplight, crowds, mobs, carrying blankets, coolers and beach-umbrellas, crossing the road in front of you, while you halted to let them pass—even when the light turned green.

What else could you do? Drive the jalopy over the tops of all the autos piled in front of you? You were stuck. For the duration. *This is what we won the war for, to get stuck here*

*and run outta cigarettes, without even a drop of water to drink.
Mother o' God.*

On a Saturday in July, there were a hundred thousand
people trying to get off trolleys and buses, and get to that
beach.

Goddam it.

It was after three by the time Patsy was finally approaching
the turn-off for Suffolk Downs.

But he wasn't so pissed off, or callous, that the sound of
a siren up ahead failed to alert him.

If only he could get out and blow his whistle and clear
up this jam passing through the gates like he used to when he
was an MP.

That siren caught in Patsy's brain.

He suddenly felt an awful foreboding wash over him.

He parked and kept his eyes on where that ambulance
went.

All the way through the paddock area and down to the
rail on the track itself.

Must be somethin' serious.

Wish I had a cigarette.

Patsy started to run.

He couldn't help it.

Up ahead, he saw the ambulance stop and the attendants
open the back doors.

He pushed his way through the mob.

They were circled around somebody down on the ground.

The attendants were trying to push them back to open a
gurney on wheels.

Patsy pushed through.

"You know this guy?"

Patsy knelt down. "It's my Pa."

He lifted Tony's hand and it felt inert.

Patsy said, "Pa, don't go."

A voice said, "He's gone, son."

Patsy jumped up.

"Don't you think I know that! I seen a dead guy before. Plenty of 'em."

The assembled onlookers edged backwards.

Another one of these vets.

It made you cautious. You stopped to think. *Watch what you say. Don't set him off.*

Patsy looked at someone, anyone.

"I got here too late. Goddam it!"

As he knelt back down forlornly next to the body, Patsy looked around at the pool of sympathetic faces who just didn't know what to say. "I shoulda got here sooner, goddam it. The goddam traffic held me up. I shoulda been here. I'm his oldest son. Did he say anything? Did he mention me? Did he ask for me? Did he say *anything?*"

Nobody answered. They didn't want to. They weren't sure if they should say anything at all.

Patsy kept looking from face to face.

Finally a weak voice said, hesitantly, "He said, 'Laura.'"

"Laura!"

"Laura. That your mother?"

"No! Laura. Who the hell is Laura? You sure?" Beads of sweat crowned Patsy's forehead as his eyes pleaded with the faces looking down on him and his dead father. "You sure?"

"That's what he said. That was his last word. *Laura.*"

BOOK I

Andy's story

Chapter 1

Memoirs of Fayette County

1921 McConnellsville, Pennsylvania

The little boy wandered through the icicle grass and dirty white snow-patches of the sloping field towards the tent-flap that was now door to his home. His name was Andrej. He was four years old and he felt damp and cold, he wanted his mother, he was hungry, and there was nothing to eat.

They were living in a cow-pasture in the southwest corner of Pennsylvania, a field full of tents, and he wanted to go back home to their house.

It was January of 1921, and the coal-miners of the Klondike Coalfield in Fayette County were on strike against the Germantown Coal Company, and the Westmoreland Coal Company, too. Andrej's family had been evicted from their comfy little wood-frame house in the newly-built model town called Shawnee, on the other side of the Mon, in Greene County.

Shivering, the boy Andrej couldn't imagine what had possessed him to leave the tent to go wandering: not to play, how could you go out and play in a place like this? Maybe it was food he was looking for. People his own size. Freedom from constant confinement. All he knew was that when he reached the leaning sticks looped loosely with barbed wire, the Federal troops who surrounded the miners' tent-camp with drawn bayonets frightened him. Sometimes, if he looked at them, they turned away. They would not look at him. They did not see him. They made him want to run back to his mother.

His mother's name was Tamara and her husband was the boy's father, Milan Petrovich. They were Serbs. Tamara and Milan spoke only their own tongue, but there were many languages in this camp, because there were Poles and Germans, Czechs and Jews, Italians, Greeks, Romanians, Croats, Bulgarians, Slovaks and Slovenes, side by side, all out on strike.

Such things were beyond the mysterious to the young Andrej. All he knew was that he had been uprooted from his comfortable house. He wanted his pot-bellied stove, he wanted his fireplace. He was afraid he would never be warm again. There was somebody called Mother Jones. She was in this camp and she gave speeches. She talked about struggle and solidarity but Andrej could understand nothing because she spoke in a foreign tongue. His mother called her Majka Jones. There was somebody else called the Organizer. He had heard the words united and union over and over. His mother said solidarity meant *solidarnost,* but what did that mean? This must be all his fault. This was his punishment. But what had he done?

His mother, Tamara, was pregnant again, for the third time. His father Milan had been a laborer in the pit at Radljevo in the Kolubara basin district back in the old country. He had worked there as a coal-picker, sorting the coal from the rocks, when he was only ten. Tamara was a farmer's daughter, betrothed as a child by her parents to the yet-to-grow-up son of the village headman. But she fell in love with Milan Petrovich instead.

Sometimes she would sing softly to little Andrej and his younger sister Adrijana in the tent in the cold evenings when sleep was the only refuge and four bodies the only warmth, four bodies thrown together on the hard ground on top of what rugs and blankets they had, and she would sing the old song full of nostalgia called *Tamo deleko*, "There, far away."

But she did not often feel like singing. It was hard living four in a tent in the winter, and two of them little ones. Cooking was impossible, you had to stand outside in the soup line if you wished to feed the children. Carrying in water from the farmer's brook down the hill in a bucket, to drink or wash with, meant guarding all day against the bucket being spilled. How do you get the children to sit still? If it wasn't for the farmer who let them use his cow-pasture, where would the strike families be then? And blessed Saint Sava be praised, the milk from his dairy cows, whose pasture they shared, was saving the lives of her children. When Tamara saw him, she had no words to thank him with. When she thought the Germantown Coal Company might never give in, she wanted to cry.

And she did cry, that time when she chanced across her velvet *jelek*, embroidered with silver and gold thread, and Milan's brilliant red sash, underneath it, in the basket. They were things they would never wear again, because it hurt too much to be ridiculed in America by strangers ignorant of who they were or where they came from. The tears came, but tears in this tent-camp were a luxury Tamara Petrovich could not afford.

Now where had that boy got to?

Milan, her husband, had left the tent to go attend a meeting of the strike committee. Not that he would say anything to them there, or even understand a word of what they were saying, but he also, from sheer frustration, had had to get out of the tent.

That left Tamara to look after little Adrijana, who thank goodness, a year younger than Andrej, was still on her hip, and less trouble.

She felt the unborn kick. *Oh, God help me.*

Suddenly Andrej was there, flinging back the tent flap.

His mother grabbed him and held him tight against the mound of her belly, swathed against the cold by two woolen *dzempers* and a donated overcoat with the lining scissored out.

"Majka, I'm hungry," the boy Andrej said.

Chapter 2

My Father's Keeper

Little Andrej was living in a house again when one morning he emerged slowly and sleepily from the cave of dreams. He knew the difference between dreams and the other, but sometimes dreams were so real. Still, as he stretched and yawned, he realized he was in his own bedroom, upstairs, with his little brother Aleksandar, still asleep, curled up beside him. This new house, to Andrej, was just not the same. The strike was long over, the tent-camp in the farmer's field a dissolving memory. But he still missed his old house in Shawnee, and now they were in another town.

What was that noise downstairs? Creaking and bumping. What was going on? Andrej decided to go down and investigate. As in the old house, here his room was upstairs, over his parents' bedroom. The alarming sounds were coming from in there. Rubbing his head, Andrej turned their doorknob and walked right in.

What he saw was not right. Not to him. He rushed over to their bed.

"Leave my mother alone, you. Stop it. You're hurting her."

He pushed at the mound of bedclothes and found it was his father rolling over to the other side. His mother looked startled at him. "Oh, *mala beba*, he's not hurting me. You come here."

She scooped him up in her arms. He was frowning because he didn't like being called a little baby. His mother was placing him between them in the bed, trying to soothe her boy down. His father wanted to protest but she hushed him. Drawing the covers up again over the three of them, she cooed to Andrej, "*Biti miran, moj dragi, i ići spavati u srpsko!*-go back to sleep!"

"But why were you crying?"

"I was not crying."

His father turned his back on them. His mother said to him, "Are you a good boy?"

"Yes."

"Then go to sleep. You can stay here—eh, Milan?"

His father grunted, meaning, *no! but what do I have to say about it?*

Crossing his arms firmly, Andrej nestled in, and quickly his anger subsided as he realized he was being transported back to what it felt like when they were all together on the ground in that tent. And he thought, *Alek is the baby now—how much longer will my mother let me? I better be good.* And he slipped back into the cave of dreams.

They were living now in a place called Pershing, Pennsylvania. It was not far from Shawnee, only across the Mon, about two miles away. But it might as well be the far side of the continent.

Their house back in Shawnee, as Andrej remembered only too painfully, had been special to him, with its fireplace and nice curtains and shades that worked, hot and cold running water indoors, and coal-fired furnace for heating. Shawnee was a company patch unlike any other, a socially-engineered small town built by the Germantown Coal Company, self-sufficient and compact, meant to house all the miners who worked below, 240 feet down the vertical shaft, in Germantown No.1. Shawnee had been designed and constructed as a model town, with curving roads hugging the hillsides, landscaped streets paved with crushed sandstone, no two houses on the same level, all single homes, mostly, only a couple of duplexes here and there, but all with running water and indoor plumbing. Four hundred and forty-one families lived in Shawnee when the mine first opened in 1917, the year Andrej was born.

When the wildcat strike of '21 was over, and the miners lost, and Mother Jones and the Organizer disappeared from their lives, there were layoffs at Germantown No. 1, and Milan Petrovich was a miner no more. The mine owner, whom everyone called Kaiser Ziggy, took his revenge by firing all the strikers. Four hundred and forty-one families were evicted. After a suitable three months when Germantown No. 1 was shut down, scab labor was imported and overnight all new families moved into the model town of Shawnee.

Forced to look for work, Milan finally found some hours as a stoker at the coke ovens operated by the Westmoreland Coal Company in Ronco, but he could not get more than a couple of days a week, or rather, nights. He still walked to work and back, but now it was two miles each way, for Ronco was on the banks of the Mon facing Shawnee, more or less, on the other side.

Gone were the flower-beds, the view of the river, the movies at the theater built into the community center alongside the company store, the dance-hall, and the rec room, the beer garden and billiards-room, the dance-hall doubling as an auditorium. Shawnee was different, a social experiment. Gone now were all of its amenities. None of the other company patches in Fayette County provided a park for the children, nor a community swimming pool, either.

This new place, Pershing, was a sprawling borough scattered along long roads going nowhere. It was a mixed, rural locality with a population something under five thousand, farmers, miners and storekeepers. Their street, Maple Street, was downhill from uptown, so-called, set among three or four back-to-back streets where the landlord was the Westmoreland Coal Company. Andrej's house now was like all the others in this patch, with the neighborhood pump downstreet, so that his mother spent all day hauling water in pails back to the house, and here he had to use the chain-toilet in the basement, which was cold as an outhouse, and smelled because the septic tank was in the vacant lot right outside the basement door.

Andrej's mother said not to mind. She said Pershing had something Shawnee did not: people of their own kind. Here she had neighbors who were Serbs. She could talk to Stella, right next door, when they were hanging out clothes to dry. They even had a new church being built out on South Washington, Saint Sava's Serbian Orthodox Church. Father Konstantin was their new pastor, and his wife, Marta, was a good soul. His mother told him to be good and not to mind and to be thankful for what he had.

Andrej tried. Though he was just five years old, he helped his mother haul water. His father would not. He said it was woman's work. Besides, he had to sleep in the daytime.

One day Andrej's mother had a surprise for him.

"Stand still!" said she as he clutched at his neck.

It was a bow-tie.

"Why do I have to wear this?"

"We're only trying it on!" She sat back on her haunches. "Oh, my little man!"

"I hate it!"

"One day soon you will have to go to school, you know. I want you to look decent. Clothes make the man, you know. Stella told me about it—the bow-tie—she said ask Marta, the pastor's wife, maybe she could find one for you. You look so handsome!"

Opening day of first grade was a shock to Andrej. There were only two or three children he could talk to. The teacher—he couldn't understand a word she said.

"My name is Miss Ledeker."

She wrote it on the blackboard. She had a pointer in her hand. She tapped hard on "Miss Ledeker," while she made a round mouth soundlessly saying it. Then she pointed at the children, who looked dumbfounded. The older children in the back laughed and told the newcomers they were expected to repeat everything the teacher said and did. Gradually the class began to catch on. Most of them had no idea what they were saying as they giggled and laughed trying to say, "My name is Miss Ledeker."

"All together," she cried. "Again!"

Now she tapped with her pointer on each syllable and made it longer and up-and-down sing-song. She swayed back and forth and the children began to get the rhythm. They liked this game. Finally she faced them and they all recited without benefit of the pointer.

"Good!" The teacher clapped her hands—and so the children did, too.

"Now." She wrote on the board. "What is your name," and placed a very large "?" after it.

The children almost squealed with delight. The bigger kids were more than happy to get the day off. This was baby-food to them.

When he got home, Tamara's bow-tied little gentleman proudly told her, in English, "My name is Andy!"

He told his father excitedly that his teacher's name was Ledeker.

His father looked dismissively at him. He said, "Hmph! A *Švabo!*"

His father might not be impressed by this *Švabo,* but in time, in a short time, Andrej fell in love. He idolized Miss Ledeker second only to his mother. There was a very round short Serb girl with heavy black eyebrows in his class who had attached herself to Andrej, to his extreme annoyance, since he was convinced it was all due to that bow-tie, and this girl was very jealous of Miss Ledeker's hold on him. One day this girl, Jovanka, brought the teacher an apple. Miss Ledeker bent down and ruffled Jovanka's spiky black hair. The teacher seemed pleased and placed the apple on her desk. Andrej went home that day determined to get his own apple.

"Majka, have you got any money?"

"You had your treats for this week."

"It's not for me. It's for an apple for my teacher."

"Well, I'm sorry, but such things are not in my budget."

Andrej was well-aware that his mother controlled the purse strings in the house. He knew because for one thing his father was always asking her for a nickel to go to the beer garden. He had to ask her because she made him give her everything from his pay packet, for her to hold onto, for the week. He didn't like it, but he did it. It was that or never hear the end of it.

"What am I going to do, Majka?"

"I don't know, little man. I don't know. But I have no money for apples."

Andrej went outside on the front steps. They were precipitously steep because this house on Maple Street, situated in the hollow downhill from uptown, and all the others in this company patch, built and rented out and neglected by the parsimony of the Westmoreland Coal Company, had a tall cellar of white-washed cinder-blocks so that the chain-pull toilet, housed in the basement, could drain into the cesspool, which was in the field left vacant beside each house. Andrej sat down to think. He did his best thinking on top of these tall steps because they gave him a little privacy. Where was he going to find an apple? He decided to try the company store on Pine Street. He walked over there. He pointed to the apples and asked the man, in the English he was learning at school, "How much?"

The man squinted at him. He was thinking, *not by the bushel for this kid.* The man held up one finger.

Andrej nodded, yes!

The man held up five fingers.

That was a lot of money, thought Andrej. He didn't blame his mother, then. He began to walk along scouring the ground and the gutter for any penny he could spot. No luck. Then it came to him. *Apples grow on trees.* And he knew of a place where a local farmer had an orchard full of golden apples, and so *my apple will be better than Jovanka's, she just had a plain old red apple.*

He walked all the way out to South Washington to where the new Serbian church was. He liked the church. It was made of yellow bricks. It smelled good inside and the icons and candles and stained-glass windows were so much more beguiling than his house, or even, his one-room schoolhouse. But especially he looked forward all week to every Sunday after mass, when all the children and all the families gathered at a picnic in back of the church, with plenty of good things to eat, provided by Father Konstantin and his wife Marta, from the collection box for the poor. She did the cooking and her husband went round all the benches serving. They even had a band with violins and an accordian and somebody who played the Serbian *tamburitza*, and they played under an elevated tent-canopy with tall steps and a wooden dance-floor, so there was music and dancing, every Sunday afternoon, after mass.

That was why Andrej remembered there was a farmer's apple orchard across the road from the church. *A farmer's orchard full of golden apples.*

But when he got there and picked his apple and was shining it up on his pants leg, suddenly he saw Father Konstantin himself watching him from across the street.

Andrej couldn't hide. The priest called him over.

"I saw you take that apple, Andrej."

"But it's not for me, Father."

"You'll have to put it back."

"No!—I can't!"

Andrej ran all the way home.

Along the way the cop from the Westmoreland Coal Company Police, who went up and down their streets on his horse, saw him running.

Andrej was sure the policeman could spot the conspicuous bulge in his pocket and so he slowed down abruptly and thrust both his hands into his pants pockets, hoping to make himself appear nonchalant and innocent to the mounted company cop, and to make both pockets appear equally bulging.

When he reached his own house, feeling the eyes of the policeman on his back, he ran up the steep steps and collapsed finally, out of breath, at the kitchen table.

"Majka, I did something wrong." He placed the apple on the table. His breathlessness came not solely from physical exertion, but from a guilty conscience. "I stole it from the farmer's tree. The priest caught me, but I ran away."

His mother knelt down, wiping her hands. She was tired and full of pity for the boy. She hadn't the heart to reprimand him. "Andrej, do you love me?"

"Of course I love you."

"Will you do something for me?"

"What?"

"Go up to the beer garden and ask your father to come home."

He didn't want to, but he did. He would have to pass the policeman on his horse again. The cop, unmoved, watched the boy curiously, as he thought, *where's he off to now?*

Andrej could feel the man's eyes on his back as he rounded the corner and started up the hill to uptown.

At the beer garden, the windows were high in the wall. Much taller than Andrej. He wished he could have just reached up and signaled his father. But no, he would have to go into this dark place. It was a speakeasy, but how could Andrej know that? He pulled at the heavy door. A man coming out pushed on it and almost stumbled over Andrej. The wash of stale beer whooshed through the doorway into Andrej's face. It was dim in there. He walked slowly up along the longish straight bar, trying to adjust his eyes and spot his father. There he was. At the end of the bar. Sitting on a high stool staring down at the counter. Was he asleep, or was he merely measuring, drowsily, with half-closed eye, the puddle of dark brown *schwarzbier* in his glass?

"Tata!" Andrej tugged on his sleeve. "Majka wants you to come home now."

His father looked down at him over his shoulder. He pondered a reply for quite a long time. His moustache was stippled with beer-drops, tiny white foam-flecks. Andrej thought wildly of the icicle grass in the tent-encampment.

"I am only a man. I am not a Serb. I have lost my country. I am not a coal-miner. I have lost my position. I am the man of the house! Yet, I have lost my . . . go away! Leave me alone!"

Andrej walked home by himself.

What had his mother thought he was going to do? *Lead his father home by the nose?*

He passed the policeman for the third time, and this time, he was sure the man could see into his soul, and find there, *a golden apple, stolen from a tree.*

Chapter 3

Miracle of Saint Sava

The time came when Tamara Petrovich felt the heaviness of the water-buckets she was carrying nearly tip her into hopelessness.

"Stop," she said to Andrej. "I can't go one more step."

Andrej was six years old now and he did not want to put his water-pails down. He had learned it would be harder, then, to pick them up again.

On Maple Ave., their unpaved street in the company patch, you had to walk from their house all the way to the end of the dirt to reach the water-spigot.

Andrej's mother looked at him with a moist despair. "What's wrong with your brother?" she wanted to know. "I have tried everything. I'm at my wits' end."

"He's sick, Majka."

Something dreadful was now truly wrong with Aleksandar. It frightened Andrej. The house was thick with calamity.

"I have no money for the doctor." Tamara was big with child again, and she tired so easily. "What am I going to do?"

"I don't know, Majka."

Andrej's mother was afraid of the doctor because at home they all spoke Serbian.

The doctor was one of those ferocious Americans. He intimidated her because she could understand nothing he said. "Have you prayed to Saint Sava, Andrej? Did you pray last night?"

"Alek wouldn't even let me sleep!"

"It's in God's hands now. We need a miracle."

"Come on," said the boy. "Let's get home."

They now had four at home. A girl they named Anastasija came after Alek. Andrej was thinking, *only God knows what comes next.* To him, a new baby, like spring rain, came once a year.

They had reached their front steps. Oh, those steep steps. It was July now, and hot out, and the toilet in the basement was the coolest place in the house. Why couldn't they go round to the cellar door on the side of the house and bring their water up the back stairs?

Andrej put his buckets down.

"Mama—he's only four years old!—children don't die, do they?"

"Don't say such things!"

But say it or not, there was no way around thinking it. Not when you recalled that until a few months ago everything was fine, or as fine as it ever got.

Life was a daily trial for the family. You paid your rent to the Westmoreland Coal Co. and you bought your groceries in the company store. Working the graveyard shift, Andrej's father, Milan, had to sleep during the day in the house. The days of hot and cold running water in the house and a coal-fired furnace in the basement were over for the Petrovich family, ever since the wildcat strike of '21. Now, in the company patch in Pershing, the poorer you got the further you fell behind. No one expected struggling to suddenly evaporate. But this thing with Aleksandar, this went beyond everything.

And it came on so suddenly. Everything was the same with Alek till about the turning of the new year of 1923.

The first thing they noticed was that his personality seemed to change, overnight. Sudden storms of temper derailed him, followed by gusts of remorse and self-pity.

When they questioned him, they heard Alek's complaints of being hungry all the time.

That was the first hint.

Now they began to watch. He was hungry again as soon as he finished eating.

Well, they were all hungry.

Potato-soup, boiled potatoes, mashed, it didn't matter. Nothing filled him up. Tamara made him *musaka*, specially, though she had no eggs for the custard on top, so she used flour instead. She ran up the bill at the company store buying blood-sausage and sheep's cheese. She made stewed *duvac* for him on top of the miner's lady, their black-iron coal-stove in the kitchen. If only she had a piece of pork to put into it. She couldn't afford any of this. What about the others? They had to eat, too.

But then they noticed it seemed Alek couldn't stop going to the bathroom.

Yet he was thirsty all the time and drinking pints and quarts of water straight out of the outdoor spigot downstreet, as well as draining every bucket in the house.

He stopped playing, he was up-and-down moody, constantly, you couldn't talk to him, he was picking on his sisters, hitting them. Even Adrijana, who was bigger than he was, and who slapped him back, with her tongue in addition to her open hand, soon gave way to doubled fists and began to hate her little brother.

Now he was losing weight and by every sign appeared listless and despondent until the next outburst. He seemed to have gone from sloping downhill to falling off a cliff.

When their neighbor Stella came over to have a look, she said, "Tamara, let me call the doctor."

"No, no!" she said, "I dare not spend the money. My husband can only get two nights a week as it is."

The following week, it seemed to Stella the boy was worsening, and she put her foot down. "My friend, my dear, you must."

"If it was a fever, I would bathe him. If it was a cold, he would be over it by now." Tamara relied on Stella because she had enough English to translate for her. "I just don't know what to do."

"Let me get the pastor's wife to help."

"To do what? Pray for him? God doesn't listen."

"Not to pray for the boy!—to pay for the doctor!"

When Doctor Logan was finally in the house, they all gathered round the groaning Alek in the bed he shared with Andrej upstairs, under the roof-beams. Even Milan roused himself out of his daytime slumber to hover around the circle of faces, Tamara, the two girls, Andrej and Stella.

"How long has this been going on?"

The doctor turned on the faces accusingly.

"Nevermind! There's nothing much I could've done anyway! It's the sugar sickness! He'll be dead by Christmas! They don't last long! Listen—you've got to stop loading him up with potatoes! And no bread! Now I'm going to give you strict orders—no more than 450 calories a day. Stella!—do they understand a word I'm saying?"

Tamara had taken her other children by the neck and shoulder and was squeezing them like dish-rags while Milan looked on wildly and a piercing wail escaped his wife's clamped, anguished lips as Stella translated.

The doctor grabbed Stella by the arm and pulled her out of the room down the stairway. "Goddamned ignorant people! You come with me. I'm going to write it all down for you—they've got to put this boy on a stringent diet. It's his only chance!"

At the bottom of the steps he stopped Stella.

"He'll go blind. He'll lose his limbs. First one leg, then the other. If he's lucky and doesn't have a stroke first. I'm not trying to scare you. I'm trying to make you understand that you must make them stick to the diet I order for the boy!"

Tamara followed doctor's orders, but it went against every instinct a mother had. How could she deny Aleksandar? It was so hard to see him in actual tears from the pain of hunger in his belly while she kept food from him, the same food she shoveled out to his brother and sisters. Every time she turned her back to spoon-feed her one-year-old, Stasija, a fight would erupt between the others. And always he grew thinner. He was wasting away. She was killing him. He was starving to death. She was ready when Marta, the wife of Father Konstantin, the pastor of St Sava's, offered to come over and pray for him.

Little Alek kept his back turned. While they all trooped into his bedroom, he put his face to the wall. They grouped around the bed and fell to their knees. Andrej and Adrijana were frightened. They were old enough, not like little Stasija. They had to help their mother to her knees because she was now near her time. Marta Jovanavich, the priest's wife, held out a crucifix over the boy's bed while she slowly swayed back and forth reciting. Milan peered over her shoulder. There was no room left under the eaves for him to kneel. You could feel the pity, as thick as incense, in the little bedroom under the roof-beams shared by the two boys. And something else. A sense of doom. An emotion like footsteps approaching. Tamara blamed herself. To her other woes she added this: *if he had not been born he would not now be suffering. Why did God take the feeling between man and wife and turn it to sour ashes on their tongues?* What had she ever done to deserve this punishment? She was about to do it again, give birth. Was God going to take that one away from her, too?

The day came when she went into labor. Now that Doctor Logan was involved with the family, he insisted she go to hospital to have this one. But they no longer lived in Shawnee, where Germantown Coal had their own wood-frame clinic. Here in Pershing there was nothing. The nearest hospital was ten miles off in Uniontown. Doctor Logan was afraid that he would not get her there in time. After all, this would be her fifth. He took her in his own flivver. The rest of them, Tata and the children, with Stella, too, as interpreter, all trooped out to the McConnellsville trolley stop to wait for the streetcar to Uniontown.

Doctor Logan had taken the dying Alek also in the flivver. Because the mother was on the verge, he did not disclose to her any of his plans for the boy. But Tamara knew. A mother always knows.

Doctor Logan was busy, bothered, nervous and in a hurry, and worried, so it barely occurred to him to explain. Beside which, had he wanted to inform her completely–she wouldn't understand a word!

Tamara's head lolled back and forth in the speeding, rocking vehicle. Ten miles of dirt road up and down hill did not spare her any jolts to the spine. She dared not open her eyes as it made her want to throw up. But she could not escape the dread and insistent feeling that while she was being driven to her destiny her poor innocent blameless Alek was being driven to his grave.

At the Uniontown Hospital, everything was white, if it was not antiseptic green. The light was white, the nurses all in white, the doctors white. But Tamara could only see red, blood-red, and that red blood only in her mind's eye, pouring from the stump of poor Alek's leg.

She knew they were going to take his leg. That was the very reason why the American doctor had told her nothing.

Compared to this pain, the agony of childbirth was bearable. To lose a child in his sleep, to lose a child from drowning, from anything, that was something awful, yet you could understand that the poor little one was beyond everything, that he was spared.

But to take his leg before you killed him. To make him suffer to live, yet not to walk. To make him look down and have to see every day, every hour, every minute, the place where his leg used to be—that was torment. That was the work of the devil.

And where was God while the devil did his work?

The day after she delivered her new child, which she had long since meant to call Adam, if a boy, and Andjela, if a girl, Tamara woke in her hospital bed drowsily. They had given her something that put her out completely. She was only dimly aware of all the people in the room waiting for her to come back to them.

As she woke, she tried to focus on them, but thoughts of her dreaded appointment with amputation overwhelmed her, and she was sure that this was why they all were there.

They must be afraid I'll jump out the window, she thought.

Maybe I will. Maybe I should. Oh, I can't stand it! How can anyone live like this?

"Mama."

It was her boy, Andrej.

"Mama, we have a new sister. Adrijana, come and show Mama."

His sister held up the new-born for their mother to see.

Andrej said, "Isn't she beautiful, little Andjela?"

Tamara felt only desolation. She waved her hand. Then she noticed Marta Jovanovich. And Stella—Milan, too—where was that man Logan? Why wasn't he here? Why were they all smiling so idiotically? Oh, this white light!

"What have you all done with my Aleksandar?"

"Mama, mama, mama!" It was Andrej stroking her hand. "Listen to me. I have to tell you something."

Marta leaned over. "It's something wonderful."

Stella said, "We couldn't wait to tell you."

They all urged Andrej on. He patted his mother's hand.

"It's something brand-new. It's called insulin. They get it from a pig, Mama. He's saved, Mama—he's going to be all right!"

Tamara looked back and forth at all their faces. She peered into their eyes to see if they were lying. It was true. "You mean—?" She appealed to Marta.

Marta took her hand next. "Yes, yes, he's saved!"

"Oh, my God. I take it all back."

They were laughing, giggling even. The joy was bubbling in their eyes.

Tamara gripped Marta's hand as if she would crush it. She reached for Stella's fingers. She looked over their shoulders to find her husband and when she did she found him with eyes cast down to the floor and when he looked up and saw her, those eyes were full of tears.

"It's a miracle then." She looked at Marta, the priest's wife.

"Yes. It's a miracle."

Chapter 4

Whistlin,' Whittlin' and Pickin' Coal

When Andy Petrovich was eight years old, an accordian-player pulled him aside at the church picnic one Sunday. "Where'd you learn to whistle like that, old son?"

"I dunno."

"That's a talent you got there, y'know. Fred, come on over here and listen to this."

The band was taking a break, and Fred said, "Can you whistle something I play and repeat it back to me?"

He played a few bars of *Happy Girl Polka* on his fiddle, and Andy whistled them back.

"Yup," said Fred. "Note for note."

"And such a pure tone," said the accordian-player. "He's a warbler, all right, like a bird, he is."

"Wish I could whistle like that," said Fred, as he walked away.

After that, every Sunday, Andy had to get up on the bandstand to whistle *Happy Girl Polka*.

However, Andy did not want to grow up to be a whistler. He whistled like breezes blow, when he felt like it. He never gave it any thought. He never tried to whistle. He just always could. Maybe it started back when he first thought of signaling to his Majka that it was him coming home. Just two notes. It was just like saying "It's me!" The accordion-player told him his signal-whistle was a one-step down, a B-note to an A. Andy would never have known otherwise. Maybe it started back in first grade when Miss Ledeker played the piano for them and the kids had to all sing *Yankee Doodle*, or *My Country 'Tis of Thee*. Andy would find himself walking home with this tune stuck in his head and he would start whistling the tune because he didn't have to remember the words.

In any case, no other pair of notes would have done for "It's me!" *Only those two notes.*

But it was nothing to Andy that you could make money off of. Nothing that you could do when you were grown up.

Andy wanted to grow up, and fast, in the worst way. Maybe it was because nobody ever had enough around their way. It wasn't just their family. It was everybody who lived in the company patch in Pershing. They were the poor side of town. It wasn't that they didn't want new shoes or furniture or a raincoat or some garden tools. They wanted the same things everybody wanted. They just didn't have no money.

People said the good times all started to fade away just right at the end of the war, back in '18. The problem was layoffs and layoffs and more layoffs. And mechanization. Used to be during the Great War 441 fathers found work down the shaft in Germantown No. 1. Not now, not in 1925. A single Joy machine did the work of ten hand-loaders, hell, fifteen or twenty, and those jobs were never coming back. Everybody was out of work, and if they got anything, it was two days a week.

At the Westmoreland Coal Company's outdoor coke-ovens in Ronco, where Andy's father worked a couple of nights here and there, the very ovens began to fade into obsolescence as soon as Germantown No. 1 opened, back in 1917. The problem was lower production rates and higher shipping costs. Germantown No. 1 was what was called a captive mine. They barged their output downriver 40 miles to the big new modernized coke plant opened by US Steel in Duquesne. They only had one customer. They only needed one customer. Westmoreland had to ship by rail. They didn't own the railroad, so they had to pay the railroad's rates. That was *if.* The *if* was a big one. The *if* was—if the railroad even had any gondolas available, which often, they didn't. Westmoreland, see, wasn't the only coal company shipping by rail. Half the time, all the gondolas were tied up by the competition, and Westmoreland was out of the running.

A coal miner was the only thing you could be around there. It was the one industry they had in Fayette County. Andy knew whistling wasn't going to paper any walls.

And yet Andy didn't know what he wanted to be when he grew up.

But till then, he couldn't wait till he was ten years old and he could get a job in the mines. After all, his father had started working when he was only ten years old, and in a coal mine, too, and that was back in the old country.

But for Andy, it was just for now. For now it would have to do.

However, when Andy turned ten, his mother wouldn't let him. No matter how he raged, she insisted. She wanted her little man to stay in school and make something of himself. Didn't she have enough on her hands with five little ones and his father to boot? And what about Aleksandar?

"He will never be like other children, not really," said mother. "He has to stay in and take his insulin shot twice a day. He has to be kept away from cuts and bruises. What an example to set for your brother! *He* could never work in a coal-mine, certainly not! And he's not to go down the swimming-hole in that awful brown river, like you and those friends of yours!"

Andy protested that all the kids at school who were turning ten were going to work. Their mothers let them!

He complained that he was going to get teased to death. He said the boys at school were going to call him Little Lord Fauntleroy.

His mother said, "Who?"

He turned to his father, who, as usual, shrugged, and left the house. *Things were nice and quiet at the beer garden.*

One day when he was about eleven Andy was walking along and found his future lying on the ground in front of him.

It seemed he had a habit of walking with his head down. Sometimes he had to remind himself to look up and see the sky. Not that you could see the sky around there. Between the rains of April and the heat haze of July and the dismal misery of November the sky in the coalfields rarely peeked through. The Mon was brown and the air was brown, too. Even the autumn leaves looked perennially smudged. So why would you pick up your head? Besides, if you kept your eyes peeled you might stumble across that nickel and get yourself a Hershey bar.

So this one time the dull glint of something almost shiny caught the corner of his eye.

At first he didn't know what it was. It was closed. He tried opening it. Turned out to be a knife, a jack-knife. He slipped it into his pocket. He liked the hint of glamor about it, the imitation-pearl handle on it.

He had never seen anything like this before. What an idea somebody had! He kept taking it out and opening and closing it. *Gotta be careful you don't cut yourself. Better keep this thing away from brother Alek.*

He had no idea what he was going to do with it or what it was good for but soon he never went out without his jack-knife in his pocket.

One day sitting on the tall steps at the front of the house, nothing to do, maybe go skinny-dipping, maybe just fool around, he started stabbing ants with his jack-knife. After awhile, he got tired of that, looked around, spotted a green branch. I wonder. He found that the knife was perfect for peeling the bark off a green twig. The wood underneath was soft and pliable. But hard to cut. It shredded. It wept. Soon he was looking for a tree. The maple tree down at the end of the block proved too tough. He needed a soft wood. He went hunting for that down by the river in the woods.

His exploration took him a couple of miles from home. There were all kinds of trees he didn't know the names of. Nor did he know if his knife was just too dull. When he found some evergreens, they seemed to be the softest. Andy guessed they were pine trees, but he didn't know.

He knew there was a lumberyard in Pershing, over on South Main, so he headed over there.

"Mister, do you guys sharpen knives here?"

"Sure do. Whatcha got there?"

Andy watched fascinated as the grindstone the man pedaled struck sparks off his knife-blade.

"Whatcha gonna do with that there knife, whittle, I suppose?"

"What's that?"

"Well, you just carve with your knife and make things outta wood."

"What can I make?"

"Why don't you start with a spoon? You can always use a wooden spoon, can't you? Make one long enough your mother can stir her pot with it on the stove, know what I mean, boy? Come on over here."

The man took him round the back of the sawmill section.

"This is a pile of odds and ends we got here, just scrap we gotta throw out. Here, take a couple of pieces, see what you can do with them."

Andy had a lot of trouble figuring out how to make that spoon and make it just right. He kept starting over and had to throw out so many rotten tries. But eventually, by keeping it small, he worked it out. He figured he could get bigger later.

Soon he was making a wooden sled-toy for nine year-old Alek to drag stuff around in and then a wooden doll for his youngest sister, three-year-old Andjela, to dress up. He drafted Adrijana, his nearest sister, only a year behind him, into sewing clothes for the doll. They went around town together knocking on back doors collecting rags. For Orthodox Christmas, he was going to make Alek a real wagon with real wheels that turned. Andy would never have to think about what to do again while he sat out on the front steps. It was now his workshop.

And, he knew now what he was going to be when he grew up. He was going to make things out of wood. All kinds of things. Furniture and cabinets, stuff people needed, that they would buy from him. He was going to be a woodworker.

Meanwhile, the coal mine waited.

Germantown No. 1, the shaft that went down 240 feet, hadn't gone anywhere.

It was the closest mine in the county to Andy's house, only two miles off, so he could walk there to work, easy.

"Majka, I need money. I need tools. I can't ask you and Tata to buy them for me. If I asked you, you know what you would say? You'd say, No, it's not in my budget. I'm twelve years old now. I'm in the sixth grade. I'm the oldest kid in the school. They all laugh at me and think I must be dumb or something or got kept back. What's the point of going any further? What are they gonna teach me? I know how to read. If you can read, you can do anything."

Andy regretted this last statement, because he knew his father felt badly about being an "illiterate," as they called them in this country. And his mother looked like she was about to sit down and cry.

Twelve-year-old boys were not sent down the shaft at Germantown No. 1. You had to be sixteen for that, maybe fifteen and a half if they liked you or you knew somebody. But you could make a dollar a day picking coal underneath the tipple, and at Andy's age, in his eyes, that was a lot of money. Think about it. If you could get seven days that would come to seven bucks a week, a pretty penny.

Andy's twelfth birthday came round on August 2nd of 1929, so in September of that year, instead of going back to school, he signed on at the mine.

The new bridge over the Mon had been opened back in '25. It took the old Carmichaels road high over the river. Nowadays there were so many autos around they turned it into a state road and the signage sported the white keystone with black numerals, spelling 21, with WEST in squared-off capitals above it.

The new bridge was something to see. It ran right alongside the old black-timber railroad bridge, taking green steel arches curving gracefully through the air from a concrete pier to a pair of mid-river abutments, swooping back to a concrete pier on the far shore.

As Andy walked across it that first day he paused around the middle to take a look around him and to observe that they had finally gotten a clear overturned blueberry bowl for a sky. *River's still brown though. See ripples real good from up here. Funny you don't seem to even notice them when you're standing right there down at the ole swimmin'-hole.* Seven or eight coal-barges were docked abreast at the landing on the far shore. He was leaving Fayette County behind him. On the opposite bank it was Greene County. Down there was Germantown No. 1. You could outline the tracks running from the mine entrance downhill to the barge landing with the tiny motor-engine pulling a line of cars with washed coal ready for shipping. The tipple rose up five or six stories from a cluster of trees, and behind that, the river disappeared around a bend. Behind the ridge flanking the mine you could pick out the winding, terraced streets of Shawnee. *Well. Here goes nuthin.' This ole coal mine is gonna make me, if it don't break me first.*

Chapter 5

United Mineworkers

"What the hell've we got here!" The man with his hands on his hips was looking Andy up and down. "Don't they feed you at home?"

McDougal, the straw-boss of the breaker-boys, was a company man through and through. He didn't like you any more than you liked him and he let you know it from the opening bell. "This here's a lump of coal, this is a piece of slate, this is sandstone, and this is dirt. Can you tell the difference? You let the coal go by and pick out the rest. That's your job. Now why don't you find a place over at the conveyor line and see if you can work up an appetite."

Andy opened his mouth, but McDougal stopped him. "And no back-talk. I ain't your mama and I ain't gonna wipe your ass for you."

The conveyor line sloped downhill from the tipple to the coal-loading house where empty pit-cars waited. A boy said to Andy, "Watch out for him."

"Whaddya mean?"

"You'll see."

McDougal strode up and down like a nervous billygoat. He jumped from side to side over the conveyor and went back and forth. He seemed to be trying to watch everything and everybody at once. Out of the side of his eye Andy saw him pick up a stout slice of slate and hurl it at a boy on the other side, who ducked, just barely. "Next time I won't miss!" cried McDougal.

"Did you see that?" said Andy.

"Just pay attention to what you're doing, or you'll be next," said the boy.

"No talking over there!"

"Is he allowed to do that?"

"Shut up! You wanna get me in trouble?"

Andy said to himself, *if he tries that with me!*

But the first time McDougal hit Andy it was a clip in the back of his head with the heel of his hand. It stunned Andy and he didn't know what to do. A hunk of sandstone lay at his feet. McDougal was already walking away as he said, "You missed that! Now throw it on the slag-wagon where it belongs."

Andy was thinking, *so that's his game.* Things were moving too fast. By the time Andy reacted the straw-boss was gone. And the coal kept coming down the chute. It was sized from the screenings it passed through in the tipple but the breaker-boys were the final station and they had to catch whatever got through. And there's nothing you're gonna be able to do about it. Everything's moving so fast. It's *their* system—*and if you wanna work here—*.

It was only five minutes after seven. The mass of miners were still milling around the main heading as the shift change was coming on and going off. It was going to be a long day.

By the time three in the afternoon rolled around, Andy was simply exhausted. He thought he would never have made it, if not for stopping and starting all the time. They got to rest whenever there was a slowdown or halt, the stream of the conveyor was far from continuous. You never knew what the problem was, but when it started again suddenly, it was an avalanche. You had to be ready, and you learned to hunger for a halt. Taking 15 minutes for lunch-break was a relief, you better rest while you could. Still, Andy had never been so tired in his life, and this was only his first day. On the chalk-board at the three o'clock shift change it read "1st Shift, 55 tons loaded."

"Is that good?" Andy asked somebody.

The man grunted. "We musta loaded twice that much."

Andy walked home alone. Most of the breaker-boys lived in Shawnee. That day, nobody his own age was trudging home the two miles to Pershing, only some miners who got off, like him, at three. Heads down, rubbing their faces or the backs of their necks, carrying empty dinner-pails, or maybe with something saved in them for the kids at home, they were silent, dead-tired; in any case, what's to talk about? *another day done, another dollar down.*

At home, his mother waited with water warmed up in the big tin tub in the kitchen where the kids had their Saturday night bath.

"Majka, I'm not a baby."

"You're still a baby to me. Get in."

He bowed his head while she scrubbed his back. It felt so good. "I need to talk to somebody."

"So talk."

"You don't know what it's like down there. I wish I had somebody to talk to, today, of all days."

"Talk to your father."

"I can't talk to him."

"He's a good man."

"Where is he?"

"You know where."

"Yeah. He's a good man."

After dressing, Andy traipsed uptown to the beer garden, he didn't know why, except there was trouble in his mind. Inside, he pulled up a barstool on the old man's left, the other side from his hitting hand.

His father looked at him, then turned away, without a word. It was as if he had been expecting him.

Andy pointed at his glass. "How can you drink that? It stinks."

His father raised one eyebrow and wiped his moustache with the palm of his right hand.

"This whole place stinks."

"So now you're gonna tell your old man what's what. Let me tell you. You got a long way to go to equal me."

"We loaded 55 tons today, the board said. But a miner said it was twice that. What did he mean?"

"You think the weigh-man gonna give you the actual weight? Like hell. When I worked in that mine, we had a contract, the union had their own check-weigh-man, right alongside the company man. They couldn't cheat us. What are they starting you at?"

"Two cents a ton."

"And what are the miners making?"

"Twenty-two cents."

"Hmph. In my day, they were paying us fifty cents. We thought the good times would never end. That time, it was when the war was on. You don't remember."

"I remember our house in Shawnee."

"You were too young."

"I remember the tent-camp, when everybody went out."

"By then, the war was long over. The good times were long gone. They cut our wages by 25 percent. That's why everybody went out. But the union lost the strike, and Kaiser Ziggy the First closed down Germantown No. 1—the biggest coal-mine in the world! He could afford to. He did it just so he could re-open months later with an open shop. The scabs from out of town who took our jobs when we were evicted from Shawnee? They got all the new jobs, what there was. The Joy machine killed the laboring man. On top of it. You ask why you got no weigh-man on your side at the scale today? Because the Kaiser learned his lesson well. He never did sign another union contract since then, did he?"

"I don't know. I was in school. Why do you think I came all the way over here to talk to you—I need to know these things now."

"Well, you got a lot to learn, that's true. Are you gonna learn it, or you gonna quit after one day?"

"How do you do it, Tata?"

"Did you see the mules yet? Of course not, you're not down in the haulageways yet. Maybe you see them around the main heading? You watch the mules. They pull and they haul and then they stand there, patiently, waiting for the next load. The mules bear everything on their backs. That's how you do it—*you become like a mule.*"

"Is that what happened to you, Tata?"

"What are you talking about? I told you—you got a long way to go before you stand on the same level with your old man."

Angrily, it seemed, he drained his glass.

"You come back here in ten years time—talk to me then."

After a while, he said, "Why don't you go home? This is no place for you."

Andy didn't budge.

His father looked at him narrowly.

"You know the only good thing about this country? No Turks!" He laughed, madly, deliriously. He slammed his palm down flat on the bar. "No Turks!"

Chapter 6

USS Ruby

The winter of '31 turned out to be the worst winter of their lives. Milan Petrovich hadn't worked a single day in two years. Westmoreland Coal Company had declared bankruptcy, but that didn't stop them from collecting rents in the patch. The company store was closed down. The company police were let go. Uptown at Kitka's store a loaf of bread was ten cents, a quart of milk 10 cents. But the Petrovich family had no money. They owed nine months of back rent. Andy had long since lost his two days a week at the breaker-shed in Germantown No.1. Demand for coal was down. Demand for steel was down. US Steel in Homestead had closed down the blast furnace. The coke plant in Duquesne was shut. There was no market for nice washed soft coal from Germantown No. 1. Nobody in Pershing was working. Nobody in Pershing was celebrating the soon-to-be New Year of '32. Lately, every new year had turned out worse than the last. Everybody in the steel mills was out of work, every miner for three counties around was out of work, the whole world was out of work. Where could you go to find work, Cleveland? As if you had the money or the transport to pick up and move. Look around you and all you saw was hopelessness on people's faces. The family was forced to go on relief. Andy said it stunk to high heaven. A Petrovich on relief. There was no other choice.

Yet Andy had to work hard every day. Without any English his parents were helpless to deal with the world outside their doors. The Serbian church was their only connection to assistance, but Father Konstantin and his wife Marta had by this time exhausted all private or community resources in the face of overwhelming numbers of needy. It was left to Andy to plead the family's destitution at the county poor board office uptown.

There he had to take his place in long lines standing in the street. These days, lines were everywhere. It took up most of Andy's day to shepherd his parents and brother and sisters through the bread line and the soup line into crowded church halls and schoolrooms to sit down at long tables with all their neighbors. It pained Andy to see his Majka, who had once proudly managed the family budget, sunk so low. If it wasn't for the American Friends Service Committee, perhaps they would have starved.

Or froze. After you fed yourself, how did you stop shaking and shivering inside your house? The three girls, Adrijana, Stasija, and little Andjela, huddled their human warmth in their room upstairs, Majka and Tata, too, downstairs, with baby Ana sleeping between them, and Andy and Alek in their bed. Then what? Now fourteen years old, Andy was in the flush of youth and vigor, but these nights he lay there awake, thinking, thinking. *There were six of them now, six children of Milan and Tamara Petrovich.* Sleep, if it came, was the only refuge for all of them. In your dreams you could escape, but in daylight, the landscape looked so bleak.

Sometimes Andy succumbed to a creeping sense of outrage. Maybe his childhood was gone, but now the best years of his life were being stolen. It was a daily struggle not to sink into the despondency that crept over the valley like a contagion of fog. Only one thing saved him, the daily newspaper.

He had taken out a subscription to the Uniontown Morning Herald when he first got hold of money of his own. He naturally turned over everything to Majka, just as his father had before him. But this he insisted on. It became his practice to read the paper front to back out loud to the family every evening, translating for Tata and Majka as he went. He maintained not that the truth would set them free but that information would keep them alive. "We have to know what's going on, you know?"

And to make it bearable to sit and listen, Andy had to work overtime cutting wood. The Germantown Coal Company had a mountain of slag 200 feet high piled up behind the Shawnee patch, but that was two miles away, across the Mon, and you had to pick what usable coal you could find with all the other families scrambling to pick some, too, and then trek it home in a sack on your back over the bridge. Andy thanked St Sava for sending him the foresight to buy some tools back when he was employed as a breaker-boy. Without his hatchet, axe and rough-toothed saw, he would have been biting tree-bark with his teeth to peel off and burn in the miner's lady in the kitchen.

Then he had to contend with little brother Alek, who was now twelve, the age when big brother Andy had gone to work as a breaker-boy. Alek wanted to help, but Majka was deathly fearful of her younger son getting cut and bleeding. "It's not the saw-blade you gotta worry about," Alek insisted. "It's infection. Andy, she doesn't understand! It's all some superstition to her!"

Andy had to let Alek string along. Just as well. He could use the help.

In his heart Andy realized that Alek just wanted to imitate him, to be like his big brother. Sadly, he had his affliction to overcome, and Majka didn't help. Someday they might all find that little brother would have to stand on his own.

It was the newspaper one night that caused Andy to exclaim, "Listen. Listen to this. Governor Pinchot says that the only force big enough, and strong enough, and able to act in time, to save us from the coming winter, is the Federal government. And he's a Republican! Let Hoover put *that* in his pipe!"

He shut up the paper and went out for his nightly foraging for firewood in the woods. As he left, he spotted Majka slipping Tata a nickel for his evening trip to the beer garden. Sometimes Andy felt his gall rising over that, but then he would button his lip. Just as well to have the old man out of the house. Less trouble all around.

It was something sad to see Milan Petrovich these days, bereft of his youth, robbed of his red sash, but no one had any use for a middle-aged ex-miner with no other skills who couldn't read or write or speak the language. Andy had to admit it. It might be that his father would never work again. Yet the old man was loath to relinquish the shreds of his dignity. He seemed to think it was only his just due that the family should scrub his back and cut his hair for him. His father had become useless to Andy, and worse, useless to Majka, whom he treated like a servant while she hauled water and scrubbed her fingers to the bone washing his socks and longjohns. It was a dirty rotten shame. It should have been the other way round. Andy was supposed to be the child, not the parent.

Into this vacuum stepped a Hungarian called Sandor Nagy, a refugee from Rossiter, up north in Indiana County.

The story went that Sandy, as everyone called him, had been run out of Rossiter at the time of the big strike up there, back in '27, by company goons hired by the Keystone Coal Company. He had taken to the road as a UMW organizer. He was a staunch John L. Lewis man. If you could get Sandy to stop philosophizing for a minute, you could get him to recite bloodthirsty tales of the bad old days.

It was Sandy Nagy who alerted Andy to the chance of a job.

Up till now Andy had only been able to make a couple of dollars a week with his paper route, delivering the Uniontown Herald seven days on foot to the big houses on the other side of town. But Sandy Nagy had good news for all the fathers and young men in Pershing, Pennsylvania desperately looking for work.

He had been signing up miners for the UMW by the dozen for the past couple of years, holding meetings at an abandoned machine shed of the defunct Westmoreland Coal over in Ronco. With the general loosening up of opposition that came with the hard times, he now had boldly set up at the new (since '26) firehouse, in Pershing itself, with the backing of the volunteer firefighters, most of whom were miners by trade.

"Men! Governor Pinchot has announced he's not waiting for Hoover to wake up, or turn human, whichever comes first. No siree! The Gov is gonna institute some doings by the Commonwealth of Pennsylvania, so-called, all on his lonesome. In other words, he's gonna put you lazy slackers to work building roads!"

"And worser than that! He has come right out and stated that right here in your own Fayette County we are the hardest-hit in the state! How's that for beans? We gotta be best at something, hain't it? And let me tell you right now in no uncertain terms if it wasn't for the pressure put on by the organized members of the UMW, led by none other than John L. Lewis himself, with the marches and counter-marches and demonstrations and picketing and whatnot, like the Hunger March put on by the mothers and children over in Harrisburg, we would not have come to this. Now, let me remind you—as long as you men of Local 1228 have been out of work at Germantown No. 1, we have suspended collection of dues, because, well, these are hard times, and we gotta stick together and help one another. They'll be time enough once we're back working at our trade. Meanwhile, if you boys are gonna get some paychecks coming in, we will appreciate most kindly any voluntary contributions you may wish to make."

Andy was standing in the audience and he heard voices at the back who started singing. Soon the whole room was moving. *". . . I'm stickin' to the union, till the day I die!"*

It was a catchy tune, and Andy went home whistling it.

The next day Andy went to see Sandy Nagy personally.

"Mr Nagy, my old man, he's in no condition for road work. I hate to say this but he's kinda given up. I'm the only hope my family's got, but I'm only fourteen. I can't take a chance on getting refused the work."

"Well, son, we'll just hafta get your parents to sign something to the effect that you're sixteen, shall we say?"

Andy was ashamed of the fact, but he had no choice but to bring his document, typed out by Sandy Nagy, to the work-relief hiring office with his father's signature signed with an X.

Thus, in January of '32, Andy found himself assigned to living in a tent, just as he had ten winters earlier, only this time, he was in the new road-building camp set up in Fayette County, in rural Normalville, on top of a mountain, about 12 miles northeast of the county seat, Uniontown. At 22 miles from home, there was no question he was going to be separated for months from the family.

At least he wouldn't have to sit there and watch his brother Alek shoot a needle into his arm twice a day.

They wanted to know why he was so small for his age. Andy answered, "I been on starvation rations, that's why!"

In the end, the camp provided him with his first real growth spurt. Better late than never, Andy thought, as he shot up to a grown man's height of five foot seven and three-quarters. That's what three squares a day'll do for you. They built roads through the backwoods up and down and around the mountainsides, two lanes of blacktop on top of a layer of crushed stone. The farmers back there had never had anything but dirt roads to get their produce to market. In order to employ more men, most of the work was done by hand with shovel, pick and wooden rake. The older guys who'd been down below figured they were doing the same damn thing, only they had the open air to do it in. Once in a while you got a break while the engineers and surveyors figured out how to scratch their heads. Then you graded the thing by hand. Andy didn't add much girth to his bones, but his back, legs and arms grew tight and sinewy with muscle. After nine months of regimented marching back and forth to the jobsite from barracks, living amongst strangers who became the best pals you ever had, Andy was no longer Andy. His higher education had begun.

There were only two colored men in the camp. One was Andy's age, or supposed to be, the other, a cousin of his, something in his twenties.

Andy had never been in school with any colored kids, but he didn't especially go out of his way in the camp to spurn them. It never occurred to him why he should. Hadn't they the right to make a living just as much as anyone else?

Still, he noticed right off that the two colored boys always worked together, every day, like they were watching each other's backs. In a way, he liked that they stuck together. Sometimes Andy felt like he wished that he could feel a little such solidarity coming off the white men in the camp. Sometimes, if he wandered into the lunch room and there was no other place to sit, he would sit at the table with the two colored boys, where they kept off by themselves. He got to know one of them, named Lester, a little bit. He never did find out the cousin's name. They were not exactly big talkers. In fact, they appeared downright distrustful.

However, the colored folk had to use separate toilets and couldn't shower with the whites. The shower room was communal and all the whites would just clear out. Andy could see what was going on and he figured he better do the same.

That didn't stop three men from coming to see him one day.

"We noticed you been getting kinda comfy with them coons. You some kinda nigger-lover, or what?"

One of the others said, "We never had no niggers down in the haulageways with us, and no nigger-lovers, neither, and that's the way we like it."

The third said, "See that you observe the local customs."

The next day at lunch when his colored friend sat down next to him with his tray, Andy just picked up and moved.

Can't fight city hall, he was thinking.

After nine months of road-building, when the program expired, on the last day of camp, the colored boy his own age, the one named Lester, looked at him, a certain, funny way, like, before they parted, he wanted Andy to know how disappointed in him he was. Andy just looked off and kept going.

All the way home he had a haunted feeling and wished to God almighty that he had stuck up for them or something.

Sandy Nagy, when he heard the story, told Andy he'd done the right thing.

"It's not your fault, son. There's only so much one man can do on his own. Lincoln freed the slaves but he didn't free the minds of white folks. Now you know. Now you learnt a lesson. You can't change the whole world all by yourself— that's why you need the union. And mind you, those men, as wrong-headed as can be, are dues-paying miners. We never said it was going to be easy, but now that Roosevelt is coming in, you just watch. There's gonna be changes, big changes. And someday, someday—well, you just never know. The world is changing, Andy. Don't you think I have the very same problem as you? Of course I do, only multiply it. It's called having a conscience. It's called being a socialist, and not a Klansman. It's called fighting injustice, because you're against the thugs. And right now, Andy, we can see it coming down the pike, a New Deal for everybody."

Indeed, the election year of 1932 was the biggest and most important in the whole of American history, everyone said. And they all knew long before election day itself that Roosevelt was gonna get shooed in by a landslide. Change was in the wind. People were excited by the prospects lit up by the Democrats' campaign promises: the New Deal was a slogan that had a ring to it. And the people were ready to hear it. Anything to get them back to work and out of this dad-blasted Depression. This election year was just as much a referendum on getting rid of Hoover as it was anything. The people were in such dire straits that only the government could rescue them, plain as the nose on your face.

Then, on the eve of the election, the very night before, something happened in Pennsylvania that shocked the world.

It happened back east, in the anthracite coal country of Schuykill County. Kelayres was a tiny place about the size of Shawnee, no more, just a patch, but the Democrats had organized local miners to parade through the streets on election eve. Naturally, they were unarmed. They could not have foreseen that the local Republican Party boss, Joe Bruce, with his sons, had set up an ambush from hiding at the crossroads of Center St and Fourth St. Three marchers were shot dead instantly and a couple of dozen wounded and a couple of those subsequently died in hospital over in McAdoo.

Living in the road camp, Andy had gotten used to radio. They had never had a radio at home. The radio quickly became as essential to Andy as the daily paper. Each week, out of his seven-fifty pay packet, he had mailed a money order for six dollars back to Majka from the camp post office. One week he included a note to tell her he'd be home soon and he wanted her to purchase a radio for the family.

The night of the massacre Andy was translating for Tata and Majka. The whole family was gathered. Andy was glad to be back. Everything seemed different now. Alek had been delivering the old paper route while Andy was away. The family had been taking in about eight bucks a week. Things were a little better. His sister Adrijana was calling herself Adrienne, now that she was 14. His kid brother was growing up. Stasija and little Angie were playing innocently with baby Ana on the floor while "Adrienne" occupied her usual place, crouched at her father's knee, which she draped with her elbow. Majka for once was beaming to have her boys back together. Then the news came on. Andy saw his parents, their faces, change, as he translated. A look of profound disbelief crept up on them. For once, his useless old man registered a human emotion. Andy felt oddly somehow that all of them were going through a shock, like a cold shower, or a window breaking with a crash. He could hardly believe the words he himself was saying. How could this happen? He watched "Adrienne" climb up onto her father's lap to put her head on his shoulder. He felt somehow drawn closer, closer to all of them. The Depression was a constant undertone that never went away, a slow-moving poison that thrummed inside you, but this—this was the face of evil jumping up in the room, an apparition.

And it was all due to that radio. They were a mining family. They all knew that a life of suffering and deprivation was the miners' lot. Those shot down in cold blood in Kelayres were miners, like them. Kelayres was far away, but, because of that radio, you didn't hear of it days later: the impact was instant, it was happening to you, right here, in your own house, right now.

In many ways, Sandy Nagy was right. The New Deal changed everything. It changed every little thing in Fayette County.

The temporary work-relief road-building program of Republican Governor Pinchot was just that, temporary. The new man, George Earle, was swept in on the coat-tails of Roosevelt's nationwide landslide, the first Democrat elected Governor in Pennsylvania since 1890.

The Kelayres massacre, on the night before the election, due to radio, cost the Republicans the governor's seat.

And yet the same radio, the very next night, spread joy over all their faces with the news of Franklin Delano Roosevelt's presidential election landslide.

All thought of massacres or even an historic new governor was eclipsed by this momentous cataclysm.

That summer of 1933, two things occurred. No, Germantown No. 1 did not re-open. But they were suddenly not dependent on the mine anymore. Suddenly massive work-relief programs on a much larger scale than anyone could have imagined, overnight, opened up a whole new world.

That summer they received a godsend; after the miracle of St Sava that saved Alek's life, it was a second miracle. When Andy heard about it he signed up right away. The new Works Progress Administration, out of Washington, had set up in Pershing and was going to build water and sewer into Maple Ave.—their street! It was the miracle of St Roosevelt.

By this time Andy was turning genuinely sixteen. After building roads in the mountains he was in prime condition for digging holes in the street. And baby brother Alek worked right alongside him. They were a team now.

Until the winter the boys were occupied and bringing home market-rate wages. Overnight, the family was making headway again. It seemed as if they had been rescued. Gone were the dinners made out of flour and water. They were eating lamb on the stick again. "Adrienne" was getting her hair done at Slovak's beauty parlor uptown. The radio was percolating away. Every now and then they sat down to have a Fireside Chat translated. President Roosevelt, now known affectionately as FDR, came right in to advise and support and comfort you. Because of the new water and sewer lines, they had running water in the house. Andy and Alek rigged up a shower for themselves in the basement next to the toilet, so that they could enter the house through the basement side-door and clean up before they even came upstairs. When winter came, although they would never spend money buying coal, it was practically a joy for the brothers to be going out chopping firewood together, and the house felt toasty.

Suddenly woodworking opened up for Andy. He was overjoyed. When Orthodox Christmas came that year, they had a tree and presents all wrapped up for the little ones, Stasija and Andjela. Andy's present was the announcement that the Quakers were going to open a chair-and-table-building furniture factory, right here, in Pershing.

It was the First Lady, Eleanor Roosevelt, who inspired them. She had been down below the border in West Virginia on a fact-finding tour and she had personally publicized her mission to spread the gospel of self-help. They were building some kind of model community in Arthurdale, just a few miles away from Pershing. The new town was named after the man who sold his farmlands to the federal government in a tax-default sale. Mrs Roosevelt took the idea from her friend Lorena Hickok and they were to relocate impoverished laborers, miners and farmers into the new town. The First Lady got Bernard Baruch to pitch in. Then she won over her husband who turned the whole plan over to the Department of the Interior and it became an official New Deal program.

Andy went to the Friends. "You gotta sign me up. This is what I want to do with my life! I could learn so much! You could teach me so much! I'll be the best investment you ever made!"

Like everything, the furniture factory did not last forever. Eventually it came up against market realities. But it took the place of the WPA water-and-sewer project and it carried Andy through 1934. And it gave him and Alek both a new outlook on life. Now they were enjoying themselves. Now they were no longer afraid. They had learned that they could help themselves. They were young and this was the time of their lives. Sure, there was a Depression on, but, well, maybe that wasn't going to last forever either. Alek especially was bursting with new ideas. He had convinced Andy they were actually going to team up and buy a car for the family. He was itching to get going and already he was spending money on getting the right tools. Andy wasn't the only one with a passion for a certain trade.

After all, who would've ever thunk that Majka wasn't gonna have to haul water anymore, but just stroll over to the sink and open the tap! And who would've ever thunk they'd be the kind of people who could afford a refrigerator in the house, instead of the old icebox? By the time 1935 rolled around, when the boys were out of work, miracle number three. Now they could collect!

It was called Unemployment Compensation. An unheard of thing. They would pay you half your average wages to tide you over while you looked for work. Not only that but now Social Security was coming in. Sure, it would be too late to benefit Majka and Tata, but it meant something. It meant that in future times, in the long-distant future, he and Alek would be provided for in old age.

Andy leaned back and reflected that his life was growing strong and hard just as his muscles were. He was ready for anything.

They could keep their house. They were paying rent again. Between the UMW and the coal companies everybody had agreed on writing off old debts. The family was going to stick together. Nobody was ever going to evict them again. He and Alek, together, would care for the old folks when the time came. In fact, when the FHA came in, in '34, and the government did a deal with the defunct Westmoreland Coal, it meant that, in 1935, the family was able to get an affordable mortgage and buy the house they were living in. *Would wonders never cease?*

One night Tata was home especially to listen to one of the Fireside chats. "Adrienne" wanted to sit on his lap. But he shoved her away, a little roughly. He didn't have to be mean about it. The old man sounded repulsive, as if he felt disgusted, personally, as he said to his daughter in Serbian, "You're getting to be too old for that!"

It did not escape Andy, the look that Adrienne shot around the room. Majka dropped her hands on her knees. Adrienne fled in tears.

Andy shot out of the house and followed her down the street. "Where are you going!"

"What do you care?"

"Adrienne!"

"Leave me alone!"

Andy tried to grab her by the arm, but she wrenched free. "You and the rest of them can all go to hell!"

Baffled, Andy watched her stalk off into the darkness.

That night he lay awake till he heard the front door open and he realized it was her, creeping back to bed. His own sister was a stranger to him.

By the end of that year Andy's 12 weeks on the unemployment rolls were drawing to a close. Nothing had turned up. It was going to be 1936 and in spite of the New Deal, the cavalry riding to the rescue of the common man, the marketplace was still keeping down the one industry that counted in Fayette County, and that was King Coal.

The news from Sandy Nagy was all about his man, John L. Lewis, and the fresh start the old warrior was making with the new Committee for Industrial Organization, the CIO. Ever since FDR's election in '32, said Nagy, Lewis, The UMW, and the President's New Deal had worked in tandem against the common enemy, the Morgan-Rockefeller-Mellon-Dupont gang.

"Believe me, boys, I know," said Sandy. "What happened to us up in Rossiter in '27 was nothing more than a planned campaign of destruction waged by the Gang of Four against the working man. Boys, it was an anti-labor crusade. Look at us today. Because of Lewis and FDR, we got the Bituminous Coal Code, we got the five dollar daily wage, we got the union shop and dues check-off, and we got the right to appoint our own check-weigh-off man."

Andy spoke up. "Sandy—I never saw a picture of John L. Lewis but he was dressed up in a suit with two-tone shoes on his feet. I don't own a suit. And Germantown No. 1's still shut down."

"That's the point, men! We need the CIO to organize the mass-production industries like the autoworkers and the truck-drivers, or we're never gonna get back to work in No. 1. Without we organize the steelworkers, a captive mine like Germantown's got no market."

"That ain't our job, Sandy," another man protested, "worrying about how the hell they're gonna open the steel mills again when they can't sell any steel."

"Seems like we always get the short end of the stick!"

"Yeah! The last thing the big-shots think about is the miner!"

Every meeting degenerated this way. It was next to impossible to get the workingmen of Fayette County to look over the hills beyond their horizons. But what they did know was that over the years, without their willingness to walk out, John L Lewis himself had no weapon with which to threaten the coal-operators. And that meant that it's us miners that hold the power! And here we see the old man shooting off every which way concerning himself with every worker in America but us!

The boys were angry.

"Yup. Old John L.'s made a nice career for himself on our backs."

Andy couldn't wait. He needed something now. There was a chance he could've joined another road-building or bridge project with the CCC, which was hiring at the moment, but he just felt that just now was not the right time to be leaving town again. No, not now.

There was a place uptown where he might try. Chalkie's pool-hall. Lately they'd had a sign, *Help Wanted,* on the glass door leading into the hallway stairs beside the hardware store. Up there, on the second floor of the longish building, they had three bowling alleys. Andy wasn't cut out for a bank-teller, he thought, but he might try his hand at pin-setter.

He found Chalkie himself lounging on the bench against the wall beside the Coke machine. A couple of older kids skipping school were circling a pool table, and the room was full of smoke.

Chalkie was an old Scotchman. Once upon a time he'd been a flunkie in the mines. Chalkie said, "You one of them hunkies from down in the patch."

It was not a question. Andy said, "Guess so."

"Long as you ain't no nigger."

"Don't let the coal-dust fool ya."

"Long as you know this ain't no union payscale here. I suppose you can push a broom?"

Chalkie was indoors-pale, undernourished. He looked like watered-down whisky. He never moved from his bench by the wall if he could help it. He talked about as fast as he moved.

"Well, am I hired or what? I'll be the pin-setter, right?"

"Boy," said Chalkie, "you be whatever you wanna call it."

Andy had often heard the knocking of the pins from the street below when he walked by. He never ventured in because, well, he didn't have money to throw away. Now, bank-teller, that smelled, something like *company man*. But pin-setter, there was something disgraceful about that which had an appeal all its own. Anyway, it was just to sort of tide him over, you know? Besides, at this stage of things, what else was there? Alek had the paper route. Pin-setter was only 50 cents a day but you could make tips. Supposedly, he'd get a ten-cent raise after 2 weeks. Andy could walk to work. He didn't know what else to do. Neither Alek or himself dreamed of walking to work—they dreamed about cars. And girls. And someday. And it seemed there were always cars parked out back of Chalkie's. Someday had just pulled up to Chalkie's pool-room.

Anyhow, one of these days Germantown No. 1 was going to come back. It just had to. Give me a jackknife and a slab of wood and I'll make something out of it, Andy was thinking.

I'll make something of myself, too, if I have to whittle my way out of this slag-heap.

One day at Chalkie's one of the older kids came over. He stood in front of Andy leaning his chin on his hands on top of his cue-stick.

The middle of the week was slow at Chalkie's. After sweeping up, there was nothing to do but sit. Nobody came in weekday afternoons to bowl. The only time you could make tips was the weekend nights. But the older kids who had cars and money and no jobs and nothing to do spent every after-noon shooting pool and gambling and raising some minor dust to amuse themselves.

"Where'd you learn to whistle like that?" said the kid leaning on the stick.

"I dunno. I just always could."

"Just like that, huh?"

"I guess. Can I ask you a question?"

"Sure."

"Where do you get the money to throw away on playing pool and losing bets?"

"Who, us?" The older kid laughed, and turned to wink at his friends at the pool tables. "We work at night, kid."

"Doing what?"

"We're rum-runners."

"You're full of it."

"You never heard of Prohibition?"

"Prohibition's been out for a long time now."

"Well, you gotta start somewhere. We still got the cab-in-cruiser tied up at the wharf down at the river this very minute."

His friends were stifling themselves.

"I never seen it."

"That's 'cause we keep it hidden in the long reeds due to the revenue agents, daytimes, I mean. We only take it out at night and sail downriver to the ocean where we pick up a load off the freighter from Mexico. You ever seen the ocean, kid?"

"How would I see the ocean?"

"Well, just take a trip downriver with us and it connects right up."

"You must think I'm stupid."

"Listen, all rivers run down to the sea."

"Not the Monongahela. It runs up to Pittsburgh and joins the Allegheny."

"To form the Ohio. Which then flows down to junction with the Mississippi in Cairo, Illinois. And from there, it's a hop, skip and a jump all the way down to the Gulf o' Mexico in New Awlins."

"Well, I suppose you're right. I suppose I knew that all along."

"Of course you did. You ain't no stupid Hunky."

"He's a smart kid, all right, Teddy!" one of the pool-shooting pals called out.

"What are your friends laughing at?"

"Now, don't go getting all sensitive on us. They're laughin' 'cause they're fuckin' jerks. Tell you what. If you want, you can come for a ride with us."

"I dunno. I'm pretty busy. Hain't got the time."

"Skeered, huh?"

"Nope."

"Skeered of the revenue agents."

So it was that Andy met up with a new phenomenon, rich kids from the country-club set over in Latrobe who spent their afternoons slumming at Chalkie's.

Andy had no desire whatever to get in over his head with these wise-guy types and their girlfriends. He liked Teddy's Ford, that was true, but the big but was, he didn't belong. He didn't care for being the subject of joke-ifying or the woebegone tag-along.

In a part of town called Gray's Landing, down by the river-bottom, where the colored folks lived, a lady called Dolly McAndrews had a little woodframe house. She was a white lady, although some said she was no kind of a lady at all. Her house had no street and no number and no mailbox and no paint on the clapboards, but everybody knew where Dolly McAndrews lived, even the postman. Dolly didn't have to leave her house because everyone and everything came to her, day and night. If ever there was anything Dolly wanted, there were plenty who would fetch and carry for her. Dolly was never mentioned in polite company, but somehow she was the main topic of conversation all over. In Pershing, PA, when there was an accident or an explosion in some mineshaft, or a wreck on the road, or jobs to line up for at some new alphabet-soup Federal project, they'd talk about it for weeks, but till then, they had to talk about something.

One day Teddy politely invited Andy to ride along with them to the party that night. "You see, the thing is, we promised Dolly we'd get her a fella that's never been kissed."

"I been kissed before."

"By who?—your mother? Your sisters?"

Teddy's friends were sniggering. "They kiss on the lips in that family."

"Don't mind them. They're just ignorant."

"Thanks, but, no thanks. I think I'll pass."

Teddy Robertson folded his arms.

"I guess maybe you'd better not, Andy. I guess maybe you're just too young."

That night the alleys and the pool-room were emptied out and it was just Andy and Chalkie sitting there staring at the four walls.

"I guess you better go on home," said Chalkie.

"Guess so. Ain't making no tips this Friday."

"You go on home and check on your sister."

Andy shot a look at Chalkie, but the old Scotchman was just staring down at his dirty fingernails.

Andy got home and tore into the house.

"Is she here?"

"Who?" said Alek, suddenly scared of his big brother.

"Your sister Adrienne!"

"She went out, Andy!"

"You stay here and watch the kids. I'll be back."

Andy ran all the way down to Gray's Landing. He went into Dolly McAndrews' house the same way he had his own, flinging the door open.

Teddy and his boys were arranged around sofas in the front room making out with their girlfriends while they dangled a bottle in the other hand. Andy strode over to Teddy and grabbed the girl by the arm who had that arm around Teddy's neck.

"You're coming home with me!"

"Whaddya think you're doing!" cried Adrienne.

Teddy jumped up.

"You stay out of this!" said Andy. "This is my sister."

"Whaddya think you are, my father!"

Andy pinched harder on her arm and twisted her toward the door. He didn't wait for a debating society to start, he just hustled her off her feet.

By the time they got home, he hadn't let go of her arm yet, but he had calmed down. "Go wash your face off!"

"This ain't the last of this," cried Adrienne. "Majka, you gonna let him treat me like this?"

"Go wash your face off," said Andy, "before your Tata gets home."

"I won't have you interfering with my life!"

"Well, I'll tell you something, baby sister. When you're free, white and 21, you can do what you want, and not before!"

That was the end of Chalkie's for Andy. He blamed himself for all this. Why hadn't he seen this coming? He had opened the wrong door, gone up the wrong stair. He'd stay home and whittle, he'd start building furniture again, and try and sell it, he'd do anything to keep from going crazy. And if the family fell apart, what then?

It was no use talking to the old man. There was no solace and no decency there, leastways, that Andy could see. Just an old drunk. He couldn't go to Father Konstantin, though they saw him every Sunday at the church picnic. Andy still heard his voice saying, "You'll have to put that apple back." Who else was there but Sandy Nagy?

"These are rudderless times to be growing up in, Andy. Bad as the old days was, I think I wouldn't go back to being your age now for any amount."

At least Sandy Nagy told you the truth, jimcracks and all.

Usually, the Mon plowed its sluggish and slow rut northward through the valley like a kind of moving mudslide meandering and backwashing, but once in a while it erupted and over-flowed its banks.

On the last day of 1936 the UAW walked out of the Fisher body plant in Cleveland because two brothers on the assembly line had been fired. It was a wildcat strike that sparked a tumult, and next thing you know, they had a Movement. By February, John L. Lewis was settling a violent 44-day sit-down strike against General Motors itself, in Flint, Michigan, far from Andy's valley, but not so far as the Teamster's Strike in Minneapolis or the Longshoremen's Strike out in San Francisco. The thread of connection was John L. Lewis himself. He personally had invented the CIO, and he was the head of their mineworkers' UMW. If you traced it back, the sitdown-strike in Flint had been born out of a cascade effect originating with the miners. Suddenly earthquakes were breaking out all over. The UAW in Flint had won a 5% increase in pay for the autoworkers and the right to talk during lunch. Think about that! A new world was dawning. It was all linked up together everywhere at once. The CIO in 1937 exploded up to half-a million members and opened its ranks to Negroes, too. Flint was the strike heard round the world. Soon the dam was bursting over the heads of the steelworkers in Homestead and the Gang-of-Four. In early May, Lewis signed a new contract re-opening U.S. Steel, the giant. Then the organizers went after Little Steel, so called, Bethlehem Steel, Youngstown Sheet and Tube, Inland Steel. On Memorial Day the police in Chicago shot and killed ten strikers and wounded 90 others at Republic Steel.

This was maddening. A massacre. Not since that time back in '32, the Kelayres Massacre, had there been such outrage. Andy and the rest of Local 1228 were in the midst of their own seven-day strike. The re-opening of US Steel in Homestead meant the firing up of the massive coke plant in

Duquesne, and the cascade effect was that Germantown No. 1, the captive mine in Shawnee, was brought back on line. When hiring opened up, Andy, as a former breaker-boy, had obtained a pick-and-shovel position in the room-and-pillar operations 240 feet down, Alek, too, now 18 years old, who was not about to be left behind by his big brother. At last here was their chance at those cars, and they could put the family on easy street to boot. The first thing you know, they're out on strike for a pay-increase.

It did not last long, but it didn't need to, because it was bloody and violent. Company goons appeared at the picket lines attempting to get a path cleared for scab labor to get through. Andy, Alek and the Local members fought back with whatever came to hand, rocks, coal, picket signs, tree branches. Most of the hired mercenaries on the company side were unknown to Andy, but he sure recognized a few. Amazing. Unbelievable. It was Teddy Robertson and the sewer-scum he hung out with at Chalkie's pool-room.

Andy's spleen knew no bounds. It rose and choked him. Rage boiled his eyes. He fought them with glee, with intensity, with fury in his lungs, he wanted blood, he fought them with bare fists, if he could get close enough. He and Alek, the brothers, fought them side by side. Like Alek said, all he had to worry about was infection—cuts and bruises only made both of them madder. Andy called out Teddy by name, to make sure everybody targeted him. "There's the son-of-a-bitch who's been hanging out in our town just waiting for this! You wanna know where he got the money to shoot pool? The Company!"

Lewis and FDR and the NLRB settled their strike after seven days with a victory for the miners on all counts. They needed Germantown No. 1 back on line because they needed Duquesne and Homestead working full-blast, not shut down.

They had a Depression to fight and their fight was getting old on them. They more or less forced Kaiser Ziggy the First to the signing-table with a gun to his head. The new contract called for the six-hour day, the six-day week, a standard wage of $5 a day, and the right to appoint their own union check-weigh-man.

Victory was sweet. The brothers were bloodied and ready for anything. They were on their way. Sundays at the church picnic were a celebration. They danced. They danced the polka with every pretty girl in sight. Andy grabbed them tight around the waist and whirled them hard while he kicked his heels up and stamped his feet. Jovanka from first grade still followed him around everywhere. She was chubby and five foot now and her eyebrows were still black and met in the middle but she was still after him. Andy had to tell her, "Jovanka—this is not a Ladies Choice!" Alek had found a love of his own, a pretty young thing with strawberry blond hair, a Polack called Rose Novakowski. She was innocent and enchanting and in love with Alek. "Watch out for them Catholic schoolgirls," Andy told him. Alek said, "I can take care of myself. Think I'll marry this one." Andy said, "You gonna pick up that Chevy you been talking about?" Alek said, "The one second-hand from that farmer over in Carmichaels?"

"Needs a lotta work."

"I got the tools."

"You know what I always say—never do the wrong job with the right tool!"

In 1939 Adrienne ran off to New York City, to an apartment in the 230s in the Bronx, and set up with Teddy Robertson.

There was no church wedding or nothing. The family didn't even know. Just one day she was gone.

The same year in August around Andy's 22nd birthday Sandy Nagy organized busloads to go up to Rossiter in Indiana County to hear John L. Lewis address the miners and their families in an open field.

Earlier that summer, in June, Alek and Rose got married, in both churches, St Sava's Serbian Orthodox on Alek's side, and Our Lady's Roman Catholic on Rose's. Between Polish and Serbian the two families' new mothers-in-law managed to talk to one another. The reception was held at the Polish Falcons.

Andy was happy for him. He knew it was what Alek wanted. He had a girl of his own he had taken up with, called Maggie, and, especially at his brother's wedding, all she could talk about was getting married, but somehow it just made Andy restless to listen to that.

"We're too young."

That made Maggie mad.

"Got a lot of livin' to do."

Madder. He smooched her on her neck. She melted.

"Just gettin' started," said Andy, with a sly wink, as he whirled her around the dance-floor.

Alek was now getting himself a new second-hand Chevy to work on once a year, so when the UMW Rally in Rossiter came up, the four of them piled into a '34 hardtop coupe and raced up and down the hills and curves in the caravan with the busses.

"Pass 'em out, pass 'em out!" yelled Andy from the back seat, with his arm slung over Maggie's other shoulder.

"You crazy? I'm too young to die!"

"Come on, you chicken-shit, let's go!"

"Watch out or I'll come back there and whup your ass!"

"Like to see you try!"

"Whee!" cried Alek as he slipped the stick-shift into neutral at the top of a hill. "Freewheelin'!"

That night after the Rally they were sitting around a campfire with Sandy Nagy. People's faces were glowing with reflected flickering lights. The faraway-ness of the stars floating overhead when you looked up made you feel small. You could sense the universe washing back and forth inside the body leaning close to yours. Twenty thousand people had been packed in that field to hear John L. It didn't matter what he said. Even now, they didn't remember what he said. What they never would forget was this feeling. Maggie leaned her head on Andy's shoulder. They were a part of something so big that it made you shiver to try to grasp the immensity. Twenty thousand people. And that's just a fraction. Of all the people in the world. Of all the love in the universe.

Somebody with a guitar was strumming a tune, and singing softly.

> *Hang your head over,*
> *Hear the wind blow . . .*

Andy was sitting on the stoop one afternoon whittling wood when he heard the radio coming through the screen door. It was a Sunday. Everything quiet. He had been working down below in Germantown No. 1 for four years now. It seemed like long ago when he had constructed that dollhouse for baby Andjela when she was four years old. She loved that thing. Played for hours. Happy. Alek and Rose had their own place now, an apartment, 2nd floor, uptown. Adrienne was long gone, hardly even a letter except now and then to remind them how wonderful New York was compared to Pershing, Penna. Stasija was nineteen now and worked in the Ben Franklin Five-and-Dime uptown, even little Angie was 18 already, and running around with a farmer named John Lucinda from over in Carmichaels. All Angie wanted out of life was a place of her own and babies of her own. She still had the dollhouse, saved for them. Baby Ana was the only one of the Petrovich children still in school. Things had changed. They had come a long way. Hard to believe but 1941 was almost over already. Soon it would be Orthodox Christmas and the new year would be 1942.

Then the music through the screendoor ceased, and a voice from New York came on.

In about a minute, Alek in his Chevy pulled up, with tires squealing.

He slammed the car-door but took his time coming up the steps. He sat himself down next to his brother.

"You heard?"

"Yup."

"What are we gonna do now?"

"I dunno. Wait and see. Goddamned Japs."

"Alls I know is I couldn't stand two minutes away from Rose, it would just about do me in, but if I hafta, I hafta."

"Most likely, the answer is no. They're gonna need coal-miners. They'll find some way to exempt us. We knew this was coming, Alek. We knew for a long time. FDR ain't stupid, you know."

"Yeah. I guess so. You're right. We're in the slag-wagon now."

"Lemme ask you something. You like it down the shaft?"

"Nobody likes it, brother. I can tolerate it. It pays the bills. What else you gonna do around here? How you gonna make that kind of money?"

Andy looked at his baby brother. "You'd take a mighty pay-cut then if you ever thought of joining up. You should think about that."

"Maybe we should ask Tata his advice."

"That old draft-dodger? 'Course, he faced getting drafted by either the Austrian empire to fight the Serbs or the Serbian army to fight the Austrians. No wonder he ran away."

"And landed us in the *pasulj.*"

"Well, now it's our turn to clean up their mess."

"Well, what are we gonna do?"

"Let's just wait and see, all right?"

Andy waited and he saw but he didn't see anything good because all through 1942 there was nothing but reverses, retreats, defeats, the death march on Bataan, and then Corregidor, holy smokes.

Before Christmas he enlisted in the US Navy.

He told Alek, "I've never even seen the ocean. Adrienne's in New York. She seen it before me. Maybe I'll get stationed there and we take a stroll down to the water together."

He finally told Maggie, *No.*

As he was leaving town on the bus he knew he was saying goodbye. In his heart he knew it was goodbye to coal-mining, too. *I'm sick of the muddy Mon.*

Andy Petrovich conceived of seafaring as the most impossibly opposite thing you could do from coal-mining, all the way at the other end of the pole.

After boot camp at Great Lakes Naval Training Station, they shipped him out to Jacksonville, Florida, where, he was told, he was to be assigned to a ship that was being converted in the shipyard there.

That was when he came face to face with the *USS Ruby* while standing in line dockside.

"What is this old tub?" he asked the seaman taking his papers at the table.

"This old tub, fella, is William K. Vanderbilt's personal luxury yacht which he has donated to the war effort."

"Is that a fact?"

"Yes it is. Anything else you curious about?"

"Looks big for a yacht. Big enough for a Vanderbilt, I guess. Destroyer?"

"Destroyer-escort. Length 190 feet, beam 26. Designated PY-21, painted on the bow already. Means *Patrol Yacht.* Built in Bremen in 1931. Boy, you're gonna serve out the war on a German vessel."

On board the Chief Petty Officer looked at his papers.

"See here where it says you worked for the Germantown Coal Company? Well, sailor, you'll feel right to home down in the engine-room, won't you?"

BOOK II

Peggy's story

Chapter 7

La Madrina

1972 Spicket Falls, Massachusetts

Where to begin? It would be nice if we could go back to the beginning, but how far back is that? Who knows? All I know is I'm lying here flat on my back and they're telling me I'm dying with some kind of a tumor on my brain, but whadda they know, the doctahs? I know what they're up to. *They're after the Third Eye in the middle of my forehead.*

You don't believe me? Just wait, you'll see. Those sawbones'll kill me yet, with their scalpels and their drills!

Now, Nicky, I want you to take this down, word for word. Don't change nuthin,' because I'm gonna tell you the truth. All you gotta do is take dictation, okay, ya got that? You were always a good boy. Like my Henry. Not wild, like his brother Ronnie. But Henry—when the Marines sent him to Japan, that was the end of him. He met that shake-a shake-a geisha-girl, and that was the end of him.

What? Nicky, Nicky, Nicky, always with the questions! The Third Eye, we'll get to that but first ya gotta know who am I, right? I mean, to you, I'm your Auntie Peggy, but if anybody ever reads this, they don't know who I am! Now. Let's start ovah. My name is Peggy Fabiano. I haven't been married to Fabiano for, God knows, thirty, thirty-five years, but I kept the name. It's better than LaStoria, which I was born with. I never liked that name. I never was my father's daughter, never. I came from my mother. Her name was Fabrizio—and Fabiano ain't far off. Maybe that's why I married the guy in the first place. I liked his name. It was almost like my mother's name. I wanted to change my name, I wanted to get far, far away from under the thumb, you know? So I took Henry Fabiano's name and I never gave it back. I became the wonderful, the gorgeous, the fabulous Peggy Fabiano.

You know how I know when I'm in trouble? When my sister Gerry, your mother, starts calling me Margaret!

My mother gave me a beautiful Italian name, *Margherita.* And nobody ever knew this, but she had a pet name for me, too, that was only between us. She would whisper in my ear, and call me Rita. It came from Margherita, you see? My name was never Margaret. Such an ugly name. Reminds me of that sister of the Queen they got, over there, that Princess Margaret. Such an ugly thing, poor woman.

My mother was a goddess. Nobody ever appreciated her but me. That woman gave birth to seven children and she raised them on her own without any help from *him,* and what thanks did she ever get for it? When I saw what life did to her, I said to myself, not me, it ain't gonna be me. She gave her life to her kids, her family, *that man.* That's who Gigi Fabrizio was, your grandmother. *La Madrina.* You know what that means? *The Godmother.*

Yeah, the Godmother. She was a *goddess*, I'm telling you. She gave me my life. And she gave to me the most precious gift of all, she gave me my soul. And your soul will last *longer* than your life. The spirit that I have in me, that lives inside me, that will never die, and it came from *her*. I will always be a Fabrizio, and a Fabiano, and those are both fabulous names, and that's what I am, fabulous. My mother was a goddess and she gave birth to me and that makes me a goddess, too.

So listen closely and take this down, Nicky. God knows how much time I got left. My head hurts and I'm lying here in my dead brother's bedroom, in your mother's house in Spicket Falls, this beautiful fieldstone house she's so proud of—only because she came down to Revere with your father, that bastard, and *abducted* me out of my precious little studio apartment, where I was happy all by myself, and they *kidnapped* me, so now she's keeping me prisoner here, because she says I couldn't take care of myself anymore, and I let myself go, and the apartment, too, as if that mattered, as if that was the big thing! All I wanted was to be left alone! And so what if I was behind on the rent! *Against my will,* she stuck me here in my dead brother Augie's room, with dead man's shoes still sitting there on the floor of the closet—and may God forgive him, my brother Augie, because I cannot.

I know, I know, you were away overseas while all this was going on, but now you're back, so just sit still, shut and up and take this down. Maybe you'll learn something. Maybe you'll find out why you, and your brother and sister, and all your cousins, too, all of them all said the same thing. *Auntie Peggy's my favorite aunt.* She's *fun*. She understands kids. She's one of us. Maybe, Nicky, you'll remember why you loved me, too.

When I was eight, nine years old, back in Hingham, I was in, say, the fourth grade, it musta been, when all of a sudden, overnight, I became the talk of the town. Overnight, I was a legend. My name was on everybody's lips, they couldn't stop talking about me. I know, I know, you heard it before, this story, a hundred times. Well, listen again, 'cause I'm gonna tell ya.

In those days, you know, a girl wasn't supposed to open her mouth. You were supposed to be a dainty little thing all proper and *speechless*. They never saw anything like me. I walked onto the court in front of the whole town and I was in charge. All eyes were on me. The other girls couldn't wait to see what I'd do next. Today, you know, they don't realize that we were the first generation of girls in the whole of history to play basketball—and softball, and if they woulda let us, I woulda played baseball and football, too. I was the equal of any boy! When the adults weren't around, whaddya think we did? We chose up our own sides and I was picked *before* some of the boys—they wanted me on their side 'cause they knew I was unstoppable, that I wouldn't quit, that nobody could make me.

Well, in grammar school, I was at the Lincoln, and the McKinleys, across town, we hated them, and they hated us, and believe me when I tell you, the whole town of Hingham used to turn out to watch us play. We were somethin.' All the mothers and fathers were there to cheer on their dainty little prissies, except for one, my old man. He wasn't gonna come to see his daughter play a game! Eh, when he was a kid, he didn't play games, things were tough on the streets of New York, yeah, we heard it a million times, but he didn't have to rub it in, did he? Us kids didn't know how good we had it! *He* had to work! There was no such thing as a day off for him! You'd think he held it against us 'cause we were kids! We couldn't help it. Times were changing. Those were the days when the big thing was physical education in the schools. That was on the agenda. That was gonna solve all the world's problems, phys ed. They were pushing it on you. It was the 1920s, modern times. I was only too happy to play along. They even gave us uniforms—you shoulda seen the bloomers they put on us. I useta love that uniform. Red and white were our colors at the Lincoln—those McKinleys from across town were blue and gold. I was so proud to wear the school colors. You think it meant a thing to my father? Hell, no. Jealous, that's what he was. *Jealous of a kid!* Because of him, my mother wasn't there that day! She woulda said, go get 'em, Peggy! Don't let nobody push you around! My mother loved me.

That day, the game was close. I wasn't the biggest girl on our side, but I was the pepperpot. I made things go. If we ever got stuck trying to run those dumb plays the teacher made us run, I'd just jump up and down and wave my arms and scream a lot, "Ovah here, ovah here!" till they gave me the ball back. Those old Yankee spinstahs we had for teachers never scored two points in their life, never mind a foul shot. They wanted us to throw up everything up there underhanded. I shot like a boy! For crissakes, I had a better set shot than most of the boys did, anyway! We didn't have a backboard or anything, just a peach basket hung over the back door of the school assembly room. We had to push back all the folding chairs to make room to play. Even then, it was only a half-court game, we had to take the ball out from the side after each play when somebody scored, usually me. Sometimes I could shoot it from a side-angle and bounce it in off the front of the balcony. My brother Patsy called it my ricochet shot. I was famous for that shot. One game I scored 6 points and we won. Another time I had eight. My greatest game of all time I had 14, believe it or not, we never scored more than say, twenty points in a game. Most of the girls were afraid of the ball. Instead of going after a rebound in the air, they'd jump back and let it bounce, or try to, before they flailed at it. As far as dribbling the ball, forget about it. They were a wreck and a mess. All thumbs and elbows. They had no idea how to shoot a layup. Easy, I told 'em. Just get a running start and don't let nobody get in your way. So most of my teammates were just as happy when the ball was in my hands. They just wanted to get the game ovah with and go for ice cream.

Now, on the other side, the McKinleys had this overstuffed cabbage of a girl who musta stood at least a head taller than me. In the fourth grade, I hadn't sprouted yet. But I ran circles around her. She kept reaching out and fouling me and if I hadn't missed a couple we woulda got thirty that day. But after a while, she started getting frustrated and all whiny on me. She was looking pouty and complaining to her coach what a bad sport I was but her real problem was I was licking the tar outta her. So, finally, she decided to foul me real good once and for all and as I was going by her for a layup, or around her, she was so fat, she sticks her foot out and trips me! Boy was I mad! I was up off the floor like a shot and socked her one right in the kazoo. I still had the ball in my hand so I threw that at her head. She stepped back, shocked, holding her nose, so she didn't see it coming and she forgot to duck, and the ball bounced off her head and rolled out the door just as the principal of the school was walking in under the basket. She gave such a quizzical look at the ball bouncing across the lobby floor that everybody started laughing, if they weren't already. Fatso was crying her eyes out and sobbing that I hit her and the grownups on the McKinleys side were crying out things like Foul! Foul! For shame! And the teacher grabbed me and said, "That was not a very ladylike thing to do!" so I told her "Neither was tripping me neither!" and the next thing you know some of the parents on the McKinley side were taking a conniption that any of the parents on our side would be defending me, which they weren't so much as braggin' about the punch I packed!

So I get home that night and Patsy was way ahead of me and he musta spilled all the beans and I walk up to the back door and there's my proud Papa standing there with a switch in his hand and he gives me a lickin' on the back of my bloomers which he's swearing I won't soon forget it. And you know what? I haven't, not to this day, and I never will.

Mamma came and got me. I was sobbing, face down on my bed, crying my eyes out, and she sat down and started rubbing my back and trying to soothe things over and all I could do was look up with my face buried in the pillow and throw my arms around her neck.

"Now, now," sez my mother, "my little Rita, you just got what you deserved. You know better. If you start hitting your brothers or sisters like that, I'd be the first to tell your Papa to get out the switch. But what I want to know is—what ever made you do such a thing!"

"Mamma, it wasn't my fault!" I cried, and I told her the story I just told you, Nicky.

Are you getting this all down?

My mother embraced me, in such a way as to say, *you know I love you, no matter what you do.*

I know that's what she meant. She didn't have to put it into words. I could feel it. Passing from her body into mine.

And she said, "*Allora,* I would have done the same thing. Sometimes I think, my precious Rita, of all my children, you're the only one who takes after me."

Peggy's sister Gerry, her self-appointed caretaker, crept away from the closed door of the upstairs bedroom on the right at the top of the stairs. She had been eavesdropping. She had come up the stairs to use the bathroom and when she came out, she overheard, through the closed bedroom door, Peggy, muttering to herself in a disjointed stream of wandering, disconnected phrases, sometimes exclaiming out loud. That was the bedroom that used to belong to their brother Augie, until he died one night in 1962, suddenly, of a cerebral hemorrhage, and then her son Nicky had taken over his uncle's bedroom, until he went away to college in Boston. At the moment, Nicky was overseas and his mother, Gerry, had no idea when he was coming back. So the bedroom was vacant again when Gerry's sister Peggy came to visit, came to stay awhile, lingered on, and eventually never left until she had been in the hospital in Spicket Falls, the Bon Secours, and was diagnosed with brain cancer. Peggy had no medical insurance and Gerry didn't have the money to put her impecunious sister in some kind of facility, so she shouldered the burden herself, just as she had with her mother and father, years before, and brought her sister home, to die at home, with family, where she could be spoon-fed and cleaned and changed and rolled up to have fresh bed-linen put on. Having missed the beginning of Peggy's rant, Gerry crept down the stairs muttering to herself, who's she think she's talking to, in her delirium, Ma? Gerry gave an involuntary shiver. Too many in her family had died, Pa, Ma, Augie, and who was going to be next was Peggy, and their ghosts all lived with her, Gerry, the caretaker, the one who never left home: the living who were not yet dead as well as the dead who were no longer among the living.

Chapter 8

Mamma's Boys

Now, Nicky, came the day, I discovered makeup. All of a sudden I went from a tomboy to a woman, overnight. Skipped right over being a girl. That was all right with me, I was never a girl. There was always a boy trapped inside of me trying to get out. In fact, in fact, I always wanted to be a man!

Why should they get all the privileges? All the freedoms? Nobody bats an eyelash when a man does just exactly what he pleases. A man doesn't check over the door to see if it says Ladies Invited. A man doesn't have to get his wife to co-sign a loan for him. A man doesn't have to think twice about sleeping with a different floozy every night!

Just let a woman try that and you know what kind of names they're gonna call her.

Now where did that goddam kid go? Nicky! Are you listening to me?

They've got the door closed, and I'm shut up in here. They don't wanna listen to me. They've heard it all before. Or so they think. But there's a lot I never told nobody. I'm a very private person. My thoughts are my own, or they used to be. Now everything is such a muddle I just keep going round and round living my life over again. Maybe I just imagined Nicky was sitting here, taking dictation. *Maybe I'm already dead and I just imagine that I lived.*

I can't tell if it's me thinking all this or the Third Eye dreaming it.

All I know is there are some things you can never forget.

Like my boys. Mamma's boys, every one of them. Tall and skinny short and fat roly poly doesn't matter they're all mamma's boys, every one. There's nothing a man likes better than to be mothered. It's amazing how by the time they're grown up enough to be of any use to a woman they've forgotten they ever had a mother and they're looking for you to be the mother they never had. Where did they think they came from, if not from their mother? All I had to do was crook my little finger and whisper, come to Mamma, and boy!

My own two kids, Henry and Ronnie—typical.

You think over the last 20 years either one of them ever came to see me, even once? Like hell. Henry's somewhere down in Washington working for the government and Ronnie's out in Colorado with his ski-bunny girlfriend, and the both of them's forgotten who used to wipe their little fannies for them.

But I remember. I haven't forgotten a thing. To tell you the truth, I was never cut out to be the homebody type. That's my sister, Gerry. How she ever did it I'll never know. All those years, the best years of her life, spent between four walls catering to everybody else's beck and call—I woulda committed suicide on myself long before that.

Just like I could never stand sitting down all day wrestling with that sewing machine pushing a needle and thread through miles of material and the wrinkles and the folds and the tangles never cease, the work never ends, day after day, mile after mile, the same thing over and over again. How did they stand it? Gerry, Mary, Anna, they all did it. Not me. The only one who had anything in it for him was Genie. He was the shadow of his father. Wherever his father went there was Genie right next to him. They coulda been identical twins they were so alike. But Patsy, Augie—they were just pieces in the puzzle, flywheels in the machine. I woulda committed homicide on myself long before that. I liked a well-made suit as well as the next guy. But to pinch my fingers together all day long eight hours, ten hours a day, one day after another, each one the same as the last, I would slit my throat.

Me, my life was what I made of it. I didn't fit any design. I wasn't cut out of somebody else's pattern. I wasn't a manikin in a store window. I filled out a two-piece ensemble with skirt and jacket and I made it come alive because when you saw me in that well-tailored outfit you could feel me breathing inside it, you could see that suit hugging my every curve and just clinging to my delicious derriere. That's why wherever I lived big or small, plush or down-and-out, and believe me, I lived in some swanky digs, and some day-bed studios, the one thing I always had hanging on the wall was a full-length mirror. That way when I was finished with my makeup and I was all dressed up to go out I could admire myself. I'd look myself up and down and turn this way and that and I must say I was so stunning I could make a statue melt. I didn't just put on a dress and wear it—the dress caressed me, the dress ran its hands all over me.

Now my day didn't start before noontime. I was always a night person. And in the morning I had to get my sleep. I loved to turn over and stretch like a cat in the bed about eleven o'clock and get up and put on a pot of coffee. I'd sit in the kitchen and have a cigarette while it perked. By that time the kids, Henry and Ronnie, had been up for hours. I taught them to make a bowl of cereal for themselves. When television came along, they were happy to sit and watch for hours. Then I'd call up one of my boyfriends with a car and have then come over and run the kids over to Ma's house so Ma and my sister Gerry could watch them for the afternoon. Then I'd jump in the shower, do my makeup, get dressed, while the boyfriend's sitting in the parlor, panting for me like a good little dog, and when I was ready for post-time, I'd let him drive me to the track in time for the daily double. Every day for me was a new adventure. I loved my life and I lived every minute of it.

Now the trouble came every Saturday morning when Fabiano, the father, showed up to take the kids for the weekend out to his place in Wilmington, where he was shackin' up with his new wife. As the kids got a little older, more and more they wanted to stay with him. My apartment in Revere, that little bird-cage I had at the corner of North Shore Road and Revere Street, was too cramped for them. There was no backyard for them to play outside in. If they wanted to play outside—and what kid wants to be stuck indoors?—I had to take them over my mother's house. At this time they still weren't old enough for school. I'm talking when Henry was five and Ronnie was four. They were rambunctious. Especially Ronnie, he couldn't sit still. Henry was only too happy to sit down with a book in his lap. My kids, they adored me. We had such times together. I taught them to play solitaire and forty-fives. I taught them how to play checkers. They were thrilled to shoot aggies or play Parcheesi with me, they were thrilled if I so much as made them a pitcher of raspberry Zarex. *Whatever happened to Mamma's boys?*

Henry Fabiano's new wife, that's what. Oh, I wasn't jealous of her. She could have him for all I cared. I had my own life. If it had been just their father and the boys, maybe it could've worked, maybe we could've shared them, turn by turn. But once she entered the picture, that was it. She either wanted them or she didn't. She couldn't make up her mind. The kids would go for two weeks in the summer out to his place and after a week she didn't want them any more, and back they'd come. She was a schoolteacher, Miss Prim and Proper. Then she wanted kids of her own. Once she started in on that you think she had any room left for her husband's kids? Poor Henry and Ronnie. They didn't know if they were coming or going.

Finally in the end the way it ended up as they got a little older was Henry, who was a brain, like his old man, ended up staying with me and going to Revere High School. Ronnie wanted to go to Wilmington High. He was the more athletic one at that stage. He wanted to play football and baseball out there in the country. He took after me, much more than his brother. Still, Henry wanted to, in his own way, follow in his father's footsteps, so I shouldn't have been surprised when he wanted to join the Marines, straight outta high school, while he was still only seventeen and I had to sign for him. What a battle royal we had over that one.

I remember when his father was in the Marine Corps. I was the reason why he wanted to run away and bury himself on some godforsaken sandbar in the Pacific. Oh, sure, the war was on, and my brothers, and all the boys, especially my oldest brother Patsy, he was fit to be tied, they were all in a fever to go off and kill Japs, kill Germans, they were gonna save the world. But I knew better because I had the Third Eye.

Men are strange. They live their whole life like they've got something to prove. Who do they think they're kidding? Not us women. I should know. I had plenty of servicemen on my hands during the war. Boston was full of them. Every last mother's son on their way to a date with destiny. While my sister Mary was stitching overcoats for the Russian army I was handing out racing forms at the track to the boys on shore leave from the Charlestown Navy Yard. What a way to win the war. You had to know how to fend off those conquering heroes. I was a good girl that they were hoping was a bad girl. I let them hope. I was fighting my own war right here on the home front.

The one time I came close to losing my grip it was the Third Eye that saved me.

People think the Third Eye is strictly about clairvoyance. It's not. It's about a lot of things. It can be just a feeling you get. It can be just listening to your own intuition. Sure, it can be about foretelling the future. But it also can be looking into another person. Seeing into them, or hearing their thoughts without them knowing.

It was Thanksgiving weekend, 1942.

I had a date. Some guy from Worcester. It was Saturday night. He was all kinds of ecstatic 'cause he won a bundle on the Holy Cross game that day. He put a bet down with the bookie we bumped into at the track. Holy Cross was a big underdog. I told him Boston College was gonna murderlize them, they didn't stand a chance. He wouldn't listen. He was right. I was wrong. The Third Eye doesn't kick in for the minor stuff, the chicken feed. Only when it's something important.

Let's go celebrate, sez the guy. Cocoanut Grove, here we come!

We were halfway there in the Sumner Tunnel. Suddenly I got the feeling that I was drowning. I could feel all those tons of water pressing down on me. The headlights of the cars coming the other way in the tunnel were boring straight in on *me.* They were aiming like arrows for the middle of my forehead.

I got the dreadful sense of being closed in. Suddenly, I got a picture clear as a photograph in the middle of my forehead, of my husband on Guadalcanal. I knew he was there. He was still in love with me and he was writing home to Mamma. I saw Henry Fabiano surrounded by piles of dead Japs. The picture was moving round and round like Hurley's Merry-Go-Round or the Whirlpool at the Beach. The dead Japs were piled up between the wooden horses or on the whip-around cars. *Faster and faster, round and round.* We burst out of the tunnel into the night-lights of the city.

"Let's not go to the Cocoanut Grove tonight," I cried.

"What are you talking about? We're gonna go celebrate!"

"I don't wanna go to the Cocoanut Grove tonight!"

"Whaddya mean–!"

"Let's go see your mother."

"My mother lives in Worcester."

"So—I'm not good enough for you to introduce to your mother?"

"It's fifty miles from here!"

"Good. I wanna get away. I wanna get far, far away from here."

The next morning in Worcester the papers said the dead bodies were piled up in the panic to get out, piled up *trapped in the revolving doors* at the Cocoanut Grove, burnt alive.

You know what my father said when he heard the story?

My mother told me. *La Madrina.* She said his face went ghostly white. All the color drained out of it.

You'd think he woulda said something like, *Thank God, my daughter was saved!*

Not him.

All he said was, "Some people are lucky."

Chapter 9

Ladies' Choice

Your poor mother, Nicky. We were so close when we were kids growing up. Whatever happened to us? My sister Gerry and me, thick as thieves, we did everything together, went everywhere. She always looked up to me. I was her big sister. I always looked out for her. Did she ever tell you that one about the time we got caught in the theater overnight, when we went to the show in Porter Square, the day of the Hurricane, back in '38? She did. How could she ever have forgotten? I remember it to this day.

But somehow we drifted apart.

I think it started the night she met your father.

Did she ever tell you that story? No. She wouldn't. Your mother was so shy. So shy, it was painful. So shy it hurt *me*. And now, of course, things have changed. Now, she doesn't want to look back and think on it. But there was a time she was so in love, and so happy, when you came along, and even when the twins were born. How did we ever let things get away from us like that? Oh, that night they met!

That's right. At the Raymor-Playmor Ballroom, in 1944. On Huntington Ave., in town. See, you *have* heard the story. But I'm gonna tell you the real story behind the story.

The argument started when I showed up at your house on Payson Street. Your mother had her hands in dishwater, as usual, and she didn't want to go nowhere. Meanwhile, I had arranged that your Auntie Mary and Auntie Anna were gonna meet us at the Raymor-Playmor.

"We're goin' in town," I says to your mother.

"Why?" she goes. "What's wrong with the Wonderland, right here in Revere?"

"There's a guy hangs out there I'd rather not run across," I lied.

In those days, Nicky, it was wartime, your grandfather, he never got home early, they were running double-shifts. So I brought Henry and Ronnie over and Ma was quite happy to watch them, *she* wanted Gerry to get outta the house, cause she *never* got out, I was getting nervous in case, just by chance, my father should walk in, our sisters are waiting for us, all this was arranged by phone ahead of time, Ma was in on it, only Gerry now all of a sudden doesn't feel like goin' out!

"Gerry!" I says. "They got two bands on tonight! Stan Kenton *and* Artie Shaw!"

"Stan who? Never heard of him."

"You heard of Artie Shaw!"

"Lana Turner's husband."

"Till she divorced him!"

"I know that!"

"Will you come on, already! Get in the bathtub."

"I don't have anything to wear!"

"I'll do your makeup. Don't worry! You're gonna look fabulous!"

By the time I got her on the trolley we were already late. In those days, you're old enough to remember, Nicky, well, you know, they didn't build the subway out to Wonderland till '53, you had to go all the way in to Maverick Square in East Boston on the streetcar. So, finally we get there—the subway by that time ran all the way out to Huntington Ave., almost to the YMCA, and you got out, and turned back, a few doors down, back towards Mass Ave., there was the big marquee, the Raymor-Playmor—twin ballrooms, Nicky.

Those were the days, I'm telling you. The town was hopping, Servicemen everywhere, we were young, oh, it was so, so, I don't know—alive! That night they were having the Battle of the Bands. Upstairs, you know, the two ballrooms were connected by a walkway so all the fans could pass back and forth between each band and sample one or the other, see which they liked best, who they wanted to dance to. And each ballroom was like a kaleidoscope or something because they had those mirrored balls hanging from the ceiling with the speckles of light crawling over all the walls and the ceiling with the big bands vibrating the whole building and something on the floor they used, to make it slippery and slide-y to dance on, oh, I'm telling you, you were swept off your feet!

So we're going in the glass doors downstairs, and there's this sailor, in his Navy whites, getting a polish from the shoeshine boy, and he sees your mother—I don't think she so much as noticed him—but I did. The next thing you know we're up at the top of the staircase, and I feel somebody behind me, you know, I feel the eyes. Women have a sixth sense about that, you know. Well, we're always getting the once-over, their eyes are roving like a pair of hands, all the time, looking you up and down. I can sense them from across the road, even if they're behind me, I don't know, it's something built-in, something left-over. Your mother, she's oblivious. But I knew it was him, the sailor.

So we get in there and we're looking for our sisters and all the good booths are taken and finally we find them at a round table, saving a couple of seats for us. Not so good. A booth is better 'cause you can always say no, I'm stuck in the middle here, everybody'll have to move, I can't get up. Well, Nicky, in those days I had to beat them off with a stick, the boys were in a hurry, they were shipping out in the morning!

I sit down and my sister Mary starts.

"Will you look at Merle Oberon ovah here?"

Referring to me, of course. You know, your Aunt Mary, God love her, 'cause I can't, it was something about, she was the oldest, and I don't know, she was the first married, but she had a rivalry with me! I didn't look at it that way! In her own mind she was convinced I would've never have gotten married to Henry Fabiano except that I was jealous of her!

"Merle Oberon could only wish she was me," I sez. "But, yes, if you insist, I have that look."

"That shady lady look?" piped in your precious Auntie Anna from the other end.

Oh, I could tell we were in for a night. "Don't get your bloomers in a twist," sez I to my sister Anna.

"Evermind-nay em-thay," sez Gerry.

"Isten-lay—Iway ancay ayplay atthay amegay. Utbay onight›stay ouryay ightnay."

"Don't start with that stuff," says Mary.

Already we were laughing like hell. Between the two of them they didn't understand a word we we're saying.

All of a sudden, we're surrounded. It's like Guadalcanal, the Army on one side, the Navy on the other.

A soldier asks Mary to dance. "I'm married," she says.

"I won't tell your husband," he says.

A sailor asks Anna to dance. She says, "My husband's in the Army. He wouldn't like it if I was disloyal to his branch."

"Stand aside, swabby," says a soldier, stepping up to take Anna by the hand.

They were always fighting over Anna. As dim as it was in there, with all those spinning lights, the music, the noise, she still stood out as the youngest, and some might think, the prettiest, because, of all of us, her, and your mother, Nicky, had the most All-American looks. Your Aunt Mary looked like an Armenian, and me, well, I had those exotic Merle Oberon eyes.

I held up both arms in a *Halt* sign. "Hold it, boys. This is a dance-club, not a football scrimmage."

"Say, is there any of you not married?"

"Guess."

"Only one of us."

"Not me."

"I'm divorced—does that count?"

A naval officer stepped up. "Ensign Murphy of the USS Ruby, and Shreveport, Louisiana, at your service. Who's in command of your contingent?"

"That would be me," I says.

Then I noticed— him, the sailor from the lobby, with the shoeshine boy. The eyes on the stairway. "Who's your friend?" I says.

"If I may be allowed to introduce to you lovely young ladies, my esteemed colleague, Fireman First-Class Petrovich, from Fayette County, Pennsylvania. And he does dance the polka!"

A soldier said, "An officer and an enlisted man? Ain't that against regulations?"

"You do things the Army way, we do things the right way."

"This war's off to a great start," I sez.. "Let's dance, girls!"

I got the herd stampeding whilst trying to steer your mother with a nudge or two. "That's him!" I whispered, pointing.

"Who's him?"

"The sailor who's been sending torpedoes at you with his eyes since you walked in the door downstairs. The one who looks like Errol-way Ynn-flay."

"I don't think so. Too dark. More like Yrone-tay Ower-pay."

"Well, so? *He's the one.*"

"The one what?"

"The one, stupid!"

"How do you know that?"

"I know! I know! Call it The Third Eye, if you want. Just dance with him. You'll see."

I took the Ensign and your mother took the Fireman. Or he took her. I don't know. Yes, I do. It was *serendipity.*

Those things happen, you know. They were meant to be there at the same time. How else do you explain it? In those days the whole world was crossed with comings and goings, departures and arrivals, trains, ships and planes, it was life and sudden death. You came around the corner and there was destiny staring you it the face, lying in wait for you. Why did he look up just when she went by? He was bent over looking at the shoeshine boy working that rag. All of a sudden for no reason he looks up? It was just like in the movies. You could see it all happening in front of you on a big screen.

And we all wanted the same thing. We wanted love. Death and destruction didn't matter as long as we had somebody out there who loved us. I was in the arms of the Ensign, dancing dreamily, my head full of ideas, and he's going, "What's your name?"

"Huh?"

"Hi, stranger. I'm Dan. What's your name?"

"Danny Boy."

"From Shreveport, Louisiana. You from around here?"

"I don't remember. Are we here? Or am I dreaming?"

"What about your girlfriends?"

"They're my sisters."

"You have three sisters?"

"Takes that many to make sure I behave myself."

After that first dance, the US Navy went over under the archways to the long bar to get us some drinks, and I could see them standing with their heads together.

"So what do you think?" I says to your mother.

"I think he's a dreamboat," says Gerry, and she's smirking. "Smooth dancer."

"He's a sailor, you know. Watch out. All hands on deck."

She only pursed her lips, and looked at me sideways, while she's arching her eyebrow at me, but then her gaze wanders off to where they're standing, and she gets a Chesterfield out of her purse and lights up, and she's blowing smoke, but it's like—*sighing.*

"What's his name?"

"Well, he says his name is Andre, but his friends call him Andy. He's got an accent, sounds to me like a southerner, like, oh, I don't know, Rhett Butler."

"Ohhhhhh."

"What's that supposed to mean?"

"Oh, nothing."

"Here they come."

"My guy's Danny Boy. He thinks I'm a firecracker."

"He better watch out you don't explode, Peggy."

There they are, with drinks in their hands, standing there.

"Hey, listen to that," says Shreveport. "You girls jitterbug?"

We danced all night. We danced until the dawn was coming up. We danced like it was the last night of our lives. And we were happy. *Could we just be happy for one night, one night, out of all our lives?* I looked at your mother, and I was so happy for her. She had gotten out of the house! She had gotten out of *herself.* She had taken off that apron she always wore around the kitchen to save her house-dress and she just *threw it aside* and went out and danced. We took a taxi home to Mary's house in Watertown. The boys piled in with us. They were on a weekend pass. We took them home. We didn't want the night to end. Five in the morning we're cooking breakfast upstairs on Dewey Street in Mary's kitchen. Then we send the boys to sack out on the couch in the front room and on the sun-porch swing, and we get Charlie up to go across and pile in with the kids' bedroom, and the four of us sisters are all in the one big bed in Mary's room chattering away just like we used to when we were kids.

And I remember falling asleep that night with the light in the window and I was asking myself *when, oh, when, will I meet my serendipity?*

And I heard the growl of the whisper of the Third Eye in my ear, goin' "Ix-nay!"

I shoulda listened, Nicky.

Chapter 10

Rings Romano

The first time ever I laid eyes on Johnny Romano was at the Frolics in Revere Beach.

Why my father had to move to Revere I don't know. We all grew up in the country. I have memories of Hingham when I was little and I'll always be attached to Hingham because that was my hometown. But my father could never stay put, so we were torn away. Your mother, Nicky, would tell you the same thing, I'm sure. If you ask her. Hingham was the seashore, a little clapboard New England town where horse farms from the old days were plunked down right alongside the harbor with Bumpkin Island and the fishing boats and Button Island and the sailboats and the yachts from the Hingham Yacht Club. It was nice in Hingham, nice and clean and neat and tidy. Then we were torn away. Our friends, our schools, were taken away from us. Our teenage years we had to spend in Stoughton. Why?—because my father saw a real estate deal that he couldn't pass up? But that was fine, Stoughton was still the country, back then.

Then came the war and now the country was no good. Now he had to be in town where he could be running things seven days a week. And we were all grown up anyway, he didn't need a big back yard, we were all scattered to the four winds, he wanted the streetcar stop at the bottom of his street. So he found a place in Watertown. Your Auntie Mary was the first one to go to Watertown when she married Charlie Laverna. And then Anna, who was the only one still in school, naturally, came with Ma and Pa when they moved to Watertown. It was big sister Mary found my father and mother a first floor to rent on Kimball Road, right around the corner from her and Charlie and their kids on Dewey Street. And Anna, she started over at Watertown High, she was the baby of the family, and the only one of us who ever got to finish high school.

She had a lotta nerve, that one. Who ever heard of an unmarried woman getting a bank loan? But she knew how to twist the old man round her finger and so she got him to co-sign for her. She graduates Watertown High and she finds a two-family for sale on Mt Auburn Street. She musta got the real estate itch from Pa, you know? Next thing you know, Pa's callin' in favors from old friends like the Italian bank in the North End. Now Anna's a land-lady, at age 17! Then she ends up getting married to Tommy DiPrima—who was actually one of her tenants in her house—she was his landlady!—he was the son of the family on the second floor!

But was Kimball Road good enough for the old man? Oh, no, he was fit to be tied because he couldn't put his garden out in the back. Charlie Laverna had his tomato plants in the backyard on Dewey Street and my father was dying of envy. Plus, he had money in the bank and it was burning a hole in his pocket. But the real reason was he found out he hated driving that twisty, turn-ey Fresh Pond Parkway with all the rotaries and stoplights on it over to Revere or East Boston to get to the track. So, now his mind was made up—it had to be Revere. And that was the real reason, the racetrack.

Well, Nicky, I was already living there. In Revere, I mean. When I broke up with Henry Fabiano and he ran off to join the Marines that was it for me, I was through with Wilmington and his family. Sure, I loved it in the country, up there, it brought me all the way back to my own childhood, running through the fields, picking blueberries. But Henry was the town newspaper, I mean, he was it, he knew everybody in that town and all their business, and they knew his business, and it was just impossible for me to stay there with everybody taking his side. But I had Henry and little Ronnie on my hands, you know, the Dead End kids, and all my friends were at the track. And I needed them. Henry was still crazy in love with me and he didn't want to let go and so he tried to control me with his purse strings and, you know, using his kids as bargaining chips, oh, I tell you, he was not the upstanding pillar of the community people took him to be, he was a nasty little manipulator to me. I suppose, you can't blame him, I broke his heart, and emptied his pocketbook, too, and so the next thing you know he's burying his sorrows in a foxhole on Guadalcanal.

But I still needed my friends, and they were in Revere. If you can believe it, my father took Henry's side in all this! So there was no help coming from that quarter. If it wasn't for your mammanonna and my sister Gerry I wouldn't have seen two nickels between Sundays. I needed my friends to give me rides to buy groceries, how was I gonna watch my kids—how was I gonna work? I certainly wasn't gonna hold down a sewing machine for an eight-hour shift in my father's shop like my sister Mary. Anna did, too, when she got outta Watertown High, and got married, and her husband was away in the service, like they all were. But for me, that was out of the question, the old man and me, we went together like fire and gasoline, him and me.

But Revere wasn't Hingham. Revere wasn't a quaint little seaside town. Revere was the big top. Revere was *the Beach.* Revere was the rides, the amusements, the Cyclone, the bumpercars. On Saturdays and Sundays during the war in the hot weather you could see a hundred thousand people lined up toe to toe on the beach sunning themselves trying to beat the heat in the water. They came from all over. The Beach was the place to be. I don't know, I never spent five minutes in Coney Island, but I suppose that's the only thing you could compare it to. Revere *was* the Beach. And the horse track and the dog track and the Wonderland Ballroom and the candy cotton and the neon lights. And the nightclubs. And the biggest of them all was *the Frolics.*

The Frolics had big plate-glass windows. Floor to ceiling. You couldn't see in but they could see out. It was dim in there at four in the afternoon. In the morning before they opened, the sun would be flooding in on the chairs stacked on the tables, 'cause the whole beach faced east out over the Atlantic on the rising sun, you know, but in the late afternoon, the sun was on the other side of the sky, and all the rides and amusements and restaurants and clubs would be in deep purple shadows. The Frolics didn't open for lunch. It was not that kind of place. They opened late and stayed open late. It was a supper club. All the stars went there. They kept the same hours I did. They got their beauty rest and took hours in front of the mirror before they ever set foot out the door. When the big band leaders were playing in town, or at the Wonderland, after hours, where could they go to wind down, have a cocktail, relax, schmooze with their pals, sit in with the combo on stage, where but the

Frolics? On any given night you could see Russ Colombo in there, or Vic Damone, Doris Day when she was in town—and their friends were Sinatra and Humphrey Bogart and Jimmy Stewart and Cary Grant. And Jimmy Durante. I'm not kidding you. They were all there. The Frolics was the place to be. The Frolics was the kind of place where I fit in. I belonged in the Frolics.

But so far I hadn't gotten further than feeling the smoke blow out the front door as I strolled by with a kid hanging on each arm.

Once in a while I used to push a rag behind the counter at a tavern in Orient Heights, I forget the name of the place, you know, to help out a friend, pick up some tips maybe. I wasn't making a career out of it, but I learned along the way how to mix drinks. I was a natural on the scene, if you know what I mean. I had a way with people. They started smiling when I was around. It was the same crowd we hung out with from the track. All the same people. Everybody knew everybody. There was always some guy was gonna rescue me from my fate and put me on Easy Street. I let them lead me on.

One night one of my boyfriends, if you could call him that, he hit it big that day in the Daily Double, he's gonna take me out and treat me to a big time, I says, Okay, I wanna go to the Frolics.

"You never been there? You're kidding me."

"Do I look like I'm kidding you? I know, the light's bad in here. But just drop me at my place, you know, my little studio, corner of Revere Street, give me a couple of hours to freshen up—pick me up at eight, and you're not gonna believe the transformation."

So we get there and it's about half-past-eight and it's a slow night middle of the week, no waiting. You didn't think my date was really gonna drop a bundle on me, did you? So the hostess, she's at the front door, she's got her little lectern, she's frantic, but, why? There's nobody there, there's no rush, no line behind us, it's just us standing there, and she's ignoring us, like we did something, or she expects us to do something.

I didn't like her, immediately. She was a prune.

So I says, "We'd like to be seated, please."

"Certainly, it'll just be a minute, if you don't mind waiting?" and she motions at a couple of those chrome chairs with the red seats where you're supposed to park yourself.

So I settle my exquisite derriere in for the duration and I says to my date, "What's with her?"

"She's above it all."

"Can't you tell?"

"I don't like blondes when they come poured outta the bottle."

I looked at him. With a sudden new-found respect. "Steve. I couldn't have expressed it better myself."

So, finally we get a table, and there it was, *serendipity.*

I wanted a table where I would be able to look toward the door, the front door, I don't know why, it was dark outside by this time, but instead she put us where I was looking down towards the back, by the stage where the house-band was playing and the wall of mirrors behind the stage—then I saw him. *Johnny Romano.*

He was sitting down in the rear of the club, in a booth next to the swinging doors into the kitchen.

One leg was in the aisle. He was sitting back relaxed in his summer suit, stirring a drink with a swizzle-stick, staring right at me, or past me, or maybe at somebody behind me, but, in any case, right through me. Like I say, that casual stare, one leg in the aisle, like he owned the place.

"Who is that, Steve? No—don't turn around. I think I know who it is."

I left Steve sitting there, startled. He watched me stand up, and he was surprised, but then he shrugged, a waitress approached, he was gonna order me a sloe gin fizz, I was gone.

I walked down the back and I walked right up to Johnny Romano and I stood there.

He slowly looked up and said, "Something I can do for you?"

"Something I can do for you."

"What might that be?"

"Your hostess is very rude. You could do a lot better. This is a nice place. She's not good for your reputation."

He waved his hand in the air, two fingers crooked. "Ginger—come here."

"Yes?" said the bottle-blonde, as she looked me up and down.

"Were you by any chance rude to my guest here?"

I looked at Ginger, she looked at me. "I barely said a word to her."

She did not look down at her boss, but I did. He looked at me while he recited, slowly, his eyes never leaving mine, "I think you should apologize to my guest."

"Well—I don't know why—but if you think I should— then I'm sorry if this lady thought—"

Johnny waved his hand in dismissal. "That's all."

Johnny Romano owned the place, so, when he waved his hand you were dismissed. The blonde stalked off, and Johnny gestured to me, welcoming. "Have a seat."

I slid into the booth opposite him and crossed my legs.

"You got a minute?" he says.

"I've got all night."

"Maybe there is something you can do for me."

I breathed in deep, my chest rose, and I gave it my best sigh. "I'm listening."

"My name is Romano, by the way."

"I know who you are. You're Rings Romano."

"Is that what they call me?"

"That's what they call you," I says.

"Well, you can call me Johnny."

"So-o-o, Johnny. What I really wanna know is, how come they call you 'Rings' when you only got one ring on each hand?"

He was by this time offering me a cigarette and so I took it slowly, tenderly, out of the pack in his hand. He leaned forward to light me up with a fancily-brocaded Lancel lighter that looked like it came straight out of the MGM prop department. I was staring at the rose-gold blue sapphire ring on his right hand ring finger. I took that hand by the fingertips and drew it closer across the tabletop so I could examine the polished band in some light. "What are those sparkling little speck-a-doodles, or whatever they are, embedded in there?"

"Gold flakes and meteorite shavings."

"Meteorites, huh? From outta this world."

"I call it my Stardust ring. Hoagy Carmichael gave it to me when he played the club."

"But you still haven't explained how come only two rings?—Johnny. When you got all these fingers available."

"Except one." He questioned with his eyes.

"Peggy," I sez.

"Except one—Peggy."

"You mean this one," I sez, taking the ring finger of his left hand in mine.

"That's right. As you can tell, that finger's taken."

"I see." Just to get the record straight, I sez, stretching it just a little, "I'm married." I don't know why I said that!

"That your husband you came in with?"

"Nah."

"I see."

The ring on Johnny Romano's left-hand ring finger was slightly spectacular. The jade dragon's-head ring was set in a jet-black obsidian band brushed with titanium. It was a ring with a compulsive beauty, the jade practically transparent, with a deep emerald-green color that was vibrating from within under the lounge lights.

"I got it from a Japanese colonel in Burma."

I looked up into his eyes, to see if he was lying. "Oh, he gave it to you, huh? Like Hoagy Carmichael?"

"Yes, he did give it to me. You understand, the Chinese believe it's extremely bad luck to be carving, or taking, a piece of jade for yourself, as it would anger the spirit or guardian of the jade. It's actually the spirit of the jade which chooses its wearer. So it must be *given* to you."

"And why would a Jap colonel give you that ring?"

"Well, I asked him first where he got it. And he said he stole it from the finger of a dead Chinese pawnbroker in Shanghai. So, right there I knew: this colonel had extremely bad luck. So then I told him that if he gave me the ring, I might consider letting him live."

"And what happened then?"

"He gave me the ring."

"And then what?"

"Then I shot him."

"Shot him dead?"

"No-o-o . . . he was alive when I shot him. He was dead after I shot him."

He wasn't lying. I gave a little shudder, and says, "Good. I hate those little yellow bastards."

And that was how Rings Romano and me discovered we had a lot in common.

Then Johnny sez, "Well—why don't you come in and see me, say, next Monday, about three in the afternoon, and we can have a little discussion."

"Will Miss Iceberg be here?"

"Not exactly at that hour, I don't believe. You just come right in and wait for me, right here, in my booth. I'll leave the door off the latch for you. Go around the back and let yourself in through the kitchen." Johnny Romano stood up and offered his hand. "You'll have to start at the bottom, you know—Peggy."

"As long as I end up on top."

Chapter 11

The Queen of Hialeah Park

I think Mr Romano knew, from that moment on, that I had him in my sights, and so did Miss Iceberg, whose name was, believe it or not, Madeleine McGill. She must have had a French mother or something because she came from someplace like Nova Scotia, I think. I don't know where she got that last name. But her first name I used against her. I started calling her "Made-*line,*" you know, like "wait in line," just to irritate her. It worked. She corrected me till she was blue in the face. Finally she gave up, so I started calling her Maddy, which she hated even more. She was easy. I got under her skin. She didn't stand a chance against me.

But then, I didn't stand a chance against Rings Romano.

Not only did he get under my skin he got into my soul. I won't say heart because it wasn't like that. It wasn't love at first sight or infatuation or a boardwalk romance like kids fall into for a summer. It was all or nothing, life or death, victory or final defeat. It wasn't anything he said or did but just the fact that he existed. How could a man like that exist? It was beyond anything natural. It wasn't real. I saw him and I wanted him. Not for a day or a night or a month's vacation or a lease for a year. I wanted to own him, I wanted to possess him. And I was afraid. I was afraid that already he owned me. And I had never surrendered myself before, never given myself. Sure, I was married to Henry Fabiano, I even had his children, but I never gave myself to him, not like this. I was walking on coals, but I wanted to plunge into the fire, to drown in the blaze. I couldn't help it, Nicky. I swear on my mother, I couldn't help myself.

So I was murderlizin› jealous of Made-*line*. I couldn't fathom what was the attraction there. What had he ever seen in *her?*

But I had to fight her for him.

My big advantage, which I sensed from the start, was that until the moment she came face to face with me, she never saw this coming. Complacency. She thought she fit him like an old shoe and that they were comfortable. It never dawned on her that she could lose him, nevermind that another woman could take him away from her. She just wasn't prepared, she wasn't ready for that. And overnight? Yes! It didn't take me long.

I started my campaign by switching targets and going after her job. Actually, I had thought it through and I realized that I could never have him while she was still in the club. I had to get her out, out completely, I had to annihilate her, remove her from the premises. The quickest way to do that was to take her job. *I had to become the hostess of the Frolics.*

The club was always crowded. She was always up the front, I was always down the back, since I started out waiting on tables, and he was always in his booth, by the kitchen. She couldn't always see me from her station, so I had plenty of chances to get closer to him. A little eye contact can go a long way. Pretty soon I could see that he was enjoying the game. She tried to fix me with a section on the other side of the stage but that would never work because I had to be constantly in and out of the kitchen. That put me in proximity to him and out of control to her.

But Monday nights could be slow. I made up my mind to force things at closing time. We were at the bar, Johnny and me, doing receipts, when she shows up at his other elbow.

"Since when are you the new bookkeeper?" she says to me, chin out.

I folded my cards and sighed deeply with the accent on exasperation.

Johnny turns to her and says, "Madeleine—you're tired— why don't you go home? Wait for me there—I'll be along."

"Sure. Sure, Johnny—you'll be along." She grabs her purse and slams out the door like she's had it with this.

I sez to Johnny, "How long you gonna keep up this charade?"

There is no man made in this world that doesn't love to see two women fighting over him. Rings Romano was no different. It amused him. It polished his image in the mirror. Why not keep the merry-go-round spinning? He knew he was in the catbird seat. He was the one who was gonna pick the winnah. And why wouldn't he pick me? I had somethin' Maddy didn't have: Maddy was old, and I was new. Every guy wants to be drivin' this year's model. Maddy was yesterday, and I was *now*.

But I had to let him know I wasn't a puppet on a string. I had to roll the dice and I had to roll them right here and now.

"Let's go for a ride," I says. "It's a nice night. I need a breath of fresh air, it's getting stale in here."

I knew Johnny was a professional bachelor. I also knew that, with him, it was one woman at a time. He was out to keep up appearances. He wanted to feel like the woman on his arm made him look good. He wanted to screen off the time-wasters, the *divorcées* and the debutantes. He was too self-important for that. I wasn't asking for the moon. I didn't want a ring, I wanted him.

That year he was running a new-model '49 Chrysler Town and Country, top down in the good weather. We headed out the Boulevard north. I leaned back on the plush seat and let the wind blow my hair around. It felt good, racing along.

We passed Lancaster Avenue in Point o' Pines and Johnny pointed it out. "She's waiting for me there."

It was his old family homestead. Johnny's Papa had come over from someplace near Salerno, a little place, Vietri sul Mare, I think it was called. The old guy was a bricklayer, and he started out making his fortune in America laying down patios and repairing chimneys. He built it up into a contractor's business. His son Johnny never had to scrape his knuckles, though. Whatever he wanted his Daddy bought for him and when he made his own money, he bought more.

"Where are we going?" I said, leaning my head over to gaze at his profile.

"You tell me." He pointed to the right at the Point o' Pines Yacht Club. "There's my boat."

We crossed over the channel on the bridge to Lynn and then veered out toward the night-time ocean and headed for the causeway to Nahant.

On the island we sped through winding tree-lined streets. It was late, and quiet. Nahant was different. People who lived out there weren't making a living digging a ditch. It was a different class of a place. Johnny pulled up outside a mansion. Although it was a moonless night, I could still make out that the long awning over the front walk was a little frayed.

"It's up for sale," said Johnny.

"What is it?"

"The country club."

He took me for a walk-through. The big room was plenty nice enough for functions and weddings and the floors were gleaming hardwood when he switched on the lights. They needed new drapes and furniture but otherwise it was hard to see why it was being let go. A third-grader could see it had the makings.

We let ourselves out the back and we were in the gazebo garden where they put on their outdoor weddings. We went all the way down the back and through the high hedge and came out to a patch of lawn rolling down to where the rocks were kissed by the ocean. On the lawn, there was one little rowboat and a lone park bench. We sat on the bench. Little lapping waves at our feet, making with an audible sigh.

"Should I buy it?" he says.

"Do you want it?"

"It's only nine holes."

"What difference does that make? Do you want it?"

"Yes. I want it."

"I think you should have everything you want."

"I wonder what we could make of this?" he said, and he looked at me as if trying to trace my features in the darkness and when he said that one word that put us together, that word '*we*'—then I knew I had won.

I looked straight ahead, out at the ocean, which we could hear, but not see, in the blackness of the night. "Can we go back to your boat, now, Johnny?"

"You want to?"

"Yes, I want to."

The next seven years flew by. I was the hostess of The Frolics and everybody in Revere knew me. Everybody in

Boston, for that matter, anybody who was somebody. From the governor on down, the Attorney General, the Speaker of the State House, the owner of the *Boston American*, the District Attorney of Suffolk County, *and* his favorite pals on the other side of the law. It wouldn't have surprised me one bit to see Harry Truman walk through that door. He never did, but everybody else did, anybody who ever had his name on a marquee in New York or New Jersey, anybody who ever had his, or her, name in lights in Hollywood. Judy Garland used to ask me how *I* was. Frank Sinatra comes in with Ava Gardner and he couldn't take his eyes off *me*. Then one night—but I'm getting ahead of myself—I'll have to save that for later.

Well, Nicky, that boat of Johnny's, at the Yacht Club, was a cabin cruiser built for two, and after we got the country club back in the black, Johnny buys this gorgeous 4-bedroom over-sized Cape Codder on Nectar Place, next door to Bass Point, out on the island, and he builds out a jetty or pier or something into the water, and we never drove out to Nahant through Lynn again—we just took the boat. Lucky wanted a new place for our love-nest, and you know, you couldn't park a boat on Lancaster Avenue.

Well, it was just perfect, the life we had. Free time we'd spend at the track, and I mean everywhere from Scarborough in Maine down to Narragansett, Rockingham, Wonderland, wherever. But our favorite was Hialeah.

See, a resort town—it's wide open in the summer—up north, that is. That's when we made our money. But when winter hit Revere Beach nobody was out there. The rides were all shuttered nobody was selling even a slice of pizza. By the same token, the Frolics was the only attraction that weathered the cold past Thanksgiving and even Christmas, because it was a supper club, because of the acts we booked. So winter was the perfect getaway time for me and Johnny—but he would not leave till after New Year's, he just wouldn't.

The meet at Hialeah would open the day after Christmas, and run till the end of February. Hialeah was the most beautiful place in the world. Oh, Nicky, the palm trees, the ivy-covered walls, the lake in the infield—and the flamingos! Hialeah was the place where you really could see Harry Truman, or the Gabor sisters or Jackie Gleason—not to mention Citation and Native Dancer. I would fly down to open up our place, a house we took in Bal Harbour, at the north end of Miami Beach, a few days ahead, right after New Year's, and then Johnny would drive the Chrysler down a few days later. Usually, we spent two weeks but sometimes a month or more. As long as there was racing next day at the track we were happy. When the last day of the meet finally rolled around we knew then that it was time to head back up north to the Frolics.

Now, Nicky, I know you adore me. After all, I'm your Auntie Peggy. You remember the time I sat you down with the twins and gave you each a dime and we turned on the radio in your mother's kitchen downstairs to tune in Babe Rubinstein calling the seventh race at Suffolk Downs, and you each had to make a bet? You remember the time we went picking blueberries up by the cemetery on Railroad Street?—the time we went looking for mushrooms in the woods and you wanted to know how did I know which ones were poisonous and which ones weren't? See, but things change, Nicky. Time goes by and we grow older and we don't feel the same way about things, or people. That's why I'm telling you this story now, Nicky. So that you'll realize—grab it while you can—'cause just maybe, just maybe, it's not always gonna be there.

They had a tote board at Hialeah, it was the wonder of the world. People said it was the first tote board in the whole country. It came all the way from Australia. They first put it in back in the early thirties when they rebuilt the park after the hurricane of '26. It was on the infield next to the lake and the flamingos. Nicky, if I tell you I had a connection with that tote board, will you believe me? What are the odds? Are you gonna play the longshot? Are you gonna play it across the board? Are you gonna run to the window now, or wait till the last second, hoping the odds turn in your favor? That's what most people are looking at the tote board to get out of it. But that tote board at Hialeah spoke to me. It sent me messages. Year after year it got deeper into communication with me. I almost was ready to believe it was the Third Eye, living and breathing outside of me—it had migrated from my forehead across the muddy track, over the rail, into the numbers and names on that pristine white board. It was an inanimate object with a living breathing mind. It was magical. And in our seventh winter at Hialeah it spelled out what was going to happen.

But I didn't want to hear it, I closed my eyes, I wouldn't listen.

What I didn't want to hear, Nicky, is that, as much as I loved him, as much as I was consumed with the desire to own and possess him, to keep him in my control so that I would never have to lose him, Johnny didn't want to own anybody. Possessions to him were *things*. And he didn't share his *things* with anyone. That's why he never married me. If he married anyone, he might lose his things. You might almost say, *lose his rings!*

So the two of us were locked in a deadly dance, whirling around in each other's arms, too blind to see where the steps were leading us.

One night towards the end of that winter we were supposed to be invited out to a party. We were getting ready and I had been out shopping that morning and bought something new and I wanted to surprise Johnny so when I went into the bathroom to do my makeup, I locked the door.

I sat in front of the mirror of the little vanity in the corner. When I looked into the glass I saw Merle Oberon. The thing I had bought to wear to the party was a beautiful black silk Chinese kimono, with a single pink flamingo over the heart—just a brushstroke of a flamingo, very stylized. I put it on to see myself in the mirror and I suddenly felt very oriental, like my skin had turned into the silk of the fabric. I was thinking of Johnny and the Jap colonel. I was thinking of Johnny avenging the dead Chinese. The story he told me about the Chinese and how they revered the jade. I convinced myself that Johnny loved the Chinese. I started to do my makeup, and stopped. I piled my hair up on the back of my head and pinned it, in the Chinese manner I'd seen in a cardboard cut-out at the dress shop. I noticed then how black my hair was. How black my eyes. I started to do my eyes and my hand just curved itself into a tracery of an Oriental slant, upwards at the corners. It was as if someone else was guiding my hand. *An artist.* I sat back and what I saw in the mirror now was a Chinese lady of the evening. I was short and slim and shapely. I filled out my kimono, my beautiful black silk kimono, which I now put on for the party.

Johnny was yelling through the door, "What are you doing in there? Come on, Peggy! We're gonna be late for Mac's do!"

I smoothed my hands all over my front as I stood up and unlocked the door. I went out and even my steps were mincing. I posed, I gently spread my wings, I turned slightly.

Then I saw a look of utter disgust on Johnny's face.

"Don't you like it, darling? I did it for you. I thought it would be nice to give you a surprise. For the party tonight."

He was moving backwards slowly, reaching behind himself to feel for a chair. He sat down tentatively.

"What's the matter, John! Say something! You're scaring me!"

For a long time, he didn't answer. My heart was in my mouth. Then he pointed at the front door and he said, "Get out!"

"Johnny! What do you mean?"

"I mean *Get Out!*"

I was staggered. I was mute. I couldn't move. He had pinned me like a butterfly with a dagger through my soul. I finally managed to utter words through my clenched lips, where already I tasted the salt of my tears.

"You don't mean that."

My lips were trembling as I tried to form the words.

"*Get out!* How many times do I have to tell you!"

I turned angry then. I was hurt but I was incensed. I thought, I'll show him. I turned my back and went to the door, but when I put my hand on the knob, every shred of steam left in me sagged out.

I turned back and ran to him and threw myself on my knees and buried my head in his lap and sobbed uncontrollably. "I don't want to leave. I don't want to go."

I waited and waited to feel him loosen up. His whole body was rigid with tension. I waited and waited to feel his hand on my shoulder, on my head, smoothing my hair, making it better. *He never moved his hand from where it gripped the arm of the chair.*

Finally, I tried to get my breath, between the choking sobs that were twisting up in heaving pulses from my midsection. "It's all right, darling. I'll change. I'll get into something else. We'll go to the party. We'll be all right."

But I knew we wouldn't be.

Nicky, when I'm gone, don't think of me like you see me now, you know, lying here, flat on my back, my head all twisted up with pain. *Think of me the way I used to be when I was the Queen of Hialeah Park.*

Chapter 12

Disowned

After that I was never the same. How could I be? True, I stayed with Johnny. He didn't end up kicking me out, after all, that night. He relented. He softened up. I got around him somehow. Maybe he felt sorry for me. Pity. That's the worst thing of all, to be pitied. After the pedestal he had put me on? Why, I was more popular at The Frolics than he was, in the eyes of many of the patrons. After all, he was like a shadow huddled in his booth at the back. I was the face of things. I was the one people thought of when they pictured walking in the door of The Frolics, you know, let's go out tonight, they counted on me being there to greet them and make a big deal out of them. We were like a family at that club. It was the place you went when you knew you belonged.

Do you remember a certain fine summer day, Nicky, in the late afternoon, just before dinnertime, when you were about five years old, yes, you must remember, you were old enough, your brother and sister were still infants that day when your mother brought them down Revere Beach Boulevard in that double-stroller, those two roly-polies, side by side, and people were stopping her just outside the glass door of the club to make goo-goo eyes at them, and you—you saw me at my lectern inside the door and you pressed your face up against the glass to try to see me better and I came over and knelt down to wave at you and then your mother yanked you by the arm and I could see she was saying, "You can't go in there."

And I straightened up and watched you all walk away and it was like the little overlapping circles of waves at low tide on the beach covering over and washing away all traces of the footsteps in the sand, the way the crowds of people on the sidewalk were swallowing you up, and I tried to catch a glimpse of you for as long as I could and then I had to turn back to my job, to my life, to Johnny and the club and the customers, and it was like we were separated forever by a glass door.

I never forgot that, Nicky.

Because when your life is falling apart, when things force you to find out, in spite of all your illusions, who really loves you, it's always your family you turn to.

That's why it hurts so much when I think of my brother Augie.

Even though I have a tumor in my brain and the pain is sometimes unbearable, it doesn't hurt me as much as the memory of what he said to me.

But before I get to that I have to tell you about Cesar Romero.

It's funny how one day, one night, can come along and change everything in your life, in an instant, and forever after you point to that instant and you know, that was the turning point.

On the surface as far as anyone could tell nothing had changed between me and Johnny after that fight we had in Bal Harbour. We got home and everything resumed, at The Frolics, at the Yacht Club, on Johnny's boat, at the house on

Nectar Place, our life, that beautiful, glittering life we had. We were still in love with our life. We were still putting on a show for everybody, his friends, my friends, we didn't want the party to end anymore than we'd stop booking headliners at The Frolics. It's just that inside of us something had shifted. We watched each other, we danced around each other, we watched what we said, we had become *adversaries.* The old openness, the old embrace of, I don't know how to express it—we used to dive into each other like the other person was a swimming pool and we wanted total immersion in each other. And now, we tiptoed around the edges and put a toe in first. Others couldn't tell, but we knew, we felt it, and it changed everything.

One night Cesar Romero walked into The Frolics, you know, the actor, from the movies.

He was such a handsome guy. He noticed me right way and he flashed that big hundred-watt smile of his. On his way out with his friends, he said to me, confidentially, "We're going to a party. Why don't you come along later?" and he slipped me a card.

"What's wrong with right now?" I said.

"Oh-h-h-h. Can you? Just walk away? Even better!"

I was feeling reckless that night. I don't know. I just wanted to get a rise out of Johnny. I wanted to see if he would be jealous, if I could make him jealous. It didn't occur to me I was walking out on the club, on my position, on my patrons and friends and family. I didn't think of any of that. I just thought of how wild and reckless it would be if I did. I couldn't help myself. I told one of the girls to take over, and I was gone, out the door.

It took a while for me to find out what Johnny thought. At first, it was like nothing at all had happened. Typical Italian. *Revenge is a dish best served cold.*

Johnny's beloved Papa had been sick for a while. All of a sudden he picks this time to check out. Ironically enough, the wake was held at the Buonfiglio Funeral Home on Revere Street. You know what that name means in Italian? *Good son.*

I was in the receiving line at the wake. I saw her there. My replacement. I knew, all right, who she was. The Third Eye told me.

As we were leaving, to go bury him at the cemetery in Malden, Johnny walked me to his car, his new Chrysler, and he holds open the door for me. Before I could get in, he hands me a set of keys.

"What's this?" I says.

"Why don't you ask Cesar Romero?"

He gets in his side and starts it up and we pull out. I was frozen in my seat. You would've thought *I* was the corpse. He wouldn't look at me. He goes, "I been thinking. My father's gone. I'm gonna sell the house on Lancaster Ave. It's time for a change. I got some people out at the house on Nectar Place, they're changing the locks. In your hand's the keys to your new place. Nice little studio on the corner of North Shore Road. First three months' rent's paid. Call it your severance pay. After that, it's up to you—when you get your new job."

So that was it. Just like that. I had a seven years' run of luck and this was how it came to an end.

I did him one better, Nicky. I disappeared.

The fact is I didn't want anybody to know me. After I'd been the hostess of The Frolics for so many years, how could I take a step down?

I went to see my friend Peter Chin. He had a place out on Squire Road called The Oriental Gardens. He used to come in late at The Frolics after he closed up. I went to see Peter and I told him what I wanted to do. He said okay, he'd help me out. He was a good person. He knew I was a good person. It sounded crazy to him, but it sounded crazy to me, too. That was how I became Winnie Ming, a waitress in a Chinese restaurant who had just come over on the slow boat from Hong Kong and didn't have too much English, if any. I made them point at the menu. Some of the same people I had from the Frolics. And believe me, the way I had of doing that make-up, they never knew it was me. My one word of English was "Ho-kay!" I had to pull it off, Nicky, the pressure was on, Peter Chin didn't want any of this getting back to Johnny Romano in case it would sour their relationship.

That brings us up to, oh, 1954, I think. Yes. It was the year your mother was selling Ma's house on Payson Street. My brother Gene was setting up his shop on Oxford Street in Spicket Falls. Your mother, my brother Patsy, your Uncle Augie, my sister Anna, Mary, too, they were all gonna work as stitchers and pressers and cutters, it was gonna be the family business. My mother was gone three years by then, God rest her, your Papanonni was two years in his grave, they were over in Holy Cross cemetery in Malden with Johnny Romano's father, the family was gonna leave me high and dry in Revere by myself. You were about seven or eight years old, Nicky, but my Henry was 18 already, he was born in '36. He had joined the Marines when he was just 17—against my will!— but he got his father to sign for him, the day he graduated from Revere High. And now he had come home on leave from Japan, and he wanted me to know that the next time he came home, he'd be introducing me to his Japansese bride!

I hit the roof. I yelled and I screamed, I was fit to be tied. You were there. You remember that day! You ran out the door so fast, I knew I had scared the life out of you, but I couldn't help it. You couldn't reason with Henry. That kid, I loved him to death, but you couldn't reason with him. He wasn't like his brother Ronnie. He was so damn smart it wasn't good for him. They were training him in electronics or radar or something at this Air Force base in Japan and he meets some girl in a bar! I told him I didn't want him bringing home a prostitute to introduce to his mother! He looked at me through those glasses he wore like he wanted to kill me! That poor innocent kid who was too smart for Revere High School, they had gotten him in boot camp and turned him into a monstah! I don't blame you for running out the door, Nicky!

I was beside myself and I couldn't think of what to do so I called up for Uncle Augie at the house on Payson Street and I figured if I got him over to my studio, he could talk some sense into my kid. After all, your Uncle was a veteran of Omaha Beach—the kind of guy that crazy kid Henry would look up to, like he looked up to his old man, Fabiano, who joined the Marines, during the war, when I divorced him, like he thought he would spite me, so instead he ends up on Gaudalcanal in a foxhole full of rainwater and his own pee. Yeah! These were the men my Henry grew up idolizing, his father and his uncles, conquering heroes, all of them!

Augie walked into my little studio and there we were sitting at opposite ends of the day-bed and Augie was as calm as could be, but you know me, Nicky, I love nothing better than a good argument, so I launched into a tirade. I guess I raised my voice again, but I couldn't help it.

"Will you tell this stupid kid about those goddam Japs! What the hell did we fight a goddam war against those monkeys for? Them and their goddam Emperor! Tell him what those goddam animals did to the poor, defenseless Chinese, and what they woulda done to us, if they'da got the chance! We had to drop the Bomb on them because they were gonna commit mass murder on us before they'd surrender! They're animals! They're fiends! They're sub-human! They'da loved nothin' bettah than to rape a white woman! And this was just yesterday! And now this crazy kid wants to get married to one of them! Will you talk some sense into him, Augie!"

Augie sat down on my one little armchair, as calm as could be. My kid brother. He was so big he overflowed. Six foot two, and he wasn't skinny anymore like he was when he came home from the war. He sez, "What do you want me to say, Peggy?"

"Tell him what they tried to do to his father on Guadalcanal, for crissakes!"

"It's his life, Margaret."

"Who you calling Margaret!"

"I'm calling my sister Margaret. Isn't that your name? Or do you want me to call you Winnie Ming?"

"You got a helluva nerve talking to me like that!"

"Henry." He had been glaring at me, my kid brother, but now he just coldly swiveled his gaze away to my son sittin' in my one chair, my TV chair. I swear to God, Nicky, until he swerved his eyes way, I was the target in his gunsight—I saw my brother looking down the barrel at me like I was a Nazi. "Henry, you look good all spit-shined and polished. They been treating you good in the Marines?"

"I love the Corps, Uncle Augie."

"Looks to me like it suits you. They've done you a world of good. I'm proud of you, son."

Then he turned to me again and I never in my life thought to see such cold-blooded disgust in a brother of mine.

"Margaret, it's time you let this boy be. Haven't you done enough to ruin his life by now? I've heard you myself belittle him till you would think he would be reduced to a puddle at your feet. And yet he stands before you now a man."

"You got a helluva nerve talking to me like that."

"Henry, let's go get a beer, whaddya say?"

They were leaving through the door, and his hand was still on the knob.

"You're a goddam asshole, Augie," I cried.

Before he shut the door in my face, my brother turned to me, one more time, and said,

"And you are no sister of mine."

BOOK III

Gerry's story

Chapter 13

Letters From Home

1942 Revere, Massachusetts

In 1942, Gerry LaStoria was an unmarried woman of 20 who lived at home with her parents (in her father's house, as she deemed it.) She had two married sisters, Mary, who was older, and more or less decently settled, and the other, Peggy, the family problem-child, sadly, Gerry thought, divorced. Gerry sometimes wondered if she herself would ever see the altar. But this was far from uppermost in Gerry's mind compared to some of her other concerns, and yes, daily worries. The war had changed everything. Her three sisters were only a phone call away, still ever-present in her daily round, especially Peggy, with her two sons, Gerry's nephews Henry and Ronnie, but all three of her brothers were in the service, beyond her reach, except by letters that went mostly unanswered.

At home, in Pa's latest second-hand two-family, at No. 45 Payson Street in Revere, the war seemed to hover. Gerry found it difficult to banish the war from her thoughts. It crept in the windows or waited for you at the back door or reached out through the radio and grabbed you by the throat. Useless worrying doing nobody any good made you feel so futile. The absolutely endless bad news of 1942, from the faraway Pacific, with strange new names such as Bataan and Corregidor, made you want to do something, such as scream. The war was the very reason they had moved to Revere to this new house. Pa's workload was such a strain due to the war effort; after they had moved from Stoughton, on the South Shore, where they had all grown up, to Kimball Road, in Watertown, Gerry's Pa found himself in a rented first floor, for the first time in more than 20 years, and he didn't like it. Peggy was living in Revere, at the Beach. Suffolk Downs, the racetrack was in Revere. Pa's only outlet was to get away on a Saturday afternoon to the track. But young Anna refused to leave Watertown High, because of her boyfriend. Her older sister Mary, on Dewey Street, with her husband and kids, Little Tony and Little Gerry, had no room, on the second floor, to take Anna in. Beside himself with overwork and government inspectors, Pa was in no mood to suffer a repeat of the rebellion he faced from Patsy and Mary and Peggy when they were children and he forced them to leave their schools and friends and start over in Stoughton. As crazy as it sounded, he continued the lease on Kimball Road so that Anna could stay by herself, just around the corner from Mary's house, while she finished at Watertown High. At least he would have one child of his seven, now that the Depression was over, graduate from high school. Meanwhile, he himself had found a two-family to buy in Revere, at 45 Payson Street, with old, widowed Mrs Nelson already occupying the 2nd floor to pay rent; Gigi could have her flower garden again; Pa would have room for his tomato plants and even for a new kennel of bird-dogs, as well as a grape arbor; Pa could commute to work on the trolley to Maverick Square in East Boston and the subway into town from there, and save on his allotted 4 gallons per week of wartime gas ration for when he wanted to drive himself to the track, since he wouldn't have to traverse the Fresh Pond Parkway and skirt around Everett to get there from Watertown.

Yet for Gerry these moving-to-Revere machinations were minor tribulations compared to her worries over Ma's decline. A strain of morbid sadness, blame it on the war, blame it on her condition, her weight, her bad stomach, her aches and pains, her poor legs, her varicose veins, her circulation, had overcome the poor woman.

Each morning the recital of Gigi LaStoria's latest vivid dreams, populated with the ghosts of her dead parents and deceased sister, haunted the kitchen. After all these years Gerry's mother still blamed herself for the death of Zi'Anna-Vittoria, her only sister, in a flaming automobile wreck. And that had happened in 1927.

Sometimes Gerry caught Ma staring out the open window in the kitchen on Payson Street, one arm sunning on the sill, staring forlornly, as if she expected one of the boys to come strolling up the driveway at any moment in full dress uniform. Ma LaStoria, registered enemy alien, was a mother with three boys in the service, overseas, in Europe, in the US Army, in mortal danger, as she constantly imagined it, and every doorbell, every ring of the phone, to Gigi, was the dread news she had tried, with prayers and promises and nightmares and anxieties, futilely, to put off.

Indeed, to Gerry, it almost seemed like some kind of seismic fault in the universe that her brothers, Patsy, Gene and Augie, were not there every day. Gene had been Pa's shadow, his right-hand man, Patsy was a presser, and Augie was a cloth-cutter, all three trained by Pa, just as the girls were. Mary, her oldest sister, was a stitcher, promoted by Pa to floor-lady, and she saw Pa every day, as did Gerry, every night after he got home, late as usual, from work, for the supper to be warmed up again which Gerry had saved for him. Margaret, the round peg in the family, was the only offspring of Tony LaStoria who did not fit in the square hole. The others, Patsy, Gene, Augie, Mary, if you asked them, would tell you that the smell of the shop, a combination of lint, stale sunlight, dust-motes and yards of cloth, in other words, the dull, steady odor of flannel, was the smell of existence itself.

Whether Russian army overcoats or Eisenhower jackets for our own boys, whichever the current contract at the shop, in town at Melcher Street, nine, ten, eleven, twelve hours later Pa LaStoria would return home on the streetcar by himself. He normally stayed overtime and still found it difficult to tear himself away at the end. Government inspectors were crawling all over him, and he had other shops in the Spritzka conglomerate to manage by telephone all over the map of four out of six New England states. He had a job, as a general-manager, that was important, more so than ever before, because of the war, and he had to be the man big enough to handle it.

Arriving home, he would find Gerry waiting for him in the kitchen on Payson Street to heat up his dinner for him. His wife Gigi no longer waited up for him. To Tony, it was a sign of her declining health, this loss of interest in anything, even her flowers. Mother of God. Yet he did not see Gigi in the morning, as she didn't get up anymore till he had left for work. If he had, he would have seen his wife hanging on to the shreds of her lost power and privilege: as soon as Gerry stepped into the kitchen, Ma would say, *"Gerardina, stai qua,"* and begin giving her instructions on every little thing that had to be done, as if anything changed from day to day. The peeling, the stirring, the mixing, the sweeping, the bed-making, the laundry, the dishes, the watering, (whether her mother's flower garden or her father's tomatoes) the weeding, the feeding of her father's bird-dogs, the list was endless, all the daily tasks Gigi used to carry out herself, which, now, she could no longer. *Whoever said that a woman's work was never done,* Gerry thought, *must have known what was going to happen to me.*

Still, Gerry loved her mother. She may not have liked her, the way she liked her father, but that was because she didn't feel she was her mother's favorite. With her father, she knew that she was the apple of his eye. He may never have said so, but Gerry remembered that, when she was little, he used to ruffle her hair, exactly the way he did with one of his dogs when they came running up. He would say something like, "How did we ever get a blonde in the family? Are you sure you belong to me? Maybe I found you in the street, eh? Maybe it was the ragman who dropped you off." Gerry would be sitting on her father's lap and look across the parlor and see her next older sister Peggy sitting on her mother's lap. That told you everything you needed to know.

Her sister Margaret (when you were mad at her), or Peggy, (when everything was hunky-dory) was now just about the biggest problem Gerry had to deal with every day. Gerry knew that Margaret, when her kids, Henry and Ronnie, were with her at her place, would push them out the door to school with a bowl of cereal in the morning, and as soon as the boys were gone, back in bed she would hop, pull the sheets up over her head, and stay there till noon. When Henry and Ronnie were gone to Wilmington with their father, Margaret didn't have to get up at all till it was time for the Daily Double. Afternoons Margaret spent at the race track, either right here at Suffolk Downs or out of town, whether Rhode Island or New Hampshire. So far her sister had successfully avoided finding a job, as such, although she sometimes pushed a rag behind a bar, but she certainly knew how to lean on you for a loan. The thing was, Gerry couldn't say no. Everybody loved Peggy, she was vivacious, funny and glamorous, and Gerry was no exception. Peggy would light up a room when she walked in. The only trouble was that when they were in the same room together Gerry would get eclipsed by that light. But your sister is your sister, and Gerry would have to dip into the housekeeping money her father left her *(but don't let him know.)*

Gerry did not envy her oldest sister, Mary. Her husband Serafino, who everybody called Charlie, for short, was an old-fashioned type of husband, actually from the old country, from Calabria, in fact. Charlie Laverna was the kind who felt a woman had her place and she should know it, and Gerry always had a queasy feeling about that. Gerry felt bad for Mary as she knew from experience how argumentative things got with those two when they were together. It just made it hard to feel comfortable being around them.

But still, Mary had two beautiful children, a son, Little Tony, named after their father, and a daughter, Geraldine, named after *guess who!*

Gerry had no idea what possessed Mary to name one of her kids after her, and she was not so much flattered as puzzled. There must have been something in Mary Gerry had missed, some special feeling. Maybe that happened because Gerry was so much younger, and besides, Peggy came along in between them, and, even when they were all kids, Peggy took up most of everybody's time and attention.

But Gerry loved those two kids Mary had, just as much as she loved Peggy's two boys, Henry and Ronnie. The kids were the light in Gerry's life, the children of her own which she had not yet had.

So the war years dragged on, on the home front, radio static in the background, a constant drone, interrupted only by alarms and bulletins.

Gerry's baby sister Anna also had no children as yet, but she was married when she was only 17, early in 1944, to a fellow named Tommy DiPrima, who was about to enlist, now that he'd graduated from Watertown High, which was why they had to get married, *now.*

Anna had bought a two-family on Mt Auburn Street in Watertown, around the corner from Mary and Charlie on Dewey Street, after she cajoled their father into co-signing a loan for her. Why not? He was already paying her rent on Kimball Road, and who would've thought that young Anna could have persuaded him to do that? Lucky for her that Pa had connections with the *Banca Italiana* in the North End of Boston where he had been taking mortgages out since 1919. So they fudged a little on the loan application and made Anna 18. *Shrug.* She was such a gorgeous young lady, with the dark-haired, All-American good looks of a Linda Darnell playing opposite John Payne in a Hollywood movie called *Star Dust,* that the loan officer at the bank really didn't stand a chance.

Where Anna, still in her teens, got her nose for real estate, Gerry couldn't fathom, but Pa just shrugged and said, "At least I got one daughter who graduated. So, now, she can go to work, for me, as a stitcher, she won't even have to look for a job, and Harry Spritzka will pay her, so she can afford the mortgage payments, no? And she'll have an income comin' in from upstairs, to boot."

Yet Gerry did not resent Anna for her seeming acquisitiveness. Not even when she acquired Tommy DiPrima, quite a handsome young fellow, for a husband. Tommy, it turned out, was Anna's tenant in the house on Mt Auburn Street. He was the son of the family upstairs on the second floor. Gerry was happy for the young couple, and took her place in the bridal party when the photographer assembled them for the bridal album. Margaret was there, too, urging Gerry to try to catch the bouquet, but Gerry only blushed to her ears, and while she was busy being embarrassed, one of Tommy DiPrima's sisters snatched the bouquet just as it was hitting the floor.

So the youngest LaStoria sister, who achieved the unheard of accomplishment of becoming a homeowner as a single girl of just 17, could now hand over the keys, as a married home-owner, to her brand-new bridegroom, but, only figuratively, as he was off to boot-camp on the next bus leaving from the South Boston Army Base.

Margaret's two boys were a handful for their grandmother Gigi. The streetcar line on Beach Street in Revere ran right across the foot of Payson Street, and, each day, right after school, Gigi would expect to see mother and boys hand in hand marching up the street about two-thirty. Actually, most days they would step out of a car driven by Peggy's latest male escort.

"Now you boys behave for your mammanonna," Peggy would exclaim as she sped out the back door again. She was always in a hurry to get back to the track.

Gigi found them impossible to handle. She had only her native Italian with which to communicate and command and with these two that only made it easier to ignore her. But Gigi could not deny Peggy anything. Henry was six and little Ronnie was five. Henry needed eyeglasses and, of course, Peggy couldn't afford them. Gigi had to weasel the money out of their Papanonni without his knowing so she told her husband it was her bad legs getting worse and she needed the special support stockings, which was true. Even at their age Tony LaStoria could not refuse his Gigi anything she wished, so he shrugged when he said to himself, *those are awful expensive stockings.*

Gerry, of course, was there every day to do the actual heavy lifting with her two nephews. She would help the studious Henry as he peered at his homework through those eyeglasses of his at the kitchen table, while she put the rambunctious Ronnie out in the yard to romp with his Papanonni's dogs or play cowboys and Indians or cops and robbers under the back porch. Henry had brains, but Ronnie had imagination.

For in spite of everything, the war, her mother, her glamorpuss of a sister Peggy, her overworked Pa, the drudgery she faced stuck at home all the time; the envy she sometimes felt for her lucky sister Anna, the dismay she felt when she looked on to see big sister Mary unhappy at home; the lonely sadness she felt missing her brothers in the service, especially her favorite, Augie; still, Gerry felt young and alive and in love with, maybe not somebody special in particular, but the world, in love with life, and she wanted the same things as everybody, the same things her sisters had: someone to love, beautiful babies to shower with hugs, kisses and adoration, a grandchild to give to her Ma and Pa. She wanted to be like her sisters, somebody Ma and Pa could be proud of. And—it was wartime. So how could you hold up the home front in the face of all the sacrifice and suffering the whole world was going through if you gave in to the powerful pull of despair?

Just as Gerry was closest to Peggy among her sisters, with her brothers, it was Augie who took first place for her.

Patsy was Ma and Pa's first-born. That made him a remote big brother, too old for little Gerardina growing up. Gene came along but he was too shy and studious to compete with Patsy and Peggy's rough-necking. Augie was born next, after Gerry herself, and that made him her little brother when she was still a very young child herself, and that must have been where the attachment that grew up between them began to materialize. For as they all grew older, only Gerry and Augie evinced any desire to stay at home. Patsy, Mary and above all, Peggy, all acted like they couldn't wait to get away and establish their own places outside the circle. Even Gene got married to his Greek sweetheart Celia before he joined the service. That left Augie and Gerry at home, both single and unattached, neither one feeling like they belonged anywhere else, till the day came when Augie enlisted.

That they were the last two left at home did not seem accidental to Gerry. It seemed to be written in the special closeness between them. Gerry thought of it this way: he was his mother's son, and she was her father's daughter.

One night at the close of another very long day Gerry retired to the sanctuary of her own bedroom. There she had a little bookshelf which Augie had made for her just before he left for boot camp in New Jersey. He built it to fit in the tiny space between her window looking out on the back porch and the corner where her bed stood. In the morning Gerry swung her legs out of bed and the bookshelf was on her left and she could look out the window to gauge the day. On the three shelves she had arranged her collection of John Steinbeck novels. In handsome brown bindings that felt like velvet to the touch, she had *Tortilla Flat* and *The Red Pony* and *Of Mice and Men* and, of course, *The Grapes of Wrath*. Every time she touched that one, it made her think of 1939. That was a special year at the show.

Gerry was in the habit of giving herself one night in the week to treat herself for all her hard work, and it was usually Saturday night, when she went to see the latest movie that everybody was talking about.

She never could go to the show alone, that did not feel right to her, as, when they were all little, her big brother Patsy used to be put in charge of the whole troop of LaStorias, to take them to the Saturday matinees, going all the way back to the silent movies in the Twenties. Oftentimes she went with her girlfriend Hildie, with whom she had been best friends since they were in 4th grade together in Stoughton. Hildie still lived there on the South Shore so she and Gerry would split the distance and Hildie would take the streetcar from Stoughton all the way into Mattapan while Gerry made her way from Revere into town and they would meet on Washington Street and go see a show at one of the big downtown picture palaces, either Loew's or the RKO Keith Memorial or the Paramount. That made it a real night out. Everybody got dressed up, there were no farmers in overalls on Washington Street, or if there were, they had changed into suit and tie. Gerry saw *The Wizard of Oz* with Hildie, and it was just like they were back in 4th grade together again. *Gone With the Wind* she saw with her sister Peggy, of course. But *The Grapes of Wrath*, with Henry Fonda as Tom Joad, she went to see that with Augie.

So, naturally, after that special occasion shared with her beloved little brother, Gerry had to go out and spend some of her pin-money on Steinbeck's original novel of *The Grapes of Wrath*, to add to her sanctuary collection on the little bookshelf Augie built for her.

Even her downtrodden mother's crabby comment, "we don't need any more books!" when she came home that night with her precious cargo, could not spoil for Gerry this hour of reflection, so hard-won, out of so many days when it seemed impossible to get a moment for herself.

So that night, when she retreated to her bedroom to commune with the spirit of Tom Joad, she put her knees up in bed and propped up her lined pad and rolled back a couple of pages so as to start in the middle and poised her pencil to write to Augie, and she was thinking of the movies, and how real they were, and of how, every Saturday night, they were all following the newsreels and drowning in the latest calamities and atrocities on every front from the African desert to the Phillipine Islands to the wheatfields of Russia, and of what a horrible world this was, and yet, what could you honestly say to your brother so far away who might possibly be having a tough time of his own this very moment to cheer him or to buck him up or to make him miss you or to make him realize how much he was loved? She despaired of thinking of anything worthy of John Steinbeck's phrase-making, because, to Gerry LaStoria, her brother Augie was just as much a Hollywood hero as any Henry Fonda or Tom Joad could ever be, and how in the world could she ever express all the sentiments that weighed like shining gold in her heart, as precious to her as emeralds and rubies were to a Rockefeller or a JP Morgan?

In the dimming grey shimmer of that movie, and again, in the cool ivory pages of the novel, you could see how much Tom Joad loved his mother.

Thus was the spirit of Tom Joad joined to the soul of Gerry LaStoria, who likewise, loved her mother, and loved her family.

So she began this letter from home, propped on her knees, "Dear Augie . . ."

Chapter 14

Across a Crowded Room

In September of 1944, the war had changed from the dark days of 1942. A bottled-up American Army burst out of the hedgerows of Normandy and began charging hard across northern France towards the Rhine. Three brothers in the American armed forces who came from the same family, the LaStorias of Boston, Mass., were scattered through western Europe, from Metz in northern France to the capital of Luxembourg to the city of Florence in Italy. None of the three knew where the other two were, although, back in late August, by sheer, remarkable happenstance, Augie and Patsy had bumped into each other, for five minutes, at the Gare de l'Est railway station in Paris, while boarding trains with their units, heading for different destinations they were not allowed to disclose.

None of this was known at the time to Gerry LaStoria, and she would not hear the story about the railway station in Paris till after the war. All she knew at this moment in September, 1944 was that somewhere in western Europe, her brothers were lost to her. For how long, no one knew. When, or whether, they would return, no one knew. These questions, and all answers, were locked in an impenetrable future, leading to an unknown fate; while here at home, the four LaStoria sisters were going dancing.

It happened one night that September, with the world plunged into uncertainty, with hope hanging in the balance, that Gerry LaStoria was coaxed, prodded and pulled out of the house by her sister Peggy to go in town, to the Raymor-Playmor Ballroom on Huntington Ave., where Stan Kenton and Artie Shaw were booked with their orchestras for a show billed as *The Battle of the Bands*.

One night a week, yes, on Saturday, Gerry's parents acquiesced in her wish to go out with her girlfriend Hildie to the movies in town. But it was not as if they gave her permission, it simply never occurred to them that she might have any needs of her own, any desires, any objections to being stuck in the house all the time. Gerry was simply expected to do what was expected: *just like her brothers overseas*. After all, her father was a busy man, and he couldn't stay home to take care of his wife, who was ailing, God help her.

Therefore, Gerry hadn't been to any dances, except once or twice when Hildie made her go along to a USO dance, you know, for the boys, for the war-effort. Gerry was not exactly comfortable doing this when it came time to make up stories to tell her mother about what they saw at the show.

Nor was she comfortable being dragged out by her sister Peggy on this particular Saturday night in September. Peggy was the girl about town; Gerry was the stay-at-home stick-in-the-mud. With her girlfriend Hildie, Gerry could just be herself, but with her sister Peggy, she felt challenged to keep up. Nor did she feel exactly comfortable around any people other than family, for instance, around strangers, or anyone she did not already know. Therefore, she was feeling rushed and nervous as they tumbled up the staircase of the Raymor-Playmor, where a sea of right-in-style young women and a crush of men in uniform thronged up the steps and across the walkways left and right to the divided ballrooms where the two bands were blaring at each other.

Out of her element, that's how Gerry felt. Scanning the ballroom they entered, on the left, the Stan Kenton side, to see if they could spot their sisters, Mary and Anna, she felt caught up in a torrent bigger than she was. Those two, no doubt, would be there before them. Watertown was so much closer to town than Revere, just across the Charles. Gerry hoped they were saving seats for them, but she and Peggy couldn't find them. They had to turn around and push their way through the mob on the bridge to cross to the other side, where Artie Shaw's band was playing. *There they were.* Gerry spotted them finally through a gap in the bobbing heads on the dance floor. *Thank God.*

At a round table, Anna was canted over with her hand firmly planted on a chair, and Mary was holding tight to her pocketbook, placed on another. "What took you two so long?" said Anna.

"What do you think?" Peggy replied, plopping herself down. "She didn't wanna come."

"Who said!" cried Gerry, as she tried to seat herself in lady-like fashion.

Mary said, "That's right, let's get the argument started."

Peggy said to her, "Well, we wanna make you feel at home."

"Come on, you two," said Gerry.

"Tell her she looks nice, willya?" said Peggy.

"You look nice," Anna and Mary said to Gerry, in unison. "No, really you do."

"I wish I felt like my lipstick was on straight," said Gerry.

"Are you gonna be miserable all night?" said Peggy. "We're supposed to be out for a good time tonight."

"Yeah, relax," said Anna. "Look at me. I'm relaxed."

"You can be relaxed," said Gerry, "as long as your husband's far, far away."

"Oh," said Anna. "For the life of me, I can't see how Tommy would mind. After all, I only came for you."

"For me?" said Gerry.

Mary said, "Have a drink," as she delicately nibbled the olive from her martini. "That'll relax you."

"You buying?" said Peggy. "I'm broke."

"What else is new?" said Mary. "Maybe you'll find a man to buy you a drink, Peggy."

"Yeah. Maybe I will."

Gerry said, "I wish you two would stop it."

Mary said to Gerry, "Will you look at Merle Oberon ovah here?"

"Merle Oberon could only wish she was me," said Peggy. "But, yes, if you insist, I have that look."

"That shady lady look?" piped in Anna.

"Don't get your bloomers in a twist," Peggy advised Anna.

Gerry nudged Peggy, "Evermind-nay em-thay."

"Isten-lay—Iway ancay ayplay atthay amegay. Utbay onight›stay ouryay ightnay."

"Don't start with that stuff," said Mary.

"Hey!" said Peggy, placing a hand dramatically on Gerry's forearm. "There's that sailor."

"What sailor?"

"You'll see," said Peggy, tapping her temple. "The Third Eye knows."

A soldier asked Mary to dance. "I'm married," she said.

He said, "I won't tell your husband."

A sailor asked Anna to dance. She said, "My husband's in the Army. He wouldn't like it if I was disloyal to his branch."

"Stand aside, swabby," said a soldier, stepping up to the batter's box.

Peggy held up both arms in a *Halt* sign. "Hold it, boys. This is a dance-club, not a football scrimmage."

"Say, is there any of you not married?"

"Guess."

"Only one of us."

"Not me."

"I'm divorced—does that count?" Peggy whispered to Gerry, "Here he comes."

A naval officer stepped up. "Ensign Murphy of the USS Ruby, and Shreveport, Louisiana, at your service. Who's in command of your contingent?"

"That would be me," Peggy said. Then, right behind the Ensign's shoulder, there he was. *The eyes on the stairway.* But she couldn't get Gerry to look up, so she hinted loudly, to the Ensign, "Who's your friend?"

"If I may be allowed, may I introduce you lovely young ladies to Fireman First-Class Petrovich, from Fayette County, Pennsylvania. And he does dance the polka!"

A soldier interrupted, "An officer and an enlisted man? Ain't that against regulations?"

"You do things the Army way, we do things the right way," Ensign Murphy replied.

"This war's off to a great start," Peggy said. "Let's dance, girls!"

Several hands were pulling the chairs out for Mary, Peggy and Anna, while Gerry remained stock-still.

"That's him!" Peggy whispered to Gerry in her ear.

"Who's him?"

"The sailor who's been sending torpedoes at you with his eyes since you walked in the door downstairs! The one who looks like Errol-way Ynn-flay."

"I don't think so. Too dark. More like Yrone-tay Ower-pay."

"Well, so? *He's the one.*"

"The one what?"

"The one, stupid!"

"How do you know that?"

"I know! I know! The Third Eye knows! Just dance with him. You'll see."

The sailor they were ogling had stepped out from behind the Ensign's shoulder and was looking down at them with a bemused grin. He seemed satisfied to wait patiently and he leaned over from the waist slightly and said to Gerry, not unkindly, but in a friendly, outgoing way, "You the unmarried one? I thought so. You look like the shy type. Why, you're blushing! Oh, I'm sorry now, I made you blush—really I am. Would you care to dance, miss?"

That was how it happened that Gerry rose from her seat to have a dance with a man she had never met before who politely smiled without saying a word as he took her right hand, the hand that, like her left, was hanging straight down at her side.

She let him take her hand and she followed him as he turned his back and gently pulled her out to the dance floor behind him. What else could she do?

After that he never said a word.

Artie Shaw's mellifluous clarinet was leading the band out in a fox-trot rhythm on *Moonglow.*

It must have been moonglow, way up in the blue
It must have been moonglow that led me straight to you . . .

When the dance ended the sailor said, "Thank you, miss." And he returned to Ensign Murphy's side.

Gerry sat down, and Peggy sat down next to her and urgently prodded. "What's his name?"

"I don't know."

"What do you mean you don't know!"

The sailor returned and leaned over Gerry behind her chair and asked, "May I have this dance, too, miss?"

"Yes, thank you," said Gerry, relieved to get away from Peggy's interrogation, and when he pulled out her chair, she floated upwards and glided out onto the dance floor with her hand in his.

This time Artie Shaw lifted his clarinet towards heaven as he played *Frenesi*, but still the sailor didn't speak. Finally, Gerry said, "I guess you're in the Navy."

"Yes, ma'am."

They both burst into grins at the same time.

"Silly," Gerry said.

"Oh, good guess," he said.

"Well—my sister wants to know what your name is."

"You can tell your sister it's Fireman First Class Petrovich, ma'am."

"Why do you keep calling me ma'am?"

"Because I don't know your name."

"Well, it's Geraldine."

"Oh. Well, hello, Geraldine."

"Uh, hello. And what do they call you?"

"My name is Andrej, since we're being formal."

"Andre. Hmm. Is that French?"

"Not exactly. More like Russian."

"So you're Russian then."

"I'm American, Geraldine. But I've been to Russia."

"You have!"

"Yes. Well, thank you. The dance is over now. But I will ask you again, if that's all right? Thank you, Geraldine. If you'll excuse me, I'll have to rejoin Ensign Murphy now."

He turned to go, leaving her standing there on the dance floor, but then he stopped. "By the way—is there another name you go by with your friends?"

"Those aren't my friends—they're my sisters."

"All three of them? Well—how about that! I have four sisters, too."

Ensign Murphy had pulled up by then and Gerry said to him, "Would you mind getting a drink for my sister?"

"Oh, don't worry, she already placed her order. One sloe gin fizz for the lady. She's not shy, you're sister. Your sister!"

"There's four of them, Murph," said Fireman First Class Petrovich.

"Good thing we brought the Army along."

Petrovich said, "Can I get you something, Geraldine?"

"A glass of wine? White wine, please. We never have that at home."

"Allrighty."

Gerry rushed back to confide in Peggy that she had found out his name and also got her a drink.

"Thank you. I can get my own."

The two Navy men had gone over under the archways to the long bar to get the drinks, and the two sisters could see them standing with their heads together in their white uniforms.

"So whaddya think?" said Peggy. "Isn't he a dreamboat?"

"Well, yes, he's good-looking, I'll give him that, and very polite, like he's been well-brought-up, but for goodness sake, Peggy, I'm not about to—to–."

"To what?" said Mary.

"Fall for him?" said Anna.

"Now you're being ridiculous."

Anna said, "So why are you blushing crimson?"

"I am not! What is going on anyway—are you girls ganging up on me—is this some kind of a set-up, or something?"

Peggy said, "Well, somebody's got to get you married off."

Anna said, "I hope you're not waiting around for Pa!"

Mary said, "Take it from me, you don't wanna do that."

Gerry said, "Margaret!—I'm blaming you for this whole thing."

Peggy said, "He's a sailor, you know. Watch out, sister. A girl in every port. All hands on deck."

When the Fireman First Class asked for another dance, he heard them calling her Gerry, so, Gerry it was for the rest of the evening. And they danced and they danced. The more they danced the more he started to open up and after a while Gerry found herself wanting to find out more about him, a little bit here, a little bit there, and so she relaxed, gradually, a little, had a second glass of wine, and after a while found she didn't have to worry about dreaming up things to say and after a little while more they were actually having a very nice little conversation going and it was easy to relax and there was no pressure and she didn't have to worry about awkward pauses or wondering what subjects to bring up or not to bring up it was all very natural and she was so glad that he was so easy to talk to and after a while more they were chatting confidentially like old friends and Gerry was amazed to stop and think that she didn't even know this man, that he was a complete stranger, and yet–.

"You wanna go try the other band, Gerry? You know— that guy Kenton?"

"Sure. Let's give them something to talk about."

"Your sisters?"

"If we disappear, they'll die of curiosity."

"Let's go!"

This time she led him by the hand as they bumped and jostled their way through the bridge between the twin ballrooms, and when she turned to face him on the crowded dancefloor in front of Stan Kenton's orchestra, she felt he was no stranger at all, but her new friend, Andy.

She wanted to know what he did before the war.

A coal-miner?

She had not expected that.

What was it like?

"Well, it was a job. I didn't mind it, really. It put gas in your tank, that's for sure, if you know what I mean. I guess I coulda done without the straw boss or the big muckety-mucks. But you know, you'd have to be one of them, miners, I mean, to know that they're the most decent bunch of men you could meet anywhere, anytime, coal-miners. We look out for each other."

"You miss it, don't you?"

"No, ma'am, I do not. It was just about the gladdest day of my life the day when I realized I didn't have to travel that 240 foot down in that bucket tomorrow morning cause I was off in a bus to Great Lakes."

"Don't you wanna go back there, after the war, I mean?"

"Oh, I have my plans."

"What about your sisters—don't you miss them—what about your mother and father?"

"Well, my sister Adrijana's in New York. We have to call her *Adrienne* now, you know. Actually, I have seen her, just recently, 'cause, you know, the *Ruby* docked in Naval District

3 at Brooklyn Navy Yard while we were waiting to get a berth in dry-dock, and we got to visit at her place in the Bronx, you know, before they sent us up to Boston, which is Naval District 1, typical Navy screw-up, another ship, bigger, more damaged, came in behind us and took our place out from under us, and they had to send us up to Boston, and that's how I got to meet you, Gerry, what do you think of that?"

"And your other sisters are–?"

"Adrijana, Anastasia, Andjela and Ana. Majka never got any further in the alphabet, thank goodness."

"We both have a sister named Anna!"

"Yes, we do."

"I like your sisters' names, they're different."

"Then there's my brother Alek, he's in Burma right now, in the Army Air Force, he's a whatchamacallit on a C-47, a navigator, he flies over the hump to China."

"Let's see—there's Adrienne, Anastasija—"

"We call her Stasija, for short."

"—Ana, Alek and Andy."

"Don't forget Andjela." Gerry looked up into Andy's brown eyes. "What are you thinking?" he asked.

"Oh—nothing." She felt a rush of emotion, so, to cover it up, she said, "Tell me about your plans."

"Well—I like to work with my hands, you know, Gerry, to start with. And I got a lot of experience making furniture—did I ever tell you about that? I love working with wood."

Gerry learned all about how wonderful it was to work with wood because it was so clean, compared to digging coal, how even the saw-dust smelled so good, compared to the way the coal-dust got all over everything and crawled down the back of your neck so that it made you reach back with your hand and want to scrape it off your skin with your fingernails, about how when they got water in the house on Maple Avenue in Pershing, back home, when Andy started working as a breaker-boy, he rigged up a doo-hickey in the cellar, you know, like a sort of a shower stall, so that every night when he came home he always entered through the side door and took a shower and got all cleaned up before he went up the back hall stairs into his mother's kitchen, about how he hoped they wouldn't be sent on another mission to cross the Atlantic on the Murmansk run as a convoy escort, as poor Ensign Glenn Murphy, being a deep-south Louisiana sunbather-type, didn't much prefer the temperatures at below zero, although it didn't much bother Andy himself, as he was used to it, Pennsylvania's north of the Mason-Dixon line, thank you very much, ma'am, and anyway, I could keep nice and warm down in the engine-room whereas he had to be exposed up on the bridge, poor guy, but, you know, he's a buddy, he kind of latched onto me because I was the nearest thing on board to a good ole southern good-ole-boy, and, yes, the Ruby's a nice little ship, more like a yacht, you know, yes, it's true, I ain't kidding, it was Vanderbilt's yacht, and you wanna know what else, it was built in Germany, 1931, Bremen shipyard, yesiree-bob, I'm shipped out on a German vessel, how about that, Miss Geraldine, she's 190-foot-long, and weighs in at 508 long tons, and runs twin Cooper-Bessemer JR-8 diesel engines rated at 1600 hp, and can make 13 knots in a headwind, but you don't wanna know about all that, Gerry, do you?

But she did. And she wanted to know all about thing-a-ma-bobs, whatchamacallits, doo-hickeys, and muckety-mucks, too, allrighty?

"I just love your accent. It's so cute!"

"Well, you have an accent, too, you know."

"No, I don't!"

"Yes, you do!"

"I speak like a proper Bostonian."

"There you go—a *propah* Bostonian!"

"You can leave the ending off any word—"

"—as long as it's an '*R*!'"

They were completing each other's sentences.

"Did we just have our first fight?" said Andy.

Gerry blushed mightily, so much so that she wanted to hide her face, and she found herself burying her cheek on his chest.

June Christie, on the stage, the Kenton band's girl singer, was leaning slightly toward the silver microphone.

Don't blame me for falling in love with you
I'm under your spell but how can I help it?

Don't blame me . . .

The singer in her sequined full-length gown moved her body ever so slightly from her shoulders down as she sustained the long notes, rotating her hips ever so decorously. She was not in the least suggestive in her movements, she just seemed to sway to the emotion of the words, like a palm-frond in a gentle breeze.

Gerry said to Andy, "Do you have to go back tonight to your base?" She looked up at him. "To your whatchamacallit?"

"My berth? No. We have a weekend pass." Andy was looking down into her brown eyes and he was thinking how he and Glenn had been laughingly conspiring, on their way over to the Raymor-Playmor, earlier that evening, so long ago now, to find them a couple of girls to take them home—but he didn't want to tell her that. He didn't want anything to spoil this. "What are you thinking?"

"Well—as long as you have a weekend pass—you could stay over with us."

"Hmm. I suppose so."

"Not at my father's house!"

"No, not at your father's house."

"At my sister Mary's. It's not far."

"Okay."

"You'll have to sleep on the floor."

"I don't mind."

"We'll have to catch the last streetcar home."

"Okay."

"I'll ask her."

"We don't have to leave right away?"

"I don't want to."

"Good. 'Cause I like this song."

As they danced on, June Christie seemed to breathe the words . . .

Don't blame me for falling in love with you
I'm under your spell but how can I help it?

        Don't blame me . . .

Chapter 15

Immaculate Conception

Gerry lost Andy when he received orders to ship out on the *Ruby*, destination unknown.

They had decided between themselves that they wanted to get married, but they hadn't told anyone as yet.

Andy only had time for one last phone call and when he hung up, Gerry just sat there in the front hall at home with the receiver in her hand, for the longest time, till she realized she was cradling it in her lap and she still hadn't hung it up on the pedestal-hook.

They hadn't gotten far with their plans, there were so many obstacles, and now she was suddenly afraid she might never hear from him again. Something might happen to him, she wouldn't know where he was. Could she even remember his face, those beautiful brown eyes, that Errol Flynn moustache, his Tyrone Power cheekbones, and the rest of that dear fond smoldering countenance? How long would she be able to hang on to the sound of his voice on the telephone?

One morning her father complained to her when she was serving him his hasty breakfast. "*Caw*-fee?" In spite of all the years he'd lived in Boston, Tony LaStoria still pronounced it like a New Yorker from the Lower East Side. "What's wrong with you these days? You're moping around the house like you lost your dog."

Gerry slumped into a chair.

"Pa. I met a guy."

"You met a guy. What guy? This is the first I heard of it."

Tony LaStoria looked at Gigi LaStoria and said "You know anything about this?"

Gigi just shrugged.

"So now you don't tell even your mother what you're up to?"

Gerry looked miserable. Obstacle number one was the Captain of the *Ruby*. "Don't worry, Pa, he's gotta get permission from his Captain before he can get married."

"He's in the army!"

"No—the Captain of his ship."

"He's a sailor?" Obstacle number two was her Pa. "Your mother never even met this guy, and you're getting married. Look—I gotta get to work."

Between mother and daughter, neither one dared to object. Indeed, they wished he would leave. When he was gone, and they looked at each other, Gigi said to her daughter, "Let me talk to him."

Sunday rolled around and when Pa finally got home from the shop and was able to sit down to listen to the radio and read his Sunday papers in his favorite chair in the parlor, after he'd had a glass of wine and spilled just one drop on his nice clean white shirt, he called Gerry over.

"Get me a mopina and just wet the tip, willya?" When she brought it he twisted the tip and started to scrub next to a button. "Sit down, willya? I wanna talk to you."

"Pa, the dishes—"

He grabbed her hand, still wet. "Gerry," he said.

She stood there, wanting to go, but he held her by the fingers.

"Do you remember when you used to sit on my lap? Gerry, I don't want to lose you. You're the last one I have left at home. At a time like this when I—I don't know–from one day to the next–if your mother's gonna have to face a telegram from the War Department–."

"Pa—who says you're gonna lose me?"

That was obstacle number three. Where were they going to go to live together? Could she really expect Andy to just throw up everything to come here and live in her father's house? What about his own family? The place where he grew up? Would she make that sacrifice for him? Wouldn't he miss all of them back home? What about *his* mother? Wouldn't he want to take his bride back to his hometown? But, no, thought Gerry, she couldn't leave her mother. *Oh, it's all impossible!*

There were days, that October, that were crushingly beautiful, when Indian summer seemed to tantalize Gerry with a hint of a balmy world free from turmoil and desperation.

That week, when she had Peggy's boys, Henry and Ronnie, to look after, to get them out of the house, she would take them down to Revere Beach, on a weekday afternoon. Supposedly, she was doing this to spare her mother from the *agidu*. But in her own mind she knew she was being pulled there by the presence of the sea.

On a blanket on the sand, leaning back on her outstretched hands, the wind off the water insinuating itself beneath the kerchief knotted under her chin, she would sit and survey the far horizon. No matter how hard she tried to gaze or to concentrate, there was a point, hovering out there in the blue, beyond which she could not penetrate. Somewhere out there beyond her ken was a ship called the *Ruby* carrying a cargo more precious to her than gemstones, the burden and the weight, as it seemed to Gerry, of her hopes and her dreams. What ship could bear such a weight? What man could stand up under such a burden? It couldn't be real. It was October and sitting there by the water, the wind coming off the waves was chilly enough to make you want to hold yourself tightly. The wind, that was real. The rest was all imagination, a restive endless yearning.

After a while, she would realize she wasn't paying the slightest bit of attention to the children she was supposed to be watching over. Reluctantly, she would call them to her, gather them to her, and they would trudge home again, the three of them, Auntie Gerry, little Henry, Jr, and smaller Ronnie, nothing accomplished, all in doubt, everything suspended.

The boys would stop their boisterous play and fall in step under the spell of Auntie Gerry's somber mood and they would grow quiet and silent.

One Monday morning as she was serving her Pa, yet again, breakfast at the kitchen table, she slipped into a chair opposite him diagonally.

"Ssh," said Pa. "Your mother's still asleep—for once."

"I know, Pa. I worry about her, too."

Her father sighed, with a certain resignation. "We're getting old."

"I know. Last night you fell asleep in your chair while Jack Benny was on."

"I couldn't help it. You know the hours I'm working. Then I get home finally and there's a heaping bowl of macaroni. My eyes were bigger than my stomach."

"You missed a good one."

"Oh, I did? Okay—so—you gonna tell me?"

"I can't tell it like him."

"You're gonna keep me in suspense."

"Well, okay. So—Mary says to Jack—you know, he's trying to get her to finally tie the knot—she says to him, 'What about the difference in our ages?' And he says, 'Oh, not such a big difference. You're twenty-five and I'm thirty-nine." And she says, "I know, Jack, but what about twenty-five years from now, when I'm fifty and you're still thirty-nine?" And, you know him, he goes "Well!—I never thought of that!"

With the cup at his lips, her father gulped. "You had to make me laugh!" His eyes were watering as they crinkled up and he rushed to put down the swilling cup. "You're gonna make me choke on my *caw*-fee." He placed his hand on his daughter's. "I want you to be happy."

"Pa—I'm not getting any younger."

"You're my princess, you know that?"

"I'm gonna be 23 next year, and Jack Benny'll still be 39!"

"Will you stop it!" Her Pa had to cover his mouth with the mopina to stifle himself. "You're gonna wake your mother."

"I just want what everybody else wants, Pa. I want what you and Ma always had. I want what Peggy has, two sons that are so adorable it breaks your heart."

"Don't start on me with your sister Margaret."

"Mary, too. Don't you think I ever thought about kids of my own? Pa, how could I help it, when I look at little Tony and his sister Gerry. Aren't you proud to say to yourself that your very first daughter named her firstborn after you?"

"All I know, Gerry, is I did the best I could all these years, and for the life of me, I don't know how I let it all get away from me. It was all too much for me. I couldn't control all of you kids—what father could? There were too many of you—I was like the old woman in the shoe, I didn't know what to do!"

"Did Ma talk to you?"

"Ma talked to me."

"Well. So."

"So I have to lose you, too. My last little girl. Bad enough I can't raise my little finger to help my sons overseas—there's a man out there better than I am gonna take you away from me. Eh! It's the way of the world."

"Don't think of it that way, Pa."

"How else can I think of it? How do you know how a father feels? At least I had you all these years. Your sister Peggy I lost a long time ago."

Gerry watched from the kitchen window, her mother's seat, as her father left for work and he trudged down the driveway a defeated man. He would walk to the trolley stop at the bottom of Payson Street and he would sit on the trolley, all the way to Maverick Square, brooding. Gerry knew it. She felt it. But as he walked, or maybe ran, to the platform, to catch the next train into town, as he settled into his seat, as he straightened up, and turned to face the day, looking over his shoulder at speeding tunnel lights under the harbor, he would turn into himself again, the general-manager of the New England division, the man-in-charge.

Gerry was pensive, thinking of how he had said before he left the kitchen that he would talk to his friend, Father Spinelli, the pastor at St Anthony's.

The next time she sat on that blanket at Revere Beach, Gerry was ebullient. Back and forth with Ronnie and Henry she tossed a thick, heavy, sponge-rubber imitation-baseball, white on the outside, dinged, dented and gouged so that, in spots, the red inner spongy filling was exposed. Such toys were not available, new, to kids during these wartime days of shortages, so the ball was one Gerry had saved from her own childhood, when she and her brothers and sisters had lived in a world of fantasy and hope, shielded from the depredations of the Depression, not knowing there was such a thing as suffering, cared for by a powerful father—until it was time to leave school at age 14 and go down to the Tyer Rubber Company in Stoughton with your working papers and get a job and join the real world, the working-for-a-living world. So many cross-currents of joy and bitterness, of sunny Shirley Temple openness and dour New England nose-to-the-grindstone narrow-mindedness, conflicted within her, that she wanted to cry out, *to hell with everything, I want to live!*

But she almost died one November morning in about the middle of the week when, at almost 11 AM, the doorbell rang.

Gerry felt herself go rigid.

Nobody ever rang the front doorbell.

She thought of her three brothers somewhere at the front lines and immediately hated herself for thinking *which one?* Slowly and deliberately, drying her hands, making herself not look at her mother, also frozen by the sound of the bell, sitting by the kitchen window, she passed through the dining room into the parlor and then the front hall and faced the blank door with its useless small pane of glass situated too high to look through and she felt frozen into a statue as automatically she finally grasped the cold doorknob and twisted.

There he was in his Navy blues with a duffelbag over his shoulder, standing on her front doorstep.

She flew into his arms.

Andy had shore leave for two weeks and had spent two days on a train from somewhere in the Carolinas, that's all he would say, but didn't you get my letters, yes I did, and I read every line ten times over, but you never say anything, I can't, we have Navy censorship on board, Lt. Alderson reads all our letters going out, but how did you get here, I took a chance and I found my way to Revere, people on the subway, they helped me, I landed at South Station, why didn't you call me, I could kill you, I wanted to surprise you!

Hand in hand that very day Gerry and Andy went to see Father Spinelli at St Anthony's.

"What do your parents say, children? You know, Gerardina, your father is a good friend of mine."

"Father, with all due respect—I mean, I am 22 years old."

"Oh, I see that you know your own mind very well," said the priest, smiling kindly, "but, you understand, I have to ask, and, after all, it is wartime, the young people are, eh, shall we say, in a hurry?"

"Father," said Andy. "I have to be back on board in a few days. It's a long train-ride, two days."

"Yes, yes, my son, I understand, perfectly well, but don't you want to have your bride to be married in a church wedding, with her family around her, you might say, involved, with her father to give away her hand in marriage, as is the most usual thing, and of course, may I say, we must observe all the dictates of our most holy and apostolic Catholic Church which are required to recognize the union, in accordance with your faith, in spite of wartime and regulations and your duty and everything else, naturally, you want God's blessing on this serious step you are taking, and after all, we have our own regulations, which is my responsibility–."

"Father," said Andy.

Something in the good priest's tone, or perhaps something he had said, caused Andy to speak up, perhaps when he mentioned the word 'faith,' or maybe 'regulations.'

Andy looked at Gerry. "Listen, babe, I think I oughta tell your pastor something."

"What?"

"Well, Father—my parish back home in Pershing is St Sava's Serbian Orthodox Church."

The priest's eyes went back and forth between them.

"Oh, I see."

"That's in Pennsylvania," Andy added, though he thought *why did I say that? What difference does that make?*

Father Spinelli looked down at his folded hands and then raised his eyes to them and he seemed to be regretful. "I'm afraid I must disappoint you, my children."

"Why?" Gerry jumped.

"I'm afraid you have brought up an impediment which I cannot overlook."

"What? So, he's from the Orthodox Church. Aren't they all the same? It's not as if he's a Protestant or a Jew."

"And in which faith are the children, God willing, going to be brought up?"

"Catholic, of course." said Gerry, and she looked at Andy as if to verify this."

"Yeah, Catholic," he said.

"So you are going to convert?"

The two young hopefuls looked at one another just at the very moment when their hearts were sinking.

"Father, you're asking a lot," said Andy.

Gerry jumped up and pulled him by the hand.

"Come on, sweetheart, we're getting out of here."

Father Spinelli rose painfully and spread his hands, as if in benediction, and said, "I'm sorry, my children, but my hands are tied in this."

Gerry shot him a look in which fury was not concealed.

Outside, she said to Andy "Come on—they're not the only church in town."

"Slow down, Gerry, what are you talking about? You're upset, babe."

"Goddam right I'm upset. That priest has got one hell of a nerve. You know how much money my father gives to this church?"

She marched Andy right across town, from Revere Street, down North Shore Road to Shirley Ave., across Bell Circle, when the light brought all the cars in the world to a halt and they could cross, all the way down Beach Street to the maroon-brick monolith of Revere High School, a two-mile march.

"Cool down, honey. We coulda taken a streetcar, you know."

"I'm so mad!"

At the four-way intersection of Beach Street and Winthrop Avenue, the high school stood on one corner; across Beach Street was Foyle's Rexall Drugstore, where Gerry used to take the kids sometimes to the soda fountain; and across Winthrop Ave from that was the peeling robin's-egg-blue clapboard edifice of the Immaculate Conception Church—the Irish parish in that part of the city. And across Beach Street again from the church, on the other side of Winthrop Avenue from the high school, was the redbrick parochial grade school of the Immaculate Conception parish. With the rectory where the priests lived attached to the back of the school. Which is where Gerry next marched Andy to.

Before Andy's leave was up, Gerry married him, on a Saturday morning, at 11, in the vestibule of the Immaculate Conception Roman Catholic Church, with only one witness, Gerry's girlfriend, Hildie, who came all the way on the trolley and subway from Stoughton to be there to play the part of Maid of Honor for her best friend. No one else was invited to the church. The bride was dressed in a nicely-tailored light grey tweed suit from Filene's with knee-length skirt and a corsage of gardenias in her lapel, and wore two-toned closed-toe pumps that gave her a little upward tilt to her chin. In the crook of her arm rested a bundle of eighteen red roses from her father, Tony LaStoria. On her head she wore a stylish pillbox hat that matched her suit, with a delicate open-spaced black veil which she turned up at the end to be kissed by the groom. The groom was in his Navy bell-bottom blues and held in his hand the cap known in Navy regs as *Hat, White.* The wedding photos were taken by Hildie with her Brownie. The reception was held right after the ceremony in Tony LaStoria's parlor on Payson Street. Gerry's sisters were there, except, of course, Margaret, and Mary brought her husband Charlie. Gerry's brothers could not attend as they had commitments on another continent. Many toasts were given Gerry and Andy around a big traditional Italian Sunday-dinner, cooked on a Saturday in her mother's kitchen by her sisters Anna and Mary and her sister-in-law Mary, her brother Patsy's wife. Everybody was happy, and sad, and crying, and laughing, as Andy had to leave immediately after the reception to catch a train to Charleston, South Carolina.

Father O'Malley, the pastor of Immaculate Conception, had had his doubts, but he managed to find his way clear to marrying them in Holy Mother Church as long as they would agree to wed in the vestibule and not at the sanctified altar. He had realized at the last moment that he could just not pass up the chance to get one up on Father Spinelli at St Anthony's, and he believed that Cardinal O'Connell would relish the thought when he heard the story.

Chapter 16

Balboa Park

Christmas of 1944 was the saddest, most disheartening Christmas the newlywed Gerry Petrovich could ever have imagined. Just when she should have been so happy at the turn her life had taken, she was beset instead by the most depressing loneliness. A nameless longing seemed to overcome her, occupying her mind, excluding thought. Nothing seemed normal, nothing seemed good. She felt no holiday cheer, no new year's hope. The war had been going on too long, too long, and yet another Christmas was coming and going with no end in sight.

On top of the separation from Andy that she had to endure, there was a kind of deflation she felt—married one minute, deserted the next—a maddening development. Who could she blame for that? Herself, Andy, God? No, the war. Events were conspiring to deprive her of any sense of balance and to drive her instead to dismay. She was a married woman who had yet to experience one night alone with her husband. Where had the wedding night gone that she was supposed to have had? She found herself in rare idle moments pacing, aimlessly, from one end of the house to the other, mourning her lost childhood, feeling neglected, twisting the gold ring on her finger, feeling ridiculous. She told herself she had to buck up and stop feeling so sorry for herself, but it was no use. As soon as she had such a thought, the unwelcome news arrived that the Germans had counter-attacked, somewhere in Belgium. Where were her brothers this Christmas? Oh, when was this ever going to end?

During that last, heady week before the wedding, when they had been shopping for the wedding rings together, at shops along Beacon Street in Brookline, at a small café near Coolidge Corner, while they sat quietly having coffee afterwards, she and Andy had set up a code system for writing to each other. If he was okay and safe, he was to write 'Remember that night at the Raymor-Playmor?' If he was ever in danger, or entering combat that he could not talk about, he would write "Say hello to your sister Peggy." Gerry remembered that she had laughed and said, "Peggy spells trouble, all right." Now she winced to recall such silliness. Why should two people who loved each other so much have to go through this? Somehow Gerry could not rid herself of the feeling that it was all her fault, that she was being punished for something she had done. But what? *Punished for loving someone?*

The severe winter they were having did not help. Snow and ice piled everywhere, and she was stuck in the house. Her mother's condition plagued her with dire thoughts. Gerry dragged herself through every day, it seemed. Just pulling on overshoes to walk in the snow down to Rupp Bros on the corner of School Street for a loaf of bread when they ran out was an overwhelming dilemma.

Finally in late January the battle they were now calling 'the Bulge' in Europe broke in favor of the embattled Americans.

It was virtually the first rise in spirits Gerry could remember since the whirlwind week of her wedding and what she now thought of as its false euphoria. She determined this time not to allow her feelings to swing so high but to keep a good grip on herself. Her parents were heartened when letters going back several months arrived in a pile from Augie and Patsy; her mother, especially, was buoyed up to hear from her precious Augie; but then, still, no word from Gene.

The winter dug in to renew its blasts in February. All this time the routine at home still centered on Ma LaStoria, from whom Gerry could never hide her own low spirits. It was a trial to be cheerful around your mother when she was so ill, complaining of old age, losing her appetite, and making statements such as "What's the use? Will I ever see my sons again? I wish God would take me, if only to spare them, I would gladly make that exchange."

Indeed, when you stopped to think of it, no matter how bad the winter here, it's been far worse on our boys over there. *And I can't imagine what it must be like out at sea.*

Fortunately Andy found a way to let Gerry know, through coded hints and reading between the lines, that the *USS Ruby* had not, this winter, been repeating their mission of 1943, crossing the Arctic Circle to Russia again. In fact, she divined that his ship was on coastal patrol somewhere down south, which came through when she read, "Gee, I wish I had a coke. Besides you, that's what I miss the most." The part about the coke was her clue. The rest she could ignore, it was just padding for the benefit of—*but isn't it awful that someone else is reading our mail?*

Early in March came the stunning news of the Remagen Bridge. Suddenly, all things seemed possible. The Allies were soon pouring into Germany's interior, the Americans from the west, the Russians from the east. Her father convinced Gerry that now this couldn't go on much longer. Gerry wanted to believe it and she wanted her mother to believe it. Her father knew so much more about these things. Gerry made a concerted effort to brighten up her general disposition around the house, on the theory that it might be contagious and she could transmit it to her mother. After all, what else have we got but hope to keep us going?

Then President Roosevelt died.

The radio in the kitchen was tuned to the Tom Mix show on the Mutual Radio Network. Gerry's father loved his cowboy stars and when he was out of the house Gerry would translate for her mother, if she asked. She knew her mother liked to have his shows on when he was gone at work. It made her feel his absence less. About 10 minutes to six, the network broke in to announce the news from Warm Springs, Georgia.

It was shocking. Gerry had to sit down. She told her mother. They both began to cry. Not since Pearl Harbor had they heard anything so devastating and full of foreboding.

Gerry called her father at work.

"Pa, did you hear? God, it's so awful. What are we going to do now?"

Tony LaStoria said, "You just sit tight till I get home."

The date was April 12th, 1945.

Not even a month later, the war in Europe was over.

Just as the news of the President's death brought unalloyed sorrow into a springtime of hope, the month of May brought not only forsythia blooming in time with the seasons but also wild, unfettered joy that was out of tune with every other mixed passion of wartime life. Nobody wanted to think of desperate battles still going on in the Pacific, when they were overcome with ecstatic celebration of victory in Europe. The LaStoria family was no exception to the widespread hysteria. But in their household, they could honestly say, now at long last our brothers and sons will be coming home!

But where were they? When would they be coming? As always, for four years now, fear mixed like poison with a gulp of anticipation as you waited on the next letter delivered from the Armed Services postal system.

But one afternoon a couple of days after VE-Day, the phone rang out in the front hall, and Gerry raced to answer, sure it had to be Augie, Gene or Patsy, calling with good news—if they were alive and all right!

Instead, she thought she might faint outright when she heard Andy's voice!

"Hi, babe, how ya doing? It's me!"

"Andy!" She had to sit down. "Where are you? Oh, I'm so glad you called! Are you coming home?"

"Listen, babe, I gotta talk fast. There's a long line of guys here waiting for the phone. Go down to the Western Union office. I'm sending you some money. Remember I promised you a honeymoon? Well, grab your bags and get ready to take a trip on a train. I can't meet you at the station, but—well, just get the telegram, that'll explain everything!"

"But, Andy, where are you? Where am I–?"

"I gotta go now. Say good-bye! Do you still love me? I love you!"

"Not half as much as I love you!"

"Well, then, everything will be all right, you'll see."

"I love you, Andy!"

"That's good, Gerry. Gee-whillikers, it's good to hear your voice! But, be a good girl, now, and say good-bye! I gotta go right now, but we'll be together soon! Now say good-bye, and go get your telegram, and do what the telegram tells you to do, will ya? That's a good girl! I love you!"

Gerry's bags were packed and she was loaded and cocked for an argument by the time her father got home, but to her immense surprise her father said that, of course, she had to go.

"You're married now. He's your husband. By the way, where are you going?"

"Pa!—Los Angeles!"

"Los Angeles! There's no naval base there. What does the telegram say?"

"I don't know, Pa. I've read it ten times and I still don't know. Oh, this is so exciting, I can't breathe. All I know is when I get there I call this phone number."

Tony LaStoria grabbed the telegram, scanned it and said, "Must be San Diego."

They were in the kitchen. Gerry had been so steeled for a fight that she had met her father at the back door as he was coming in. Now her father turned to her mother, sitting there, and explained in Italian that he believed Andy Petrovich must have been transferred to the Pacific Fleet. That made sense as the focus of all the war effort now had to turn to the enemy in Japan. His wife and his daughter both deferred to him as the expert in the family. Gerry had been so preoccupied with her jolting wish to join up with Andy again that, now, she suddenly remembered her mother and felt crestfallen and stupidly, stubbornly selfish. There sat her mother glowing with joy and pride and yet crying as if at a funeral or a wedding, and all Gerry could think of was her own happiness.

"Don't you worry, I'll take care of your mother."

"I'll be back, Pa. It won't be forever."

"Oh, will you stop! We'll manage. You're not the only daughter I have! Your sisters will have to help out. Not Margaret, mind you! You just go. That's all you have to worry about. And, listen, Gerry—please try to understand that you go with the blessings of both of us. All we want is for you to be happy. Don't you know that?"

The next day they all met at the shop at ten in the morning and walked together over to South Station. Mary had gone to stay over in the house in Revere with her two children and it was Pa and Anna who accompanied Gerry to the train. She was crying as she was getting on board, thinking of the day they had last seen Augie, at this very spot, as he set out for boot camp, and Pa was putting money in her hand and Anna was giving her flowers and magazines.

All the way to New York she felt like crying but she told herself she just had to straighten up and fly right.

She was riding the *State of Maine*, the flagship train of the Boston and Maine Railroad, which had pulled into South Station with passengers already on it traveling from Portland, Maine to New York City. The instructions from the telegram had been to proceed to Grand Central Station and take the Twentieth Century Limited from there to Chicago and then change trains to the Super Chief the rest of the way across the continent.

For Gerry Petrovich, who had never been anywhere outside Boston and its environs, who could only picture Rockingham

Park in nearby New Hampshire from the races called on the radio, this trip was a revelation.

Crossing New Jersey and then Pennsylvania, she kept looking out the window at houses and intersections passing by, trying to picture what life could be like in these unknown places. She certainly could not imagine anyone living in those houses. It must be so different, to be from another place, and yet these towns and cities in the middle of nowhere resembled what she knew of, what she was familiar with, and at home with. If only she could find out. Would she be surprised? Would she find out that people and families were the same everywhere?

The *Twentieth Century Limited* was another complete surprise to Gerry. Her father had paid her way onto a luxury train as a going-away present. This was costing him $51.80 to get his daughter from New York to Chicago, but for that, the treatment Gerry got was unparalleled in her experience. It started with the red carpet you had to walk along the platform to get yourself to the train. When a lady boarded, a Negro porter gave her flowers and perfume. Gerry thought, *this is not like riding the subway in Boston.* In fact, this train was pulled by a new-fangled engine, brand new that very year, which combined electric and diesel power. Gone was the smokestack and the dirty coal. Wait till she wrote home to the folks about this! Departure time from Grand Central was 6 pm sharp, Eastern War Time, and it was going to take only 16 hours to get all the way to Chicago.

The mountains of western Pennsylvania were certainly a surprise. And those tunnels! Although it was dark outside already, nothing could have prepared her for the deep, total blackness, and the roar, inside those tunnels. It was frightening. When the train emerged with an audible whoosh, and the sound of the cavernous, echoing mountain closing in on you suddenly evaporated, it felt like a giant sigh of relief. Gerry had to settle herself in. It was going to take a good three days to cross the country. Wasn't it somewhere around here that Pershing, Penna. was located, where Andy grew up? She tried to imagine that but fell asleep with the realization that it was impossible. The train was loaded with young fellows in uniform, middle-aged men, too, which had surprised her, and how many different uniforms does our Army have, anyway? Not to mention the sailors and civilians on board. Gerry twisted the wedding ring on her finger, hoping to display it auspiciously while she dozed off, which kept happening. She must have been rocked to sleep many times by the rhythm of the rolling train.

Once she figured out that she was so exhausted she couldn't stay awake one minute longer, she climbed into her single berth and shut the curtains.

In the swaying dark she was thinking, *wonder what Chicago'll be like? If it's anything like New York* . . . what little she had seen of it . . . *tall buildings, so many people . . . everybody seems to be happy on this train . . . they're going somewhere . . . even the porters and conductors . . . hard to believe that was the place my Pa thinks of as his hometown . . . New York, New York . . . Andy's sister Adrienne is living there right now . . . wonder what the Bronx is like . . . living . . . in . . . an . . . apartment . . .*

She woke up in the morning feeling so rested that it was as if she'd been rocked in a cradle all night by her mother. She had breakfast on board in the dining car at seven, and by 9 am, right on time, they were pulling into the LaSalle Street Station in Chicago, where—*they rolled out another red carpet?*

Well, no time to think, no time to register how enormous the buildings, or imagine where Marshall Fields might be, which Gerry had heard was the world's biggest department store, she had to get to Union Station by ten AM to catch the *Super Chief* to the West Coast. Another new departure for her—she had to hail a cab in one of the biggest, most congested and bustling cities in the country. With a laugh, she thought of sticking her leg out like Claudette Colbert did in the movies that time, which so shocked them all, back then. *How times have changed!*

The *Super Chief* turned out to be, if anything, more luxurious and well-appointed, by far, than the *20ᵗʰ Century Limited.* This, as Gerry knew from the magazines she and Peggy and Anna habitually devoured, *Screen Gems* and *Hollywood Confidential,* was the "Train of the Stars." Judy Garland, Frank Sinatra, Hedda Hopper, too, they rode this train—even President Truman, she had heard. The *Super Chief* was pulled by a gleaming diesel engine with a distinctive nose, painted red and yellow, war-bonnet colors, pulling seventeen cars across prairies, rivers, mountain passes and deserts. The dining car looked like something that should be standing on a set in the back lot at MGM. The last car of the seventeen was an observation car with a unique rounded tail. You could stroll back there and find a comfortable seat from which to view the Rocky Mountains all around you for 180 degrees through the wide-open spaces of picture windows. The names of the places you were going to pass through along the route by themselves sounded so romantic—Kansas City, Dodge City, Kansas, La Junta, Colorado, Albuquerque, Winslow, Arizona, Barstow, San Bernardino, Pasadena—weren't those the very names from that hit song they're playing on the radio, *yes, from that movie that just came out, with Judy Garland, The Harvey Girls, what's it called? no, yeah, that's right, The Atchison, Topeka and the Santa Fe . . . imagine riding a train they write songs about . . .*

And the boys on this train, or, should she say, young men? although they acted like boys in fourth grade, well, they were all young and heading for California, so—*why shouldn't they be happy? even if they were in the service, which many were, though certainly not all, because, stop and think, we're winning the war, some of these boys are already due to be discharged and are heading home, and somebody bought them a ticket, like Pa did for me, maybe their parents, or their wife, or sweetheart, and wouldn't it be rude to refuse to talk to them?*

Thus it was that the reserved, shy, stay-at-home Gerry Petrovich, a newly-wed from Boston, who had never been anywhere in her life, found herself actually flirting with young fellows she was not married to and had no intention of ever writing a mash-note to, no matter how much they begged or slipped her their home addresses and telephone numbers. She kept insisting that she was honest-to-God married, see this ring? and that her husband was in the Navy, and, yes, he was a coal-miner from Pennsylvania, and, *listen, what's a nice girl from Boston like you doing with a coal-miner, anyway?* but these boys were so starved for love and affection and a touch of home and the girl they missed, that it made your heart break to stop and think what they all had been through in this war, together, *all of them, everywhere, all over the world.*

It was going to take about thirty-six hours or thereabouts to get to Los Angeles, about two days and one night, and the last thing Gerry was going to do was to have a drink with one of these boys, no matter how many times they pressed her to take a stroll down to the lounge car for just a little nip, *do you good, you need to relax.*

My God, thought Gerry. *These mid-Westerners sure are different. How friendly they are! Don't they just love to talk? Why, back in Boston I would never in my life have thought to behave this way, people would just think there was something wrong with you. But here, you just slide into it, like a pair of old slippers. And they're nice, really. You can't blame them. Aren't we all looking for a friendly face, a smile along the way? You don't want to be stand-offish, do you?*

But no matter how much Gerry wanted to loosen up she had bred into herself a defensiveness that came from years of fending off dumb guys who worked in the Tyer Rubber Factory in Stoughton, Massachusetts, and had no polish or savior-faire, and that street-wise attitude of *the best defense is a good offense,* that came with the territory of *born and raised on the streetcars of Boston,* that attitude you always got, and gave back to, the people back home.

It was one thing to open up to Andy on a certain night at the Raymor-Playmor, when, after all, her sisters were all there with her, and quite another to have all these men telling her she was the most gorgeous thing since Rita Hayworth—*well, anyway, it was flattering, wasn't it?*

"All the Way with Santa Fe." That was the slogan of this train. But from the way they behaved, you would have thought it was the operating credo of some of the soldiers and sailors on board the *Super Chief.* So Gerry adopted a strategy. She figured out that nobody was getting off this west-coat express except to get something to eat at one of the Harvey House dining stops somewhere along the way, so she picked out one particular young man who turned out to be, of all things, a college man, who'd become an officer and a gentleman through the Reserves at UCLA, and she turned this gentleman into her dining escort. His name was Richard Berman, a handsome Jewish boy from Los Angeles, which rendered him perfectly safe, because of the religious barrier; and anyway, he was none too happy to be saddled with a Catholic girl from Boston, Italian, to boot;

an additional reason why he was perfectly tame to be with, as far as Gerry making a show of openly linking his arm. And so Richard, which is what she called him, to keep it formal, yet friendly, became her dining escort, and Gerry was amazed at herself, because she had prevailed upon him, as a gentleman, and succeeded. She had never been so forward, or resourceful, in her life!

And finding a guy who was too polite to say no to a damsel in distress, that was the way to make sure you slept safe and sound in your single berth at night for the one night it would take to get to California. After a while, since they only had thirty-six hours, and she wasn't the only fish in the sea, the other fast-workers gave up.

On the second day Gerry relaxed and gazed out the window at the staggering vision of the Sierra Nevada range as they made their way to the promised land, while she chatted amiably with an educated man, mostly about how wonderful it was to be having the time of your life taking the trip of a lifetime to join the man you love, something which Richard Berman distinctly stated he knew nothing about.

They parted company and shook hands wishing each other luck in Union Station in L.A., and a more gorgeous place Gerry had not seen in New York or Chicago. The palm trees, the balmy breeze, the Art Deco décor transformed with the influence of Spanish mission architecture, was simply breathtaking, and the first thing Gerry did was to have a cup of coffee in the stunning atmosphere of the Harvey House restaurant inside the station, just to finally get a moment to herself.

Her honeymoon began right there. She had left behind a whole continent. She had left behind every single day of her own past. She was starting a whole new life from right here, right now. She was going where she had never been before, and now, she was ready. She was Gerry Petrovich now. She had accomplished things she never thought would come to pass and she herself had become something she had only dreamed of, a woman in love. She had been kissed before, and kissed by him. She wanted to be kissed again, and by him. She had no idea what it was going to be like on that night of nights, the first night they would spend together, alone, away from the world, but she felt that it was all right, to be ignorant, to be surprised, on that night. Good girls of her background and upbringing were not supposed to know all about it ahead of time. Nobody ever told you anything, not even your sisters. That was good. You were supposed to find out for yourself. You were supposed to make it up as you went along. You were supposed to trust your man. She knew in her heart that she was going to follow Andy's lead, just as she had when they were out on that dance floor the night they met, and she knew this because she knew that she loved him with all her heart and that love was going to pull them through and that when you loved somebody you couldn't do anything wrong because love made all of it alright. Of one thing Gerry Petrovich was sure—*it's not a sin to love somebody.*

So Gerry discovered that Andy Petrovich, her husband, was indeed in San Diego, that her Pa had been right, and that if she went to Gate 43 of the Naval Base at 32nd Street and Norman Scott Road, in San Diego, ASAP, and waited for her husband there, that she would meet him when he got off his shift, and they would go home. This she found out when she called up a phone number long distance from a telephone booth in the Harvey Restaurant, the number Andy had given her to call, in the telegram he had sent to Gerry back home in Revere. At this number, a woman came on the line who was the wife of a Chief Petty Officer in Maintenance at the Navy Yard, a woman who knew Andy, whose husband knew Andy, and this woman explained that *ASAP* meant *As Soon As Possible.* And that home was a little apartment in Mission Beach, across the road from the water, as, at this stage, they were permitting the married men to live off-base and bring their wives to town.

So Gerry discovered that she would be moving from the beach on the Atlantic in Revere, outside of Boston, to the beach in San Diego, on the Pacific.

And she discovered that the *USS Ruby* had traveled from the Caribbean Sea through the Panama Canal to join the Pacific Fleet, just as her Pa had thought.

And that they would have the whole summer together as the war out there on the vast ocean would have to wait on repairs and refitting before the *Ruby* could get new orders to escort troop convoys across the Pacific for the expected, dreaded invasion of Japan.

Then Gerry Petrovich discovered that her first night together with her bridegroom was sweeter than peaches and smoother than cream, and that she could push back from the table still wanting more, and that most of all, she cherished the moment, and then went on cherishing every moment, the rest of the summer and into the Southern California autumn, which she and Andy spent entwined together in bed, or sitting on the balcony of the apartment on the second floor, watching the water, with the bougainvillea hanging down over their heads as the sunset descended, blood red, over the Pacific, while they were curled up together on the porch swing and she had her knees drawn up, her head resting on his shoulder as he puffed on a Camel, lounging in his tee shirt and Bermuda shorts, his arm around her.

And she discovered that they were saved, that the whole world was saved, when they heard the news about Hiroshima, and then Nagasaki, and then Unconditional Surrender, and that they had been saved by the Atomic Bomb.

This thing which had happened was so unexpected, so unfathomable, so immense and so awe-inspiring that it could only have been an Act of God.

And she discovered, the next time she and Andy took a stroll languidly arm in arm through the shaded walks and beautiful grounds of Balboa Park, as they were gazing at the softly swaying palm trees and the dazzling white buildings of the massive Naval Hospital, as she realized that they had been spared, spared by God, for something special, something unknown that yet lay in the future, something neither one of them could yet envision or know, an entire new world, an uncharted land yet to be explored, Gerry Petrovich discovered that they were not really walking through Balboa Park—*they were the first two people in the history of the world, they had tasted the golden apple of the Sun, and they were walking under the shade of the green boughs of Eden.*

Chapter 17

Death of a Matriarch

Fireman First Class Andrej Petrovich was discharged from the United States Navy on November the 8th, 1945, from Camp Elliott in San Diego. His Honorable Discharge stated that he was entitled to wear the World War II Victory Medal, the American Area Medal, the Honorable Service button, and two Blue Honorable Service Emblems, for the Murmansk run. The Discharge specified that he had served for three years, two months and 21 days. During his separation interview, he told the clerk he had been a coal miner, and the clerk typed that into the No. 38 box marked *Main Civilian Occupation*, although his clacking typewriter ran it together as one word: 'coalminer.' Under Box 39, *Job Preference (List Type, Locality, and General Area)* Andy stated 'Carpentry, Boston, Mass.' and the clerk looked at him askance, which made Andy want to expand upon that with all the details of his chance meeting and meant-to-be romance and beachcomber honeymoon and just his whole life in general, but there was no time: he had been standing waiting in one of four lines leading to four desks for two hours, and the typist had been typing all day. So as soon as 'J. H. BAKER, Lieut. jg. USNR' had signed the document above his typed name 'By direction NTC, San Diego, Calif.' Andy took the document in his hand, felt its heavy, stiff grade of paper, turned it over and saw for the first time that it looked exactly like a high school diploma, and, thinking that this was the closest to a diploma that he was ever going to get, took a moment to examine the etching showing an obsolete, pre-Pearl-Harbor battleship steaming full speed ahead with black smoke pouring from the stacks. Then he carefully folded his discharge in four neat folds so that it would slide into the back pocket of his bell-bottoms and placed it there, along with the $100 he had received under Box 32. *Initial Mustering Out Pay*, plus $35.40 in *Travel Allowance*, Box 31. The war was over.

Gerry Petrovich gave a great big hug and squeeze to her new best friend Isobel Rodriguez, beside whom she had worked sewing dresses at Pacific Apparel and both women were crying, promising to write *if you write me back, I will, you better*, as Gerry and Andy boarded the bus for Los Angeles.

When they had settled into their seats, she squeezed Andy's hand. Her mascara was running as she looked up into his eyes and said, "I'm gonna miss this town *so* much."

At Union Station in LA, to save money on the fare, the newlyweds, as they still thought of themselves, boarded the Union Pacific's *Challenger*. At Pacific Apparel, Gerry had been pulling down a decent $36.50 a week or thereabouts on piece-work, but their rent in Mission Beach for the apartment had run $60 a month, so they still had to count their change. The *Challenger* was an affordable alternative to either the *Super Chief* or *The City of Los Angeles*, and it still provided them with a dining car and a sleeper, although the route took them from San Bernardino to Las Vegas through Salt Lake City and

Omaha, Nebraska before it got to Cedar Rapids and, finally, Chicago.

They didn't mind. Gerry had been given a book as a going-away gift from Isobel, who said *"you have to read this,"* and she treasured the prospect of reading what promised to be a romantic saga, if you went by the back cover, a novel which, at 1176 pages, could last the whole trip, a novel by a woman called Marguerite Steen, *The Sun Is My Undoing.* Gerry had a superstitious sensation that this book was going to magically prolong her happiness on the way back east, that somehow it was connected in some uncanny, subterranean fashion to the thrill she anticipated when she thought of occupying a double berth with Andy this very night: for it was something delicious, written by a woman, given as a gift, by a woman, to a woman.

The first leg of the trip and the night spent together was everything Gerry had hoped for: the new sights out the window in the daytime, the shared meals in the dining car, looking across the table at the man she loved, the spectacle of the soaring mountains, the panorama of the plains stretching out to infinity, the disquieted passion of the book in her lap, page after page.

But in Chicago they took the Pennsylvania Railroad to Penn Station in Pittsburgh.

The closer they got to Andy's hometown the more nervous Gerry became. By the time they reached Uniontown, she was a wreck.

"What if your mother doesn't like me?"

"You just keep saying 'dobra' if she gives you anything to eat."

"What does that mean?"

"Good."

"Oh, great. I know one word of Serbian."

But everyone loved Gerry "just fine," as Andy had predicted. It was the season of love in Fayette County. It was Christmas of 1945 and all the soldiers, sailors, marines and flyboys were coming home. The houses in Pershing and the people, too, were lit up from the inside out. Sweethearts, wives, sisters and mothers could kiss, coddle and comfort their boys again. The whole town was one big reunion between miners and servicemen, both of which groups had stories to tell of hard labor and hair-breadth escapes on the way to winning the war. There was such an unmatched-in-living-memory out-pouring of pent-up emotions in Pershing that Christmas that you would have thought they were inventing the season of goodwill for the very first, original time; that no one had ever laughed, danced, sung or embraced ever before in the annals of the world.

It made Gerry miss her own home, her own family. She had heard on the phone when calling her mother and father that her three brothers had all made it home safely and here she was, missing out on the miracle of their return. If only she could have cut herself in half and been in both places at once. She had talked to every one up there in Boston on the phone, but it wasn't the same. *And they all kept saying, when are you coming home?*

They had gone to see Andy's sister Angie on her husband John Lucinda's farm in Carmichaels. His sister Stasija was still working uptown in the beauty salon on North Main and living at home. Gerry was thankful for her because it gave her someone their own age to talk to, in American, too, someone to chat with while they washed and dried dishes together, someone to be there for her if Andy was gone out of the house. Stasija was her intermediary if her new mother-in-law, Tamara Petrovich, attempted to converse with her new daughter-in-law. Gerry acquired one other Serbian word, *Majka*, so that she could make a gesture at being properly respectful and call Tamara "Mother." Oh, if only there wasn't this language barrier!—or if only in moments alone, Gerry didn't find herself protesting silently in her own mind, 'but she's not *my* mother.'

Andy could slip out of the house, but for the women it was awkward. Andy would take a walk uptown to Kitka's store or be sent by his mother chasing after his father at the German beer garden. And of course he had friends in this town to look up and carry on a confab with. So Gerry found herself alone at times, staring out a window, feeling uncomfortable. Andy's sister Adrienne was the only family member she hadn't yet met because she lived in New York City—but Gerry dreaded the idea they might have to delay and stop there on the way home up to Boston. She asked Andy to show her the coal mine he worked in over in Shawnee, because she was curious about that part of his life, she wanted to see for herself, but he said, *naw,* it was nothing for a woman to see.

People always were saying things like, make yourself at home, but Gerry couldn't. They were already there going on two months, it seemed to her, and she still felt so out of place. Even the local accent Andy fell into with his sisters was laughable, at times, Gerry was ashamed to admit to herself. Why did they have to say '*over to Uniontown*' instead of '*in Uniontown?*' Gerry knew she was being snooty about it, but why did they have to say '*hain't it*' all the time. They made themselves sound like somebody trying to ridicule hillbillies on the radio. Andy took her out to a Christmas dance at the country club 'over to Latrobe,' and she found that everybody there talked that way. He even took her on an excursion to Lookout Point in West Virginia, where you could see seven states from the top of a mountain, on a freezing cold day. He took her window shopping in Uniontown, but it only made her miss a real city like Boston or, yes, *San Diego,* so much more. *Oh, why had she been so happy there, and here, she was so miserable?*

But Andy wanted to hang on, hoping by New Year's and then the first week of January, that he would get to finally see his brother Alek, who had to return home all the way from Burma. Gerry had already met Alek's wife Rose, and she was so nice, a strawberry-blond Polish girl, somebody who reminded Gerry a great deal of her own best friend, Hildie, back home, who had been her Maid of Honor. Finally, Alek got home, and of course, that meant another three weeks of boys being boys. Gerry could only laugh with Rose about how stupid men could be and the rest of the time, wish she was happy, and wonder why she wasn't.

In the end it didn't go unnoticed by Andy.

"What's wrong, babe? I think I know. You wanna go home. I'll talk to my mother."

They were upstairs in the room under the roof on Maple Ave in Pershing, the room Andy had shared with Alek back when they were kids and Alek was going through that God-awful suffering with his diabetes before he was saved by insulin. It seemed to Andy so long ago now.

Gerry was whispering. "Why do you have to talk to her?"

"Well—I haven't exactly told her—"

"Andy, we had a plan, didn't we?"

"I know. I know, babe. But—well, I was trying to string her along and not have to raise the subject—"

"She doesn't know? You haven't explained it to her!"

"Judas Priest, Gerry. She's my mother. How do you expect her to feel? Same way your mother feels. She just got her sons back, and now—."

What a mess this was turning out to be. Gerry was appalled at the way Andy's mother carried on. Crying and beating her breast, fit to be tied. You would think they were trying to kill her. Why couldn't her mother be stoic about it and show a little fortitude, the way Gigi LaStoria would have? Are the Serbs so emotional that they can't control themselves? And why do they kiss each other on the lips? Even Gerry had to submit to this from her father-in-law. Gerry just wanted to flee. All she had succeeded in doing was to make everyone so unhappy.

On the bus on the way to New York, Andy nudged her in the ribs. "Come on." He tickled her, he tried to get her to laugh. "There. That's better, hain't it?"

"Will you stop it?"

"Well, I just wanna get my little lumpkins back."

"I could kill you."

"Does that mean the honeymoon's over?"

"Yes, and we're broke, too."

"I'm gonna get a job, babe. You'll see. Soon as we get to Massachusetts."

He tried to get her to look at him so he could make funny-faces. "And I promise we won't stop in New York."

Gerry just burrowed into her 1176-page book, *The Sun Is My Undoing*, which she still hadn't finished, because she was honestly afraid for it to end.

Back home in Massachusetts at last, Gerry found no comfort or relief in the prospect of running out of land to traverse, of having to finally stop, and say to herself, *this is it, there's no more, it's ovah.* The city sliding by on the other side of the buswindow, although, to her, these were the most familiar streets in the world: why did everything look *different?* When they landed in the bus terminal on Stuart Street, she was virtually disappointed to find this wasn't San Diego. But what had she expected? She told herself it was only natural after all this to feel a letdown. On the subway and the streetcar back to Revere she almost had a sense of foreboding.

However, everyone at home greeted her and Andy with open arms, and that included not only her brother Augie, home from the war, but even her Pa's bird-dogs.

Oh, they had so much to talk about! How was your trip? *I thought it would never end.* What's San Diego like? *You wouldn't believe it if I told you.* Did you miss us? *Not a bit, I had no time.* "How's Ma? How's Pa? Augie, how are you? We gotta talk. Later, later. Okay. It's so good to see you, let me put my arms around you." Gerry was crying, sobbing on her taller brother's soft shoulder, saying, "You know, I hope you got my letters, I thought about writing you every single day, I'm sorry I didn't write more often, you know, they talk about the veterans having to re-adjust when they get back home, but what about us sisters, who could only work and wait and work and wait, it's a big re-adjustment for us, too, have you gone to see Mary and Anna?"

They were standing right there, since the whole family, excepting Peggy, of course, had come to the house in Revere to make a happy homecoming for the late-comers from the West Coast, but not everyone could fit in the kitchen, so her brother Patsy, her sister-in-law, Mary, his wife, and their little boy, Anthony, now four years old, Anna's husband Tommy DiPrima, also home from Europe, Gerry's brother Gene, home from Italy, and her sister-in-law Celia, Gene's wife—Gerry could see nothing through her tears, she had no idea why she was crying, everyone assumed they were tears of joy, it was an impossible night of mixed emotions which no amount of cleverness, experience or wisdom could have prepared Gerry for, and all she could hope was that they all knew how much she loved them all, and how happy she was to be home with them at last.

The very next morning life began all over again, on a cold day in late January of 1946, and by the end of that year, just before Christmas, on the sixth of December, Anna DiPrima had a baby boy, which she named after her husband Tommy; Gerry Petrovich had a baby boy, also, on the night before Christmas, whom she named after jolly St Nick, because he was a Christmas baby, so that she and Andy had their own little Nicholas; Celia LaStoria had her second child, Leon, in early 1947, followed by Patsy and Mary's new daughter, Linda, in March.

It was a season of new grandchildren for Tony and Gigi LaStoria, who had given birth to seven of their own, so they naturally expected more to come, and Gerry's letdown after her honeymoon didn't last. She was home now, and in charge of her own life, she was a new mother, with more to live for than ever before, she had an infant she became absolutely absorbed with. Andy signed up for the GI Bill and got a job making 40 bucks a week as an apprentice carpenter at Page's Woodworking shop on the corner of Broadway and Mountain Ave., right here in Revere. He could walk to work in the morning, he'd take a bag lunch out of the icebox that Gerry made up for him the night before, or, he was close enough to walk home for lunch. And Gerry made sure he turned over his paycheck every week to her, so that it went into the kitty for the house, and the whole family was the better off for it. Gerry had to admit that maybe Andy's mother had brought him up the right way after all, and she shouldn't begrudge the poor woman. Nor did Andy mind one bit. He was pleased to be fitting right in and his out-going, down-home, aw-shucks nature just made him a pleasure to be around.

Pa was still working for Spritzka Industries as a general-manager, New England-wide, and the plant manager at No. 10 Melcher Street in town, and, of course, his son Gene, the ex-Sgt LaStoria, resumed his position at his father's side as Assistant Plant Manager, which he had left, it seemed, just yesterday, in 1942, though, at other times, it felt like several lifetimes ago. Patsy LaStoria was the head presser, in charge of that department, and Augie worked with them as the cloth-cutter, still single, still a non-smoker, because, as he always said, "I'm in training."

In training for what was the only question. Augie was the only guy they knew of who went through the European campaign without taking a single cigarette to help him get through, at a time when they were being handed out like candy by the quartermaster. And he was the only guy they knew who came home from the war and resumed living with his mother; and the only guy they knew who never went out except to the racetrack or the ballpark or the bookie parlor; and the only guy they knew who had no interest whatsoever in getting his driver's license and couldn't see why he should. And he was the only guy they knew who suffered from disabling migraines that sent him to bed behind a closed door with a towel wrapped around his head.

Gerry worried about her brother, as did everyone else. He had always been the biggest in the family, in spite of being born the second youngest. At six-foot-two, he towered over everyone. They had always thought of him as that unstoppable backfield runner they knew from the Stoughton High football team who had seemed gifted with talent and clothed in a shining, indestructible light.

And he was in fact the same old Augie, carefree and happy and always with a wisecrack on the tip of his tongue, the brother who competed with Patsy for the position of family comedian, the guy who would pick up the shovel and go dig up the garden for his Pa in the springtime so the old man didn't have to strain himself: the Augie they all loved.

He was the guy who could crush you with a handshake, and yet, he was the guy who lived at home with his mother, the guy who for all the world could see no interest at all in girls. Even his sisters didn't dare to try to fix him up with anybody. They knew their Augie was more interested in the standings in the American League or the next bout coming up for Joe Louis than any woman he had ever seen or heard of.

And you didn't bring up the subject of the war around Augie. At least not face to face or in a quiet moment.

Whenever the family got together in Pa's backyard in Revere for a cookout around the picnic table, Patsy would start in on how they shoulda let him and General Patton take care of the Russians when they had a chance. Patsy never let go by an opportunity to show off his wounded leg from his time in Germany as a military policeman in a motorcycle patrol. Patsy would tell the funny story of what he did to the ten-year-old boy when they caught him, the boy who had shot him with a hunting rifle.

"I pulled his pants down and gave him a good lickin,' that's what I did, just like Pa used to do with me when I was a kid if

I did anything wrong–if he could catch me. Then I told him it hurt me a lot more than it hurt him, just like Pa used to say to me. The kid didn't understand a word of English, so I sent him home with a chocolate bar."

If Patsy told them that story once, he told them a hundred times. And he would always pull up his pant-leg, to show you the scars on the back of his left calf, where the bullet went in and where it went out. That was the kind of thing you could count on with Patsy.

But Augie would become uncommunicative at times and at times would withdraw from the rest of the family and you wondered if it was another headache coming on, maybe. And when Patsy started telling war stories at the picnic table, most often, Augie would get up and walk away.

His brother Gene would say, softly, "Eh—just leave him alone."

But Gerry did not worry about Augie. To her, he was her special kid brother, who belonged to her. Patsy was a lot older than they were—even Gene was older. But Augie, when they were kids, was, to Gerry, growing up, almost her twin brother. So now, with so much going on in her own life, Gerry still had the gift of being able to say quietly to Augie, "You okay?"

And he would answer. "Sure. Of course. What else? Mind your own business."

Gerry was a lot more hopeless about her mother.

In the summer of '47, Alek Petrovich and his wife Rose and their new baby, Roseann, just a bit younger than Gerry and Andy's Nicholas, drove up the 500 miles from Pennsylvania in Alek's brand-new Chevy to visit Andy, Gerry and the nephew they had never seen at the house in Revere.

It was the last happy time for Gigi LaStoria. She went outside to her beautiful flower garden which stretched the length of the driveway inside the chain link fence beside the house in Revere. There was something new out, color film for the Kodak box camera, the one that you flipped up the lid on and then held at your midsection and looked down into the viewfinder to shoot your picture. They took color pictures of Gigi and Tony posing as the grandparents in the flower garden, with Gigi seated on a kitchen chair and Tony kneeling on one knee at her side. Gerry posed with Nicky on the little patch of front lawn near the driveway gates, and somebody caught her turning her head with Nicky looking over her shoulder. The two cousins, Roseann from Pennsylvania, and Nicky from Revere, were propped up on the lawn together for a boy and girl portrait. Andy's brother Alek had insisted on taking the push-mower out of the garage and trimming every grass-blade around the place. When he washed his new Chevy in the driveway he also washed his brother's father-in-law's Buick. And of course everyone had to gather for the spectacle of watching Alek inject his arm with a syringe of insulin in the evening. The Germantown Coal Company was going great guns, the latest contract with the UMW was the best they'd ever had in terms of hourly wages, vacation pay and benefits, and Alek had a pocketful of rattling change. His older brother Andy certainly didn't have two weeks paid vacation on his apprentice program at Page's Woodworking, but, no, he wasn't going back to work in the mine, he was doing just what he always had wanted to, and it would all work out in the end, baby brother might be making a lot more money right now than he was, but, no matter, don't spend it all in one place, someday Andy was going to be a master carpenter, just you wait and see, yes-siree-bob. Gerry's Pa just adored young Rose

Petrovich, who was so friendly and nice, it made an old man feel young again, and they posed for snapshots with Rose's arm through his. Prosperity was a wonderful thing and didn't they all deserve it, after what they'd been through, what with the Depression first, and then the war, and all?

The life of the LaStorias on Payson Street in Revere continued apace in 1948, but Gigi LaStoria, the matriarch of all this, did not.

She seemed to worsen imperceptibly day by day, and months later it would dawn on Gerry, her constant companion in the house, with a shock, that her mother was dying.

Gerry had a son barely a year-and-a-half, talking, walking and running, on her hands, and she wished devoutly that she would always have her mother on hand, for any and every moment when she doubted herself, just to turn to for advice, or to ask a question; although with the encouragement of their family physician, Dr Graham, down at the end of Payson Street, who was a general practitioner, and cheaper than a mere pediatrician would have been, she was also consulting Dr Spock, and his baby book, which she had picked up off the drugstore rack down at Foyle's on Beach Street. Ma LaStoria and Dr Spock did not always agree and Gerry was determined to be an up-to-date, modern mother, and she did not always appreciate the constant lectures about testing the temp of the bottle, especially since her mother had never used one, having always breast-fed her babies. She was tempted to say, "I heard you the first time. And yesterday. And the day before." And she did say so.

But to think that she might lose her mother . . .

By 1949 Gigi LaStoria did not get out of bed anymore. She would raise her voice to make herself heard to Gerry in the kitchen through the open bedroom door. It had become a chore that Gerry was ill-equipped and ill-prepared-for, to turn her mother in bed, to bathe her in bed, to feed her, to dress her. Dr Graham had to school her on how to keeping changing position on the bed-ridden old woman to prevent her from getting bed-sores, which could be a serious thing. Days when little Nicky's cousins Henry and Ronnie were on her hands she would fall way behind schedule on the house and the cooking and her mother and everything. Her mother was still issuing instructions while lying on her back. "Don't forget the laundry is today. I can't see out. Is it nice enough to hang out to dry?"

By the autumn of 1949 Gigi LaStoria was no longer issuing orders.

In 1950 Dr Graham said she was dying of congestive heart failure.

There came the day when Gerry knew she would have to pick up the telephone and call her sisters. She sat on the chair in the front hall and wiped her hands in her apron. "Mary, if you wanna see her, you better come today. Call Anna. I'll call Patsy. You call Gene, and Peggy—but tell her she better get here before Pa gets home from work."

One by one they went through the closed door of their mother and father's room to say goodbye to their mother and receive her last blessing.

To each one of her seven children, Gigi LaStoria gave a special word, and begged each of them to look after their father when she was gone. To Patsy, the first to go in, she said, "You were my first-born and there was never another like you." He emerged from that closed door and shut it behind him, out of respect, and he was a grown man, weeping silently, as he never had during the war. One by one they took their turns. To Mary, her second child, she said, "You were the only one who was a proper bride in a church wedding and always remember, I made your father find a marriage for you because he forget to notice how beautiful his oldest daughter was." To Peggy, who arrived in haste and out of breath and who left in tears, she said, "Don't ever tell the others, but you are my true daughter, the sister of my soul, the only one who was like me." Gerry was told she was the only one her mother wanted to keep at home with her, "my precious diamond, the best of all my jewels." Augie came in late, with his father and his brother Gene, all coming in after work at the shop. Gene was told that he was the one who was destined from birth to follow in his father's footsteps and that he must never let his father down when she was gone. Augie was told that he was her champion and that during the war when she prayed on her rosary beads in her chair by the window, she reminded the Holy Mother, that she herself, God's Mother, had saved her son as an infant, that day in the hallway at the Massachusetts General, "because the Heavenly Father must have meant Augie for something special." Anna was the last to go in, as she was the last to be born, and her mother said to her "Anna, Anna, my baby . . ." She told Anna that after her, she could have no more children because God had made Anna the most perfect and beautiful child anyone had ever seen, and God was content, then, that He could not surpass Himself.

At last she called in her husband, Tony LaStoria.

He knelt by her bedside and took one of her hands in his.

"Come closer. I don't have long, and I have something to ask you."

"Anything, Gigi, mi amore, anything."

"Do you remember the night of our wedding?

"How could I forget?"

"Well, now the time has come, and I want to know your secret."

Tony was stunned. He said nothing. About that, he had truly forgotten.

She warned him. "Do you want to rob me of my last wish so that I can't die in peace?"

"Gigi, Father Spinelli is coming, you must be given the last rites of Holy Mother Church."

"He's already been. Did you think your children would omit that? They're not stupid, your children. Forget the priest. *I want to know.*"

Tony found his hand was trembling as he tried to put her hand down.

Gigi said, "And don't try to lie to me. I will know."

He bowed his head as he confessed. "There was a young girl, before you."

"What was her name?"

"Her name was Laura."

"Did you love her?"

"Why do you want to torment yourself?"

"Did you love her?"

"Yes, I loved her. God help me—I loved her."

"Ah—I knew it. I knew it. You never loved me."

Tears were streaming down Tony's face, tears of anguish, and shame, and guilt.

"And why did you not marry her, then, instead of me, if you loved her so much?"

"Because she died."

"Oh."

Gigi took away the baleful eye she had kept fastened on him until then, and looked away, to somewhere far off, within herself.

"Ahhhh . . . ah, me . . . I always knew that I had taken someone else's place. But I didn't know that I had tried to take the place of the dead. That, the living cannot do."

Tony emerged from the closed door and his children observed him, as he closed the door softly again behind him, and said, "She's gone."

They saw that he was crying, but why he was weeping, they did not know.

And they did not question why because, in their minds, they thought they knew.

Chapter 18

The Fieldstone House

When he lost Gigi, in 1951, Tony LaStoria was 61 years old. *Well,* he thought, too often, *that's it, my life is over.* He had journeyed to America all alone by himself when he was ten years old, brimming with notions, floating on his hopes, driven by the need to make a buck. Now his future was gone. His hopes were buried in the grave with Gigi. What was left for him? For all his striving to succeed, where had he gotten to? For all his scheming and manipulating, what had he controlled? Nothing. Life had gotten away from him. It was slipping through his fingers at this very moment. He looked around at his dogs, at his tomato plants, and he thought, *what's the use?*

He tried to trace back the thread of one thing and another and how the winding and twisting of fortune and fate had led him to *this,* or just where exactly his grasp had eluded him. And inevitably the path led back, back, back, through the twists and turns of one child born after another, one house lived in only to be left behind, one town and the next, beyond Gigi, beyond Boston, back to New York, to the Lower East Side, to the day he met his childhood friend, Harry Spritzka.

It was a testimony to the strength of their faith and belief in one another that this alliance, which they had first formed in the flush of youthful fancy, had lasted over 45 years; yet they had, perhaps inevitably, who knows how or why, become estranged, of that, there could be no doubt. The world had changed too much. Their partnership had not been a matter of business, it was mystical. They had worked hand in hand through the fever of the First World War days, through the Roaring Twenties, through the agonies of shrinkage and loss during the Depression, only to reach a peak with the desperate crisis of the Second War. Tony had not put even fifty cents of his own money into this partnership, but he had put in his soul.

Tony had not calculated that Harry might one day no longer need him.

He had never envisioned that Harry would lose interest in making money from garment-making.

Now, in the end, to simply cease operations of a network of garment industry facilities that stretched from Philadephia to Maine?

He knew, of course, that Harry had long ago diversified, and had turned his attention to real estate and banking, in partnership with his brother Robert. For Harry the time had come to divest himself of what was fast becoming, in the late 'Forties, an obsolete business model. Surveying the horizons, Harry could see the industry moving south, abandoning New England, New York, New Jersey, why? Labor costs, pure and simple. The unions had finally driven their old foe Harry Spritzka out of the industry. Why should he carry on the fight with them now, when he could see no future for himself in it, when, in fact, they had beaten him in the past, going all the way back to 1909? And Harry had not the heart nor the stomach for transferring operations to Carolina, Tennessee, Georgia, where he would have to practically start over again, searching for corner properties to buy. Not only that, but his carefully built-up chain of Richard Paul retail stores throughout the Northeast with their selected locations on urban streetcar lines, were now, suddenly, when everywhere they were digging up the trolley tracks to make room for more cars—what? suddenly located in the wrong place!

Harry Spritzka was the one in this spiritual partnership, this brotherhood of the boyish heart, with the business acumen. Tony LaStoria was a manager. Another way of saying, glorified hired-hand? Point him in a direction, give him the materials, the power, the structure, the premise, and he would do what he was bid. Harry was the hunter. Tony was his bird-dog.

When the time came Harry simply made a business decision, which had led to a phone call, in late 1947.

"Naturally," Harry had said, after enquiring whether Tony was sitting down, and advising him to do so, "naturally, I'm gonna take care of you with a very nice little severance package, but, Tony, maybe you wanna think about retirement now, at this point, anyway, because, listen, brother, the future of the whole industry is heading south. Look at what's happening right now up where you live, in Lowell, in Milltown, Fall River, New Bedford, Manchester, Hartford, Providence, New Haven—and then take a look at the tax breaks they're handing out in North Carolina! And it's not just us, Tony, it's across the board, it's textiles, it's shoes. It's our old nemesis, you know? our old foes, our old adversaries, that you and I fought together, toe to toe, the unions. They're killing the goose that laid the golden egg, Tony. And I, I can't evade the consequences, it's an epidemic, and, Tony, I'm not immune, there's no vaccination, I'm bleeding from the main vein, I can't go on forever throwing good money after bad, no, no, no, I'm losing my shirt, and I'm not about to start up everything from scratch all over again, down south, I'm not as young as I used to be, you know, and neither are you, my friend, besides, I got other ways of making money, eh, I shoulda listened to my brother Robert long ago, he always said real estate was the only way to go, you remember, Tony, but would I listen? no, I had to have my own empire, and besides, Tony, these days it's a different world, not like when we came up, who knows what's gonna happen in Palestine, in '48, all's I know is it's gonna be something, we can't go on like this, after what happened to us during the war, we just cannot depend on the rest of the world, we can only depend on ourselves, Tony, don't get me started."

When Tony put the receiver back on the hook he was still seated. He was not angry. He was not upset, except at himself. He was just more or less sick and tired of the whole thing.

He's sitting there on the fifth floor of his mansion on Third Avenue, and I'm out of a job.

It was the death of an organization man. When Gigi passed, *that was the big one. This was just a little death. Instead of going on to a better place, I'm still stuck here. I'm still alive, but, for what?*

The next question that occurred to Tony was *who do I know?*

A lifetime in the garment trade in Boston meant that Tony knew everybody who was anybody and they knew him and what he could do. So he picked up the phone again and started making calls.

He found a position. Plant manager at his accustomed payscale, but it was out of town, north, 30 miles from Revere, on Route 28, or you could take Route 1 to 114 north, all the way to the Merrimack Valley, bordering the New Hampshire line. Either way was full of rotaries and traffic. To Tony, it was a world away. He still, after all these years, thought of Milltown, Massachusetts, as the place where the Wobblies in 1912 led out 20,000 textile workers and all those housewives and mothers in the notorious Bread and Roses Strike—*all the way back in 1912!* The only time Tony had ever passed through Milltown was on the way to place a bet at the 2-dollar window at Rockingham Park in New Hampshire.

But he had moved too many times in his life. If only he could just stay in one place for a change. In Revere, he had a tenant, old Mrs Nelson, the widow, who lived up on the second floor, and he could count on her for forty bucks a month, he didn't want to raise the rent, she was quiet, never a bother, never had visitors, never complained; if he kicked her out, who the hell would he get in there?

He bought himself a brand-new '47 Buick to commute in. He needed it. He needed something. After all, he had worked hard, all his life, he deserved it.

Pappagallo's in Milltown was located on the second floor of the Everett Mills, at the foot of Essex Street, the main shopping street of the city. This building was so enormous it blocked out the sun. At one time Milltown had been the biggest woolen textile manufacturing city in the world. Now famous mills such as the Arlington Mills, the Wood Mills, the Malden Mills, and the Ayer Mills competed against each other trying to fill empty space, at dirt-cheap rents. Pappagallo had been a buyer at Filene's, and he thought he knew how to make a buck. He branched out on his own to start making knock-offs of the women's fashions he used to buy for the store. He hired Tony because he wanted to spend his daytimes on the road, selling.

Pappagallo hired Tony and Tony hired his son Gene as his floor boss and he brought in his son Augie as the cutter and Patsy as the presser department, and he said to Gene, "You learn everything you can here, and when I'm gone, you go out on your own."

"Who you kidding, Pa, you're gonna live forever."

But he did not. He did not even last barely a year after Gigi went.

The day he died was a Saturday, and he died at the finish rail at Suffolk Downs.

For some time after that, his daughter Gerry, whenever she looked out the kitchen window, where her dying mother had spent years sitting in her stiff-backed chair; when Gerry saw her dead father's empty Buick sitting there in the driveway idle and unattended; she would think *who's gonna drive it now?* and it would be all she could do to keep the weeping from starting again.

Her husband Andy didn't want it. He couldn't see going to college on the GI bill when he could be getting paid every week to get an education through his apprentice program at Page's Woodworking in Revere (besides, he never graduated high school, so college wouldn't take him); nor could he see paying for gas when he could walk to work, and besides, he was only making $40 a week take-home, Gerry was pregnant, with twins, this time, and they had lost the support his father-in-law used to provide. True enough, his brother-in-law

Augie pitched in, but Andy still had to apply for extra compensation under the GI Bill, which, he was entitled to, since, if he had gone to college, he would have received $500 a year for tuition and fees (but not room and board). The extra five hundred a year sure came in handy. It was going to take 4,000 hours at Page's for Andy to earn journeyman status as a carpenter with the Massachusetts Carpenter's Union and come in for the big money, union-scale. The future looked bright ahead as long as they didn't spend on things like car insurance.

Gerry had never learned how to drive. Whenever she thought of that, she heard her father's voice telling her, *if you need to go anywhere, I'll drive you.* It was funny, though, because her old girlfriend Hildie, from Stoughton, that was the first thing she had done after the war was to get a license. Hildie told Gerry that it was the best way she knew how to come and visit Gerry in Revere, now that they were tearing up all the old streetcar lines, as they both were married now and had kids and, in fact, wasn't it funny, but Hildie was having twins, too. Hildie had two boys, identicals, whom she named Peter and Paul. Gerry had a boy and girl set of fraternal twins and she named them Jack and Jill. Every time they got together the girlfriends laughed like hell over that, and Hildie always said, at least you can tell yours apart!

It was 1952 when Pa passed away, 1952 when the twins were born, and still 1952 when General Eisenhower was elected President. Well, he was going to end that war in Korea, that was a good thing, but what to do about that Buick?

Gerry's brother Augie showed no interest whatsoever in learning to drive. Ever since the end of the war he had gone to work every day with his father in the Buick. That way Augie didn't have to worry about the driving, the traffic, the boredom, or the expense. If he wanted to go anywhere else besides to work every day, well, he just took the streetcar. You could go anywhere in metropolitan Boston you wanted to, and the only places Augie ever wanted to go was the dog track, the horse track, Fenway Park or Braves Field, or Boston Garden—or the bookie parlor—and you could walk there.

Augie was a race fan and he was just as fanatical about big league baseball. The family all thought of him in their own minds as occupying the pedestal they had placed him on, long ago, before the war, when he was a three-sport star playing for Coach Puffy O'Brian at Stoughton High. And the only thing Augie had ever told them about the war was how, when he was in the camps in England, before D-Day, he had gone up against some major-league players who were in the Army, and the big-leaguers had all told him he had more than held his own over there at first base, both fielding-wise and with a bat in his hands.

The family all agreed. Augie coulda been a big league ballplayer himself if he had wanted to. That was the reason, in fact, that he didn't smoke. Cigarettes were always in the house. Gerry smoked Chesterfields, like her Pa, Andy smoked Camels. But Augie didn't smoke because he was in training.

In training for what never occurred to them. It might have seemed to an outsider a little odd somehow that here was a big, strapping guy, a veteran of Omaha Beach, who lived at home with his sister, never went out, showed no interest in women, didn't drive a car, and didn't drink, except for once in a while when he'd stick a quart of Miller's in the icebox (he swore by Miller's, *the Champagne of Bottled Beers.*) Augie would have a glass when the Game of the Week, usually the

Yankees, came on television on a Saturday, especially during the '49 season, when the Red Sox went neck and neck with them to the end. He would have his glass of Miller's, put the quart back, and stretch out on the sofa in the parlor, to watch the game, whereupon he would fall asleep.

None of this struck the family as unusual. It was just Augie being himself, and you didn't question Augie. He was big, imposing, didn't say much, kept to himself, never bothered anyone, was always quietly helpful, would do anything for you without you having to ask, and suffered from mysterious headaches, which caused him to withdraw to his bedroom and shut the door, with a towel wrapped tightly around his head, so you had to go around the house being quiet so as not to disturb him.

The one stranger in the house, who had to get used to Augie, who had never known him before the war, was Andy.

Nor had Andy really expected beforehand, when he was contemplating a life and a home with his sweetheart, Gerry, and leaving his own family behind, when he pictured all that, he had never imagined having to share her with a brother-in-law.

But he quickly found that Gerry always deferred to Augie, even though she was the big sister. Augie got asked before anyone, even Andy, if he wanted a second helping. Even Gerry's Pa, before he passed, had noticed. He had not hesitated to remind his daughter Gerry, at the supper table, in front of everyone, to show a little respect to her husband. Andy noticed that. And Gerry didn't take kindly to Andy noticing.

However, to Andy, all this didn't seem like a big deal, not really. After all, back home, his own brother Alek had his wife Rose living in the house in which the Petrovich kids had all grown up, on Maple Ave., in Pershing, with her sister-in-law

Stasija—and didn't that come to the same thing? Didn't everybody these days live with their in-laws in the house? *We're not rich people, you know, just ordinary folk. We're all in this together.* Andy was actually more or less just grateful they had taken him in and seemed to accept him and tried to make him feel at home, like he was one of their own. Especially his father-in-law, Tony, who went actually out of his way to show everybody that Andy was all right with him, and that Pa was thankful to know that, after he was gone, his new son-in-law would be there to take care of Gerry. *And so handy around the house, he was, the guy could fix anything.*

It was Gerry's sister Margaret who claimed that it was their father who had spoiled everything for Augie because he insisted Augie had to quit school and go to work, like the rest of them. If not for that, Peggy was sure that Augie would have been recruited by Boston College, or even Boston University, on a full scholarship, and become a star halfback. If only he had graduated high school.

But nobody paid any attention to Peggy, with the Third Eye and everything else, because she was always making trouble: that was her job in life.

The professional driver in the family was Gerry's brother-in-law, Tommy DiPrima, her sister Anna's husband. He had driven a truck during the war in Europe. Afterwards, that's what he went in for to earn his daily bread, truck-driver. He used to stop in to see Gerry for lunch two or three times a week, for a sangwich and a bottle of milk, which Tommy said he had to drink a lot of on account of his ulcers, which came from bouncing around in that furniture truck all the time.

Sometimes Andy was home for lunch on the same day Tommy would drop in, pulling his truck into the driveway behind the Buick. Gerry found out from Tommy that all she needed to sell the Buick was the registration in the glove compartment. Her girlfriend Hildie told her the same thing. So, she sold the car because they didn't need the car, they needed the money.

As for money, Gerry was now the one in the house who held onto the purse strings. She never asked her brother Augie for anything, but he always kicked in. Her husband Andy, of course, was diligent in turning over his weekly paycheck. Gerry's parents were gone, she had her older boy, Nicky, starting school in the first grade at the Shurtleff, across the street from their house, in the autumn of 1952, and it seemed that the boys were satisfied to have everything fall on her shoulders. As if she didn't have enough on her hands, what with a first grader, and two infants to raise.

She didn't have to worry about getting Andy to help with the dishes as Augie always took care of that, as if he were still on Army KP. That suited Andy as he could sit at the kitchen table and read his paper, which he did religiously. He would hand over the sports page to Augie when he sat down and they had coffee. The only other thing he had ever seen Augie read was the Green Sheet and the paperback novels from the drugstore with the lurid covers of half-dressed women in peril that Augie kept in his bedroom.

Gerry was running out of room since the twins were born. She had Nicky and them in the one room that used to be their mother and father's bedroom, Augie in the back bedroom and herself and her husband in her own room. That was the year that Gerry fell into the habit of feeling like she just couldn't keep up with everything. She had to get Andy to help her changing one baby while she changed the other, but Augie was actually easier to ask. She just didn't have enough room in this house, and she wanted to go up on the rent for Mrs Nelson upstairs, but every time this crossed her mind, she'd hear her father's finger-wagging voice scolding her from the grave. Where was she gonna put that enormous double baby-carriage she had had to buy for the twins if not in the back hall, which was already occupied by her mother's old-fashioned washing machine tub with the wooden rollers? How was she gonna fit Nicky in a bed in his room now that she had to make room for not one but two cribs and a bassinet? Sometimes she thought that if it hadn't been for Dr Graham down at the bottom of the street she would have lost her mind. Andy wasn't a lot of help. He suggested she could have put the infants in makeshift cradles using a couple of bureau drawers, like his mother used to do. Gerry wanted to throw Dr Spock at his head. Andy began to complain that he never knew what kind of mood he'd come home to find her in, but he couldn't really blame her when he thought of how Gerry had gone through a Caesarean section for the second time with the twins, and a mis-carriage, to boot, in between Nicky and them. Andy figured that kind of thing might put any woman off her feed-bag.

If it hadn't've been for her brother Patsy and his wife Mary, Gerry didn't know what she would have done.

Gene LaStoria, Mary Laverna and Anna DiPrima, Gerry's other siblings, all lived in Watertown, but Patsy and Mary and their kids, Anthony and Linda, lived right here in Revere, on Reservoir Ave., right off Broadway. Patsy's wife Mary had already had her first-born, Anthony, in '41, before Patsy enlisted in '42. During the war, she lived at home in

Somerville, with her own family, the DiOrlandos, where she had grown up. When Patsy came home from Germany in '45, they moved to the house in Revere on Reservoir Ave., which they bought with a GI Loan.

Tony LaStoria did not want his sons coming home from the service to be wanting for a job to support themselves and their families, nor to be stuck for a place to live, after all they had done and been through, he wanted them close by, no further than arm's length. So Pa LaStoria made sure Patsy, Gene and Augie all worked for him in town on Melcher Street at No. 10. But Gene and Anna had spouses whose families, parents and siblings, lived in Watertown, so naturally they wanted to stay there, nor could Mary and Charlie Laverna be expected to sell their two-family in Watertown just to move to Revere. But at least Patsy should bring Mary from Somerville, which was closer than Watertown, to Revere, since they didn't have a home of their own already.

When Gerry's Christmas baby, Nicky, and Mary's Linda were born, close together, in '46 and '47, Gerry and Mary had grown closer because they used to walk to each other's houses with their toddlers in strollers, to visit and get the kids out in the fresh air, to play.

Now it was her sister-in-law, Mary LaStoria, who came to the rescue for Gerry in '52, when the twins came along.

Gerry was reeling in the aftermath of her latest Caesarean, and Mary LaStoria had nothing but sympathy for her. Gerry knew her to be a good soul and now that they were seeing each other so much because of the infant twins, Mary had become almost a new sister in Gerry's mind—especially since she was a better help than her own useless sister Peggy, who continued to drop off Henry and Ronnie for Gerry to mind while she was out, completely oblivious to what was going on in Gerry's life.

It was dismaying to Gerry to think that Mary LaStoria cared more about her than her own sister Peggy did. Things had certainly changed between Gerry and Peggy since they were kids, that was for sure.

Dr Graham, too, was concerned about Gerry. Nicky, her first, had been born in the Revere Children's Hospital by Caesarean in '46. Gerry had had two miscarriages since then. Dr Graham knew that Gerry had never told her husband about the first one. The twins were born at the Winthrop Hospital and Dr Graham was cautioning Gerry. After all this which she had been through, she better not be having any more pregnancies. She better take steps to prevent it. Her pelvis was just too narrow, or something. Dr Graham explained it, but Gerry wasn't sure she understood. She could only focus on the idea that, if she had any more kids, she would have to have them by Caesarean, and Dr Graham wasn't the only one who didn't know if she could go through that. Gerry was aghast. She was already feeling exhausted and worn out from nine months of carrying twins, the both of them. She blamed herself for having had those two mis-carriages; she just couldn't help feeling it was her own fault, though for the life of her, she didn't know what she could've, or should've done, that she didn't do. Now her dream of having as many kids as the old woman in the shoe, or, at least as many as her mother had had, you know, a big happy Italian family, was being snatched from her, just when she was already at her lowest. She fell into a depression.

Dr Graham said it was the postpartum blues. He took Andy aside and wanted to know if any of those lessons from the service about using prophylactics had stuck, or did he want to be responsible for his kids having to grow up without a mother?

Thank God for Mary LaStoria and *I Love Lucy*.

Augie had brought home a television back in '48. He had bought it down on Broadway in Revere, at the new television store, Barron's. He said it was better than the ones they came out with in '47. He used to walk downtown to watch TV through the store windows. A couple of times he had gone into a barroom just to watch a ballgame or a Friday night fight on TV. But he hated hanging out in barrooms with people he didn't know and whom he considered lushes. So the new TV was his gift to the family, and to himself. A Zenith, with a 9-inch screen. A beautiful console model with its own cabinet. It would actually fit in the parlor as another piece of furniture. One Saturday afternoon, he had called Pa in from outside to say, "Look, Pa, it's Joe DiMaggio!"

"Who's he?"

"You know who he is!"

"Who doesn't know Joe DiMaggio." Pa was delighted. He was from New York and the Yankees were his team. "Can you fix the picture?"

Now, in '52, after the twins came home, Gerry's sister-in-law Mary moved in for a week or two, sleeping on the couch in the parlor, and she took over Jill, the girl, while Gerry cared for little Jack, so that in effect, Gerry's workload was cut in half during the daytime, till the boys got home after work. Little Nicky would just have to put up with it. He was halfway through his first year in school and he was causing quite the problem as he wasn't getting all the attention anymore. In fact, his father and his Uncle Augie had to pick up some of the slack there. His father took him to see a movie on a Saturday afternoon at the Rialto on Broadway, a western with Kirk Douglas called *The Big Sky*. Uncle Augie took him on a Saturday afternoon to a game at Braves Field between Boston and Brooklyn. Nicky had to promise to be good and do his homework and mind his mother for a whole week to get to do these things on Saturday. In return, some weeknight evenings Uncle Augie took him out in the driveway to throw the ball around and get the new baseball glove he had bought for the kid broken in. The Buick wasn't there anymore so they could use the garage door as a backstop. Nicky loved it when his uncle played ball with him. Now he was getting the attention again. Besides, Nicky didn't have his Papanonni around anymore to pal around with, the dogs were all gone, including his own dog, Daisy, which his grandfather had given him, all because the neighbors, the Sullivans, complained to the police about the barking. And his father never went outside to play with him. He was always too tired from working or busy fixing the slats on the back porch or a leaky faucet or the cement wall at the back of the garden or the broken grape-trellises or cutting the grass or something.

So, every Monday night, at 9 pm, it was time for the whole family to all sit down together and watch *I Love Lucy*. There was Nicky sitting on the floor, the one night in the week he was allowed to stay up this late, Gerry with Jack on her lap, Mary sitting with little Jill squeezed in beside her, Andy and Augie on the sofa, Uncle Patsy come to see his wife, with their kids, Anthony and Linda visiting, and Gerry would laugh and laugh at Ethel and Fred and Ricky and Lucy, and it was the best medicine she could have taken.

One Sunday in the summer of '53 the whole family was getting together in the backyard of 45 Payson Street for one of their regular cookouts. It was already a year almost since Pa had passed away. Everyone was there except, of course, Peggy. Gerry would call her to let her know about a family get-to-gether and then she wouldn't show up, but let her find out you hadn't let her know, and sparks would fly. On this occasion Gene LaStoria had something important he wanted to bring up, but he was pre-empted by his older brother, Patsy, who had an announcement.

It seemed that he and Mary were going to sell their house on Reservoir Ave. in Revere and move to a new development in Peabody and buy something there before Patsy's GI Bill ran out and they lost the chance for a cheap loan. They had a nice three-bedroom picked out on Reynolds Road, a brand new street, right across the road on 114 from the brand-new shopping center going up in Peabody which was supposed to be, if anything, even a bigger deal than the one they had put up out in Framingham, which supposedly was the wonder of the world. It was time to make a move.

"Well," said Gene, "I have some news, too."

And he proceeded to explain that ever since he had worked under Pa at Pappagallo's, up in Milltown, the dream of duplicating what Pappagallo had done, setting up his own shop, and becoming independent, had become his own ambition. "You know, Pa never would take that step. All his life he was dependent on Spritzka, his connection with Spritzka. And look where he ended up—at Pappagallo's in Milltown."

"You mean you wanna open your own shop?" they all said.

"Our own," Gene corrected them. "It's gotta be a family decision. I couldn't do it all on my own without all of you."

They hashed it around and Gene revealed that he had locked up a chance to get a contract with London Fog to make raincoats under license from their brand. Not only that but he had located space to rent in an old mill complex dating way back to the middle of the nineteenth century in Spicket Falls, the little town north of Milltown, between Milltown and the New Hampshire line.

"Actually, it's good, Pat, that you and Mary are moving to Peabody. It's that much closer and the drive to work is a lot less trouble on 114. Right now, you're driving to Pappagallo's from Revere round-trip six days a week for an hourly wage plus Saturday overtime—next month you could be driving to your own place from Peabody for a slice of the pie."

"That soon?"

"Time is of the essence."

Gene was regarded as the brains in the family, the one who followed their father in that respect, by everybody. *If you could not trust your own brother in something like this, who could you trust?*

"Now, I'm not saying you have to come up with any cash up front to put into this. That's already all taken care of. I've been to the bank with the London Fog contract and they're gonna issue a line-of-credit to cover all the start-up costs as far as the equipment we have to buy, you know, the presses and the machines—hey, I don't have to draw a diagram for youz, we been doing this all our lives, haven't we? And we'll get the machines second-hand, don't worry, I know just where. The thing is we're gonna own all this, not work for somebody else who owns everything. All the commitment I need from youz is that you work for your regular wages and we make a go of it together because we're gonna help one another and at the end comes the big payoff. Believe me, we're gonna make a lot of money. And you'll get your share. Andy we could use you, brother, there's a lot of fixtures, tables, benches and what-not we're gonna have to build into this space, it's two floors on a wing of the mill complex on Oxford Street, and, would you believe, the windows on one side look right down on the Spicket Falls itself, it's a beautiful location, big parking lot, loading docks, we can open our own factory outlet, right there, sell straight to the public, I'm telling you, we're gonna make a lot of money."

"Eliminate the middleman, eh?"

"Line our own pockets for a change."

"Gene, you could sell coal to Newcastle."

"What are you gonna call it, Gene?"

"I'm gonna call it *Gigi Sportswear*."

"You gonna name it after Ma?"

"Oh, I like that. It has a ring to it."

"By the way, Gerry, as long as Mary and Pat are moving out of Revere," said Gene, "why don't you sell Pa's house and come work for me?"

"Genie, the deed's not in my name, how can I?"

"You occupy it, don't you? You were the one who stayed here taking care of Ma and Pa. I got my house in Watertown, Patsy's buying in Peabody, Mary, Anna—none of us are gonna object if you wanna sell Pa's house. Listen, Gerry, you don't even need advice of a lawyer, don't go near them, I've got a real estate agent—."

"Or you could hook up with ours, she's good," Patsy and Mary interjected, agreeing with one another.

"And she's right here in Revere," said Gene. "Knows the local market, that's even better. Listen, if I was you—we'll take it through the probate court if we need to—just put it in the hands of the real estate agent, for their 6 percent, they'll handle it for you, you won't have to think about a thing."

"Six percent!" said Gerry.

"And worth every penny," said Gene.

That settled it. Gene, Patsy and Gerry were all on board. Nobody expected Augie to say or do anything but follow along with Gerry in lockstep. He hadn't left his mother's house, now his sister's, since the end of the war. He didn't even have a driver's license and to make a living he worked for his brother Gene. Nobody gave a thought to their divorced sister, Peggy, who had always gone her own way. Anyhow, Peggy was glued rib to rib with Johnny Romano, owner of the Frolics in Revere Beach, and married or not, as hostess of the hottest nightclub on the Boulevard, was certainly not about to go to work for her brother Gene as a stitcher: she might ruin her nails.

Although it was not until almost a year later, in the spring of 1953, that Gerry and Andy were able to finally sign a purchase-and-sale on the house, Gerry had gradually begun to envision what might be and make plans. Finally she was going to have a home of her own. It was going to be her dream house.

Gerry had sold the house on Payson Street for six thousand. Her father had bought it in 1942 for four grand. Inflation since then had sent prices sky-high on everything, but wages had gone up, too, and it was the 1950s now and people had jobs. Gerry paid off the fifteen hundred left on the mortgage and thought she had done well. With $3900 hundred dollars coming in from the sale of the two-family in Revere, she could aspire to a single-home, such as Patsy and Mary had on Reynolds Road in Peabody. But she didn't want that. They had a three-bedroom bungalow, very nice, but new construction, everything plywood and sheet-rock. Gerry wanted something with a little class. She would keep looking.

Gigi Sportswear, the LaStorias' newly-opened family business, was already underway on Oxford Street, in Spicket Falls, right behind the redbrick Fire Station with the square tower, right in the town Square. They had two floors of a wing of the old 19th-century redbrick mill-complex directly overhanging the Spicket Falls itself. Lowell Street carried over the Spicket, where Jan's Diner, the old-fashioned red-and-white-trimmed railroad-car, stood at one end of a tiny bridge. They were in the heart of town.

Come to think of it, Spicket Falls was a nice little town. A population of about only 12,000. It would be like going back to the country, back to a place like Hingham, or Stoughton, where Gerry had grown up. In fact, Spicket Falls was a kind of yesteryear New England town, with fine dining at The Red Tavern (very horse-and-carriage), an MSPCA farm, ballfields, nice little brick schools, very 1920s. It had none of the slums of Milltown, right next door, or, very little, three or four streets at most, right on the Milltown city line. There was the sprawling estate of Searles Castle occupying the middle of the town behind faux-medieval stone walls, and on Broadway, just a few steps below Oxford Street and the family's new place-of-business was the redbrick edifice of the Organ Hall, built specially, in 1909, to house the enormous pipe organ which had originally been meant for the Boston Music Hall. Why look anywhere else but Spicket Falls itself?

Meanwhile, the people who bought the house in Revere exercised their rights and Gerry, Andy, Augie and the kids, all had to pick up and leave by the end of May, in 1953.

In the emergency of being forced out before she was ready, Gerry did the only thing she could, she took a temporary rental, no lease, on Grove Street in Watertown, near her sisters Mary and Anna, where she could get help with the twins, still only a year-and-a-half. Eight-year-old Nicky would have to leave the third grade at the Shurtleff in Revere immediately and go to the Coolidge in Watertown for one month, the month of June, the last month of the school year.

On the Saturday when the furniture truck driven by Tommy DiPrima, who had it on loan for the day, stood out in front of the house on Payson Street, Tommy, Patsy, Gene, and Augie were loading onto the truck Ma's furniture, beautiful pieces Tony LaStoria had purchased, long ago, for his beloved Gigi, a bedroom set and a matching dining-room, bureaus with cedarwood drawers and sea-wave scrolls scalloped into the dark burgundy-stained surfaces and old-fashioned brass fixtures with ring-handles that you picked up with two fingers to pull out a perfectly-balanced drawer; the big bed that had belonged to Tony and Gigi, from the same bedroom set, which Gerry and Andy now slept in; her mother's vanity with the tilt-mirror in the middle and three drawers on each side standing on carved legs.

Andy was destroying Pa's player piano on the tiny front lawn with a hatchet, a saw, and an ax. They didn't have room for it on the truck and nobody else wanted it. These days people had record-players in consoles that fit in your parlor like a piece of the décor. What would they want with a player piano?

Eight-year-old Nicky was running around and crying and wailing that he wasn't going to leave Revere and his friends, Billy and Paul, who lived next door, at No. 47; that he couldn't leave his school and Miss Clark, the principal of the Shurtleff, his beloved old Yankee spinster who had white hair and dressed in blue serge suits and who was his second-grade teacher; that if they tried to take him with them, from *his* house, he would only run away and come back to Revere.

They lived in Watertown that summer, in the house on Grove Street, and, though Nicky complained vociferously about smelling cat's pee in the back hallway, he was compensated by having his cousin Tommy DiPrima living only two streets away, on School Street, and they spent the summer playing baseball at the Hosmer School and raiding the Golden Cookie Factory on Grove Street, across from Nicky's house, on the days when they had free cookies to give away in the bakery-showroom on the first floor.

By the following September, Nicky was starting fourth grade at the Packard, on Winthrop Ave. in Milltown, across from the South Milltown branch Library and the St Patrick's parochial school. Gerry had found a first floor to rent in South Milltown, on Winthrop Ave, at the corner of Boxford Street, which backed onto the South Milltown railroad yards operated by the Boston and Maine. Her landlord, Mr Torrini, and his family lived upstairs. He owned Torrini's Market on South Union. Gerry was still looking for her dream house.

In the summer of 1954 she finally found it, in Spicket Falls, and it was a beautiful, oversized, two-story single home on a corner lot on Elm Street, distinctive because it was a fieldstone house.

It was on the other side of Tower Hill, which began rising around the seedy sections of North Broadway in Milltown. This tremendous hill, which rose directly from the northern banks of the Merrimack River, on the west side of the city, was a counterpart to Prospect Hill, which flanked the river on the east side. On top of Tower Hill was a perfectly level space engineered to hold the city Reservoir. Next to the Reservoir, like a sentinel standing guard, rose the octagonal brick water-tower with its turret-style, grey-shingled roof that looked like a witch's cap. It was this magnificent relic of the 19th century founding fathers of the city which gave its name to Tower Hill. Bordering the parkland which enclosed the reservoir was the stretch of stately homes on the crest of Tower Hill, which were all that remained of the glory of the old industrialist ruling-class of Milltown, capital of the wool trade.

When you came down the steep incline from Tower Hill, after two more streets, you crossed the city line into Spicket Falls; one street over from the city line, on a corner lot on Elm Street, at Glenwood and Elm, within sight of the Tower, stood a fieldstone house.

This house had been built originally to serve as the rectory for the French-Canadian parish of St Therese's, in Spicket Falls.

It had four bedrooms upstairs and four big rooms on the first floor. Around a central hall and stairwell, upstairs there would be a bedroom for Augie, facing northwest, a bedroom northeast for Gerry and Andy, a bedroom of their own for the twins across from their mother and father, and a bedroom of his own for Nicky in the middle of the hall, opposite the stairwell railing, and next to the bathroom, which was not small by any means. Downstairs there were, on one side of the central hall, a parlor and a dining room, closed off for privacy by solid doors, and on the other side, an open den, with a fireplace, from which there were two exits into the kitchen, which was at the rear of the first floor, through the central hallway and through a doorway next to the fireplace in the den. The front door of this fieldstone house opened on Elm Street, but the kitchen occupied the entire back of the house, with a connecting door leading directly into the dining room.

It was obvious the house had been built for privacy, so that four priests could each have their own bedroom upstairs, and so that the priests could talk with a visiting parishioner, in private, in the parlor, on one side of the hall, behind closed doors.

Yet it was the den, with its fireplace, that Gerry fell in love with.

The only trouble with the house was that it was going cheap: a family of French-Canadians, the Rancourts, who were fonder of whisky than religion, had bought it when the parish built a new church with an attached rectory on Plymouth Street. When Gerry walked through the upstairs bedrooms with the real estate agent, she had been so enthralled, by that time, with the den and its fireplace, that she neglected to look inside the closets, only noting that they looked large enough for her.

When she and Andy took possession after the closing, she heard Andy whistle upstairs, and yell out, "Come and look at this!"

Empty whisky bottles were stacked in the closets in every bedroom, from the floor to the ceiling.

It was obvious that the place needed a lot of work. No wonder the asking price had only been 12-five. Gerry got it for eleven flat.

Andy calculated that it was going to take months to get the place ready for his bride. He was going to start by tearing out the kitchen and put in all new cabinets, designed and built by himself. On the outside he had to point all the stonework and repair the shingled second-floor exterior. The property had an apple tree and a fieldstone garage, one-stall; a long driveway opening out on Glenwood Ave at the back of the house, and a wide lawn bordered by quince bushes, a lawn big enough for another house-lot. Two tall, very tall, pine trees flanked the concrete sections of the front walk that led up to a full-width-of-the-house front porch with fieldstone pillars that held up the porch-roof under the second-story bedroom windows. Andy would have to start by re-shingling the roof up on top of the whole house and work downwards from there. It would take time. Andy was now a rough carpenter, and had been accepted as a dues-paying member of the Massachusetts Carpenters' Union—he was working on housing developments every day as a framer, throwing up the skeletons for new homes, for whatever contractors the Carpenters' Union sent him to, so all this work had to be done in his spare time.

Finally there came a Monday evening when Gerry sat down with Andy and Augie and the children in the den.

Andy built a fire in the fireplace, using scrapwood he had collected on the construction lots he worked at. Now that they had moved to the distant suburbs far outside metropolitan Boston, it was necessary for them to have a car of their own, and Andy had bought a Willys jeep station wagon, maroon-colored, boxy, but to him, beautiful because it was utilitarian, nothing like the Chevy four-door sedan family car his brother Alek preferred, and which Alek, flush with the latest UMW contract's raise in wages, bought new, every two years, like clockwork.

Nicky was now in another new school, the Ebenezer Baker, starting the fifth grade in Spicket Falls. The twins were almost three years old. The new season was starting on television and that evening they did something novel, they had their supper in the den. When nine o'clock finally arrived, with the dishes done, the little ones put to bed upstairs, it was time to sit back and laugh at *I Love Lucy.*

Once in a while they would hear a pop-and-crackle as a stick of wood split in the fire. Sparks would scatter and Andy would turn his head to make sure the firescreen was doing its job, and then, even so, he kept getting up to fiddle with and adjust it. Augie sat back in his new white naugahyde recliner. Gerry sat in her adjustable-back wing-chair with the wide fore-arms where she held steady onto a tall glass of cherry Zarex with a bowl of popcorn on her lap. Nicky was sprawled on his stomach in front of the television with his chin propped up on both hands.

Gerry was happy. She was living in her dream house and life was good.

A few days later, Peggy Fabiano pulled up into the driveway behind her sister Gerry's new house, in a station wagon. She and her new friend Otto, who was about twenty years older than she was, had dropped off a load of race-track habitués from the Revere-Everett-Malden-and-Melrose route at Rockingham Park, just over the line in New Hampshire, and then swung back to Gerry's house. While Peggy went up the back porch and into the kitchen, Otto sat waiting in his scratchy tweed suit-jacket in the July heat out in the driveway behind the wheel of the station wagon, which had jump-seats built into the back cargo section so that Otto could fit in two more paying passengers.

Gerry didn't know that her sister was out of work. Peggy hadn't yet told her that Johnny Romano had thrown her out. Gerry thought of her sister Peggy as the untamable black sheep who'd turned in her wooly cloak for a neon-pink cashmere sweater. She didn't yet know that Johnny's 4-bedroom 2-bath Colonial with the 2-car garage and the circular cobblestone driveway hidden behind the tall hedges in Nahant was last week, and this week, for her untamable sister Peggy, was a dingy studio flat with two rickety wooden steps: a beach rental, at the corner of Revere Street and North Shore Road.

Peggy plunked down her pocketbook on the kitchen table, sat down, and said to her sister Gerry, "I've got a bone to pick with you."

BOOK IV

Augie's story

Chapter 19

The Jasco Men

1944 Southampton, England

It was warm, early in the evening of June the 4th, 1944, and to 19-year-old Augie LaStoria, the air was sleepy as the JASCO men boarded LCI 39 in Southampton harbor, on the Channel coast of England.

Corporal LaStoria was a member of the 2nd Platoon of the 293rd Joint Assault Signal Company, called, for short, the 293rd JASCO, a US Army Signal Corps outfit attached for this mission to elements of the 6th Engineers Special Brigade, a highly-trained and specialized group composed of a unit of Combat Engineers, a Demolition Team, an M.P. detachment, and a chemical-warfare unit. There were 45 men in Augie's JASCO platoon, and it looked like about a hundred men or so in the 6th Engineers assemblage, and they each took one half of the main deck of the LCI, the Engineers on the port side, the JASCO men on the starboard.

The boarding was orderly. In fact they had actually practiced and drilled on boarding techniques, so it was all very efficient. But the settling-in, this time, felt different. There was a subtle, barely detectable mood of suppressed tension as the thought in every man's mind, 'This is it,' had to be prevented from passing the lips.

Augie himself was sick and tired of the phrase. He wished to God Almighty he could prevent himself thinking it every thirty seconds. They all knew from the intense sensation of increased readiness and especially tightened security that this was it. The operation for which they had been training assiduously and preparing repetitively for two years now was actually on. Augie's platoon and the engineers had combined to practice their landing together at Slapton Sands in Cornwall, true enough, practiced till they were sick of each other, but this was no rehearsal, this was no drill.

Across the gunwale came a taunting hollering. "All aboard for another Sicily!"

It was the First Division, loading up on LCI 56 right alongside theirs. They had seen action aplenty from North Africa onwards. Augie's outfit was 29th Division, and his whole entire Division were untested rookies.

One of Augie's team members yelled back the 29th's battle cry, which had been pulverized into them on close-order drill, "Twenty-nine, let's go!"

From the other ship, a First Division wise-guy piped up, "Go ahead, Twenty-Nine, we'll be right behind you!"

Augie LaStoria had enlisted at the Boston Army Base on Summer Street in early 1942, a month after Pearl Harbor, with the promise of being given his choice of training; his first choice was the Signal Corps because he liked the idea of the new, the up-to-the-minute, field of electronics. But after he was sent by train to Fort Dix in New Jersey, he was told there was a war on and he would go where he was assigned. *Fair enough,* thought Augie. From there, he was shipped out for 8 months of basic training at Fort Jackson, Carolina, assigned to—Signal Corps School. *Welcome to the Army.*

He was actually quite pleased to find out at Fort Jackson that he had been right about the Signal Corps. It was a helluva lot more than climbing poles and stringing wire. He was trained on Morse Code, a variety of combat radios, switchboard operation, field repair and maintenance, radar, advanced electronics, the list was extensive. He was not bored, and he was glad of that. It was keeping him out of the infantry, and he was glad of that. The last thing Augie LaStoria wanted to be was a grunt.

And the words of his father, Tony LaStoria, on the day Augie had embarked on the train for New Jersey from South Station in Boston, still recited themselves in his mind every day: "Do me one favor, don't volunteer for anything. The Army's got plenty of heroes, they don't need you. Your mother needs you—so come back to us in one piece when this is all over."

Nevertheless, Augie had taken to the Army life. He liked it that you were up early and out in the fresh air. He liked it that every minute of your day was scheduled, you never had to think of what to do with yourself. He liked basic training because it was physical, and he was a physical, six-foot-two young fellow who had been a star halfback in high school before his father made him quit school and go to work to help out the family. But that was all right, too. After all, that was his father and he owed him respect and obedience. It was his father, Augie often thought, who had been his first drill-sergeant. Augie liked guns, and he got that from his father too, who, early on, had taught Augie not to be afraid of a gun, but how to handle it, how to clean it, how to be careful with it so you didn't shoot yourself or somebody else. His father's code had taught him that you never shot something for sport, or out of meanness, that was perverse, you only shot something if you needed it for the table and to feed your family.

Also, Augie liked the Army because it made him a member of a team.

Besides his father, his other mentor had been Coach O'Brian at Stoughton High School. And his team there had been nicknamed the Black Knights—just like the cadets of West Point and their football team, which was practically the most famous, and greatest, in the land. Augie had been a star on that team, the fleet-of-foot, dodgy, rangy halfback, the only time he had ever been a star of anything, and he loved to lay back on his bunk and rehearse in his mind his best moves, the plays he had invented on the spot, on the fly, that made fans jump up in the stands, his teammates crowding around him, looking up to him, wanting to be his pal; the adulation had been intoxicating, and he would lie back and watch it like a newsreel in his mind.

It was funny that his father and Coach O'Brien had not started out as friends, not at all, back when Puffy O'Brien had been Police Chief in Stoughton. But then when political opponents, in other words, most of the town, forced Puffy to resign, he had gone over to the high school instead, to coach three sports, and then Coach had become practically a member of the LaStoria family, famous for never missing one of Ma's Thursday night dinners, praising her meatballs, and especially her sauce, to high heaven. Augie, of course, had always thought he himself was the reason Coach O'Brien was hanging around their house so much.

On the other hand, you could never forget the Indian in the woods, either.

That was Tobias Haskins, who came from the Pocassets of Mashpee, down on Cape Cod, part of the ancient tribe of the Wampanoags of Nantucket and Martha's Vineyard. Haskins was the groundskeeper and forester at the Appalachian Club in Ponkapoag. Augie had first met him when he was only twelve years old. He had ventured into the woods of Ponkapoag by himself, thinking to stalk deer with his Pa's 12-gauge shotgun. Mr Haskins had taken him under his wing and made sure Augie was taught the rules and regulations of deer-hunting, the seasonal restrictions, the licensing, and so on; and finally, Haskins was the man who accompanied Augie on his first kill and taught the boy everything he knew about how to dress a deer.

These three men were the mentors who had shaped Augie into what he was today, and he was hard put to say which was the greatest or most influential, although he did grant his father pride of place.

Augie was always ranking things. Public enemy No. 1 was, of course, Adolf Hitler. FDR was the greatest president the US had ever had. The US Army was, naturally, the best and finest in the world. And England was the country with the worst food in the world.

Augie had first come to England, in September of 1942, along with the rest of the entire 29th Division, on board the greatest, and fastest, luxury ocean liner in the world, the *Queen Mary*.

What other Army in the world did things like that?

When they got there, the 29th Division took over Tidworth Barracks, near Salisbury, which everyone, but everyone, agreed, was the best barracks in England.

Which didn't improve the food any.

Out in the field, when doing an exercise, say, crawling under barbed wire with live machine-gun fire just inches overhead, or a field problem, say, attacking a town or an artillery emplacement, or using satchel charges to blow open holes in barbed wire, they were provided by the local Ladies' Auxiliary with sack lunches, which always consisted of two sandwiches, on brown bread that looked and tasted like cardboard, with, inside of one, a blob of jelly, smack in the middle, and in the other, a slab of greasy pork luncheon-meat sliding off-center.

But they marched all over southwest England, staying outdoors overnight, sleeping in foxholes, using bayonets to probe the ground for hidden mines, utilizing Bangalore torpedoes to neutralize fortified bunkers, executing poison-gas drills, first aid, airplane and tank identification, the use and detection of booby traps, spending countless hours on the firing range. For a year the 29th was the only large American combat aggregation in England, and they became famous, in their own eyes, for being as competent to fight in a war as any green outfit in history.

They were also true believers in the theory that all work and no play made Jack a dull boy. A weekend pass was a coveted commodity. The first place the boys headed was London, obviously. The pay they were making was twice as much as the British Tommies had to spend, and their uniforms were much smarter, according to the English girls. They were young, impressionable, and hungry for a night on the town and all the pleasures they imagined came due to a sailor on shore leave.

Augie tried it once, but for him, it was not a success. Like any clean-minded all-American athlete, he didn't care for waking up the morning after with a swell head. Nor did he smoke cigarettes, despite the fact that the Army was always pushing them on you. No, no. An athlete needed his wind if he wanted to run fast. Nor was he looking for a girl. He loathed the barracks braggadocios and he wasn't looking out to settle for a one-night stand. For him to be with somebody, it had to be special, it had to be sincere, serious, once-in-a-lifetime. Besides, he was on a crusade. He didn't think of himself as especially saintly, or cut out for the priesthood, or anything like that, but on the other hand, he hadn't come here to fool around. If anything scared him, to be honest, it was all those posters with an attractive young woman beckoning over the warning, *She may look clean to you, but* . . . and all those Army training films about VD . . . and all those guys in the barracks whining in conspiratorial whispers about catching a dose of the crabs. Augie could only think *I'll bet they don't write home to their mothers about that* . . . And Augie didn't care what anybody thought about it or said about it, either. He had come to England for a reason, this was the time of his life, he was young, strong, and in the best shape of his life, he had never been more alive, but he was not about to spoil his own life. The fellows all would have liked to tease him about it, but, he was a guy who didn't say much, who kept to himself, stuck his nose in a SCR-609 training manual, and kept his eyes open. Besides, in the boxing ring with the Division contenders, Dick the Bruiser, and Jack the Hammer, and the like, all the popular ones, Augie showed that he was a guy who could take one and give one, and so, you didn't mess around with Augie.

This particular time, when he went up to London, Augie got caught in the wrong place at the wrong time, in a pub where an all-out brawl broke out between American uniforms, between the whites in the joint and the Negroes, and Augie ended up having to explain to the MPs that he was just sticking up for the poor colored boys, and of course, anyway you cut the mustard, he came out on the wrong end of that good deed.

The next time he went up to London on a weekend pass, and there were only two times, he played it safe and spent his time at the British Museum and the National Gallery.

But it was on the baseball diamond that Augie excelled.

He played first base and hit over .350. He was calm and upright at the plate and kept his hands about mid-section with the bat straight up and unwavering, but, though he didn't crouch, he somehow got into motion with a lightning-fast, explosive uncoiling that, a couple of times a week, sent the ball over the trees at the back of centerfield. He was a regular, a starter on the Division team, and he played against major-leaguers, and they all gave him a pat on the ass.

"Keep it up, kid, you're gonna make it."

Now, Augie had been a football star, but he loved baseball. As he was wont to do in all things, he ranked girls third, football second, and baseball first and foremost.

His exploits on the diamond had a secondary effect on him that made Augie smile to himself.

His unit had pulled in guys from all over the map back home and some thought he was not the friendliest fellow they'd ever met. They tended to put it down to his New England reserve, which they took for granted as a cold and frosty facet of the American character, sort of like New Hampshire granite.

That puzzled Augie. He thought of himself as a hot-blooded Italian, a person of passionate likes and dislikes, with an explosive temper, to boot. Anything but reserved. But he poured his passions into baseball. He didn't stop to analyze it, he just did it. He didn't know how to be any other way but to be himself. Augie found that baseball had made him one of ours, a JASCO man. It even revived his old high school nickname, "Moose." *The Moose is loose* became the latest catchphrase. Suddenly Augie had a lot of buddies. And without a doubt he owed his promotion to Corporal to baseball.

Then their time in camp changed. The JASCO men moved on from war games and the target range to an intense period of devising, learning and practicing amphibious assault techniques, combining, for the first time, with strangers, with another unit, from another sphere of specialization, the combat engineers. Both sides were called upon to meld and fuse as one. It was a tense time.

Now it was time to think of other things. Tonight they were shipping out. About time, too. Augie thought there wasn't a man aboard that ship, soldier or sailor, officer or rank and file, who didn't consider this coming day, tomorrow, to be the single most important day of his life.

Augie felt in his bones they were as ready as they could possibly be. He had taken steps to ensure that not only was his body and mind at rest and ready to go, but that his soul, too, was unburdened and free of guilt. This was a Saturday and it felt natural to go to confession and receive, as he had done already so many Saturdays and Sundays as he was growing up. It was the rule in his house and his parents had enforced that. Today when the Catholic chaplain passed through the ranks offering communion, Augie requested that he hear his confession first. He had nothing to accuse himself of but impure thoughts. The priest told him to say three Hail Marys, and later, after he passed through the ranks, he came back with the Host for Augie. Augie received and bowed his head.

After that, he felt better about lifting his head and keeping it held high. He would need it for the coming day. He heard his mother's voice, inside his head, say to him, *A mali estremi, estremi rimedi* and *mantenere il vostro spirito su di voi.*

Now with his back up against the gunwale, sitting on his pile of equipment, in his assigned place in the LCI, Augie pulled his book out of his field jacket pocket.

It was an Armed Forces Edition of *Anthony Adverse,* which his sister Gerry had sent him in a package with a letter.

In the letter she had said that she picked out this book because she remembered taking her little brother Augie when he was 14 years old to the Saturday matinee on a summer day in Stoughton to see the movie of the book, and that she thought he would like it better than *Gone With the Wind.* "Women love that book," Gerry had written, "because they'd loved to be spoiled like Scarlett O'Hara was," but at least *Anthony Adverse* had a main character who was a man. "Besides it has our Pa's name in the title so I know you'll love it."

Augie remembered the movie mostly because Frederic March was in it, and he stood by the rigging of a sailing ship in a storm with his jacket blowing, that's what Augie remembered. But the book was a different matter. It was very, very long. It was so long that the war would probably be over before he finished the book. The Armed Forces edition was so compact that the print was very very small. That was also good, it made you concentrate. Books were good for the troops, Augie believed, because they took you away. At the end of another long day you needed something to divert you. And—they put you to sleep.

Augie was deep into the book, almost halfway through. Anthony Adverse was now a grown man, the Master of Gallegos, a slave-trader in Africa, and he was deeply involved with a mistress called Neleta, who was a mixed-race Spanish woman from Barcelona.

Augie glanced at his buddy next to him, who was reading *Candide,* by Voltaire.

"Any juicy parts in that one, Phil?"

"Nah. You ain't missing nothing. The biggest thing that happens in it is an earthquake in Lisbon. I didn't know they had earthquakes over there. The jacket says it's one of the 100 most influential books ever written, and I quote, but I don't know why."

"You got a ways to go to finish the other 99 and find out."

"I don't know if I'll bother."

"Listen to this."

Augie read from his chapter.

"Matter was about to get the necessary business of its preservation in a certain form accomplished, and the means to this end now violently emanated heat as a preliminary to the process. Anthony was aware of all this. He did not think of it in so many sentences as he stood for a minute looking upon Neleta asleep in the barred moonlight; he apprehended it all as though it were expressible in one deep-breathed word, the exquisite hieroglyphic of which was the form of the woman before him with all her secrets bare."

"How do you like that, Phil? 'All her secrets bare,' huh?"

"Yeah, that's pretty good. Does your mother know you read stuff like this?"

"I gotta have something to confess next time I go."

"It don't count if you're only thinking it."

"That's what you say."

Augie stifled a yawn. They had found out that they were not departing that night, but they didn't know why. All they knew was that they were not going to disembark. No other information was forthcoming.

Augie went to sleep that night assuming the invasion of Europe was still on, just postponed, the same assumption everyone on board LCI 39 was making that night as they slept where they lay, on lumps of packs and rifles, dreaming of earthquakes or women naked in the barred moonlight.

The next morning was Sunday and the Catholic chaplain conducted Mass on the main deck of LCI 39 and all the men from both the JASCO platoon and the 6th ESB detachments took communion, no matter the denomination. The men wanted to make double-sure they were right in the sight of the Lord. After Mass, the chaplain read out aloud General Eisenhower's message to the Allied Expeditionary Force. After that, everyone milled about, asking, *does anyone know when we're shoving off?* When the chaplain, a Captain, who did things the Army way, distributed printed copies of Ike's address, some of the Coast Guard crew who ran the ship went around getting their copies signed by all the olive drabs they could, as if they intended to keep them for souvenirs when this was all over. Somebody shouted, "Get Augie's signature." "Yeah, one of these days it's gonna be worth a lotta money!" "Make him sign it 'The Moose is Loose!'"

As the afternoon wore on the boredom increased, the decks of cards came out, crap games started up against the gunwales, men grumbled about the nuisance of making their 'toilette,' and a rumor started that they were getting set to sail that evening.

No such luck. The skipper eventually was prevailed upon to tell what he had heard.

"The first elements of the invasion fleet went out all right, the slowest ones, but they encountered rough weather out in the Channel and had to come back, so I'm told, 'cause they wouldn't have made it to their destinations in time to be on schedule."

"That's strike one," somebody said.

Strike Two arrived on Monday morning when the first copy of *Stars and Stripes* came aboard and gave everybody something new to grouse about. It seemed that back in the States the Associated Press had sent out a premature invasion report, and in the atmosphere now laden with disgruntlement this news caused more than a little consternation. "Shit and shinola—now the goddam Krauts are tipped off we're coming!" "Yeah—they'll be ready for us!" "Maybe the whole shootin' match'll be called off!"

To change the subject somebody laid out a waterproof on the main deck and got a round-robin game of Texas Roll'em going, with side bets, so that the worriers and the old ladies among them would get their minds taken off of jumping overboard.

Then, in the late afternoon, the skipper, after going ashore for a brief conference, came back with the word that "we're shovin' off at five sharp."

In the wake of that statement, Augie could hear loud and clear the thought-balloons from the Sunday funnies popping out all around him: '*This is it.*'

The next mass hysteria that swept over them was "Please, God, don't let me get sea-sick."

The sailors on board were all too ready to laugh at the landlubbers, who, in turn, craved the chance to deny them the excuse.

The last thing on anyone's mind was the tasks they were supposed to perform tomorrow, which they had rehearsed it seemed like a million times. First, they had to sleep, so they could be fresh and ready to perform tomorrow, and before that, they had to eat, so that they could sleep, and then perform functions, so that they could sleep, and then, hope they could sleep.

Augie slept. He slept like a milkfed infant. He read *Anthony Adverse* and it put him to sleep. He slept safe and sure in the knowledge that he was a member of the best-equipped, best-trained Army in the world, and that the Army Air Force was going to bomb the living creation out of the Germans, and that, in any case, where he was going, which was code-named Omaha Beach, the only opposition he would have to face was going to come from a second-and-third-rate outfit called the 716th Infantry, which was composed of Polish slave labor and Russian prisoners-of-war, who, most likely, could be counted on to throw down their weapons at the first opportunity of surrendering; at least, this is what he had been told, and why in the world would he doubt it, since he had received this information in briefings from officers who got it from US Army Intelligence, the best in the world.

And, secondly, the B-17s who usually bombed industrial targets on the continent in daylight runs so awe-tingling that they covered the sun and made you want to cover your ears, those were the bombers, the best bombers to be had by anybody anywhere, that were going after whatever bunkers and big gun emplacements the Germans had on Omaha, with precision bomb-sights—so the opposition was going to be obliterated before Augie had to land, and, for his convenience, they would also leave a lot of craters on the beach for him to duck into when he needed to find cover, just in case anyone was left who had a mind to take a potshot at him. *The sky-jockeys were gonna dig Augie his foxholes for him!*

Thirdly, there was the Navy. And not just the US Navy; they had Brits and Frenchmen, even Norwegians; all first-class sailors, not to say, gunners; and the naval bombardment, which was scheduled to sweep the beach after the Air Force finished their run, would culminate in a rocket-ship barrage of what was called LCTR rockets, which were going to finish off anything left alive and moving after the B-17 attack.

Lastly was the fact that (and this was undisputed, since Augie could see it with his own eyes) once they got out of port, long before he thought of going to sleep, on that Monday evening of June the 5th, the armada setting out to cross the English Channel was so vast it stretched out further than the eye could see, beyond the horizon. Since they were under British double summer time, twilight lasted forever. Like every other man on board LCI 39, Augie could see it, as it gradually faded into the fog of night: they were sending 40,000 men of the most highly-trained, highly-specialized troops in the world, men like himself and his JASCO comrades and the combat engineers, the Navy demolition men, the M.P.s, the chemical-warfare boys: 40,000 men were going to land on Omaha Beach, to be faced with, manning the defenses, Intelligence reckoned, one battalion—of about 800 men.

It was just like General Eisenhower always said, and had said, that time he visited Augie's camp at Tidworth, "Nothing's sure in war, boys. Unless you're gonna send a battalion against a squad."

Augie woke up about three in the morning.

It was a little spooky the way he had sensed a shift in the motion of rockabye lulling beneath him, and an audible alteration in the sonorous, smooth accompaniment of the ship's engine.

He felt like a bird waking up on a branch. Suddenly alert.

They were floating now and he realized they had arrived at what the briefings had referred to as the transport area, their destination. Checking his watch, he thought, *on time.*

Nothing to do now but wait.

He had slept with his clothes on, and now he tried to exit his bunk without waking the other sleepers. He went up on deck as quietly as he could and located his stack in the pre-dawn darkness and sat down on it. There were several of his comrades already there, shadows like himself.

Augie knew they wouldn't start in to the beach until about 0730. At 0630 the first assault wave was scheduled to hit. The first wave would comprise two battalions of the 116th Regiment of the 29th Division, on Augie's end of the beach, the right flank, or west end, under the cliffs of the Pointe-du-Hoc. This landing was elaborately organized down to precision detail. The first wave assault teams were organized into the 116th RCT, or Regimental Combat Team. They would be led in by amphibious tanks, which could swim onto shore wrapped in flotation gear, a Navy demolition team, and Army amphibious engineers. Assault teams of infantry would cover every inch of the beach with M-1s, .30-cailber machine guns, BARs, or Browning Automatic Rifles, bazookas, 60mm mortars and flamethrowers. The Army and Navy demo-men would blow lanes in the steel and concrete obstacles and place markers for the landing craft to follow, to keep the successive waves from hitting Teller mines the Germans had attached to the obstacles. All this had been mapped out in a diagram of linear boxes with vertical and horizontal lines on the big white easel-mounted demonstration-boards at briefings, and gone over endlessly. Augie had not only memorized it all, but noted in particular that, curiously enough, LCI 39 was all alone, in a wave by and of itself, scheduled to hit the beach at 0810.

That meant that there were 4-1/2 hours to go till they would start to head in at 0730.

Augie relaxed, secure in the knowledge that everything was going to be 'softened up' for him by the time he got there. He took a peek over the rail, but there wasn't much you could make out. The ship lazily rode the swells up and down. Everything quiet. No sound of airplanes. That was a good thing. That meant the Luftwaffe hadn't detected them. Riding out there in the dark was a big blob of blackness. Augie realized from the size of it that it could only be the invasion fleet command ship.

He withdrew his head. He sat down again. Nobody was talking. The fleet was under orders to maintain radio silence. The very idea insinuated itself into your head. Nobody wanted to say the wrong thing. Nobody wanted to tell a joke that fell flat. Nobody wanted anyone asking them, how are *you* doing? They waited and they watched.

Once in a while an officer came by and whispered, "Make sure you've double-checked your equipment."

Augie would pat himself down to make sure he was all there, no parts missing, and then go through his checklist. He was sitting on top of his SCR-300 field radio. It weighed thirty-two pounds, was wrapped in a waterproof casing, and had straps, so you carried it as a backpack. Augie's assignment for the landing was to accompany Lt Weatherby of the combat engineers team wherever he went so that the Lieutenant could simply turn and pick up the receiver on the SCR-300, which had a reliable range of 3 miles, and get orders or information or talk to upper echelons, anything he wanted. Augie also carried a letter-H shaped spool of 1350 feet of military field phone wire which weighed forty pounds. That had a shoulder-strap attached to the DR-8-B spool with its RL-39 reeling tool spliced onto the strap. The reeling tool was important because it had a handle and rods, U-shaped, that fit into the spool-holes so that you could actually run with the spool and pull it behind you to get the wire laid out quickly. Then there was his M-1, on another shoulder strap, and encased in an oilskin bag to keep it dry till you needed it. Then there was his musette-bag and his pouch with four percussion grenades, his ammo belt with snap-compartments stocked with .30-caliber ammo—altogether, Augie was hoisting 85 or 90 pounds of stuff, but he was a big kid, as he said to himself, and of course, he patted his head and his helmet was there. All the guys on board kept their helmets on at all times because the easiest way on this ship to lose your helmet was to take it off your head. Last of all, he patted *Anthony Adverse* in his field-jacket pocket. And of course, over the top of everything, his Mae West, although he couldn't imagine why he would need that. He fully intended to step out and stroll through wavelets, at most, maybe up to his instep, and step right onto the beach.

By 0830 they would be proceeding up the draw riding in jeeps heading to the 116th RCT objective of Vierville, getting ready to lay field wire and start installing switchboards in trenches and foxholes.

It seemed to be getting lighter out. The wind was picking up, too, pretty cold.

About 0530, just when it was scheduled to be low tide on the beach, they heard the drone of approaching aircraft.

After this, there wouldn't be anymore element of surprise. It was hard to sneak up on the Germans with 700 B-17s roaring overhead.

At 0545 the naval bombardment began, from several large warships, if Augie could tell anything from the sound. Things were heating up and the noise level increasing—it wasn't quiet anymore.

Then at 0625 it suddenly hushed.

Checking his watch in what was now full daylight, Augie realized that the first wave was going in right about . . . *now*.

Aboard LCI 39 they still had another hour to wait before it was their turn.

Augie went to the head, he waited in line, he came back and sat on his pile; he waited.

The hour went crawling by. They were still in the transport area. He wouldn't know anything by looking over the rail. They were still a mile and a half out in the water. You could hear the sound of battle drifting out to where they were, mostly puffs of explosions, nothing that sounded like small-arms fire, and when he did look, the shoreline was becoming obscured by a low-riding cloud-bank of smoke that was peeling off to the left at a brisk pace that looked pretty windy. So you really couldn't tell what was going on.

Then the engine started up, they circled, and swerved and to Augie, it felt just like a halfback swooping in to hit the hole in the line.

They were picking up speed, quickly. These things can scoot, Augie thought. Already they were probably halfway there.

To his surprise, Augie saw waterspouts spring up over the top of the rails, out in the water around them. Water colored black.

Christ, they're shooting at us.

Lt Weatherby was looking toward shore. Suddenly, he spotted the church spire of Vierville. He shouted, "Where the hell's the Air Corps!"

Augie took a peek and saw the same thing and realized they had been told that all such landmarks would have been, by now, no, long before this, obliterated by the preliminary bombardments, and they had been cautioned not to expect them to be there to use to orient themselves.

They hit a sandbar and came to an abrupt stop.

At the start of the run-in everybody on board had stood up and assembled into two files. The 6th ESB teams were lined up on the left for the port ramp. Augie's platoon was pointed to the starboard ramp in the right side of the bow. Augie had his backpack radio on, he had his thumbs hooked through the shoulder strap on the left, his rifle, and the strap on the right, his 40-lb wire-spool. The winch motors on board started whining as the ramps went down and the whole ship jerked backwards from the anchor starting to pull them off while everybody was still starting to jump down the ramps and somebody was yelling "For Chrissakes, get off the ship!" when a shell hit the port ramp vaporizing Lt Weatherby and six men behind him, leaving a gaping hole in the bow, smoking with tendrils of cordite-smelling smolders.

Augie was running down the starboard ramp and then through the instep-high water-swirls he had anticipated. He wasn't looking around but somehow he was aware of body parts floating, and the red color of the water. He was looking up to where he thought he was going, a gap in the swirling smoke that suddenly parted to reveal about 100 yards away dark blobs of huddled soldiers crouching down at what appeared to be the seawall, which they had been told would have been penetrated by now, penetrated with openings blasted out by the engineers, along with the swamp-ground of barbed wire and mines behind it, which they had previewed in aerial photographs.

Augie was still looking up and studying this when he stepped off into a hole and there was nothing there to put his foot on and everything fell away underneath him.

A drowning man doesn't think. He thrashes. He flails. He knows he is drowning and he panics. Augie threw off his rifle first, then his wire-spool. They were dragging him down. He hadn't touched bottom yet and he was unable to propel himself upward. He knew he had to get rid of them, his helmet, too. He punched his Mae West to inflate it when suddenly he was propelled sideways by what felt like a hand, an enormous hand, shaped like a paddle, or a dust-pan, which just swept him aside to his left–he felt he was sweeping left and his body was trailing out behind him, when his head popped above the surface.

Immediately a crashing surf-roller swept over his head and submerged him again, and again he was swept away on a current, irresistible, powerful, and he was struggling to get rid of the 35-lb radio on his back and the Mae West was impeding him; he couldn't breathe, he was hoping the Mae West was going to bob him up to the surface again; he needed air and a thousand pounds of fear was penetrating his lungs and choking him.

All this time he hadn't opened his eyes except the single time he broke the surface and automatically gulped air, but now he felt a hand, a human hand, brush his back, between the radio and his back, and slip in there, and yank him up out of the water, using the radio for leverage.

Augie gasped and looked at a man he didn't know.

The man was hanging on to the steel upright on a C-element gate-obstacle. Behind his shoulder Augie could see a Teller-mine was pasted to the top of the gate.

The man said, "I think the water's about six feet deep here. Can you swim?"

Augie said, "Yeah."

"Well, we can't stay here. Sooner or later they'll target us. I'll go first."

The man dove head first into the water and broke the surface with a powerful arm stretching out as if he thought he could pull the shore to himself, when a ripple of tracers and spouts tip-toed across his back, his head went up as his back arched into an inverted bow, and then his head hit the water face-first and he sank from view.

In spite of what he had just witnessed Augie knew that his only chance was to do the exact same thing so he slipped off his radio and he then dove into the water in the same place as the other man, thinking, *odds are, they can't hit the same spot twice, if luck is with me.*

He dove and he kicked and he kept his head under with his hands palms together and tried to swim underwater as long as he could. When he broke surface again he saw water-spouts kick up several yards away. He then dove again and he now thought his best odds were to try a dead man's float. He reasoned that the Germans wouldn't waste the ammunition, efficient bastards that they were. He also was certain now that an undertow had taken him left of his landing zone, which was the Dog Green sector, and he might as well forget about his mission, all his equipment was gone, he had no rifle, not even a helmet, he thought *it must have been the undertow, that's what saved me, plus that guy, whoever he was;* it was time to think about saving himself. *If only I can get to shore.*

He tried the dead man's float and he found it worked. *I was right. There's a current carrying me left. So, I'm heading eastward.* He felt his body rise and fall with the swell and ebb of the rollers, from trough to peak, that were heading inevitably, eternally shoreward, and would be, with or without him, *forever and ever, amen.* If he did nothing at all, the breakers should carry him in.

He placed his cheek on the water and let his head sink, with his face turned away from the shore, till one nostril was left above the water, and he breathed through that, and kept his mouth shut, for what he surmised was the first time in his life, and he felt the rise and swell of each roller, and he felt, each time, he was fluttering like a leaf, closer and closer in. He had his right eye open above the water but who could tell that? Besides, he might have died with his eyes open, *stuck open,* he'd heard of that, he didn't know, *probably I'm going to find out, and soon,* and then—his foot touched sand.

He sank himself under with one big gulp and crawled for his life along the bottom until there was no more water left and there, six or eight feet away, was the seawall, with the crouched forms of men in various assorted postures of agony and desperation, all of them his buddies, now.

He crawled up on his hands and knees along the sand and looked around like a dog hunting for a spot in the kennel to lie down.

"You all right, buddy?"

"Yeah."

"We thought you was a goner."

"I was just play-acting."

"Huh."

"I didn't want to get shot."

"You mean you ain't been shot yet?"

"No. You?"

"Yup. Got me in the hip. That's why I didn't try to help you in."

Somebody else said, "Well, you made it."

Another voice chimed in. "Welcome to shit crik."

Augie said, "Well, we can't stay here."

He said it because someone had said it to him, but a moment ago, it seemed. Nevertheless it was true. The enemy had mortars and they were using them. What few words had passed between Augie and the others had been shouted because the noise level was terrific, even if the man was right next to you. There were incessant machine guns, 88s, 75s, mortars, which descended with a vicious howling scream that you thought *had to be* headed straight for you.

"What outfit you guys from?" Augie yelled.

"Every outfit there is," somebody shouted.

"What about you?"

"Signal Corps."

"Halleluljah, a radioman. Now we can dial up Ike and tell him the plan didn't work."

Somebody said, "Anybody got a smoke? Mine are all wet."

Somewhere further along down the wall somebody screamed, "Medic!"

This is hopeless, thought Augie. He put his back up against an inch or two of seawall and then he spotted a BAR floating in the water. He might not be getting anywhere with these men but he could get himself a weapon.

Augie scrambled into the water and brought the BAR in.

"I'm gonna clean this thing," Augie said. "Anybody got a waterproof?"

"There's a dead man here, you can use his field jacket."

"Might as well."

Augie was thinking, *somebody's gotta show some initiative,* although he also thought he wasn't gonna get anywhere with these men as a mere corporal.

At that point a 2nd looie came crouching along.

"What's your name, soldier?"

Augie said, "Corporal LaStoria, sir."

"What outfit you with?"

"Signal Corps, 293rd JASCO."

"Well, my name is Armstrong. Nice to meet you."

"Nice to meet you, sir."

Augie could tell that Armstrong had an accent. He was some kind of Southern gentleman, maybe Louisiana, Mississippi, Texas?

"You ever done this before?" Armstrong asked.

Augie knew he didn't mean cleaning a BAR. The lieutenant seemed a little anxious. Augie said, "No."

Armstrong said, "Me neither. Guess it's that way with the whole 29th."

"Yeah."

"Well, we gotta get started somewhere."

"I guess so, sir. Between you and me, sir, I'm glad you're here. I wouldn't get anywhere with these men as just a corporal, you know?"

Armstrong said, "Listen. I need you. I'm going to round up five or six guys who aren't injured and I'll be back. You stay right here."

The lieutenant started to crawl off, but he came back. "What did you say your name was?"

"LaStoria. Corporal."

"Okay. Stay right there. You got anything else besides that BAR?"

"Some .30-caliber ammo and 4 grenades."

"Okay, we gotta find some ammo for the BAR."

The lieutenant departed.

Augie checked his watch, and said to himself, *0830.*

He hoped to hell that lieutenant was coming back. He didn't favor sitting here waiting for a mortar to sight him in. Not after making it this far. Not after seeing the man who saved him a minute before lose his life a minute later. And the hell of it was they all had orders not to stop and help a fallen comrade. That's not your job, they'd been told. We got medics for that. You keep going. And Augie had kept going. He hadn't stopped to help the man who helped him. And the hell of it was here he was up shit crik like the guy said sitting soaking wet still dripping and he could bite it any minute and now he didn't know if he'd done the right thing or not.

The 2nd looie came back. "Okay, LaStoria—Corporal. I got the ammo—helmet for you, too. Here's the deal. We can't all bunch up together, so—I'm going over that wall first. We reconnoitered a little and we figure there's a bunker right up above us with an 88 or something, maybe a French 75, but it's sighted down the beach, and they can't see us from here, because they got concrete wing walls facing seaward protection. So, I used to be pretty good at tracking rabbits. I figure I can spot a trail through the minefield over the wall. There's got to be one, however tiny, for the Germans to use. I got some ammo here, you give me the BAR. I go over the wall, you watch, and when I'm set up with a firing position, I'll wiggle a bush. You watch over the wall where I've went and stay in my same tracks. Then you and the others creep up on their blind side and when you hear the BAR open up, that's your signal to rush them and dump in your grenades. I think it'll work."

"We gotta do something," said Augie.

The lieutenant went over the wall, which at that point was about four feet high. Augie peered over as much as he dared. He said to himself, *I gotta give him credit. He's got balls to do a thing like that. Glad it ain't me.*

The lieutenant spotted the path he was looking for and crawled on his stomach the way they all had been trained, probing the ground in front of him with a bayonet. Augie watched to make certain he knew he could follow the same route. It looked pretty easy as Armstrong's crawl was going to leave a distinct trail, like an alligator bellying himself through tall grass. The area he covered was about a hundred yards of scrub-bush and low-lying swampy ground before you got to the bluff, the escarpment they had all examined in the photos. That went straight up, too steep for vehicles, but not for a single climber. It was up at the top, on the high ground, looked like about a hundred feet up, where the Germans had tactically placed their artillery and machine-gun emplacements to give them clean sightlines for both plunging fire and grazing fire. They had the whole beach covered and the Americans were easy prey. *Fucking animals*, Augie thought.

The bush wiggled. Augie went over the wall.

As he had thought, it was not difficult to make it through the swamp following Armstrong's marked-out path. Augie saw four other men dump over the wall behind him. They all were armed. Augie had no rifle but he figured he was there to use his grenades. When he got to the bluff, he made sure to use the wing walls to shield himself from sight. As he climbed he could see that they must be at the west end of the strongpoint around the Vierville draw, which meant that eastward, the Germans weren't looking back in his direction. Pretty smart. *We're picking off the last trooper in line. After that, we'll get the rest from the rear.* The only concern Augie had was to use the natural outcroppings on the climb to conceal himself from any German machine guns further west of him, or east of him, on the far side of the draw. He only hoped they were too busy concentrating on Americans in the water or on the beach or along the seawall. From up here Augie could see they had plenty of targets there—too many.

Everybody was in position. The other men were behind Augie, backing him up. He was closest to the roof covering the opening of the artillery piece inside the bunker. He could feel the whole mountain shudder went the gun went off. *Jesus— must be an 88. Sounds like a bomb going off in the London tube.*

The BAR opened up. *Good boy, Armstrong. Give it to 'em.*

Augie clung to the cliff with his cheek pressed up against it, hoping like hell that Armstrong's aim was true and that he himself didn't get any chips flying in his face off the rock or concrete.

He inched closer to the opening. He had a grenade in his left hand ready to pull the pin. He was sprawled against the incline with his legs spread-eagled. *If they see me up here exposed like this they could shoot off my balls.*

A white flag appeared, waving from the opening, about a foot from Augie's left hand. *The Germans in the bunker were surrendering!*

The BAR stopped firing, and Armstrong stood up, tall and lean, and waved his hand at them to come on out.

The Germans then shot him between the eyes.

Lt. Armstrong crumpled and slipped down, like a bunched-up curtain that just slipped off the rod.

Fucking Jesus.

Augie inched forward and, pulling pins, he poured all four of his grenades through the slit-opening of the bunker, as fast as he could.

Too late! Too late!

He slipped down and the next man behind him did the same with his grenades.

Augie was kicking up rockdust as he propelled himself toward Armstrong's position, which was screened with scrub-brush. He didn't care if he fell off the side of that cliff, he was going to get that BAR.

He got Armstrong's BAR and he used it to pour fire into the mouth of that bunker, the first shots he had ever fired in anger in his life.

They were all dead inside there already from a dozen grenade blasts, but Augie didn't care.

The BAR shaking and shuddering in his hands kept repeating, *too late, too late.*

Chapter 20

Homecoming

Technical Sgt. Augie LaStoria of the 293rd JASCO, 116th Regiment, 29th Division of the victorious United States First Army, after his discharge, in late July of 1945, was not able to convince himself that he was really, *really* home again until the moment he was in Revere and turning the corner from Beach Street onto Payson Street for the long walk down to No. 45.

Payson Street was perfectly flat and level, till the dip all the way at the end down to the brickyards. He remembered that. Passing houses on both sides of the street, he took his time, walking slowly. He wanted to gauge their familiarity. Was this the street the way he remembered it, the way he had so often tried to picture it? There was Stuart's house, and, ah, here's Sullivan's, next door to us, across the vacant lot. The vista of the back of the Shurtleff, the redbrick elementary school with the granite cornerstone that read 1898, opened up, directly across the street from Augie's house; the Shurtleff was buried on a level below Payson Street because the front of the school faced School Street, but what was this? *The old dirt playground behind the back of the school, that used to be here, at the bottom of the embankment, dipping down from the Payson Street sidewalk? was completely paved over with tar! . . .*

It was an unaccustomed luxury to walk slowly. To stop and think. To take things in, without being preternaturally alert for danger. He had been in an awful hurry for 335 consecutive days after D-Day, except at the end of June, in '44, when they finally captured Cherbourg.

The Germans had done their indecent worst to destroy the port and make the city uninhabitable before they fled or surrendered or were captured. The assignment for Augie's unit, after they had fought their way up the whole Contentin peninsula, had been to work to restore the communications infrastructure in Cherbourg so that the French civilian population and the new occupiers, our side, could utilize a port badly needed to re-supply a stalled campaign.

When the breakout came, and the drive through Northern France to the German heartland rapidly accelerated, Augie and his unit were kept constantly close to the leading edge of the wave. The high command, the middle echelons, and the lower levels all combined to create an urgent demand for secure, telephonic communication lines. The Signal Corps was sorepressed to keep up.

Augie and his comrades in the 293rd JASCO worked every single day seven days a week without a single day off, especially when the Red-Ball Highway was established, and it didn't matter if they never caught up on First Army assignments—they were already way behind on restoring the French, and German, civilian systems, which turned out to be their job, too.

Augie remembered every one of those 335 days, all the way from the Normandy beachhead to Pilsen, Czechoslovakia: especially the first one, when he crawled out of the English Channel onto Omaha Beach.

But did he remember his own street back home?

With his hand on a picket fence, he paused at a house to his right. The next house had a chain-link fence around an undersized lawn. The Sullivans' was the next house. Then came the vacant lot, and after that, his house.

It all seemed so small. So narrow. Still and quiet. It was like looking at a miniature inside a glass. Payson Street didn't seem as long as he remembered it used to be.

Opposite the vacant lot, diagonally, was the schoolyard. And the squarish redbrick two-story school-building with its slate-grey pitched roof, in the Victorian manner. *It's summer, school's out.*

With its staid back porch, painted butter-yellow, the only dab of color in the midst of dull brick and dour windows, the school was a relic from a previous century. *Long before I was born.* But the school was not a ruin. It was intact. The second storey, the roof, *isn't caved in.*

All the time I was away, kids came here every day. To play on the swings. Climb the jungle-bars. How? Did ordinary life go on and on as if nothing was happening?

How could that be?

I can't accept it.

I couldn't accept it on the train from New Jersey, I couldn't accept it on the streetcar from Maverick Square.

Nothing has changed.

They just went on. Oblivious.

Around the corner of Tree Valley Road, up ahead, a car came nosing, creeping, because of the steep incline of Tree Valley Road coming to an abrupt stop where it joined the dead level of Payson Street.

Augie registered the sensation as odd because it occurred to him, *now, if that had been a tank . . .*

His house was No. 45, on the right, the tall two-family with shingles painted brown and all the trim cream-colored, facing the school across the street, to his left. Because of the vacant lot, Augie could see the entire house, front to back, in profile, as he approached. Had it shrunk? *Didn't it used to be so big?*

The driveway had a strange car parked in it. His father's customary Buick wasn't there.

At least he thought he remembered Pa drove a Buick, before the war.

But those memories had all been replaced.

He wished he could turn his nerves off prickly alert. His eyes were scanning everything, taking note. Yes, he wanted to remember this, this moment, so looked-forward to, so longed for, yet there was so much that he couldn't forget that was blocking it, adamantly.

Gigi's flower-garden. The colors were vibrant, un-smudged, insouciant, free of fear, full of innocence. Tended by his mother's hand, her loving self-expression. Her flowers painted a portrait of the self that dwelt within her, her real self, her heart and soul.

Augie hoped he wasn't going to cry. He hoped he wasn't going to make a blubbering baby out of himself.

He remembered the day they had found out the war was over. He was in a communications trench when he heard the news. There were a lot of Americans crying in Pilsen, Czechoslovakia that day. Some of the guys shot themselves, they were so happy.

A lot of those Joe-jerks did stupid stuff like that. They got drunk they got laid they got VD. Then they were mad when they weren't allowed home.

But he had to stop thinking about all that.

He had to get on with his life.

He now dreaded the moment he could no longer forestall, and moved up the driveway between the parked car and the house, until he saw his mother in the kitchen window, timidly waving with a handkerchief in her hand.

Augie flung his duffel bag down, charged up the back steps and burst through the screen door, the hall door, into the kitchen. His mother had swiveled herself in her chair to receive him.

He fell to his knees and buried his face in her lap, and the tears flowed freely, from her, and from him.

"Mamma!" Augie managed to say through clenched, wet lips twisted grimly downwards. "Non si sa quante volte ho pensato a te."

"Lo so," his mother said, sobbing, "ma ora sei a casa con me—mio bambino, mio bambino prezioso." Then she lifted his head and said, "Stand up and let me look at you."

Heads were crowding through the door from the dining room, looking over shoulders. Soon Augie was wrapped in arms, hands and fingers, pulling and tugging from every direction. They all wanted to touch him. They all wanted to embrace and kiss him and every face was wet. The whole family was there, Mary, Anna, Peggy, his brother Gene, home from

Italy, Gene's wife Celia and their little girl, Joanne, Patsy's wife Mary with her four-year-old, Anthony, and Augie could see, through the door, his sister Mary's kids, Tony and Geraldine, sitting in the parlor, waiting politely, their hands folded on their laps, being minded by their father, his brother-in-law, Charlie, the whole family except for Patsy, who had not been discharged yet and was still in Germany.

"Where's Gerry?" said Augie.

"She's in San Diego," they chorused, all laughing through their tears.

"Eh—the war's still on in the Pacific," somebody said.

"But what's she doing in San Diego?" said Augie.

"She got married! Her husband's in the Navy! Didn't she write to you?"

"I've got letters in my duffelbag. I still haven't opened them."

"She was so excited," somebody said, excitedly, but then faces fell, as they started looking at each other—*he didn't open our letters?*

"Where's Pa?"

"Not home from work yet!" voices bubbled again.

"Sit down, sit down—come on—we're gonna eat!"

"When's the last time you had a home-cooked meal?"

"We've been waiting for you all day!"

"We're starved!"

"Whose car is that?"

"Mrs Nelson, upstairs—Pa's tenant—her Pontiac. She drives!"

"Boy, you got a lot to catch up on!"

Oh, no. Was that the wrong thing to say?

Voices all talking at once. "How was your trip?" *That was a safe enough question.*

"I took a little ride on the battleship *Nevada,* out of Le Havre, courtesy of the Navy. But I must say the accommodations weren't as luxurious as on the way over when we took the *Queen Mary.*"

"The Queen Mary!" they all said at once.

"You never told us that!"

"Listen to him! Talks like a Limey now."

"Didn't you get any of my letters?"

Brother Gene interposed, "Maybe that information was restricted."

There's a lot the boys know that we're not entitled to.

"Listen to the voice of authority," the cynical Peggy interjected.

"Shut up, you," said Mary.

"Show some respect to your brother," said Anna.

It's good to be home. It's good to be home. Dear God, it's good to be home . . .

They dried their eyes and they sat down and Mary and Anna started serving. Augie had been outprocessed at Fort Dix in New Jersey and called home to let them know he was on the way from there. Although it was Saturday, he was going to get the traditional home-cooked Sunday dinner of his foxhole dreams. First came the soup with shredded meatballs floating amongst flat noodles—"we're still on meat ration!" The next course was the macaroni dish laden with his mother's tart garlic sauce, this time sweetened with raisins she had dried herself on the window sill, from last summer's grape bounty in Pa's arbor out back of the garage. *Home.* Next came veal and pork chops, roast beef—"I thought you were still on rationing!" "You know your father, he gets his meats from Fabrizio's the butcher in the North End, just like he used to when nonno was alive!"

Home.

Everyone kept interrupting one another, it was impossible to talk with your mouth full, everyone had so many questions they wanted to ask, but they didn't ask them, they hesitated, they didn't dare, they wondered if they should, *better not, we'll wait, if he wants to tell us, he'll tell us, I don't want to spoil this for him.* Meanwhile, whenever his glance chanced to land on his brother Gene, an unspoken agreement seemed to pass between them, through their eyes, without having to say a word—*we'll talk later.*

"Why's Pa working on Saturday?"

"War contracts, Augie."

Nobody wanted to say what they thought. *Pa and Peggy can't be in the house at the same time.*

It wasn't fair. The boys have been through such an ordeal. What do they care who isn't talking to who? They should be spared. *They've seen troubles enough of their own.*

Augie announced, when the salad arrived, "First thing I'm gonna do—have a nice hot bath for myself—then I'm gonna sleep for a month—then I'm gonna get up, and—well, I don't know what I'm gonna do!—we'll just have to see!"

He pushed himself back from the table.

"I gotta let my belt out!"

"You came home so skinny! Same as your brother Genie. Both of you."

"You look wonderful!"

"Never better!"

"We're gonna have to fatten you up!"

Augie and Gene never did get a chance to have their little talk.

When August the 6th arrived, the day they first heard of a place called Hiroshima, the shock was almost as deep as Pearl Harbor, or the day FDR died.

But the sense of relief was also immense.

Now the war's bound to come to an end.

But it took another three days, and Nagasaki, and still no surrender.

Hirohito's a madman. They're all out of their minds. The Atomic Bomb . . .

Finally the never-ending war was over, and Augie could begin thinking about other things—*if he could.*

He still hadn't had a chance to get together with Genie. Nobody knew when Patsy was going to get his ticket home. Pa was working at the shop at No. 10. Some things were eternal—*and some things had to change.*

But first of all he didn't know what to do with himself. There were lotsa things he wanted to do, but try to pick one!

They were all giving him a wide berth. Nobody was saying, hey, it's time to get up, come on, Pa's leaving, get in the car, time to go to work, you don't wanna make him be late.

That first evening when Augie returned, and he had just pushed back from the table, and in walked Pa, and Augie stood up. They embraced, they held each other as if they would never let go, and Pa said, "You're home. You're home. There is a God. My prayers have been answered."

It was Pa who buried his face in his son's chest, Augie was that much bigger than he was.

Augie said, "Pa—there were so many who didn't make it."

He said it in Pa's ear, for only him to hear.

He couldn't help it—it was like the truth slipping out another door.

Everything else he said that night—was covering up, just—hot air—just passing the time of day—all to save their feelings.

From what they didn't know that they didn't want to know.

Or did they?

Now as he lay there thinking, do I wanna get up or not? he felt nauseous.

He tiptoed out to the kitchen.

It was September and his sister Anna was minding their mother. It was her turn this week. Anna was not exactly happy. She wanted to be happy, her husband Tommy was sitting right there, just home from Europe and the Army motor pool last week, and Anna did not want to spend a minute apart from him, so she had brought him along with her that morning on the long trolley-and-subway trip from Watertown. This routine of Gerry being away in California was wearing thin. Just to get from Watertown to Revere you had to go all the way in-town from Harvard Square and change for the subway to East Boston, then take a trolley from Maverick Square all the way out to Revere. They didn't have a car, Tommy wasn't working yet.

"Why is the light so bright?"

Anna looked up from the sink. Her brother Augie's face was twisted up with hurt.

He said, "Stop making all that noise."

Offended, Anna put down a dish in the rack, carefully.

Augie turned and went back to his room, shutting the door in their faces.

"What's wrong with him?" Anna said to her husband.

Tommy shrugged.

When this had happened two or three times, and Pa witnessed an episode while he was in the house, he became worried and sent for Dr Graham, at the bottom of the street.

Dr Graham came and he said it sounded like it was migraine, take two aspirin, and call him in the morning.

Augie was baffled. "I never had this before. Why, all of a sudden?"

He noticed that he would start to feel different a couple of days before. You know, lethargic and uninspired. He might get a sore neck waking up in the morning. He was sure that was all there was to it—he was sleeping the wrong way. But on other occasions, no sore neck, but instead, a fit of yawning—and then would come on the pulsating waves of pain on one side of his head. It would go on for hours. It was debilitating. He had to reduce all noise and light. Sometimes it settled right behind his eyes. He would close the door to his darkened bedroom and lie there writhing. Groaning. Even to crinkle the sheets hurt. He took to wrapping a long white towel around his head and his ears, to block out the noise, to dull the pain in his forehead and temple.

This went on for a while. They were all sure it was the war that was behind all this, at bottom. They wouldn't say that to Augie's face, but naturally, they discussed it among themselves. Now they had two sick-patients in the house, Augie and his mother both. Mary and Anna each spent the money calling Gerry out in California long-distance to tell her they needed her back home, they couldn't go on like this, they had their own houses, their own families to take care of. Anna and Tommy were trying to have a baby, and—.

Pa told everyone to just calm down and take it easy and you'll see everything will be fine. "As long as we keep Peggy out of this—that's the last thing I need."

Pa could not conceal that he was worried.

But in the end he turned out to be right. In October, Patsy got home from Germany and Augie was fine, he was happy, he got through another round of celebrations, in fact, he was exhilarated, they hadn't seen him like this since he returned home himself back in July; he struggled a bit through the Thanksgiving holiday; then, Christmas was a trial. Everybody had to visit everybody else's house, they were all laden down with presents, everybody had a tree you had to exclaim over, and Augie wasn't the least interested. Half the time he begged off and he didn't care what kind of feast he was missing. They'd come home in Pa's car and find both Gigi and Augie stretched flat out, each in a bedroom behind a closed door. It was not exactly like coming home to a house full of Christmas cheer.

But they made it through the New Year, it was 1946 now, the war was falling behind in the headlines now, everyone was dying for a new, fresh start on something better, maybe *the rest of their lives*, and finally, at the end of January, Gerry and Andy came home.

It was magic. Gerry came home and suddenly the house was set to rights again. Anna and Mary could get back to their own lives and Gerry was where she belonged. Pa could sit back and relax for the first time in months. Ma was happy she had Gerry back in the kitchen to do things *her* way. That Anna was so sensitive you just couldn't talk to her. Even Mary, angel that she was, had a mind of her own. But Gerry was back and only Gerry would do. Gerry was the garlic in the sauce—she was the ingredient that made the whole thing go. Without her, well, it just wasn't the same.

And it did Gerry's heart good to see that her new husband and her precious kid brother Augie hit it off so well.

Of course, it never occurred to Gerry that Andy would have the least trouble fitting into her house and her family, whatever the situation going on at the time. It never occurred to Gerry that the awkwardness and ineptitude and sense of not belonging that had plagued her in Andy's home in Pershing, Pennsylvania, could happen to Andy, too, when the shoe was on the other foot.

But in fact, it did not. Compared to the LaStorias, Andy was easy-going, relaxed and happy. Neither he nor Gerry were really prepared even though they been told about Ma, and Augie, too, by Gerry's distressed sisters. But Andy just figured he was damned lucky, by hook or by crook, to be out of the coal mines, forever, and, he was never going back, he had just escaped, yet again, the first time was when he enlisted in the Navy, but now he had a wife who loved him, she was his ticket out, and there was no way he was going to screw this up, he was lucky he had been able to resist the pressure from his own Majka to sink her claws into him, not that he didn't love his mother, but, hell, a guy wants to have a life of his own, don't he? not to mention his sisters back home, and his brother Alek, heck, even his sister Adrienne had to put her two cents in, all the way from the Bronx, New York, that long distance telephone sure is a hell of an invention.

It helped that Gerry's Pa already had met Andy and gotten to know him and, no two ways about it, the old man made him feel welcome in his house, made him feel not like a son-in-law at all, but like Andy had found a second father, and a better one than his own, goddammit. Now as to this new brother-in-law Augie, who, in fact, he had heard a great deal of—this was the first time they were meeting, head to head.

But he turned out to be a hell of a guy. Andy wasn't sure he didn't like him better than he liked Gerry.

For it happened that there was no sign of illness in Augie as soon as Gerry showed up.

Augie instead felt euphoric. Suddenly he had a new pal to show around town. He took Andy to the track with him, *over to Suffolk Downs*, as Andy might say. Augie was used to all kinds, he had met them all in the service, from *everywhich-where*, as his new brother-in-law said, and Augie could tell Andy wasn't thrilled with the horses. He seemed to spend the afternoon fidgeting and looking around, he was not the least interested in letting go of a couple of bucks at the two-dollar window. Augie tried Fenway Park, but there was a great deal of fidgeting there, too. It seemed that Andy had never played much sports at all, unlike himself, and of course, that was a key thing, a guy doesn't go all in for spectator sports unless he has played them himself in his youth.

But Augie thought, wasn't it remarkable that here he had a brother-in-law who'd actually been a coal-miner, of all things, Navy, too, and, since neither one of them drank much, or cared to spend a nice afternoon in a dim, stale-smelling barroom, well, come to find out, what Andy did like to do was stuff like cutting the grass, weeding the flower-garden for his mother-in-law, and fixing stuff around the house that was broken, he was a wizard with all kinds of things, didn't have to be wood, could be plumbing and pipes, or anything that could be taken apart and put back together, it was amazing how Andy could figure things out, he was like Augie's brother Patsy that way, it was a talent that had skipped over Augie himself altogether, although in the Signal Corps he had been obligated to find a way around his own disinclinations.

And after the mild seashore winter they had that year in Revere, Massachusetts, spring came to Gigi's flower garden and Gerry was expecting.

Andy had found work through the GI bill at Page's Woodworking shop at the corner of Broadway and Mountain Ave. in Revere, and he was embarking on a future for himself that involved his apprenticeship program for woodworking, which he explained would lead ultimately to his qualifying as a master carpenter in the Massachusetts Carpenters' Union, where the big money was.

Augie caught the contagion from that, the spillover of good feelings in the house, his father's nod of approval for the industriousness of his new son-in-law. Augie began to feel competitive.

The next thing you know, Augie decided he would get back together with his brothers Gene and Patsy, and his Pa, and they would all be working at their trade again, the family trade.

The garment business was a decent way to make a living. It was something you didn't have to be ashamed of. They hurt nobody, they made a decent buck, they provided for their families, won friends and influence, and bestowed upon their fellow humans something they needed, clothes on their naked backs. Sure, in some other family you had to be a doctor or a lawyer, or own a restaurant, or have a fancy title on the door, but sewing, stitching, cutting and pressing cloth was a skill just as much as carpentering. And in the LaStoria family, their skills had been handed down from father to son through generations, some of them forgotten generations, without benefit of any government GI bill or job-training program. Garment-making was something any man, or woman, for that matter, could take pride in, and the LaStorias did.

And, yes, now Augie absolutely had to get up in the morning, and, no, he couldn't be making Pa late on the commute into town in the Buick, he would get a lift to work and back each day with his Pa; Gene had gotten himself a car, a Buick, like his Pa's, so that he could commute from Watertown; and Patsy, too, had his own car, another Buick, but of course, second-hand;

Patsy had been working on cars since he was a kid; he and his wife Mary were also trying to have another child, Anna was having a baby, her first, they were all getting back to having normal lives again, and Augie—*Augie had found his team.*

Augie was not a joiner, now that the war was over. There was an American Legion Post down on Beach Street, more or less a few doors down from the foot of Payson Street, and they also had a VFW in Revere, but Augie was not about to sit around all day in a room with wooden floorboards, a room full of cigarette and cigar smoke, with a lot of boozers fighting the war all over again.

But in going back to work Augie had found the team he wanted to join, the team he had lacked since the day he left the JASCO men behind, the team he had always had, going back to high school.

Back then he had Coach O'Brian in his life. Back then there was Tobias Haskins, the Indian in the woods. And his father, Tony LaStoria, a well-respected man who could be depended upon to support his family.

These three had been Augie's three chosen mentors.

The life he had had, before the war, *before the war*—it was resuming now, in all its glory, its splendor, just—in a different form—if you could recognize it for what it was.

The war. Had interrupted him. The war was the interlude. The war, it turned out, Augie could see it now, *the war was not real life.* This was the real thing. This was him.

Augie knew. He knew because when the war ended he had felt absolutely no desire to stay in the service.

He knew now that he never wanted to go through that again.

He didn't need the profession of soldiering. He didn't need to find any profession. He already had a trade.

He knew where he belonged, he knew where he fit in, he belonged with his family, at the shop. *He looked inside and found he had already forgotten everything he ever learned in the Signal Corps about electronics, telephones, communications, or cable.*

In 1948, the Boston Red Sox were going for the pennant again. They had lost the World Series in '46, but in seven games. Their turn was coming up again. The town of Boston was alive with pennant fever. It was three years since the war ended and nobody wanted to be reminded that the Russians had put a blockade on Berlin. Dewey was gonna be the President, so what? What did the Red Sox and the Yankees do today?

What was more, the Braves were leading the National League. There was a real chance that they were going to have a subway Series involving both teams from Boston. It was incredible to think of. *Pennant Fever Grips Hub.*

Augie tried Braves Field on Andy, because the Pirates were in town, and guess where Andy was from? fifty miles from Pittsburgh, that's where; but that didn't work, either, so he just gave it up. The guy was just not thrilled with baseball.

In the end, the Cleveland Indians, of all teams, Boudreau shift on Williams, and all, beat the Sox in a one game playoff because Joe McCarthy, *that Yankee has-been,* that infiltrator, started the immortal Denny Galehouse instead of Mel Parnell, the rookie sensation, in the last game of the season.

Who needed Commies in the State Department when you had Joe McCarthy on the Boston bench?

Then in 1949 the Yankees beat the Red Sox, *again,* on the last day of the season.

Augie had installed a replica of the Fenway scoreboard on a wall at the shop at No. 10, and for four seasons now had faithfully kept up with the changing standings of all eight teams in both leagues.

And this was how his faith was rewarded. Maybe Andy had something there. Augie was going back to the racetrack. At least there you could place a bet without a bookie.

Chapter 21

Memento Mori

When Tony LaStoria died, in 1952, it did not surprise his sons and daughters that there were many people who wished to visit to pay their respects. Only a year earlier, they had buried their mother, and they had received people in the family home. But times were changing, and nowadays people were holding wakes in funeral parlors. It was just as well. How would they have fit all those people in the house at No. 45 Payson Street? There were parades of people who had worked with Pa at No. 10, in town, down through the decades, worked with Genie and the rest of them, too, women, mostly, stitchers from their big, extended family from Spritzka's shop, some of whom they hadn't seen for years. There was even a man no one remembered, a man in his late sixties, from the North End of Boston, a newspaper editor named Stephen diBenedetto.

Of Tony's sons, Augie LaStoria arrived last, at Del Valle's Funeral Home, on Beach Street, opposite the foot of Payson Street, right in between Dr Graham's office and the Knights of Columbus. He was last to assume his place in the receiving line because his sister Gerry had asked him to take little Nicky out, for diversion. It was her wish that the boy be spared the ordeal of looking upon his grandfather, with compressed lips, cold and unmoving in a coffin. Gerry's girlfriend Hildie Razilko was minding the infant twins, Jack and Jill, who had been born in February, at the house. Now, Nicky's father Andy took his turn keeping the five-year-old entertained and Augie took his place with the other six children of the dead man.

The first in the line was Tony's eldest, Patsy. Yes, it was true, as he affirmed over and over, Tony breathed his last at Suffolk Downs, at the finish rail of the seventh race. Many people wanted to say at least he died happy. He was doing what he loved. The visitors waiting to kneel and cross themselves before his coffin were Tony's people, the stitchers and pressers and cutters who over the years going all the way back to the Depression and before had come to see him as their benefactor, simply because he gave them a job: they were the people you saw smiling, laughing and waving in those group photographs Tony had taken year after year in the shop at the annual Christmas party. They wanted their Tony to have had a happy death.

Patsy LaStoria was not so sure. To him, his father's death had been troubling. Patsy welcomed the chance to step outside when his brother Gene motioned to him and Augie to take a walk with him out to the parking lot.

When they got there it was a pleasant May afternoon towards five o'clock and the world was going on without them, and Gene and Patsy lit up.

Gene was picking tobacco off the tip of his tongue when Patsy heaved a sigh as he blew smoke.

"Gene, did you ever hear Pa talk about a woman named Laura?"

"No. Why?"

"Because that was the last thing he said."

Augie said, "What was the last thing he said?"

Patsy turned to him. "He said a woman's name—*Laura.*"

"Who's Laura?"

"That's what I'd like to know."

"Are you paying attention now?" said Gene to Augie, amused. "This is like Abbott and Costello."

Patsy turned on Gene. "I'm serious. There was something going on there that we knew nothing about."

"Such as what?"

"I don't know, but there he was, dead, on his back, with his eyes wide open staring up at the sky, and when I asked the bystanders, did he say anything? they said, 'He said Laura, is that your mother?' and I said, No!"

"You did?" said Augie.

"Like that?" said Gene. "Like you were upset?"

"Damn right I was upset."

"Why?"

Wasn't it only natural that he had hoped his father would have said something about him, his oldest son? Would have reached out to him, Patsy? Or, at least, had the name of Patsy's mother, Gigi, his own wife, on his lips? Instead there was an unknown 'Laura' on his father's mind, at the moment of all moments. "Look, don't you understand, Genie, it was the way he said it. He was surrounded by strangers, it was like he was trying to tell them something, you know? But this Laura, whoever she was, is not our mother."

Gene said, "Look—there never was any Laura."

"Well, how do you know!" Patsy exploded.

"Because I would've known!"

Now it was Augie's turn to be amused. He took a poke at his brother. "Say, Patsy, when he was looking up at the sky, was the look on his face like the one you get when you're looking at the Marilyn calendar hanging on the wall over your press?"

Augie's hands were gesturing circles in the air, in the va-va-va-*Voom* outlines of the naked Monroe on the famous red draperies.

Gene said, "The press opens, clouds of steam rise, he's in love!"

"Forget about it, I'm sorry I mentioned it," said Patsy.

"Good," said Gene. "Because I called you two out here because I had something important to discuss."

"This *is* important," said the wounded Patsy. He was always miffed, yet again, to find out that his standing as the eldest counted nothing at all with any of his siblings.

Now it was Gene who displayed the family temper. "Look, Patsy, it's all in the past. He's dead now. He's not coming back, and we just have to move on with our own lives."

"You don't think he could've had a secret that you didn't know anything about?" said Patsy to Gene.

That stopped Gene in his tracks because he himself *did* have a secret that he had never told the other two about.

It was a secret he had sworn he would take to the grave with him. A secret about Patsy and Augie's grandfather—the two brothers he was facing now, in a parking lot, with their father lying in a coffin inside.

Gene's entire manner changed as he said, slowly and seriously, "Patsy, there are things about another person you can never know. We just can't look into another man's heart and soul and mind, even if it's our own father, or even our own brother."

"Yeah," said the disgruntled Patsy. "I know." He did not like it one bit that Gene was eye to eye with him and asserting himself.

"So—is that the end of it?" said Gene.

"If you say so," said Patsy. "But no, not really."

"Can we move on now to what I came to say?" said Gene, exasperated.

This is the way it always was with these three brothers. Gene was the man with the agenda. The other two knew from the start he hadn't called them out here to the parking lot just to have a cigarette or a group hug.

Patsy said to Gene, "I know what you're gonna say. You're gonna tell us that Pa told you that after he was gone it was gonna be up to you."

"No, that's not what I was gonna say. Pa never once in his life thought for a minute we should go out on our own. It just wasn't in him. He left all that to Harry Spritzka. Pa wasn't gonna take the chance. As soon as he had you, Patsy, and then all of us, yes, Peggy, too, he had all he could do to take care of his own, and he couldn't take the gamble. Two bucks at the window on a horse he could chance, but not his whole wherewithal—what if he lost? What would've happened to those who depended on him? Pa never would take that chance. But he's gone now. Now it's our time. And personally, I'm never gonna work for somebody else again."

Patsy said, "You always were his golden boy."

"That's beside the point. I'm nobody's golden boy now. He's gone. And we have to take our own lives into our own hands. It's time we went to work for ourselves. And that's what I'm gonna do, start working on this, starting now, and see what I can do."

Augie said, "Of course we're with you, Genie. We're your brothers. We're a team. You gotta know we're always gonna back you up." He turned to Patsy. "Isn't that right, brother?"

"Yeah. We're the three musketeers. All for one and one for all."

"Abbot and Costello," said Augie, referring to the movie version, trying to lighten things up as the three of them turned and started to walk together through the parking lot back to the side door.

"That was the Ritz Brothers," said Patsy, who was in the mood to correct somebody.

Gene said, as he was holding open the door for the other two, "You know, when I was in Italy, I met a guy, one of those eggheads, you know, went to Princeton. He was a dogface, but he went to Princeton, like Einstein, and he could never let you forget it. Anyway, this guy was telling me that the Romans, when they had a winning general, they used to throw a big parade for him in Rome when he came home from the wars, and he'd go down the street on a big float, triumphant, like Patton in Palermo, and the crowds cheering for him, and meanwhile, they'd have a slave right behind him on the float, whispering in his ear, 'Memento mori, memento mori,' which means 'Remember that you will have to die.' So, you see, Patsy, it don't matter if you're a golden boy. Pa was a golden boy, once. Look at him now."

Chapter 22

Duel in the Snow

Spicket Falls, Massachusetts, was a town of about 12,000 people in the Merrimack Valley, wedged between Milltown, a city of 100,000, and the New Hampshire line. The foothills of the White Mountains began right there in Spicket Falls Square. The Oxford Mills, on Oxford Street, adjacent to the Square, was a nineteenth century mill complex, built in the 1850s on the lip of the Spicket Falls itself, to take advantage of water-power. The LaStoria family business, *Gigi Sportswear*, was located in a separate but attached two-story wing overlooking the Falls. The rest of the ell-shaped complex was five stories tall, extending out towards Oxford Street, which took the same precipitous drop past the mill buildings as the waterfall did on the far side. The loading docks were at the junction of the ell. The other end of the ell wrapped around yet again with another five-story extension which followed the sidewalk inside black iron railings down the steeply descending Oxford Street to where it flattened out to cross a bridge across the bend in the Spicket, which sped from there between granite walls down to

Broadway, where the river crossed under and broadened out to flow between meadows past St Monica's Church.

It was a peculiar place, originally, to situate the heart of a town. The Oxford Mills came first, and then the 3-story brick Town Hall with its pair of cream-colored columns flanking the front door was built on Milltown Street, on the northern, shouldering ridge above the river, which narrowed after the Falls skipped past the rear of the Oxford Mills between sheer rock walls, on its way dipping steeply down to Broadway in a torrent of rushing whitewater.

Broadway was the main north-south artery through the Square. It carried Route 28, the state road built in the 1920s, which began far south of Boston, on Cape Cod, as it passed through Milltown and Spicket Falls. North, Route 28 crossed the line into New Hampshire, running through Derry, where Robert Frost had his farmhouse; but southwards it traveled, flat and arrow-straight through North Milltown, across the Merrimack River on the Broadway Bridge, where the Great Stone Dam formed the falls of the Merrimack, traversing South Milltown, crossing into Andover, and then down through Reading, Stoneham and Melrose, to where it began to wind through Medford and finally Boston itself, thirty miles distant.

The result of this nature-mandated, rather than manmade, town center, was that the Square was wedged into a triangle formed by three streets which skirted around the Oxford Mills. On the north, Milltown Street curved past the Town Hall east to west, perched high upon the ridge of the northern rock wall of the Spicket, and had a few stores, the Merrimack Valley Co-op Bank, the 1867 House Restaurant, a tiny Kresge's 5-and-10, and Dillon's Drugstore on the corner of Broadway. Milltown Street stopped at the intersection of Lowell Street, which was carried across the Spicket on a short bridge. Lowell

Street left the Square at the three-way junction with Pelham Street and Oxford Street. Oxford Street then dipped down steeply, following the descent of the river and the Mills, to rejoin Broadway, closing the triangle at the point where the levelness of Broadway, going north, took a sudden leap up a gigantically steep, two-humped hill through the Square: the beginning of the White Mountains.

Only stubborn New Englanders with heads as thick as rocks themselves would have perched a town square on such an inauspiciously stony, steep hillside.

Inside *Gigi Sportswear*, Gene LaStoria's office was next door to the loading dock. The office and the windows of the first floor looked out on the hilly, unpaved, steeply-rising dirt parking lot, which seemed to be strewn with every famous rock and boulder in New England. The Spicket Falls Fire Station, at the cross-roads of Oxford, Lowell and Pelham, with its square belltower, then stood sentinel on the level shoulder of Lowell Street, next to Jan's Diner, an old railroad car painted red-and-white, which was perched on the end of the bridge across the Spicket.

In the mid-1950s, the fire bell was no longer in use, they had gone over to an ear-piercing siren, which was used to halt all traffic when the fire engines had to race out of the building. There were no stoplights back then at that end of the Square where Lowell Street and Pelham Street merged. In those days Spicket Falls was still a country town. No big multi-lane highways came near it, or criss-crossed it. The Interstate system that would shortly come to be was a thing people had not yet imagined, nor could they imagine it. Rte 28 north and south and Rte 110 east and west were the state roads bisecting the town. These were the roads people had grown up with and were accustomed to, and travel was slow on two-lane blacktop, full of stoplights, and choked by big trailer-trucks.

Apart from the Square, the town of Spicket Falls meandered widely east and west north of the Merrimack River, a kidney-shaped municipality draped around Milltown on both sides. In the 1950s it was still a farming community. Rte 110 passed by the flattened banks of the Merrimack with its low-lying farmlands, the section of Spicket Falls called Pleasant Valley, which was where the Italians in town grouped their gardens in several streets around St Lucy's Church. After cruising Pleasant Valley, 110 entered Milltown from the east, surmounted Prospect Hill, descended, twisted and wound through and around the city, past the Milltown Common and the huge yellow-brick High School whose most famous graduate was the poet Frost, crossed Broadway at right angles, arrowed past three-deckers and corner stores, traversed the heights of Tower Hill, and emerged on the west side of Spicket Falls, which was known as the Glen Forest section. The big hospital that served both Milltown and Spicket Falls, the Bon Secours, staffed by nuns from French-speaking Canada, sat atop Daddy Frye Hill, in the middle of Spicket Falls, east of the Square.

Many people who had grown up in the city and the town could honestly say they had never been to Boston in their whole entire lives. The big city of Milltown rivaled its companion mill cities on the Merrimack, Lowell, to the west, and Haverhill to the east. But it had actually been carved out of the original towns of Spicket Falls, north of the river, and Andover, on the south bank.

Andover was famous for Phillips Academy, which gave the world Edgar Rice Burroughs and Humphrey Bogart, and, most recently, graduated Capt. Tom Hudner, first Congressional Medal of Honor winner of the Korean War.

Spicket Falls, going back to colonial times, was the place that gave birth to Robert Rogers, the Northwest Passage pioneer who, with Rogers' Rangers, was a hero of the French and Indian War.

At *Gigi Sportswear*, Gene LaStoria ran the family business and he had a factory-outlet showroom next to his office, the windows of the showroom facing the parking lot.

On the other side of the first floor, his brother Patsy's pressing section had three steam presses floor looking out the windows on the Falls. From there, the view was about level with the top of the Falls. On the bare janitor-green-painted bricks of a pier between two windows facing Patsy he had Marilyn Monroe in her calendar pose hanging amid clouds of passionate steam rising from the presses.

Augie LaStoria's wide and long cutting tables occupied the rest of the first floor. They had been built, rock-sturdy, by Andy Petrovich. He had used Masonite for the table-tops, slick to the touch, so that heavy layers of stacked cloth could slide on them easily. The tables were big enough so that Augie at six-foot-two, when he leaned over from the waist, and stretched out one arm as far as he could, could reach barely half-way across the tables. Andy had built them in four sections to Augie's specifications and afterward pushed the squares together to form one extensive rectangle and then jointed them so they supported one another. He had told Gene what he needed for lumber and Gene simply wrote a check out to Appleton's Lumber Yard for him.

Andy also devised and built a chute that came down from the second floor and emptied into a canvas wagon with high sides and little rollers. That way bundles of finished raincoats could speed downstairs without being carried down the stairs to drag on the floorboards, nor did they need to wait for the freight elevator, and Gene could keep all his wheeled coatracks downstairs.

The second floor was where all the stitchers worked at rows of sewing machines. At the top of the chute on the second floor, up against the wall over the opening in the floor for the chute, that's where Augie placed his Fenway Park scoreboard with the National League on the left and the American League on the right. He had Andy build him a catwalk with a railing so that he could walk across and make his entries, for which he used stiff white shirt-cardboards. The scoreboard covered the whole sidewall, from the stairwell on the left all the way over to the windows on the right which overlooked the parking lot.

Gerry and Mary worked with the stitchers upstairs. Mary traveled to work each day from Watertown with Gene in his '54 Buick on Rte 28. Their sister Anna had young children at home, the same age as Gerry's, so she could only come occasionally. Patsy came up from Peabody on 114 in his Pontiac. One of the reasons Gerry had wanted a house in Spicket Falls was so that Augie, who didn't drive, could walk to work if he had to. From the fieldstone house at 34 Elm Street it was about two miles to the Square. Gerry would take a bus to the town square after she got the kids fed and off to school. She would work until it was time in the afternoon to get back for her kids coming home from school.

Andy was working on housing-development sites building suburban homes and he was using his Jeep station wagon to commute. He had to travel anywhere from Middleton to Danvers to Burlington to Chelmsford or Tewksbury, depending on where the Carpenter's Union Local 59 sent him when one project was finished and another began. It was the 1950s and the Boston suburbs were rapidly expanding into bedroom communities.

Peggy Fabiano was the only one of Tony and Gigi LaStoria's seven children who did not work with their son Gene and his brothers and sisters at *Gigi Sportswear.*

None of her brothers and sisters seemed to miss her. They knew they would see her soon. She would turn up on their doorstep when she needed a place to stay for a few days. Or she would just drop by for something to eat, especially if she had a friend who drove her. They knew that Peggy knew that they all had been brought up the right way, with old-fashioned South of Italy customs of peasant hospitality: if someone was in your kitchen and you asked them to sit down, you offered them a cup of coffee, you said, "Okay, let's eat."

Peggy was still living in Revere. She would get a cheap studio flat in rundown beachfront properties, fall behind in the rent, and move out in the middle of the night, then repeat the routine at the next landlord's. When she wasn't working waitressing, she would collect. She managed to not get fired, but somehow always got laid off, usually just when she was getting tired of the boss, the other help or the customers. She was always on the verge of her next big bonus payday at the track. She had perfected the art of living well. When she was hungry, she got a job in a restaurant, they always fed you instead of paying you, when she had gained too much weight, she quit and went on a diet.

Peggy would then show up at one of her sister's or brother's houses standing on the doorstep with a suitcase in one hand and a vanity case in the other, packed with all her makeup. "Can you put me up for a few days, I'm between jobs—just for a few days." Three months later the few days would come to a sudden ending.

Her own children, and Mary's, were too old now to be fooled, but not so at Gene's house, at Anna's, or at Patsy's or Gerry's. There the kids would be still young enough to be captivated by Auntie Peggy. She was a breath of fresh air compared to their parents. She would sit there and play games with the kids all day. Scrabble, Monopoly and especially Solitaire. She would get the kids fascinated with Solitaire, and then move on to Chinese Checkers. She would teach her nieces all about makeup and dresses and then run outside and play softball or badminton with the nephews. Auntie Peggy was all about games. And expeditions. She knew how much kids loved to go barefoot. She loved to go barefoot herself, and she was a grownup. She knew all the places in Watertown, in Peabody or in Milltown or Spicket Falls where you could find blueberries. All her nieces and nephews who were still young enough in the Fifties had been to a cemetery with Auntie Peggy to pick blueberries. It seemed they grew wild best at the edges of a graveyard.

The day she came to pick a bone with Gerry at her new house, she had been staying in Peabody with Patsy and his family, just previously, so it was there that she found out all about the fieldstone house.

She timed her arrival that day for the afternoon, after two, when she knew Gerry would be home for the kids, and before Andy and Augie came home from work. It was about the time of the fifth or sixth race at Rockingham when she walked in the back door.

"I've got a bone to pick with you."

Suspicious, and on guard, Gerry said, "What's that?"

Peggy looked around. "Nice house."

Gerry did not like her tone. She sometimes hated Peggy and this was one of those moments.

"I'll stay in the parlor, on the couch—if you don't mind."

"Why should I mind?"

"Just for a few days—till I get settled."

"Help yourself."

There was a pause, not awkward, but a fencer's pause. The two sisters were getting ready to spear one another, with bitter glee on Peggy's part, with the savagery of cornered prey on Gerry's.

Said Gerry, "You were saying?"

"Musta cost you a pretty penny, the down payment."

"I had it in the bank."

"Yeah, you got it from selling Pa's house in Revere. So, where's my share?"

"The same place where's all my babysitting money from all those years of minding Henry and Ronnie when you were out running around."

"Is that so?"

Gerry was shaking with defiance.

"So that's the way you wanna play the game," said Peggy.

"Don't think you're gonna make me feel guilty."

"Don't worry, I'll get it out of you one way or the other."

"You are—."

"What?"

"I can't say it."

"That's all right—I forgive you."

"You got a hell of a nerve, forgiving me."

"Why? What have I ever done to you? Tell me one thing I've done to you."

Gerry was speechless.

Peggy said, "So, you like the new house. You even love it, maybe. I don't blame you. It is the kind of a house somebody could fall in love with. Well—I wish you luck with it."

"What does that mean?"

"I wish you luck with it, that's all."

Gerry was so angry her fists were clenched.

Peggy said, "I, uh, I heard from Patsy that it used to be a priest's house. Is that right?"

"What's that got to do with anything?"

Peggy sat back and laughed softly to herself, as she reached into her bag for a cigarette. She took her time lighting up. Then she looked directly at her sister through a cloud of smoke. "And then, after that, I'm told, there was a family of French winos took over."

"They drank Crown Royal, if you must know. So?"

"So, nothing. It's just that I'm sure when the priests were living here, I'm sure they blessed the house, they always do, sprinkling a little holy water in the corners, you know? And then maybe when the Canucks were here they maybe, you know, sprinkled a little Crown Royal around. You know. You know what I mean, Gerry. They disrespected the house. So who knows? Who knows what kind of an effect that could have? Who the hell knows about these things? I heard from Patsy that it took your husband Andy a year to get the house ready for you to move in with the kids, while you were paying rent to Torrini in South Milltown. It took him a year just to get rid of the stale smell of booze in the closets. You know, some things linger. Some things never go away. So, I guess we'll find out, won't we?"

That winter, after Peggy had come and gone, when her usual three months were up, and she moved on, this time, back to a place of her own, a studio in Revere; when her checks had run out, and she needed to look up an old flame for a restaurant job; when Christmas had come and gone, and Gerry had reveled in the new snapshots she had collected of her three kids opening presents for the first time in her new house; then New Year's came and went.

And it was now the new year 1956. Which year brought her sister-in-law Adrienne to visit, all the way from the Bronx.

Gerry knew Andy's sister Stasija, the hair-dresser, and she knew Andy's sister Angie, the one who was married to John Lucinda and lived on his farm in Carmichaels, and she knew the one called Ana who worked at the Creamery. But Gerry had never yet met Andy's sister Adrienne, though she had heard plenty about this sister from her husband. She knew all about Adrienne running away to New York to shack up with Teddy Robertson, as Andy had put it; she knew all about the falling out between her husband and his sister Adrienne, and all about who Teddy Robertson was, and all about his gang at the pool hall in Pershing, and all about the scab-labor battle between Andy and his brother Alek and Teddy and his company goons at the time of the UMW's seven-day strike in '37.

And now Gerry was going to be meeting Adrienne for the first time in the twelve years since she had been married.

When Gerry heard Adrienne was coming to visit from the Bronx, she got that awful caving-in feeling in her stomach, thinking *oh, now she's coming to meet me, at long last, because she's dying to see this house!*

Andy's sister Adrienne waltzed into Gerry's kitchen in Spicket Falls after taking the Trailways from New York City to Milltown, and from there, a taxi to the fieldstone house. Adrienne waltzed into Gerry's kitchen, planted herself down on the wrap-around bench-seat section with the diner-style red naugahyde cushions her brother Andy had designed into one corner of the kitchen (between the side window overlooking the lawn and the back window looking out on the clothesline and the driveway) and then plunked a six-pack of *Rheingold* on the table, saying to Gerry, "Get me a glass, willya, honey?" and Gerry had the dreadful thought *Oh, my God, No! another Peggy!*

All of a sudden without any warning or any apparent reason or trigger, Gerry's brother Augie's severe, disabling migraines returned, and he had to shut himself up for two days at a time in his bedroom upstairs, on the northwest corner of the second story, the coldest spot in the house, in an extremely cold, snowy winter with temperatures hovering over zero, never rising out of the teens. The inference obvious to Adrienne and everyone else, true or not, was that Augie had taken an instant dislike and was snubbing her.

Gerry's daughter Jill, now four years old, heard that in another year she would have to leave the house to go to school, and decided to throw up in the morning every day for a week.

Gerry had an awful, upsetting argument with Andy about when in the blazes he was ever going to finish putting that door on the compartment of the kitchen cabinets he had designed and built where Gerry stored her rolling pins and breadboards, the ones she never used anymore since her mother was dead and they didn't roll out spaghetti, noodles and ravioli on

Sunday mornings anymore, and Andy told her it was part of his design that the compartment should not have a door, that there was no room to place hinges there, and finally told her "Judas Priest, woman, dry up!"

Andy had never spoken to her this way before. But now his sister Adrienne was camped out in her kitchen with a six-pack of *Rheingold.*

Gerry was so stunned and offended that he would talk to her that way that she burst out crying, and he tried to put his arms around her and apologize, and she wouldn't let him touch her, but drew in her shoulders and cringed into a corner over by the telephone on the countertop across from the cellar door.

She started thinking unwelcome thoughts that intruded on her mind the idea that ever since his sister Adrienne had come into her house, Andy had seemed different, that he had changed.

One day, during that awful winter, she went to the mailbox Andy had fixed to the doorjamb outside the front door, that front door, installed brand-new from the factory, with the full-length oval window in it, and the handsome door-handle with the trigger-action; that door that Gerry was so proud of because she thought it was such a dignified door and graced the welcome to her house perfectly; and sadly, when she went to retrieve her copy of her brand-new subscription to *The Saturday Evening Post,* which she had bought from the magazine-salesman who come to the house one afternoon in the snow, she found the cover wrinkled and spoiled because snow had blown across her fieldstone porch, wide open to the wind, and filtered itself into the top of the mailbox, propped open as it was by the too-tall *Saturday Evening Post,* and she thought as she tried to straighten it out on her bosom, *why does everything have to get spoiled?*

Then in February, long after Adrienne had come to the end of her two-week winter vacation off work and returned to the Bronx on the next Trailways, a blizzard struck, an old-time New England nor'easter, the kind that drowned sailing ships, and snow drifted up to the tops of the windows on the house, and the big lawn, looking out the windows of the den, looked like a field of creamy mashed potatoes two feet deep, no lumps, but scalloped by the wind, and dazzling white.

Nicky, now in the fifth grade at the Ebenezer Baker, was thrilled to wake up in the morning and find out *"No school today!"*

Andy came in after shoveling out the back porch and steps in front of the kitchen door, stamped his feet in the hallway, and called out "I could use some help out here!"

Augie was feeling uncannily energetic that morning and he eagerly got dressed to go out, pulling on rubberized over-shoes and a red, black and orange checked winter jacket that he'd gotten from his sister Gerry for Christmas.

Nicky, too, wanted to help. He was going on eleven years old now and big enough, he said. The grown-ups said they didn't have enough shovels to go around, but Nicky would not hear of it, he had to be let to go. So his mother dressed him up with ski-cap and scarf and gloves and the whole rig while he fidgeted at her fussing.

Once outside the eleven-year-old romped through the snow, splashing and showering. He started making snowballs to throw at this uncle and his father. His dad was stomping through the snow piled and drifted in the long driveway, pulling one leg and another out of two-foot-high drifts. He had a hell of a time getting the garage door open, plowing snow aside with his hands. This garage door was the one thing he had yet to modernize on the house—it had straight vertical slats, no windows, and fixtures so rusted that it was a wonder they still worked. There was only one way to open the door, by pulling it out and up from the handle at the bottom, which was buried in snow. In summer, it was fine, no problem, the door lifted and slid back into the ceiling area of the fieldstone garage on the rusted runners. Finally, Andy got it to work. His only snowshovel was the one he kept leaning by the back door, with which he had shoveled off the back porch and steps. Now he emerged from the garage with two of his father-in-law's wide-mouth spades, which he had kept from the house in Revere all this time, just in case in the spring, Gerry wanted to start up a garden in the back yard, like her father used to dig every year.

They were the kind of shovels that stable-hands used to shovel horseshit. They had straight, sharp-edged mouths, flat beds and curved sides, taller at the front. The handles were long and solid as baseball bats, longer, for better leverage. Andy had often admired these old-fashioned tools for the sheer beauty of the wood in the handles and the utilitarian design. These shovels came from the cast-iron world of fifty years ago. Tony LaStoria had employed them to dump fertilizer into his garden soil.

Andy struggled through the deep snow in the fifty-foot driveway and when he got to the foot of it, handed one of the shovels to Augie, who suddenly said, "I'll race ya!"

Andy looked at him like he was a foolish kid.

"First one to the door!" Augie cried as he jumped aside to claim the right half of the driveway.

Now Andy couldn't resist the challenge. He'd show him. That a coal-miner knew how to wield a shovel! He didn't care suddenly whether Augie was that much bigger than him—he wasn't any stronger, though he had never tested him, and Andy was pretty sure, though he was five-foot-eight, and his brother-in-law six-foot-two, that Augie couldn't beat him anymore than the steam-engine coulda beat John Henry.

Nicky was jumping up and down for joy. The grownups were turning this into a game, and he could have a ringside seat, and be the cheerleader. He didn't have to do anything, just watch them—they wouldn't let him play but he was seized with the feeling that this was somehow deadly serious between the two of them, in a way he didn't understand why or how, but, *sheez, who cares, what fun!*

His dad was looking all the way back to the garage door, making sure he had remembered to shut it. He didn't want to have to walk all the way back down there. Yes, he had shut it. It was automatic of him, as in winter weather like they had been having, the whole idea of having a garage was to protect his used '51 Jeep station wagon. *What good was a garage in the winter for the vee-hicle in it if you left the door open?*

"Okay," said Andy, "now look—you have to completely clean down to the ground *all* the snow on your half, from here to here—no leaving it half-done just so you can get ahead of me!"

"And the same thing when I get to the door," said Augie. "I don't win till I get the whole door cleared on my side."

"If you think you can!"

"Oh, I know I can!"

"You ready? Nicky!" his dad called out. "You do the one-two-three!"

The two shovelers planted themselves, backs arched, knees bent, shovels poised, one hand low, the other high, elbow sticking up. They were both right-handed so Andy figured he had the advantage since he could scoop to his left while Augie had to lift and throw to his right—two motions to one.

Nicky was nearly jumping out of the snowsuit with excitement as he called out, "Ready—set—Go!"

The first shovel-full from his Dad went right in his face but he didn't care as he staggered out of the way.

"You stay back now and don't get in the way!" his father yelled.

His uncle shouted, "You wanna put money on this, Andy?"

Andy said, "You know I don't gamble, but just this one time, I'll bet you a quart-bottle of the Champagne of Bottled Beers. Now shut up and quit wastin' my breath!"

Their heads were down and their tails up in the air as furiously they sent the snow flying.

Nicky just could not believe how hard they worked and how fast they cleared the snow.

It seemed that he blinked and already they were halfway there.

Nicky plowed his short legs though the snow past the weighed-down-with-snow clotheslines suspended from the rectangular frame at the back window of the kitchen. He looked up to see his mother inside the kitchen window, standing there with the twins, Jack and Jill, soon to be five years old, and all three faces pressed against the glass, watching, so the window kept clouding up. Nicky didn't care if they were nice and toasty warm inside while his hands (especially since he had made snowballs) were frozen and hurting inside his mittens, he just didn't care if his ears tingled and his nose was runny, he wouldn't have missed this for the world. He struggled with might and main to get past the two shovelers and far enough ahead of them—but they were going so fast, it was a miracle, *it's like Bob Mathias in the decathlon in the Olympics!*

The thought crossed Nicky's mind right then and there that he would never be able to work hard enough or grow up enough or be disciplined enough to equal these two men, his father and his uncle, who were shoveling snow neck and neck down to the finish as if their very lives depended upon it.

Nicky didn't even have a favorite. He wanted both of them to win! He could never have chosen between them.

But if he did choose, he realized that he would've gone with his uncle, only because his uncle once in a while would go outside and toss the ball around with him, which his father never did.

He knew it was disloyal and unfair of him to be thinking this about his father, just now, just at this moment, but—

He had to get ahead of them! Or else how would he know who won!

Nobody won. They all won. All three of them.

When the two men got to the garage door and both of them scraped the final shovel-full right down to the tar on the driveway, they stood up and faced one another and started laughing.

Each of them realized they had not had this much fun in a long, long time.

"First drink's on me," Augie said, big breaths pouring out of his mouth like a locomotive puffing in the cold.

They straightened up and each one seemed to reach for his back with one hand while they stood up the shovels in the other.

"No, no," said Andy. "We tied."

Nicky was jumping around ecstatically. "It was an absolute dead heat! I never saw anything like it! There's never been anything like it in the whole history of the whole world!"

The two men reached out to him at the same time, pulling him into them, each with one hand on one of his narrow little shoulders.

Augie said, "I don't know if we ever had a drink together!"

"Oh, sure we did. Many's the time at Thanksgiving or Easter the wine was on the table."

"Yeah, but I mean, having a drink together."

"Well, we just never got around to it."

"Yeah. We never had occasion to, till now."

Andy said, "I'm not much for drinking anyways."

Augie said, "Me neither."

Nicky looked up, beaming.

"Well, kid," said his uncle.

"Yeah," said his Dad. "Who won?"

Nicky hugged them both, and said, "You both did."

He looked over his shoulder to make sure his mother was watching to see the three of them like this.

She had moved to the side window of the kitchen to keep the garage in view at a better angle.

She was there in the window all right, but the twins were gone.

She had cleaned out a circle of vapor-frost on the window with her hand, so that, looking out, her face was framed in a halo, with the kitchen light white behind her.

And her face in the halo was a serious one, not smiling, not laughing, not happy, but full of concern.

Chapter 23

The Greatest Game Ever Played

In the basement of the Oxford Mills, down in the bowels of
the building, at the very bottom, where nothing but gigantic
asbestos-wrapped steam pipes ran, was Jack Lane's lunchroom.
Augie was down there one day buying coffee when he met
someone new.

Usually once a week his brother Gene would send him
down to get a box of donuts, on a Thursday or a Friday, so
that he could prop open the box, with a couple of dozen of
different varieties, on a table outside his office, alongside a
coffee urn. In the morning, the stitchers could help themselves
as they came in. Sometimes Gene had pizza delivered from
Jackson Street. He liked the thick-slice pizza they made there
and so did everyone else.

Sometimes when things were slow Augie would drift
down to Jack Lane's and sit by himself and brood over a
coffee. It was small in there, a straight counter and three swivel
stools without backs. The walls were painted apple green and
unadorned. Jack Lane would sit turning over a newspaper leaf

by leaf in the corner behind the counter all day long. He made a little book on the side. There was a payphone hanging on the wall opposite the counter. Usually Jack had a girl waiting on customers because breakfast could get busy up until about 8.30 or 9. Then at 10 am there was a coffee break rush. Then, nothing doing until lunch, and Jack closed it up by two in the afternoon. Jack flipped the pancakes and burgers on the grill and the girl took the orders.

This particular day Augie looked up when he went to place an order and was startled to be looking directly into the eyes of the new girl. She had on a white butcher's apron and a dark blouse and had straight, short hair hanging down the back of her neck, no flip. Maybe because she was wearing glasses her eyes seemed big and brown. Augie was embarrassed enough to look away quickly.

Later on he began to wonder why it seemed to him that she had made personal eye contact with him. All she did was take his order. She, too, looked away. She, too, must have felt it was too intimate of a moment, that it was an intrusion on her part that perhaps was accidental, that she hadn't really meant to do that. When she brought his coffee she avoided looking at him, but the cup slipped on the ring in the saucer, and a small spill trickled over the lip of the round white ceramic cup. The girl scooted away quick.

She wasn't young. She was maybe mid-twenties. It was 1958 and Augie was 37. Lots of girls had come and gone in Jack Lane's lunch counter. Jack couldn't be paying them more than 50, 75 cents an hour. Augie always left a tip, anywhere from a nickel to a quarter. She wasn't any different from all the others. But for some reason he couldn't stop thinking about her. Augie wasn't the kind who hung out in barrooms trying to establish eye contact with some woman on the other side of the horseshoe.

Eventually, the girl became pregnant. Or maybe Augie just noticed one day she was starting to show. Augie hadn't yet spoken to her. Other than ordering something, not a word. He still didn't know her name. He still didn't know why he wanted to know her name. She wasn't anything special to look at. But then again, neither was he, or so he reasoned. If he had had to describe the color of her hair he would have called it mousy-brown. She seemed shy enough, but so was he. But then she couldn't be all that shy if she was pregnant. And if she was pregnant she must be married. So it was all right to talk to her. He ventured to say, "Congratulations."

"On what?"

"You're having a baby."

"So?"

"So you and your husband must be very happy."

"There isn't any husband."

She walked away.

The next time Augie was in Jack Lane's he said to her, "What's your name?"

"Carol," she answered, and walked away.

Augie felt he was hopeless at this. She hadn't even asked him his name.

Another time he asked her, "Where are you from?"

"Maine," she said.

"Where?"

"Millinocket."

"Pretty far up, isn't it?"

"Yup."

This was getting nowhere, and Augie knew it. But in that case, why couldn't he get Carol off his mind?

He had begun to fantasize about her. They were going to run away together, get married and she was going to have her baby. Augie was going to take care of them both. Her child, didn't matter if it was a boy or a girl, was going to be his child. He would love that baby as if it was his own. Didn't matter if she didn't love him, maybe after a while she would learn to care a little about him. Maybe he didn't love her, but he wanted to take care of her. She needed someone to do that. He wanted—. . .

Augie was sitting up on the edge of his bed in his bedroom in his sister's house one afternoon going round and round in his mind over and over this same ground for what seemed like the twenty-second time when he stopped himself to say, in that way he had of endlessly talking things over with himself, *this has happened to me before.*

He meant that there had been other times when he had been stuck in a fantasy that he couldn't get over for a good while.

Back in '48, a book had come out, in time for Christmas, that swept the nation. Augie had come across it on the rack at the Rexall drugstore in Revere, Foyle's, across from the Immaculate Conception Church, where Gerry and Andy had been married in the vestibule by the Irish priest—a story Augie hadn't heard till he got home from the war, when he discovered Gerry was still upset and angry over the way the Church had treated her, the Catholic Church, the Church that they and all Italians had grown up in, their Church.

Augie never passed that drugstore without going in to see if there was anything new on the rack. This time he found a best-selling paperback, a book about the Church, their Church, the Catholic Church, a book his sister Mary had told him he should read. The cover price was 50 cents. He bought it. It was *The Seven-Storey Mountain*, by a monk named Thomas Merton.

In that book Augie found a Church he did not recognize, issues he never knew existed, a life-story so unlike his own that it might be from another, different human race, and, although he thought the author was a spoiled boy from a privileged childhood, he had kept reading and reading just to find out what the Seven-Story Mountain would turn out to be. Was it Purgatory? Was it seven steps to salvation? Was it a ladder to Heaven? Was it real or just symbolic?

He never found out because he never finished the book but he never threw it out, either. It was in this bedroom of his at Gerry's house this very moment, on top of his bureau. From time to time he would take it out and re-read passages he had already read and forgotten, without trying to finish the book, without trying to solve the mystery.

But it was a powerful book that got under your skin and it left him with a nagging fantasy that he had found it, or been told to read it, for a reason, and that reason was that he should go in for the monk's haircut himself.

After all, what was he doing with his life?

This bothered him for the longest time, ten years now, and never really left, but in the end, he rejected it as a fantasy. *I am no more meant to be a monk than Swaps the racehorse was meant to be President.*

Then there was the idea that he should write a book. After all, wasn't there somebody who said that there was a book in all of us, if we could just let it come out? And didn't Hemingway himself say that the great American novel had yet to be written? And what would Augie write about? *Why, the war, what else was there?* Wasn't that the most important thing he had ever done, to be a part of that?

Another book that came out in '48 put an end to that fantasy. This one Augie also found on the rack at Foyle's. It was by Norman Mailer. *The Naked and the Dead.* Augie read the opening passage in that, about the troop ship in the Pacific, and realized that Mailer had described it photographically, with almost total recall. The guy was the real thing. If the book ever went on that way it would turn out to be a monumental mental effort. Was Augie the kind to put himself through that? *Hell, no.* What he wanted to do was forget the war, every last day of it, and the trouble was, he couldn't.

So that put an end to that fantasy.

Then there was his flirtation with the idea of boxing.

After the war, a number of Italians had become prominent in that game. Some of them, indeed, were local, which brought it right into the realm of actual possibility. Augie took a lot of pride in that fact. There was Rocky Marciano, from right down the road in Brockton, heavyweight champion of the world. There was Tony DeMarco, who came from the North End, where Augie himself had been born. If they could do it, why couldn't he? After all, Augie recalled very well that he had held his own in the ring back in the camps in England, and he was a big guy, still young, strong, didn't smoke, didn't drink. *So what was he in training for?*

Then in '55, they came out with that notorious photo of Carmen Basilio, in the sports pages of the *Boston American,* with his eye swollen shut after his middleweight title bout with Sugar Ray Robinson. It was his left eye. That meant Robinson had hit him there repeatedly with his right. Augie took one look at that picture and he shut the newspaper.

It reminded him of guy's faces he had seen during the war. A mask of pain. All the humanity drained out. *All the glory gone.*

And somewhere he heard that Basilio had said that he couldn't concentrate anywhere but in the ring, because in the ring, somebody was trying to kill him.

That was it.

That was it.

Augie, sitting on the bed, realized that when the war ended, he had lost his concentration.

Outside that arena where they were trying to kill him, he had lost it.

For 335 consecutive days, from the moment he dragged himself soaked and heaving up onto the shingle at Dog Red, and found himself separated from his JASCO unit, among strangers, without a weapon, without a helmet, from that moment onward every fiber of nerve in his body had been stretched to preternatural alert, and he had spent each and every one of those 335 days *alive*, as he had never before been, and never would be again.

Compared to that, all the intervening years since then he had spent more than half dead.

Because now there was nothing important about what he was doing.

Augie stood up from his bed that afternoon and walked across the hall to the bathroom.

On top of the built-in linen cabinets that Andy had installed there on the landing, Gerry had placed their father's favorite work of art, a thing the dead man had valued almost above anything else he owned, a copy of DaVinci's *Last Supper*, encased in glass, inside a trapezoidal wooden box made of polished oak.

Augie went to the mirror in the medicine cabinet over the sink in the bathroom.

Andy had redesigned the bathroom window with a crank-handle so that it was placed high in the wall opposite the mirror, for the sake of privacy.

The afternoon sun slanted in that window from above and made it difficult for Augie to see his face in the glare coming over his shoulder.

He peered at himself.

His nose was too big. It had always been too big. No wonder back in high school on the football team they gave him the nickname *Moose*. The guys in his squad when he was Tech Sergeant used to kid him that no matter how long it took them to get to Berlin, his nose would beat them there.

And yet that ugly, unlovable face that could not even be called ruggedly handsome and obviously held no attraction for somebody called Carol from Millinocket, Maine, somebody who had been gazing on dairy cows and tree stumps all her life, had been loved.

Yes, he had been loved.

He had been loved by his mother. He had been loved by his sisters. Even his brothers put him on a pedestal he did not deserve.

It was love that had kept him home all these years.

Where in the world would he find love like that? Where, outside his family? Why did anyone ever look for love when they already were showered with it at home?

Could a woman love you the way your mother did?

That kind of love was the antidote to the war.

That kind of love, which is given without asking, which is free for the taking without being sought after, was the medicinal agent to the poisonous hate, the balm to the crippling anger, the precious ointment to all the pain he had given and suffering he had received in the war.

That was the love the dying German soldier had been reaching out for in his last extremity as he staggered from the bunker at Omaha Beach and fell to the ground clutching his neck in two hands, crying *"Mutti, Mutti!"*

Looking in the mirror, Augie said to himself, *Things are gonna have to change.*

It was a laugh to think, *and I don't mean plastic surgery.*

Suddenly he felt nauseated.

He knelt over the commode but nothing would come up but dry retching.

He realized that he had worked himself up into another migraine. It was coming on rapidly as he pressed his right temple and tried to massage it away with his fingers.

He grabbed a bath towel, went back to his bedroom, wrapped the towel as tightly as he could around his head, shut the door, and fell on his bed, shooting lights blinding him.

He did not emerge from his room for two days.

On Sunday morning he woke up feeling fine. He jumped out of bed and went to the bathroom, ran one hand across his unshaved face in the mirror, and said to himself, headache's gone–halleluljah!

It was only 6.30 and nobody was up, so Augie went downstairs and put on some coffee. He must have woken up his nephew Nicky because he heard somebody coming downstairs.

Nicky had just turned 12 years old four days earlier, the day before Christmas. His little brother and sister, the twins, Jack and Jill, were still only six, and had started school that year in the first grade at the Ebenezer Baker. Nicky's mother had put her older boy in charge of making sure the little ones got to school and back each day without getting run over or beat up, and Nicky was enjoying the Christmas vacation week respite from these onerous school duties.

"Hi, Unk, what are you doing up? You feeling better?"

"Nicky, I never felt better in my life! Do you know what today is?"

"Sunday. We gotta go to Mass. You coming?"

"You go and I'll meet you there."

"You always say that!"

"Listen, the important thing is today's the Championship Game! The Giants are playing the Colts, and the Giants have the home field!"

"Are we gonna watch?"

"Are you kidding me? I wouldn't miss it for the world! I been waiting all year for this—haven't you?"

Naturally Nicky thought there couldn't be a better climax to school-vacation week, but also he mimicked his uncle in all things and held a special shrine of reverence in his boyhood heart of hearts for this special uncle, who was an actual living sports-hero and war-hero all rolled into one, and therefore someone whom Nicky could unbashfully worship—it was like having Johnny Unitas living in the house with you, and he was definitely the greatest quarterback of all time! "I'm taking the Colts, Unk!"

"I dunno, Nicky. The Giants are a pretty tough defense, and you know, defense wins in the big game. The Giants won it all two years ago—and just last week they beat the Lions in the playoff game, and you know who was last year's champ? Detroit, that's who!"

"Unk—you can't go against Johnny U!—he's the greatest of all time!"

"Well, Baltimore is an up and coming team, I'll grant you that, but they've never won anything! I just think this is the Giants' year! Besides, who told you Unitas is the best? He's never won anything, either!"

"It was in *Sport* Magazine! You bought it for me for Christmas!"

"That was from Santa Claus!"

"Oh, come on, Unk. That stuff's for the twins!"

"All of a sudden you're too cool for Santa Claus, huh?"

"Well, you don't think I would've believed it came from Dad, do you?"

Nicky regretted saying that as soon as the words were out of his mouth. It wasn't fair, to prefer his uncle over his own father, but he just couldn't help it. There was a secret reason also why he liked Johnny U so much—because in the feature article on the big game in *Sport* Magazine, he had found out Unitas came from his dad's part of the country, down around Pittsburgh, and that went a long way to even-ing up the playing field. And Unitas had a funny name, like his dad's name, Petro-vich, an ethnic name, like one that you didn't see every day, that was uncommon, you certainly wouldn't find that name around this neck of the woods. And after all he had seen with his own eyes his dad tie his uncle in the snow-shoveling match, and who would've ever believed that? So Nicky had built up Johnny Unitas in his mind to where he was almost as big a hero as his Uncle Augie.

Nicky ran off to the foot of the stairs, and yelled up. "Ma!—Ma!!—get up and come make me some pancakes. I'm hungry. And bring down my *Sport* Magazine from my bedroom!"

From the kitchen his uncle whispered loudly "Ssshhh! Let her sleep! Get over here, you."

"What? What? What did I do?"

"Don't you think it's about time you learned how to make pancakes for yourself?"

"Unk!—you know Ma won't let me near the stove! She's afraid I'd burn myself!"

"You're too old for that excuse now—just like you're too old for Santa Claus. You come over here, Nicky, and I'm gonna show you how to make the best pancakes you ever had."

Nicky ran to the fridge and pulled out a box. "Ma says we gotta use Bisquick, 'cause they make the best-tasting pancakes."

"Well, I would have to agree with her about that. Get the bowl out. Now you only need one egg."

Nicky had a million questions. It wasn't enough to tell that kid you only needed one egg. He would then ask three questions why? What if you used, two, what would happen? Why did you need an egg at all, what did that do? He'd been driving them all crazy for years. Of course, the biggest question of all was, "Where did you learn how to make pancakes, Unk?"

"In the Army. Where do you think?"

The Army was an off-limits subject. Nicky had learned long ago that you never asked Unk to talk about that. If he mentioned it at all, it ended right there. Which increased the mystery ten-fold. The next thing Uncle Augie did was to look narrowly at his nephew and say, "Don't believe everything you see on television."

That's right. You didn't want to grow up to be a dope, did you? You wanted to grow up to be just like your uncle—*and* your dad.

"Now watch this. You see the bubbles grow?"

"Yeah."

"When they start to burst—"

"That's when you flip them over?"

"That's right. That's why we used to call them flapjacks." He didn't need to add '*in the Army.*' Augie looked upon his nephew as a smart kid. *Too smart for his own good.* He picked up on things. You had to watch what you said. But all in all the kid managed to be just like a son to him—*a son he had never had.* But still, a son he would have liked to call his own, if he had ever had a son. In fact, Augie had always had a scrupulous practice in dealing with Nicky, which was never to let the word "son" slip out when he was talking to the kid—and many's the time it was a near thing—but he wouldn't have wanted the kid to get the wrong idea, that wouldn't have been right. The kid had his own father.

"You know what, Unk? I'm gonna go out for football when I get to high school."

"You just try to make it through junior high first. Come on, let's eat."

"Ma doesn't want me to try out in junior high. She thinks I'm too young."

"And right after this we're gonna walk up to the Hillside Market and buy the Sunday papers—get ready for the game. That way these flapjacks won't sit on our stomach."

"She won't even let me try out for Little League. She thinks a hardball's gonna hurt me. Can't you talk to her, Unk?"

"Well, she saw me get beaned one time. But that was 'cause I was leaning out over the plate too much."

"You can talk to her, Unk. Dad's no good for things like that. He won't go against her. He just takes the easy way out and says, 'your mother said so.'"

"You finished? Go get dressed and let's get outta here."

When Nicky came downstairs again, after waking the whole house getting dressed, the two of them left the kitchen by the back hall door, went down the steps of the back porch, which Nicky's Dad had built, crossed the brick walk he also had built, and turned right on Glenwood, down the cracked and frost-heaved sidewalk where the two maple trees erupted on that side of the fieldstone house, the side that faced MacPherson's white house behind its tall green hedges on the other side of Glenwood. At the corner of Glenwood and Elm, they turned right on Elm Street, passed under the two tall pines flanking their front walk, and after six or seven houses, came even with the back parking lot of St Theresa's Church. Nicky was twelve now and this spring he was going to have to attend Confirmation classes at St Ann's Orphanage, across Haverhill Street from the Ebenezer Baker, and he was dreading the prospect as they passed the church, as it set him to recalling the terror of the fires of hell the Irish nuns at Immaculate Conception in Revere had inspired him in him when he had to go there for Communion classes. He was struggling to keep up with his uncle's big strides as they started up the hill to the top of Elm Street where it come to a stop at Haverhill Street, which was the Route 110, which indeed ran all the way from Haverhill, through Pleasant Valley, across Prospect Hill, then Broadway and Tower Hill in Milltown, until it passed through Glen Forest, past Nicky's school, the Baker, and from there, hugging the coils of the Merrimack River, where it became the Lowell Boulevard, all the way to Lowell.

Nicky was tracing this route in his mind, because his father had taken him and the twins in his Jeep on a Sunday excursion up to Salisbury Beach by Rte 110, back in the good weather. Nicky had found that beach but a second-rate, cheap imitation of Revere Beach, as far as the lights and the rides and the amusements were concerned. Besides, he was loyal to his hometown, like a boy should be, and he had never yet found anything around here that could compare with his memories of Revere. Huffing and puffing to keep up, Nicky ventured to tell Uncle Augie, "I still think of Revere every day, you know."

"Why?" said his uncle over his shoulder.

"I miss it. I don't think I fit in around here."

"Why? You have friends, don't you? What about that Jimmy kid you brought over? Or Billy Wade? You been over his house, haven't you?"

"Yeah, but when Jimmy's mother invited me over for supper once, Ma didn't want to let me go."

"I'll talk to your mother."

That was what was so good about Unk. You could talk to Unk, and he'd understand how a kid felt.

They had arrived at Haverhill Street, but it was too early yet, and the Hillside wasn't open till 8 on Sunday morning. So they crossed Haverhill Street by the Texaco station and went to the Glen Forest Variety on the corner of Cypress Avenue.

On the way back past the church again, Nicky was still thinking about Revere. "How come they don't have any Spas around here—everything's a Variety Store—remember the Broadway Spa, back in Revere?"

His uncle said, "Comes to the same thing. Different places have different customs, Nicky."

"Yeah, but I don't like it. It's not the same."

"Nicky, you can't live in the past."

Nicky left it at that because that sounded like a pronouncement. He was already feeling bad enough about leaving his childhood behind and being forced to grow up—supposedly, Confirmation was going to be the beginning of his manhood, that's what he had been taught. And it was just awful, awful being caught in between, like he was right now, being dragged backward by all he had lost, and could never retrieve, and yet faced with a future unknown, with people telling him things like, *wait'll you get to junior high, if you think you got homework now, boy, just you wait.*

His mother had the twins all dressed up and now it was big brother's job to get Jack and Jill to 9 o'clock Mass in time. He got scolded yet another time about making sure he held onto *both* of their hands when he was crossing Elm Street to the church's back parking lot. Of course, Nicky had to change, he couldn't go to Mass looking like that! His father came down the steps scratching under his arm as Nicky was being pushed out the front door with the children. None of *them* ever went to Mass, his father wasn't even a Catholic, his mother was mad at the church, God knows why, his uncle acted like Rockingham Park was his church, I tell you, *it just isn't fair!*

In the end Nicky sat through the whole Mass, genuflected, stood up, and sat back down, every time he was supposed to, and made the twins follow suit, like a dutiful miniature parent, leafed through his brand-new Sunday Missal, which he had got for Christmas, a present his mother gave him because he was going to be going for his Confirmation, read a bit, trying to follow the ins and outs of the litany of the Mass, understood not a word of the Latin that was being recited almost audibly on the altar by the parish priest, with his back turned, even though, by now, Nicky had memorized *Dominus Vobiscum,* which sounded to him like *Give us the Biscuits,* and *Et Cum Spiritu Tuo,* another favorite, which sounded like you were getting ready to spit a nice, ripe, round lunger.

But after Mass, Nicky felt great. He felt about as great as Uncle Augie had felt that morning, when he said *I never felt better in my life.* It was amazing, truly amazing, how great you felt when Mass was over!

Now he could get on with a Sunday, and not just any Sunday, but maybe, just perhaps, the greatest Sunday of his life, because the big game was on today and they were gonna watch it!

Of course, there was more torture to get through, courtesy of his mother, before they could get to the big game. First of all, she wouldn't move the Sunday dinner, which is what Gerry Petrovich always called it, *Sunday dinner*, up to 1 o'clock, just because some game was coming on. "Sunday dinner in my house is 2 pm, and you know it!" And, no, you *can not* eat in the den! We're gonna eat right here in the kitchen, just like always, no, not in the dining room, we're not having company today, everybody's home for Christmas, *sometimes I wish that kid would button his lip!* Then, of all things, when the grown-ups had dawdled and gabbed and delayed and vociferated and spooned and forked their way through a whole hour of the usual same old wasn't that delicious Gerry you oughta open a restaurant if people knew what they were missing macaroni and meatballs and roast chicken and potatoes and finally salad-'cause-it's-good-for-the-digestion Sunday dinner, then of all things, they had to wash the dishes before they were allowed into the den. *Mamma-mia!* We're gonna miss the start of the game!

Uncle Augie said to Nicky, "Come on. Won't take us a minute. Let your mother sit down and relax, she's been slaving over a hot stove all morning. You wipe and I'll wash."

Finally they got to the game, halfway through the first quarter. And when Nicky finally sat down, he had to yell at his brother Jackie, who hadn't had to lift a finger. "Get out of the way! I can't see!"

Chris Schenkel, the Giants' play-by-play announcer, was saying it wasn't looking good for the Giants at half-time, behind 14-3, but then in the second half, the Colts' announcer took over, whoever he was. The game was being broadcast on Channel 7 from Boston, a CBS network station, which carried the New York football team because Boston didn't have a pro team of its own. So, Nicky and Augie had seen every Giants game every Sunday all season long, and Nicky knew the New York lineup by heart. Sam Huff and Frank Gifford, of course, were his favorites, they got most of the publicity, their names seemed to be on Schenkel's lips more than any others, but he also liked all of them—he especially liked Linden Crow and Emlen Tunnell, because of their unusual names that just sorta kinda rolled off your tongue, but he also loved Andy Robustelli and Rosey Brown.

Now in the second half, when the Giants had gone to Charlie Conerly at quarterback, they not only caught up, but went into the lead, 17-14, and the fourth quarter was almost over. Nicky was so upset that he had missed the first quarter, but now, he couldn't stay in the room, he kept running in and out, he couldn't watch because the Colts had gotten the ball with only two minutes left in the game.

"Well, it's time for Robustelli to stop them," Uncle Augie said. He was a true blue Giants fan because he thought they were just head and shoulders superior to the rest of the league, they had all the stars, their defense was invincible, they had a lead, now was the time.

Nicky followed Uncle Augie's lead, and had done so, all season. When they watched games they always picked out the Italian names on the rosters to root for. But Gino Marchetti, defensive end, for the Colts, was now on the screen being carried out on a stretcher, after making a touchdown-saving tackle of the Giants' star halfback, matinee idol Frank Gifford. The Baltimore announcer was saying that Marchetti broke his leg when defensive tackle Gene 'Big Daddy' Lipscomb of the Colts fell on him as he was tackling Gifford. What a game! A game for the ages! "Well, you just gotta go with Robustelli and the Giants," Uncle Augie declared, "now that Marchetti's outta the game."

But then the Giants, inches shy of a first down on Marchetti's tackle, decided to punt on fourth down, rather than go for it, and the punt pinned the Colts back, 85 yards away from the goal line.

There was little more than two minutes left in the game.

Uncle Augie told his nephew, "Well, we decided to put it on our defense, and we got the best defense in the league, what did I tell you, Nicky? Looks like the Colts are cooked now."

But then Unitas had completed a pass, 11 yards, to Lenny Moore, after throwing two incompletions. The Colts were still alive. They still had a chance.

Nicky couldn't watch. He kept running out of the den, then returning to peek around the corner from the hall by the stairs.

Unitas was moving them down the field! He completed two in a row to Raymond Berry and Berry went out of bounds to stop the clock!

The Baltimore announcer was going nuts, and he was swaying Nicky from his loyalties.

It was that guy Unitas. There's something about that Johnny Unitas!

He certainly had a name for a football hero! *Johnny Unite-us!* Nicky was thinking.

The Colts' quarterback was turning Nicky into a Colts fan in spite of himself.

Now, after Unitas threw two more darts to split end Raymond Berry, who nimbly stepped out of bounds to stop the clock, the Colts, they were down on the 13 yard line! Time was running out. Could they make it? Only 7 seconds to go! They're gonna kick it! They're going for the field goal and a 17-17 tie! Can the Giants block it? Nicky's fingers were crossed, but now, he didn't know any more for which side! He couldn't watch. He couldn't move, he couldn't run out of the room. He closed his eyes. He opened them. The kick went through!

"I don't believe it! They tied it! Unk, what's gonna happen now?"

"I don't know, I don't know. Listen!—they're saying something."

"But the game's over!"

"Nicky, shut up! I think they're saying they're gonna have to go into overtime. Because it's the final game of the season and they have to have a winner, or the league won't have a champion. Wow. This has never happened before."

Nicky thought back as far as he could remember. He could remember back to Jim Brown and the Cleveland Browns winning it in '56. Then last year, the Detroit Lions with Bobby Layne at QB and Dick 'Night-Train' Lane in the defensive backfield. But before that—well, probably he was too young and hadn't been a fan, hadn't been paying attention back then, heck, he was only nine years old back then.

Nicky turned to his uncle, who would know so much more. "Is that true, Unk? It's never happened before."

"Nicky, they never had a tie game in this situation before."

"So what's gonna happen?"

"We don't know yet. We'll just have to wait and see. They said they're going into something called sudden-death overtime. Meaning whoever scores first wins the game."

"Oh, no. This is incredible."

"Nicky, keep your eyes open. We're gonna see history made right in front of our very eyes."

Together, they went out to the kitchen for refreshments. Nicky got tonic and this was a rare occasion when Uncle Augie popped open the quart of Miller's High Life, the Champagne of Bottled Beers, that he had been storing up in the fridge for several weeks, and which, now, he was glad he had saved, because this was turning into something special. They brought back a bag of chips into the den and placed it between them. From one side and the other they reached and hunted for the bowl as neither one of them now could take their eyes off the screen. Nicky was growing up all in one afternoon and his uncle was becoming a 12-year-old kid all over again, eyes wide in anticipation of thrills he hadn't felt since he was out there on that field himself.

The Giants won a coin toss and they were going to get the ball.

"Oh, Unk, it's all over now, they can't miss, they've got the ball, all they gotta do is score, the Colts don't have a chance!"

"I hope so, Nicky," his Uncle Augie said. He didn't want to say it to Nicky but while the children had been at Mass that morning, he had called up Jack Lane at home and placed a bet, but Jack had made him take the Giants and give points, because the Colts were favored by the oddsmakers by 3-1/2 points. So that meant that Augie would win his bet even if the Giants lost the game, because if they lost by three, two or one point, Augie still won, and he also won if the Giants won the game outright–but the Colts, for Augie to lose his bet, would have to score a touchdown, because they had to win by four points or more, and a field goal could only give them 3 points. And they didn't have the ball to start the overtime, which was going to last 15 minutes, like a whole quarter. So, at this point, it wasn't likely the Colts were going to win the game, or that Augie could possibly lose his bet. Complicated, but Augie ran all the possibilities in his head, and he just didn't see how the Colts could do it.

But Augie hadn't reckoned on Johnny Unitas, who lost him his bet, and Nicky hadn't counted on Johnny Unitas, who won his heart.

The Giants took the kickoff and went nowhere. Three downs and they were out. They had to punt the ball. The Colts got it back on their own 20.

Eighty yards to go. *Impossible.*

But methodically Unitas began to move them down the field. An 8-yard pass on third-and-8, to the fullback, Ameche, of all things, looked ominous to Augie. Berry made another two catches and suddenly Unitas was taking his time setting them up deep in Giants territory. To Augie's eye, it looked like the Giants defense was dog-tired. Huff and Robustelli were nowhere to be seen. It could be they had nothing left. Augie had been there on the winning end when it was the waning minutes and you were wearing them down, just shoving them aside, grinding. He recognized the signs. Unitas threw a completion to a little-heralded end called Jim Mutscheller and Augie was thinking, it's all over. *Unitas thinks he can do anything he wants and they can't stop him.* The TV cameras showed the Giants in enormous game-cloaks watching from the sidelines, Giants stars like Gifford and Conerly crowding the line, clutching their cloaks like they were shivering in Yankee Stadium. They had the look of defeated men written all over them. Augie had seen it in the war. The Colts were down to the one-yard-line and it was third down. They were going for the touchdown. *Did they somehow know about Augie's bet?* No, no, no, it can't be that, it's just that they have one more down, then they'll kick the field goal—I can still win. *If the Giants can stop them here on third down.*

Ameche the fullback went in on a one-yard plunge into the line on a hand-off from Unitas.

The Colts win, Augie loses.

"I can't believe it!" yelled Nicky, dancing around.

"I can't believe it, either," said Augie.

Well, they played it safe. They kept it in the middle of the field for the field-goal. It was an absolutely safe play, straight ahead into the middle of the line, minimize the chances of a fumble, don't make the quarterback have to sneak it for a whole yard on the goal-line. The Giants just couldn't stop it. They melted away. They were whipped.

Just at that moment Nicky's Dad appeared in the doorway to the left of the fireplace that connected the den and the kitchen.

He had spent the afternoon outside, even though it was cold, because it wasn't snowing, and he was building a brick-oven fire-place between the apple tree and the garage, so that, next summer they could have cook-outs and wouldn't have to use one of those cheap, flimsy, three-legged charcoal thingama-bobs they sell down at Sears and Roebucks on Essex Street. He had poured the concrete base all the way back to September and now he had wanted to get her finished before the real winter weather set in because he had let himself get distracted by Thanksgiving and Christmas and a million other things that

Gerry or her brother Gene or the rest of them wanted him to do with his weekends. He thought he had gone all-out for the kids and the wife and he was proud of himself—it looked good the way the job had turned out, a chimney in the rear and two slabs on top of the side-bricks, so you could have wing-tables on the barbecue to put your pans and utensils on. The grill itself was sunk in the middle between the wing-table-tops, it was neat. Andy had gotten the design out of *Mechanics Illustrated,* which he subscribed to.

Now as he stood in the doorway to the den, Andy said to his son, "Nicky—wanna come see what I finished out in the yard?"

"In a minute, Dad. We're watching the game."

Nicky's Dad went away, evidently taking no special notice of Nicky's comment, but—Augie noticed. *Maybe the little kids'll want to go see. Maybe Gerry will look out the window.*

Later that evening, after all the excitement of *the greatest game ever!* as Nicky called it, had somewhat died down, when it was bedtime for the little ones, and another family Christmas, with a long weekend tacked on, drawing to a close, and work looming tomorrow morning, a resumption of the daily humdrum, when Nicky had finally been persuaded over the most strenuous objections that he had to go to bed, upstairs, now! *there's school tomorrow, you know!* when it was just Gerry and Andy and Augie left sitting around the kitchen table, when Andy went upstairs to use the bathroom, Augie leaned over to Gerry and said,

"We gotta talk."

"About what?" Gerry was already alarmed. Augie never acted like this and he had been so happy all day, after those awful couple of days of suffering shut up in his room with the migraine.

"Tell him you're out of cigarettes and send him out."

"Augie, you're scaring me!"

Andy objected that he was dog-tired, and couldn't it wait, or—couldn't Augie walk to the store before it closed?

"I can't wait that long," said Gerry. "You smoke, Andy. You know how it is. I›m havin› a nicotine fit. For Crissakes, just go up to the Glen Forest. It won't take you a minute in the car. Geez—I pay enough in gas money for the thing."

Andy didn't have to be urged any further after that comment.

"Now what is it, Augie."

"Well—I been thinking."

"Thinking what? Are you all right. You're not sick or anything?"

"I'm fine, I've just been thinking it's time I made a change."

"Whaddya mean? What kind of change?"

"Gerry, you need a chance to have your own life. Your own house, your own life, with your husband and kids. I'm in the way here."

"You are not in the way!"

"Yes I am. If you can't see it, I don't know what to tell you, or how to persuade you, but Gerry, you're my sister, I love you, I may not say it much, but, you know it's true, and you know I wouldn't be saying this now unless I felt like it was time I needed a life of *my* own, a new start for myself, to start over, somewhere on my own."

"But I don't want you to go." Gerry was crying.

"It's not up to you, Gerry. It's not what you want, it's what I want."

Gerry had always deferred to the men in her family, her father, her brother Gene, especially Augie, and Augie knew it, he depended on it, and Gerry knew that he knew it. Hadn't she opened her home to him, and always made sure he knew he had his place in her home, and in her heart? *How could it come to this, that it was never enough, no matter how hard she tried?* "This is making me very sad."

"Go dry your eyes, Gerry. Your husband's gonna be home in two seconds."

Gerry rushed away from the table.

Augie said to himself, *Goddammit, I'm just no good at this. God knows I love that kid Nicky. But why wouldn't I want a son of my own, someday, maybe? Gerry, I'm only doing what I think is best for everybody.*

Chapter 24

Sudden Death Overtime

"So you gonna tell me what's going on?" said Augie's brother Gene.

They had just climbed into Gene's Buick, parked at the foot of the driveway at Gerry's house in Spicket Falls. It was a cold day, the morning of Saturday, January 3, 1959, so the windows were rolled up, and Gene took the first chance he had to talk to his brother where they wouldn't be overheard or disturb the family—*in other words, a private chat,* Gene was thinking, *man to man, brother to brother, away from the others—what in the hell is going on?*

"Nothing's going on," said Augie as he settled himself in the front seat, in his long overcoat.

"Tell that to Gerry. Why did you have to go and give her a case of *agidu?*"

"I couldn't help it."

Backing out onto Glenwood, Gene was straightening out the Buick when Augie touched his arm on the wheel.

"Wait a minute."

"You changed your mind."

"No! Where's my duffel-bag?"

"You put it in the trunk."

"Oh."

"Yeah. You're ready to live on your own."

Gene veered the Buick onto Elm Street and powered past the church smoothly, then up the hill, when he felt the automatic transmission shift. His 1957 Riviera still felt new to drive. He would never have driven anything else. Buicks were good enough for his father, they were good enough for him.

Augie was thinking about the day before, walking up this same street with Nicky, *having that talk*, on the way to pick up a loaf of bread at the Hillside Market, *that talk* where he was going to explain that he was leaving. He thought it was going pretty well, pretty well, the kid wasn't saying anything at all, then he goes, *Will I ever see you again?* And Augie had said, *Of course you're gonna see me again, what's the matter with you?*

And yet Augie knew he was going to move far enough away so that he would not be tempted to walk by the fieldstone house and see the lights on, and see them moving around inside the house, and have to walk on by without going in. *Because it wasn't his house anymore.*

"I'm waiting," said Gene.

They were passing over Tower Hill, heading down to Broadway in Milltown to pick up Rte 28 south. Augie said, «Let's wait till we get out on the highway, you got a lotta stoplights and turns you gotta watch out for going through the city."

Gene was thinking, *he acts like driving a car is like piloting a tugboat or something.*

And Augie: *See, this is the very reason why I had to say no when Andy offered to take me in the Jeep. If I gotta put up with a million and one questions, the third degree, from my brother—how the hell was I gonna tell Andy, I think it's better for your marriage if I leave?*

They were cruising down Rte 28 through Andover, and after passing Andover Square and Phillips Academy, they hit an open stretch between there and the turn-off for 125, and Gene had so often, in his life, driven this road, he could have done it with eyes closed. Indeed, he often found his mind wandering and had to bring his attention back to the road. He decided to try again. "Remember that talk we were gonna have?"

"Which one?"

"That talk—the talk we were gonna have later.

"Oh—and later never came."

"Yeah. Later never came. You know, Augie, I am your brother. You can talk to me."

"I know, I know."

"So everybody wants to know, your sister Mary, Anna, your brother Patsy, the whole family wants to know, what brought all this about, all of a sudden? They're asking me, like I know. What am I supposed to tell them?"

"Tell 'em to mind their own business."

"Come on, Augie. We're not kids anymore."

But then the guy falls silent.

And when he does speak, it's just to try to change the subject.

"How's your kids, Gene? How's Joanna? And Leon, and—and–"

"Marie."

"Marie."

"They're fine, Augie. But we're not talking about my kids, we're talking about you."

They hit two or three stoplights in Reading Square and so Augie waved him off again with, *wait'll till we're out on the highway.*

That did it. If Gene's mind wasn't made up before, it was made up now. Normally, he would continue straight south on 28 after Stoneham Square, as, on his everyday commute to work, that was the quickest way home to Watertown, through Medford, Somerville and Cambridge–but now he took the turn-off to the new sections of Rte 128, which was still under construction, a highway he normally avoided, if he could, for that reason: too many slow-downs and lane restrictions.

Augie, who was not a driver, said, "You sure we can get to Providence this way?"

"Okay. Let's start there." Gene was adjusting himself in his seat behind the wheel for a nice long highway ride. "How in the hell did you decide on Providence?"

"It's a hundred miles away."

"Good reason."

"Look, you don't understand, but, to be honest with you, Gene, I just couldn't see moving across town. It would be like I never left. I would be back on Elm Street every other day, visiting. I would be tempted. This way I won't be tempted. I'll be a hundred miles away."

"And so you stick me with having to bring in a new cutter. Thanks."

"Who you gonna get?"

"I'm gonna give Frankie Merano a ring, a guy I used to know at Pappagallo's, see if he's looking, or if he knows somebody."

"There you go. You're all set."

"Yeah, but, Augie, it's not gonna be the same anymore—it was always you, me and Patsy, the three brothers, in this, together. Now what are you gonna do in Providence? You don't even know anybody there."

"So I'll meet people. Look—it's not that far away. In fact, it's just like Boston. They got an Italian section there, Federal Hill. Hell, Genie, we know all about Providence—how many times we been to Lincoln Downs, Narragansett, the ponies, the dogs, the trotters in Foxboro. What's to know about Providence that we don't already know? At least it's in another state—and I have never lived in another state—except the state of war."

"Now he's making jokes."

"And I quote, 'since Sunday, December the 7th, a state of war has existed between the United States and the Empire of Japan.' Remember that one, Genie?"

"How could we ever forget?"

"Yeah. How could we ever forget."

"Well?"

"Well, I'm waiting. For that little chat we were gonna have later. Here it is, later, only thirteen years later—no, let me correct myself, it's already 1959, so, it's fourteen years later—and I'm still waiting to find out what happened to you in Italy."

"And what happened to you on D-Day? What about that?"

"You wanna hear about D-Day? You sure?"

"Well, Augie, you were the only one of the three of us who had to go through that—."

"Yeah, and to listen to Patsy, he took the whole thing as one big joke."

"Listen, you can't blame Patsy for that. It was just his way of dealing with it, that's all. And let's face it, he was the only one of the three of us that got wounded, wasn't he? So Patsy bled for his Purple Heart, you can't take that away from him, he's entitled to talk any way he likes. Besides, you had the same chances to say whatever you wanted to say, all those times, at the family picnic table, but you used to just get up and walk away—so, the rest of us figured—you know, leave the guy alone—with his memories."

"My memories, huh?" Augie was looking out the car window on his side, and had his face averted.

Gene said, "Sometimes it helps to talk to somebody." *God help me. I should know. If I didn't have Celia to talk to, I don't know what I would've done.*

Augie said, "Hey! I got an idea. Why don't we swing over to Stoughton, have lunch? I haven't been there in years. I haven't been there since before the war! We got all day, don't we? We're in no rush—we'll get to Providence—it's Saturday!"

"You wanna?"

"Now you're talking."

"We're talking? We're talking. But first, before we get into the other, I gotta know, 'cause I'm dying of curiosity—why the move out of the house?"

"I was just in the way."

"In the way of what—are you telling me Gerry's having some kind of trouble—?"

"No, no, no, nothing like that. It's not Gerry, it's Nicky. The kid needs to have a chance to get to know his own father, and I was just in the way of that."

"Yeah . . . yeah, I can see that could happen."

"I was turning into his substitute father, Genie. The kid was picking me over his own father. It wasn't right."

"I can see that, in a certain way. But are you sure that was all there was to it?"

"I'm sure, I'm sure. I'm sure it didn't escape the notice of Gerry, either, or Andy, himself, for that matter. But Gerry didn't want to draw any attention to it, because she didn't want to blame me. After all, it's the kid's fault. But how could you blame him—he's just a kid, he can't help it. And Andy—poor Andy—he was caught in the middle because he didn't want to piss off Gerry. Jesus, Genie, I'm well out of it. I mean, how would you feel if that happened to you and your son, Leon?"

"I guess I wouldn't like it, all right."

"Yeah. Because you love your son. Don't you?"

"*Of course* I love my kids."

"Just like I love that kid Nicky, God knows. But he's not my son. And if I ever wanted to have a son of my own–."

"That's it, that's it! You found a woman, and she lives in Providence!"

"No, no, no, nothing like that! But if I did find someone, what would be wrong with that?"

"I always thought you were scared of girls."

"What? Come on!"

"You were scared of girls in high school."

"How would you know, you weren't there."

"That's right, I was working with Pa as his gopher."

"Gopher this, gopher that. But I wasn't scared of girls in high school. I just didn't have time for them. I was too busy being '*Moose.*' Captain of the football team, captain of the baseball team. I just preferred hanging out with the guys, that's all. Say—is this the way to Stoughton? Is that why you turned off back there?"

"Well, we're gonna go through Dedham, I think, and then Norwood—and we'll see from there."

"Why didn't you just take 135?"

"'Cause I don't think 128 extends down that far as yet—look, who's driving this car?"

If Gene was going to get them lost, he wasn't going to let on to his brother Augie.

They were on Rte 1 in Norwood, when Augie saw a sign for Canton.

"Take that turn, left hand turn. Gene, I'm telling you, if we get to Canton, we'll get to Stoughton."

Neponset Street from Norwood took them into Canton and they somehow made their way to Pleasant Street, and Gene knew where he was. He took that all the way to Stoughton Square.

Augie said, "Oh, boy, I don't know the place anymore. Everything's changed."

"Let's go to the *Town Spa!*" said Gene, who was hungry.

"The pizza! But first, swing out to Pearl Street, Gene—I wanna go by the High School."

The High School had been expanded. The old foursquare red brick two-story classroom building had grown wings.

"Look at this! I can't believe it! Pull in, Gene. Let's go up to the ballfields."

As they drove the winding road alongside the high school, Augie marveled at the low-lying, one-story modernistic extensions, which completely altered the image in his mind of his old school. But the football field—that was the same. Across the road from the baseball diamond, almost a half-mile from Pearl Street, the wooden bleachers with the press-shack perched on top where the local reporters from the *Stoughton Journal* and the *Brockton Enterprise* hid out from the autumn chill to write their stories and take photos—Sarno Field.

They got out of the car and walked out onto the field. Augie stood under the goalposts at the near end and pointed. "I scored once in this end-zone in '39, and twice down at the other end. Louie Arsenault scored the other one and we beat the Canton *Bulldogs* on Thanksgiving Day that year, 28-0. Remember?"

"Yes, I do. That was your sophomore year."

"Yeah. And the next year I was in the CCC."

"Pa wanted you to go to work with him—he was gonna make you into a cloth-cutter."

"And he did, later. But first I had to go my own way."

"I still think it's a damn shame you had to lose your last two years of ball."

"Come on, let's go eat. You know what the man says that wrote that book."

"Which book?"

"*You Can't Go Home Again.*"

"I dunno. All I ever read is trade publications. You're the book-reader, Augie. Out of the three of us."

"Ah," said Augie, dismissively.

"I remember when you were so deep into that book by the Trappist monk, what's-his-name, Gerry was worried she was gonna lose you to the priesthood."

"There was never any danger of that."

When they got to the *Town Spa,* they took a booth separated from the bar area by the low wall. It was musty and brown in the *Town Spa,* the one place where nothing had changed in decades. The pizza was thin-crust and so oily you had to blot it with a paper napkin. It was as dim and private in that booth as a church confessional. The two brothers leaned their heads close together as they bent over the booth-table endeavoring to curl the thin, hot slice between pursed lips onto a burn-testing tongue without dripping oil onto shirt-fronts.

"So tell me about that day," said Gene.

"That day?"

"The sixth of June."

"Well," Augie began. "Oh—this is hot—but so good— just the way I remember it—"

He told Gene that nothing had gone according to plan. He told Gene the part about being underwater, admitting frankly that he panicked because he thought he was going to die. He blamed himself for being stupid because in spite of all their training, all the year-and-a-half spent in camp and live-action amphibious rehearsals, he had somehow treated the whole thing as just another football game—when the whistle blew, he'd be ready to go. But he wasn't ready. He wasn't ready to drown, he wasn't ready to die, and as he struggled for air, and struggled for life itself, that—was the beginning of his fight that day. And his fight wasn't over, that day, until the moment his war began—his personal war of suppurated hatred and festering revenge against an enemy who wantonly violated the rules of the game. And at the end of that day, he had sat down on the brow of the cratered and pock-marked bluff overlooking Omaha Beach, with a dead man's helmet on his head, and watched, feeling, personally, spent as an empty cartridge, watched the unloading of trucks, tanks, half-tracks, jeeps from wobble-waisted landing ships onto the beach far below, through spandrils of drifting smoke, and he thought *they have lost the war, they just don't know it yet . . . and I don't care . . . I've taken human life, and I don't care . .*

In the present moment of that Saturday afternoon in the Town Spa, with the pizza consumed, and the grease gone cold, coagulated on paper plates with curling edges, Augie looked at his brother Gene and concluded, "So, that day, I started that day a kid of 19, and by the end of that day, I was still 19, but I was, uh, oh, kinda like the light went out, you know what I mean? like when the pilot light goes out and you try and turn on the gas and nothing happens, except you die of asphyxiation . . . "

They left the Town Spa with what appetites they had arrived with gone. Augie was being quiet and Gene did not want to intrude on his thoughts. After settling into the Buick, they proceeded onward because there didn't seem to be anything else to do. Gene thought about doubling back to Rte 1, which would take them straight into Providence, but he didn't want to backtrack, so he headed out Washington Street southwards, which was Rte 138. He knew that would take them around Brockton instead of through it, and on down to—Taunton. The thought made him remember the moment back then, on his bicycle, outside Salerno, when he had been faced with getting past the German battery in the woods, and the American lieutenant had called over a private from the artillery platoon who happened to come from southeastern Massachusetts, and Gene had to pass the identity test—*what road would you take to get from Stoughton to Taunton?* The road he was now on. That was the answer—*Rte 138.* He passed the test. *They helped him get past the Germans on his bike, with covering fire, to distract them, to keep them busy while he sped by, pumping furiously, head low.*

Gene found himself lost in thought. It had happened before, too many times. Especially when driving, which seemed to lull you into vacancy. You could easily miss your turn. You could go off the road—hit a truck oncoming. *You had to pull yourself back out of the war.*

He swung left, in South Easton, onto Rte 123. That would get them to Attleboro, instead of Taunton. And Attleboro was practically in Rhode Island. Attleboro would get them to Providence.

All this time, Augie had still not said a word.

Gene said, "You okay?"

Augie was looking out the window. Gene could not see his face, it was turned away.

Augie didn't know if he had filled in a gap in his life, or opened up a hole.

"You feeling all right?" said Gene. It worried him that his brother had gone so silent.

Augie said to the car-window, without turning his head, "I don't know if I feel better, or worse."

Gene had seen this before, at the shop, at family holidays. "You got a migraine coming on?"

"Huh? Oh. I hope not."

"What are you gonna do, all alone by yourself, down there in Providence, when you get one of these things, and you're laid low for two days? Huh, Augie?"

"Maybe I won't have them anymore." Augie had turned to look at Gene, with a strange smile on his face.

"Will you cut it out now! You're making me nervous. There is no way I'm gonna drop you off in Providence on some street corner tonight if you're gonna have an attack of migraine."

"So stop talking about it, all right? You wanna jinx me, or what? It's too late to stop now. We've come all this way . . ."

He trailed off, still with that strange smile lingering on his lips—*like he knew something nobody else knew, and he wasn't going to tell you.*

It was getting dark now. They were sailing past the outskirts of Attleboro on 123, when stoplights appeared out of the mist ahead—Rte 1.

When the light changed, Gene took a sharp left onto Rte 1 South.

It wouldn't be long now. They had been on the road for more than an hour since leaving the Town Spa. It was the time of year when it got dark early, almost at four in the afternoon, it seemed. Southeastern Massachusetts was a dense forest with roads winding through it seemingly going nowhere, past houses set back in the woods, with lights flickering, and then you would pass a gas station. With Augie silent, Gene had wandered back in his mind to the mountainous route he had taken to Avellino, and beyond, to Alta Villa, so many years ago. Those woods were similarly deserted. Those woods similarly held out unknown threatening recesses, and occasional twinkling hope. *It was all a passage you had to go through to get where you were going, a kind of a tunnel bored through the darkness, and when you got to your destination, then you would come face to face with the answer, and the answer would tell you why you had made the passage.*

Gene wanted to reveal this knowledge to his brother. He had always wanted to. He had thought that by bringing on the revelations of the sixth of June which had been hidden for so long, back at the *Town Spa*, that he would open a door, through which he could get out the secret which he had kept so long from his brothers, and all the others, *the secret he had sworn an oath to himself, that he had vowed to himself, in a sacred, secret vow, that he would take with him to the grave.*

But now he could see that it was still not the right time. His brother Augie had troubles of his own. *Now was not the time.*

They sailed on with only the headlights piercing the darkness.

Gene quickly found himself lost in the streets of the city when they arrived in what unmistakably had to be Providence.

He was peering about looking for street signs and asking Augie, "Where do you want to be let off?"

Augie turned to him and, in the dimness, with no interior light on in the Buick, but colored lights and the glare of a slight rain outside sending deceptive, confusing bolts of shadow and light through the front seat of the car, Augie was trying to say something.

"I—I feel—funning—"

Then he grabbed his head in both hands and Gene could feel the shock of pain roar through the middle of his brother's head as Augie cried out in stifled agony.

His body was thrown back against the car door, his head twisted away, and suddenly an eruption of vomit poured out of him, down the front of his overcoat, his head fell back against the glass, his body slumped against the car door, and the hands grasping his head on both temples went limp and fell to his sides.

"Augie! What's the matter!"

OH MY GOD! he's passed out . . .

Gene panicked, as he realized he had to get Augie to a hospital immediately, and he had no idea where there was a hospital in this town.

He cursed himself for all the times he and Augie had driven together down to Lincoln Downs or Narragansett to pursue the ponies while purposely avoiding the logjam of traffic in downtown Providence. Now at the critical moment when he needed to know where to turn immediately, he was stuck at a redlight in the rain and the dark with no idea.

When the light changed he shot ahead with no more plan than to look for a large building. He quickly realized that he was heading the wrong way, in a direction taking him away from the center of town, and the smell of vomit swimming up in his face penetrated his nostrils and his open mouth straight to his brain bringing an odor of death that sickened him with a guilty fear. *Hurry up, hurry up!*

Gene spotted a man emerging from a corner liquor store. He went to roll down the passenger side window to yell at the man to ask directions when he realized he couldn't get at the crank-handle past the slumped over Augie in his heavy winter coat. He jammed on the brakes, jumped out, stood up in the street and yelled across the roof. "I've got an emergency here! I gotta get to a hospital right away!"

The man was heading for his own car, and when Gene opened his door and the interior light went on in the Buick, the man could see through the raindrops on the car window the shadow slumped against the door. "You're going the wrong way!" he hollered to Gene. "You'll have to turn around. Turn your car and follow me!"

The two cars were in the middle of this maneuver on the dark and busy street when the Providence Police appeared out of nowhere with lights flashing. Gene jumped out and so did a wary patrolman in the two-man squad-car. Gene stopped and gestured back to his car.

"My brother just took violently sick! I gotta get him to a hospital right away! Can you help me?—please, Officer!"

"Well, pull over a little and let us get by and we'll take you there."

They sped through stoplights with the police, siren sounding, in the lead and Gene in the Buick following. At the emergency entrance one of the policemen ran inside while

Gene waited with his hand on the door-handle and Augie slumped inside. Two attendants came running out with a gurney on wheels and Gene raced around the car to hold onto his brother so he wouldn't fall out when they opened the passenger door. But he wasn't thinking, they already had him out, onto the gurney. He sped after them in time to see one of the attendants shaking his head at the other. Inside, they told him to wait and take a seat, they'd be right with him when they could, and the last Gene saw of Augie was the top of his hatless head disappearing through two doors that closed after him with a soft pneumatic sigh. A nurse with a clipboard was asking him questions and he remembered to tell her this was his brother, Augie LaStoria, but he really did not remember filling out the forms she handed to him with the clipboard.

All Gene did recall later was that he took a seat on a wooden bench, forgetting all about his car, not looking at the people already on the bench who silently pushed over and squidged up in a semblance of commiseration, and he plunged his head in his hands, not wanting to deal with anyone else, anxious to find a dark place to hide in with this own thoughts.

If he dies *it's all my fault, all my fault . . .*

Within five minutes someone from the hospital came over to advise him gently that he would have to move his car.

That gave him something to do and think about for a few minutes before he would have to go back and confront the situation again.

When he came back there was no longer any room on the bench seat, so he stood leaning his back up against the wall. He hadn't taken off his overcoat and it was very warm and stuffy there, inside the waiting room of the emergency department, but when he touched his cheek, sometime later, he didn't know how much later, but a good deal later, both his hand and his face and his nose were cold. And his eyes were not registering anything that was right in front of him, in reality, but were seeing only a grey cloud of uncertain provenance that seemed to be dwelling inside him and which felt like the only reality there was.

In another five minutes, Gene bolted from the wall and made his way quickly to the admitting nurse's window. "I wanna see my brother. Where is he?"

"Well, sir, he's in emergency surgery right now. As soon as he's done there, and we find him a room, then you'll be able to see him. I'm sorry, sir."

After about thirty minutes more, standing, then sitting, then standing, in the Emergency waiting room, a nurse approached him, to inform him that the doctor would like to see him.

A doctor came by who said his name was Blumenthal and pulled Gene aside to a little more private space, and said softly to Gene, "I'm sorry to have to tell you that your brother has passed away."

This man was very much the same height as Gene but thinner and slighter and trimmer, but he looked directly into Gene's eyes, and, not without sympathy, but seeming to be trying to gauge the depth of feeling in Gene's response, and choosing his own words carefully, he then said, "There was nothing you could have done."

"What do you mean, Doctor?"

"It was a cerebral hemorrhage, Mister LaStoria."

Now Gene perceived that the doctor held a clipboard loosely in the fingers of his left hand hanging at his side. The doctor was saying, "I think that when the medical examiner pronounces he will probably have to declare that your brother was dead on arrival."

"If only I could've gotten here quicker—."

"There was nothing you could have done. Most likely, it was instantaneous."

"So—he didn't suffer?"

"No, he didn't suffer." The doctor reached out his right hand to touch Gene on the forearm. "I hope you can understand, sir, that there was nothing that you or I or anyone with the best intentions in the world could have done. It was an act of nature, or God, if you like, and it could have happened at any moment, without warning."

"I'll never believe that, Doc. There was plenty of warning. Years of warning. It was the war that killed him, and so we've had, oh, years of warning."

"I understand how you feel—but, for what it's worth, I can only say—he could have had a malformation of blood vessels in his brain, a weakness of some sort, from the day he was born, and neither he, nor you, nor anyone would've known about it, or could have done anything to prevent this—."

"Cerebral hemorrhage."

"I'm sorry."

Four hours later, Gene was sitting on the wooden bench, staring. They had taken Augie's body to the hospital morgue. There was nothing to do but wait. They wouldn't release the body to him until the medical examiner had pronounced. Then the funeral parlor people would arrive to take the body on the long ride back home in a hearse.

About two in the morning the emergency room was deserted except for two or three people and Gene LaStoria. The nurses at the main admitting desk had gone through their change of shift at around eleven o'clock or thereabouts. All this time Gene had been sitting there, long after he finally stopped weeping, with his head buried in his hands, all this time he had been sitting there with nothing but his thoughts for company.

Augie, I was going to tell you, and now I'm glad I didn't. You suffered enough. You didn't need to know this. I needed to know this. For some reason, God decided I needed to know this. And God knows I vowed, I swore, I would keep the secret to myself, and take it to the grave with me. None of you needed to know. Especially Pa.

It's funny but he never said much to us, about his father, or his mother either, for that matter. For all we knew, when we were kids growing up, he never had any parents, and we didn't ask, we had grandparents on Ma's side, the Fabrizios, we grew up in their midst, we spent family holidays, we didn't need any other grandparents, we already had them.

But what we didn't know, I found out. And when I found out it was the worst moment of my life. You had a grandfather you never knew about, Augie, and his name was Enrico LaStoria. And he was a Fascist. That's right. He was on the other side. He was an enemy of his own grandchildren and everything they knew and thought that the country they grew up in stood for or meant to them. I didn't want to believe it, even when I met him, even when I heard it from his own lips, but . . . he convinced me.

Do you want to know how? I'll tell you how. I'll tell you now because I know it can't hurt you anymore. And I've taken all the hurt from it that I can.

God knows it hurt me. It damaged me more than I can ever know or maybe I'm willing to admit. That I know because I failed to keep the secret. In spite of all my swearing and vowing, over and over, I had to tell someone—I had to.

Thank Christ it wasn't Pa who had to hear it. Thank Christ I kept it from him.

It was the night of his funeral, when we finally laid him to rest, beside Ma, in the Holy Cross Cemetery, in Malden, you remember, Augie. I held it together all through the days after he passed and the wake and the funeral and the burial and then I got home that night to my own house with my wife and kids in it and I just couldn't keep it in any longer. The kids were put to bed, Celia's mother and father were sound asleep, you know all these years they've been living with us so that Celia could take care of them, she's a good woman, Augie, I wish to hell you could've found that in your life, only God knows if it would've helped you, but all I can say is that all these years I don't know what I would've done without my wife.

Every time I looked at her, and at Joanna, Leon, Marie, I took that vow over again and over again, never, never, never would they know.

But Celia was there for me when I needed her most.

The night we finally put Pa to rest, I was crying in the bed and she thought it was over Pa, and she was trying to comfort me and I said, no, no it's not that, it's something else, Celia, go put on a pot of coffee, bring it back here to bed with us, grab the cigarettes, I have to tell you something, tonight, or it's gonna be the death of me if I don't.

I scared the hell out of poor Celia. She thought I was gonna tell her maybe that there was another woman or maybe that I murdered someone, I don't know what she thought, but when she came back, we sat up in bed together and she put her arms around me and I told her the story.

How I met our grandfather in the partisans' camp. How I managed to save him from them. How he took me back to the family home in Alta Villa, the very place where Pa lived when he was a kid, before, and after, he went to New York, the home he ran away from in the end.

It was a narrow house, Augie. It was built like a coffin and from the moment I stepped into it, I was afraid something was going to happen to me there. But what did happen I could never have imagined in my wildest dreams.

We sat there, the old man and me—for all intents and purposes we were two Italians in their own home, since the mission that brought me there, I couldn't wear an American uniform—I had to go undercover, masquerading as a local Italian, which meant that if the Germans caught me, they could have shot me as a spy.

But when I got to the partisan camp, and afterwards to our grandfather's house, in Alta Villa itself, there were no Germans there. I had seen them down in the city of Avellino, I'd observed them from a height, but I skirted the city, to avoid them. I was alone. I had no help. I had a sidearm, and that was it. I couldn't trust the partisans—they were out to hang your grandfather when they gave him over to my custody instead, because I pleaded for his life.

Afterwards, I wished I hadn't. I only did it because of the crazy coincidence, or string of coincidences, that led me to find him and meet him, without wanting to, without actually searching or looking for him, completely by accident. Something about the whole crazy affair convinced me I was meant to be there at a certain time and place to save his life. Never in a million eons did I think he would betray me the way he did.

Unbeknownst to me, although I should have been more on the alert, since I knew all about the American paratroopers in the vicinity, and it was my mission to bring the field radio to them, which I handed over to the partisans— unbeknownst to me the Germans, their intelligence, knew all about the paratroopers as soon as they made their midnight landing.

Well, why not? The Germans were in headlong retreat at that very moment, as they were giving up on Salerno, and pulling back. And their units from the Adriatic side, in Bari, who were heading north at all speed to the Gustav line, or whichever one it was they were gonna take a stand at next—they passed right through Avellino, 50 miles from the Salerno beachhead.

It was those units I had seen from above that were setting fire to Avellino and murdering and plundering. Every territory they passed through in Italy they divided into friends and enemies. They didn't trust their friends and they killed their enemies, among the civilian population. So, two days after Enrico LaStoria and I landed back at his house, where do the Germans show up—in Alta Villa! They're searching for the American paratroopers which they knew all about from their informants.

This is the story I'm telling Celia the night we put Pa in the ground. And she's listening, while I'm crying, and telling her the story and she's rubbing my back and I'm telling her she must never, never tell anyone what I was going to tell her—what happened next. I made her swear to take the secret to the grave with her. And she did swear it.

What happened after the second day I'd spent in the old man's house was the arrival of the Germans, and they had American paratroopers, a bunch of them, captured and tied with their hands behind their back, and they were marching them through town to hang them in the central square.

In two days time I'd had a chance to talk to Enrico LaStoria. Why did my Pa run away from home? He was no good, your Pa, said the old man. He was your son. He was no son of mine. Back and forth we went. And I got a sense of just exactly why Pa had never breathed a word to us of this man who was his father, and my grandfather.

But still, still, I never expected him to do what he did.

The Germans had executed some of our boys in a public hanging in the square. We heard about it from neighbors. We were cringing behind the walls of the narrow house. I was hiding from the Germans. He was hiding from the partisans, and he didn't trust the neighbors, who knew he had been Mussolini's Fascist mayor of Alta Villa.

But then the Germans were attacked—it might have been the townspeople, more than likely it was the partisans who had infiltrated. As usual, the Germans took some casualties and immediately started reprisals.

The partisans and the townspeople were fighting back for their very lives and the Germans were trying to burn down the town. This went on for the whole day. We were watching from the one window at the front of the house when the local fighters went running by. Around the corner came the Germans in pursuit.

Your grandfather, Augie, flung the door open. I lunged for him but I missed.

There was a firefight going on in the street, but the crazy old man went out there in the middle of it, yelling at the Germans and waving his arms.

"Da questa parte qua! Da questa parte qua! C'è un nascondiglio Americano in casa mia!"

The Krauts shot him down in the street like a dog.

A nurse came over to Gene sitting on the bench.

"Is there anything I can help you with, sir?"

Gene looked up. His reverie evaporated.

"No, I'm all right, thanks. I'll be all right."

"The Carney Home has arrived, sir, and they're getting your loved one into the vehicle."

"I suppose I gotta go, huh? You'll be glad to see the last of me, huh?"

"Oh, no, sir, nothing like that. We're used to it. We see everything around here."

"Well, thanks for putting up with me. You've been very kind."

"I don't mind at all. You just take your time."

The nurse was getting ready to go back to her station, but she stopped to listen when Gene said,

"He was my brother, you know. There were seven of us, to begin with, four sisters and three brothers. I've just been sitting here trying to think of how in the hell I'm gonna call them all and tell them their brother's gone. I don't know how I'm gonna do it, nurse. It's just not right. I wish God had taken me instead of him. He was a far better man than I could ever be."

About the Author

Eugene Christy is a novelist, poet and musician currently enjoying retirement in his home in the Berkshires. His maternal grandparents Antonio Scioscia and Giuseppina Fabrizio came from Alta Villa Irpina, near Avellino, in the South of Italy. He has studied under Sean O'Faolain, James Dickey, and Larry McMurtry. Appearing as Gene Christy, he was previously known around the Berkshires as the singer-songwriter and accordian-player who led The Dossers, the Irish-themed pub-band trio featuring Bill Morrison and Rick Marquis. His current project, six years in the making, is called The Twentieth Century Quintet, five novels telling the saga of Antonio

LaStoria and his descendants through three generations in America from 1899 to 1972, to be published by Adelaide Books, New York, in 2020 and 2021.

www.ingramcontent.com/pod-product-compliance
Lightning Source LLC
Chambersburg PA
CBHW051158190726
48288CB00006B/1705